BAEN BOOKS EDITED BY HANK DAVIS

The Human Edge by Gordon R. Dickson

We the Underpeople by Cordwainer Smith
When the People Fell by Cordwainer Smith

The Technic Civilization Saga
The Van Rijn Method by Poul Anderson
David Falkayn: Star Trader by Poul Anderson
Rise of the Terran Empire by Poul Anderson
Young Flandry by Poul Anderson
Captain Flandry: Defender of the Terran Empire by Poul Anderson
Sir Dominic Flandry: The Last Knight of Terra by Poul Anderson
Flandry's Legacy by Poul Anderson

The Best of the Bolos: Their Finest Hour, created by Keith Laumer

A Cosmic Christmas
A Cosmic Christmas 2 You

In Space No One Can Hear You Scream

To purchase these and all other Baen Book titles in e-book format,
please go to www.baenebooks.com

A COSMIC CHRISTMAS 2 YOU

Edited By
HANK DAVIS

A COSMIC CHRISTMAS 2 YOU

A Baen Book

Baen Publishing Enterprises
P.O. Box 1403
Riverdale, NY 10471

ISBN 13: 978-1-4516-3942-1

Cover art by Sam Kennedy

First Baen printing, November 2013

Distributed by Simon & Schuster
1230 Avenue of the Americas
New York, NY 10020

Library of Congress Cataloging-in-Publication Data

A Cosmic Christmas 2 You / edited by Hank Davis.
    pages cm
  ISBN 978-1-4516-3942-1 (pbk.)
1. Science fiction, American. 2. Christmas stories, American. I. Davis, Hank.
PS648.S3C673 2013
813'.0876208--dc23

                              2013033170

Printed in the United States of America

10 9 8 7 6 5 4 3 2 1

CONTENTS

ACKNOWLEDGEMENTS

My thanks to all the contributors,
as well as those who helped with advice, permissions,
email addresses, and other kindnesses,
with extra thanks to Connie Willis,
who revamped one of her early stories
until she was no longer unhappy with it.
And to Toni Weisskopf, whose idea
the whole thing was, including the title.

Teachers in Kentucky in the 1950s
weren't paid generous salaries, but come
December 25, my mother and father managed
to put a lot of cool stuff under the tree for their
two rotten kids. This book is for you,
mom and dad.

A COSMIC CHRISTMAS 2 YOU

THE SHAPE OF CHRISTMASES TO COME

by Hank Davis

LAST YEAR, in the introduction to *A Cosmic Christmas*, I publicly mused that it was hard to find anything to say about Christmas that hasn't already been said. Now I have to say something about Christmas that *I* haven't already said.

Well . . .

How's the weather out? Read any good books lately?

Welllll . . .

Let's take a stroll down Memory Lane (watch for the landmines).

Last time I considered how science fictional some of the gifts under the present-day tree would have seemed just three or four decades ago, such as laptop computers, cell phones, GPS units, etc. That reminds me of the high-tech toys from the 1950s when I was a rotten kid. "High-tech" for the time, that is.

One of them, from Christmas 1955 if memory serves, was a battery powered thing shaped like a futuristic bus. I don't remember its name (and I'm too lazy to try to find it online), but it had a plastic radar-dish-like antenna on its top that was really only a directional guide. It came with a spherical whistle, a very low-pitched whistle. The bus moved slowly across the floor, but when the aforementioned rotten kid blew on the whistle, something inside would turn the front wheels. The "antenna" would also rotate, so that you could gauge which way the bus was about to turn, and stop blowing when the antenna was pointing in the direction you wanted it to go. The bus would also have unanticipated changes of course if the TV happened to be on and a voice or sound on TV happened to hit the right pitch, briefly redirecting the angle of the wheels.

Now this seems very primitive now, what with cars, tanks, helicopters and robots which are electronically, rather than sonically, remote-controlled. But it was an unusual item then.

Or there was the gadget (again, of unremembered name) which looked like a cartoonist's idea of a radio station, complete with two plastic antenna on top which did absolutely nothing but look decorative. It came with two handheld communicators. When both of them were hooked up to the station by wires (yes, wires), the holder of one communicator could talk to the other and almost hear what the other was saying, as long as there was no loud ambient noise in the room . Of course, the wires that came with it weren't very long, so you couldn't talk much more than from one room to another. It was an advance on the old tin cans connected by string setup, but not much of an advance.

Then there was the airplane flight simulator, though I don't think it was called that. It was mostly mechanical. There was a small pilot's wheel on the front, and a window with a little airplane silhouette on a wire that went across the window. The airplane cutout would move left or right as you turned the wheel, while a strip of paper inside the gadet rolled from the top of the window to the bottom, as if the plane were flying over terrain. On the strip was a red line that moved from side to side, and you moved the plane to stay on the red line as it wavered back and forth. If you got off the line, you supposedly were off the radio directional beam and there was a beep.

I could go on—I haven't yet mentioned Robert the Robot, with a tiny acoustic phonograph inside, so that he would talk when the crank on his back was rapidly turned—but I'll stop there.

It isn't surprising that these toys seem downright neolithic now—there have been considerable advances in electronics in nearly six decades, after all—but consider the shape of toys to come, circa 2013. Barring atomic war, worldwide plague, an unexpected visit from an asteroid, or mass entinction due to watching reality shows, the toys of the present day will probably seem just as primitive by 2073. (Which, come to think of it, will be three years before the American Tricentennial. Lay in a supply of fireworks early, they may be completely outlawed by then.) What then will be a state-of-the-art high-tech toy?

Science fiction has thoroughly covered the idea of robots made to look like children to be playmates for the old-fashioned human children, or maybe child substitutes for parents, but that might be a possibility. Or maybe a holographic image of a child would be even better. They're intangible and can't break. And they can't break those fragile human kids if they go out of skew on treadle.

One thing about the mid-1950s toys is that they could only do one or maybe two things, and that was it. Which led to them ending up in the attic or a closet once the thrill was gone. Unless imagination took over, and the airplane simulator became the control wheel of a spaceship, zoom! zoom! That's still true of some modern toys, but not with electronic games. If you get tired of one game, you can plug in a different cartridge for another one. (Anybody remember board games?) Maybe toys can be made to be modifiable. Suppose you get tired of a toy, and can push a button to make it change shape to something else, like the soft weapon in the Larry Niven story.

Or maybe the ultimate toy will be something like the "feelies" in Aldous Huxley's *Brave New World*. (Are there *still* English professors who insist that novel isn't science fiction?) Put an electronic thingy on your head and suddenly you're *there*, wherever *there* is. Back in time with—hmmm, probably not cowboys and Indians, unless the 21st century flushes the currently omnipresent Political Correctness crap—but maybe the age of chivalry with knights in armor (without the fleas and lice, of course), or the stone age (will Neanderthals have to be treated with Political Correctness?), or be the first on your block to be a T-Rex in the Cretaceous. Or go forward in time with starships of the future (will *Star Trek* still be popular?). Be John Carter of Mars. Be a Gray Lensman. Be Eric John Stark. Be Jirel of Joiry. Be Ferdinand

Feghoot. (They'll all be in public domain by then.) Of course, the grown-ups will have to make sure that the kids don't get hold of the *adult* feelie recordings . . .

Or maybe the kids will visit the more recent past, like the 20th century when the kids had toys that didn't have electronics. Or even moving parts! (I direct your attention to Isaac Asimov's story, "The Fun They Had.")

But there's one toy that I don't think they'll have to play with via virtual reality. I'm sure that the Slinky will still be around . . .

—Hank Davis

INTRODUCTION
🌿🪷🌿
ANGEL OF LIGHT

HERE'S A TALE OF OLD-FASHIONED horse trading in a future that's not unusual just because the aliens are here, and getting in on the horse trading. Omar Khayyam (as channeled by FitzGerald) wondered "what the vintners buy/One half so precious as the stuff they sell." I don't think either party in this yuletide transaction would have asked that question. Nor, I think, would they be likely to want the Moving Finger to do a rewrite of events as they came to pass.

🌲 🌲 🌲

JOE HALDEMAN is a Vietnam veteran whose classic novels *The Forever War* and *Forever Peace* have the rare distinction of having won both the Hugo and Nebula Awards for best novel of the year. He has served twice as president of the Science Fiction & Fantasy Writers of America and is currently an adjunct professor teaching writing at the Massachusetts Institute of Technology. Stephen King has said, "Haldeman writes with wit, grace and ease. If there was a Fort Knox for the science fiction writers who really matter, we'd have to lock Haldeman up there." His most recent work is the trilogy comprising *Marsbound, Starbound,* and *Earthbound.*

ANGEL OF LIGHT

✤✦✤

by Joe Haldeman

IT BEGAN INNOCENTLY ENOUGH. Christmastime and no money. I went down into the cellar and searched deeply for something to give the children. Something they wouldn't have already found during their *hajjes* down there.

On a high shelf, behind bundles of sticks waiting for the cold, I could just see an old wooden chest, pushed far back into a corner. I dropped some of the bundles onto the floor and pushed the others out of the way, and with some difficulty slid the chest to the edge of the shelf. From the thick layer of dust on top, I assumed it was from my father's time or before.

I had a warning thought: Don't open it. Call the authorities.

But just above the lock was engraved the name, JOHN BILLINGS WASHINGTON. John Washington was my father's slave name. I think the Billings middle name was his father's. The box probably went back to the twentieth century.

The lock was rusted tight, but the hasp was loose. I got down from the ladder and found a large screwdriver that I could use to pry it.

I slid the chest out and balanced it on my shoulder, and carefully stepped down, the ladder creaking. I set it on the worktable and hung one lantern from the rafter over it, and set the other on a stack of scrap wood beside.

The screaming that the screws made, coming out of the hardwood, was so loud that it was almost funny, considering that I supposedly was working in secret. But Miriam was pumping out chords on the organ, singing along with Fatimah, rehearsing for the Christmas service. I could have fired a pistol and no one would have heard it.

The hasp swung free and the top lifted easily, with a sigh of brass. Musty smell and something else. Gun oil. A gray cloth bundle on top was heavy. Of course it held a gun.

It's not unusual to find guns left over from the old times; there were so many. Ammunition was rare, though. This one had two heavy magazines.

I recognized it from news and history pictures, an Uzi, invented and used by the old infidel state Israel. I set it down and wiped my hands.

It would not be a good Christmas present. Perhaps for 'Eid, for Ibriham, when he is old enough to decide whether he is to be called. A Jewish weapon, he would laugh. I could ask the imam whether to cleanse it and how.

There were three cardboard folders under the gun, once held together with rubber bands, which were just sticky lines now. They were full of useless documents about land and banking.

Underneath them, I caught a glimpse of something that looked like pornography. I looked away immediately, closed my eyes, and asked Mohammed and Jesus for strength. Then I took it out and put it in the light.

It was in a plastic bag that had stamped on it NITROGEN SEAL. What a strange word, a tech word from the old times.

The book inside had the most amazing picture on the front. A man and a woman, both white, embracing. But the woman is terrified. The man seems only resolute, as he fires a strange pistol at a thing like a giant squid, green as a plant. The woman's head is uncovered, and at first she seems naked, but in fact her clothes are simply transparent, like some dancers'. The book is called *Thrilling Wonder Stories,* and is dated summer 1944. That would be 1365, more than a hundred years before Chrislam.

I leafed through the book, fascinated in spite of its carnal and infidel nature. Most of it seemed to be tales—not religious parables or folk tales, but lies that were made up at the time, for entertainment. Perhaps there was moral instruction as well. Many of the pictures did show men in situations that were physically or morally dangerous.

The first story, "The Giant Runt," seemed at first sacrilegious; it was about a man furious with God for having created him shorter than normal men. But then a magical machine makes everyone else tiny, and his sudden superiority turns him into a monster. But he sees an opportunity for moral action and redeems himself. The machine is destroyed, the world is normal again, and God rewards him with love.

Nadia, my second wife, came to the door at the top of the stairs and asked whether I needed help with anything. "No," I said. "Don't wait up. I have something to study here. A man thing." I shouldn't have said that. She would be down here after the morning prayer, as soon as I left for work.

I looked at the woman on the cover of the book, so exposed and vulnerable. Perhaps I should destroy it before Nadia or Miriam were exposed to it. A present for Ibriham? No; he would like it, but it would lead him away from proper thought.

I put both lanterns on the table, with the book between them, for maximum light. The paper was brown and the ink faded. I turned the crumbling pages with care, although I would probably burn the book before dawn. First I would read as much of it as I could. I composed my mind with prayer, reciting the Prophet's *hadith* about the duty of learning.

In 1365, a war was raging all around the world, and various pages took note of this. I think this was only a year or two before America used nuclear weapons the first time, though I found no mention of them. (There were several exhortations to "buy bonds," which at first I misread as bombs. Bonds are financial instruments of some kind.) There were short pieces, evidently presented as truth, about science being used against the enemies of America. The ones that were not presented as true were more interesting, though harder to understand.

Much of the content was religious. "Horatius at the Bridge" was about a madman who could find the "soul" of a bridge and bring it down with the notes from a flute. "Terror in the Dust" and "The Devouring Tide" described scientists who were destroyed because they tried to play God—the first by giving intelligence to ants and then treating them as if he were an almighty deity, and the second, grandly, by attempting to create a new universe, with himself as Allah. The last short story, "God of Light," had a machine that was obviously Shaytan, trying to tempt the humans into following it into destruction.

The language was crude and at times bizarre, though of course part of that was just a reflection of the technological culture those writers and readers endured together. Life is simpler and more pure now, at least on this side of the city walls. The Kafir may still have books like this.

That gave me an idea. Perhaps this sort of thing would be rare and sought after in their world. I shouldn't accept Kafir money— though people do, often enough—but perhaps I could trade it for something more appropriate for a Christmas gift. Barter could be done without an intermediary, too, and frankly I was not eager for my imam to know that I had this questionable book in my possession.

Things are less rigid now, but I sharply remember the day, more than forty years ago, when my father had to burn all of his books. We carried box after box of them to the parking lot in front of the church, where they were drenched with gasoline and set afire. The smell of gasoline, rare now, always brings that back.

He was allowed to keep two books, a New Koran and a New Bible. When a surprise search party later found an old Q'ran in his study, he had to spend a week, naked, in a cage in that same spot—the jumble of fractured concrete in the middle of the church parking lot—with nothing but water, except a piece of bread the last day. (It was an old piece of bread, rock-hard and moldy. I remember how he thanked the imam, carefully brushed off the mold, and managed to stay dignified, gnawing at it with his strong side teeth.)

He told them he kept the old book because of the beauty of the writing, but I knew his feelings went deeper than that: He thought the Q'ran in any language other than Arabic was just a book, not holy.

As a boy of five, I was secretly overjoyed that I could stop memorizing the Q'ran in Arabic; it was hard enough in English.

I agree with him now, and ever since it was legal again, I've spent my Sundays trying to cram the Arabic into my gray head. With God's grace I might live long enough to learn it all. Having long ago memorized the English version helps make up for my slow brain.

I put the old book back in its NITROGEN SEAL bag and took it up to bed with me, dropping off a bundle of sticks by the stove on the way. I checked on both children and both wives; all were sleeping soundly. With a prayer of thanks for this strange discovery, I joined Nadia and dreamed of a strange future that had not come to pass.

The next day was market day. I left Nadia with the children and Fatimah and I went down to the medina for the week's supplies.

It really is more a woman's work than a man's, and normally I enjoy watching Fatimah go through the rituals of inspection and barter—the mock arguments and grudging agreement that comprise the morning's entertainment for customer and merchant alike. But this time I left her in the food part of the medina with the cart, while I went over to the antiques section.

You don't see many Kafir in the produce part of the medina, but there are always plenty wandering through the crafts and antiques section, I suppose looking for curiosities and bargains. Things that are everyday to us are exotic to them, and vice versa.

It was two large tents, connected by a canvas breezeway under which merchants were roasting meats and nuts and selling drinks for dollars or dirhams. I got a small cup of sweet coffee, redolent of honey and cardamom, for two dirhams, and sipped it standing there, enjoying the crowd.

Both tents had similar assortments of useful and worthless things, but one was for dollar transactions and the other was for dirhams and barter. The dollar purchases had to go through an imam, who would extract a fee for handling the money, and pay the merchant what was left, converting into dirhams. There were easily three times as many merchants and customers in the dirham-and-barter tent, the Kafir looking for bargains and the sellers for surprises, as much as for doing business. It was festive there, too, a lot of chatter and laughing over the rattle and whine of an amateur band of drummers and fiddlers. People who think we are aloof from infidels, or hate them, should spend an hour here.

Those who did this regularly had tables they rented by the day or month; we amateurs just sat on the ground with our wares on display. I walked around and didn't see anyone I knew, so finally just sat next to a table where a man and a woman were selling books. I laid out a square of newspaper in front of me and set the *Thrilling Wonder Stories* on it.

The woman looked down at it with interest. "What kind of a magazine is that?"

Magazine, I'd forgotten that word. "I don't know. Strange tales, most of them religious."

"It's 'science fiction,'" the man said. "They used to do that, predict what the future would be like."

"Used to? We still do that."

He shrugged. "Not that way. Not as fiction."

"I wouldn't let a child see that," the woman said.

"I don't think the artist was a good Muslim," I said, and they both chuckled. They wished me luck with finding a buyer, but didn't make an offer themselves.

Over the next hour, five or six people looked at the magazine and asked questions, most of which I couldn't answer. The imam in charge of the tent came over and gave me a long silent look. I looked right back at him and asked him how business was.

Fatimah came by, the cart loaded with groceries. I offered to wheel it home if she would sit with the magazine. She covered her face and giggled. More realistically, I said I could push the cart home when I was done, if she would take the perishables now. She said no, she'd take it all after she'd done a turn around the tent. That cost me twenty dirhams; she found a set of wooden spoons for the kitchen. They were freshly made by a fellow who had set up shop in the opposite corner, running a child-powered lathe, his sons taking turns striding on a treadmill attached by a series of creaking pulleys to the axis of the tool. People may have bought his wares more out of curiosity and pity for his sons than because of the workmanship.

I almost sold it to a fat old man who had lost both ears, I suppose in the war. He offered fifty dirhams, but while I was trying to bargain the price up, his ancient crone of a wife charged up and physically hauled him away, shrieking. If he'd had an ear, she would have pulled him by it. The bookseller started to offer his sympathies, but then both of them doubled over in laughter, and I had to join them.

As it turned out, the loss of that sale was a good thing. But first I had to endure my trial.

A barefoot man who looked as if he'd been fasting all year picked up the magazine and leafed through it carefully, mumbling. I knew he was trouble. I'd seen him around, begging and haranguing. He was white, which normally is not a problem with me. But white people who choose to live inside the walls are often types who would not be welcome at home, wherever that might be.

He proceeded to berate me for being a bad Muslim—not hearing my correction, that I belonged to Chrislam—and, starting with the licentious cover and working his way through the inside illustrations and advertisements, to the last story, which actually had God's name in the title . . . he said that even a bad Muslim would have no choice but to burn it on the spot.

I would have gladly burned it if I could burn it under *him,* but I was saved from making that decision by the imam. Drawn by the commotion, he stamped over and began to question the man, in a voice as shrill as his own, on matters of doctrine. The man's Arabic was no better than his diet, and he slunk away in mid-diatribe. I thanked the imam and he left with a slight smile.

Then a wave of silence unrolled across the room like a heavy blanket. I looked to the tent entrance and there were four men: Abdullah Zaragosa, our chief imam, some white man in a business suit, and two policemen in uniform, seriously armed. In between them was an alien, one of those odd creatures visiting from Arcturus.

I had never seen one, though I had heard them described on the radio. I looked around and was sad not to see Fatimah; she would hate having missed this.

It was much taller than the tallest human; it had a short torso but a giraffelike neck. Its head was something like a bird's, one large eye on either side. It cocked its head this way and that, looking around, and then dropped down to say something to the imam.

They all walked directly toward me, the alien rippling on six legs. Cameras clicked; I hadn't brought one. The imam asked if I was Ahmed Abd al-kareem, and I said yes, in a voice that squeaked.

"Our visitor heard of your magazine. May we inspect it?" I nodded, not trusting my voice, and handed it to him, but the white man took it.

He showed the cover to the alien. "This is what we expected you to look like."

"Sorry to disappoint," it said in a voice that sounded like it came from a cave. It took the magazine in an ugly hand, too many fingers and warts that moved, and inspected it with first one eye, and then the other.

It held the magazine up and pointed to it, with a smaller hand. "I would like to buy this."

"I—I can't take white people's money. Only dirhams or, or trade."

"Barter," it said, surprising me. "That is when people exchange things of unequal value, and both think they have gotten the better deal."

The imam looked like he was trying to swallow a pill.

"That's true enough," I said. "At best, they both do get better deals, by their own reckoning."

"Here, then." It reached into a pocket or a pouch—I couldn't tell whether it was wearing clothes—and brought out a ball of light. It held out the light to a point midway between us, and let go. It floated in the air. "The light will stay wherever you put it."

It shimmered a brilliant blue, with fringes of rainbow colors. "How long will it last?"

"Longer than you."

It was one of the most beautiful things I had ever seen. I touched it with my finger—it felt cool, and tingled—and pushed it a few inches. It stayed where I moved it.

"It's a deal, sir. Thank you."

"*Shukran*," it said, and they moved on down the line of tables.

I don't think it bought anything else. But it might have. I kept looking away from it, back into the light.

The imams and the white scientists all want to take the light away to study it. Eventually, I will loan it out.

For now, though, it is a Christmas gift to my son and daughter. The faithful, and the merely curious, come to look at it, and wonder. But it stays in my house.

In Chrislam, as in old Islam, angels are not humanlike creatures with robes and wings. They are *male'ikah*, beings of pure light.

They look wonderful on the top of a tree.

INTRODUCTION
AND TO ALL A GOOD NIGHT

IT'S CHRISTMAS TIME in a totally artificial environment where everything's under control and nothing unexpected happens. But the universe, as a scientist once said, "is stranger than we *can* imagine," and a bit of undisciplined, inexplicable strangeness was coming for Christmas . . .

♠ ♠ ♠

TONY DANIEL is the author of five science fiction books, the latest of which is *Guardian of Night*, as well as an award-winning short story collection, *the Robot's Twilight Companion*. He also collaborated with David Drake on the novel *The Heretic*, and its forthcoming sequel, *The Savior*, new novels in the popular military science fiction series, The General. His story "Life on the Moon," was a Hugo finalist and also won the *Asimov's* Reader's Choice Award. Daniel's short fiction has been much anthologized and has been collected in multiple year's best anthologies. Daniel has also co-written screenplays for SyFy Channel horror movies, and during the early 2000s was the writer and director of numerous audio dramas for critically-acclaimed SCIFI.COM's Seeing Ear Theater. Born in Alabama, Daniel has lived in St. Louis, Los Angeles, Seattle, Prague, and New York City. He is now an editor at Baen Books and lives in Wake Forest, North Carolina with his wife and two children.

AND TO ALL
A GOOD NIGHT

by Tony Daniel

ANDERSON STOOD BY the outer shell window in his room and gazed at the Big Dipper. Some people called it the Great Bear or the Plough, but Anderson could *see* a scoop pattern in the arrangement of stars. The other forms he had trouble picturing.

What is a plough, anyway, he thought. *And don't answer that, Gear! Something to do with Earth-style farming. I'm not stupid.*

But it was a hard thing to imagine what it did even *after* you had seen photos. Like trying to figure out how a sewing machine worked. *A plough is a kind of "sowing" machine. It sows seeds.*

Incorrect, said Gear. **A plough prepares the soil, while—**
Mute.

The artificial stimulus, which translated as spoken words in Anderson's brain, ceased. Gear could be so annoying at times like this. Anderson's mind was racing. He didn't want all the regular answers. It was Christmas Eve.

In his hand was a snow globe that had originally come from Earth. Inside was a figure of Santa, his sleigh, and eight tiny reindeer.

"Where's Rudoph?" he'd asked when his mother had given it on Christmas Eve six years ago, back when he'd been six years old.

"This was made before Rudolph came along," she'd answered.

She'd come into his room to find Anderson in his pajamas, looking out his bedroom window at the stars, just as he was tonight. He'd told her he would probably not be able to sleep no matter how long she read to him, so instead of a book, she'd given him the globe.

"Your Nana gave it to me when I was about your age," she said. "It's nearly seven hundred years old."

"What if I break it?"

"Don't worry about that," she replied. "It's been treated with hardener. That's why it lasted so long."

He shook it and the snow swirled. The sleigh, forever suspended over a rooftop with a chimney, traveled through the blizzard bringing toys.

"Back then, they didn't know Santa came out into space, did they?"

His mother smiled. "No, they didn't know," she told him.

He'd fallen asleep holding the snow globe. The next morning when he jumped up to go check for presents, he shook it from the covers and the globe fell with a bang onto the floor. It didn't crack. His mother was right; it was hardened against breakage.

Christmas was pretty big in the North Bottoms, the part of the Sphere where Anderson lived. That didn't mean everybody celebrated it, though. It was always weird to see neighbors and kids at Education who you thought you knew pretty well, but who didn't *do* Christmas. This was even some people who went to churches. Zens like Mr. Timehound next door, and Basics like Anderson's friend Sigi, didn't go in for Santa Claus or giving out gifts at all, for instance.

Anderson was twelve now. He didn't believe in Santa anymore. He hadn't for a good two years. He'd had the talk with his parents after Sigi had told him she thought it was all made up. And after that, Gear had filled in the details and provided the breakdown of the psychological justifications for pretending to little kids there was such thing as a magical being known variously as Santa Claus, Father Christmas, or St. Nicholas.

But like a lot of things, there was part of him that *still* believed, despite his parents' gloomy faces when they'd informed him of the truth, and despite the dry info-dump that was Gear's special form of torture when he was in explaining mode.

"One day you'll appreciate having a Gearbox put in when you were born," his father had once told him. "Some people don't get one until the mandate kicks in at sixteen and then it can take years to learn how to really use it. And Angsties never get one at all, of course."

One day maybe I will, Anderson thought. But not tonight. Not when some drawn-out lesson from Gear could totally ruin Christmas.

Anderson looked at the outer two stars on the Big Dipper. If you drew a line through them and followed the part that left through the lip of the dipper the line would point at Polaris. This had been the North Star for planet Earth, more or less hanging right over the Earth's North Pole. Now it was just a star. But you could see it a lot better here than on Earth. The Sphere contained the Sun within it, of course, and blocked off almost all light. There were energy regulatory vents and inertial transfer pistons that bled unused energy into interstellar space. But for the most part, the Solar system was shut up in its own vast ball. Only people who lived in the Shell, like Anderson, could see out, could see the stars and the Milky Way, whenever they wanted. The others had to go on special vacations to the viewports, and some people had never seen a night sky at all.

Anderson felt sorry for them. He liked the Sun okay, but he couldn't imagine living in the perpetual day of the Insiders. Sure, they had the Flukes, the rotating shading blanks in the interior sky that provided the day's dark periods according to old Earth seasons. But it never really got dark-dark Inside, and even though each of the Flukes had a pattern of holes cut in it that let through pinpricks of sunlight to simulate stars, this was a far different thing than real, actual lights *out there*. Of course, nobody but the Basics who remained back on Earth had the Moon.

Anderson shifted his gaze over to the stars that made up Draco. The imaginary lines of the constellation coiled around Polaris. He always picked out the squashed square of the dragon's head first. He even knew the names of the stars, courtesy of a lesson from Gear: Beta Draconis, Gamma, Nu, Xi—

What's that?

Something strange in the Dragon's head. A red light.

Aw, come on. It can't be.

But the light was definitely red, and getting closer. Or at least brighter.

It's got to be a ship coming to dock, Anderson thought. But he resisted unmuting Gear to confirm or deny this. This was exactly the kind of thing Gear would drone on and on about, telling Anderson what the cargo might be, and the alien or colonial culture that produced it, and then going on about how the link-hoops worked to make faster than light travel possible. Gear would make it all a geography lesson and skip the interesting parts like whether or not that particular ship had been in a firefight with the Galz pirates, what its weapons systems were, and whether or not it could blow up a planet or make a star go nova—just the kind of stuff that *really* interested Anderson.

But the red light wasn't a ship. It began to move from the left side of the sky, where Draco presently resided, across to the right, while always growing brighter. Ships didn't have marking lights. Why have exterior lights when you could outrun the very shine the lights made itself? No, the glow they put out was residue from the hoop transfer differentials, whatever that meant. Gear had, of course, explained it all once.

Anderson had seen plenty of ships. This was no ship.

It's headed this way. He fought the urge to draw back from the window. Instead, pushed his head against the glass, and felt the reassuring surface that lay between him and space. The window wasn't real glass, of course, but a light-frequency-passing structure equivalent in density and strength to the interior of a neutron star or, more precisely, the nucleus of an atom. The quantum effect that held a neutron and proton glued together was ramped into the macro-world by SQUIDs, the superconducting quantum interference devices that held the Sphere together, and kept it as tight as a drum.

Closer. The red light trembled now. Moved up and down in regular motions, not precise, but fluid.

Like a galloping reindeer, Anderson thought.

Anderson squeezed his eyes shut, hard. Wiped his eyelids with a finger and thumb. Opened his eyes again.

Still there. And now it looked like something. Something with a light in the front and maybe a smaller, white light in the back. A lantern, maybe?

Not possible. That's vacuum out there. There is no way a lantern could even burn without air.

He wasn't entirely sure of that fact, but again he resisted the urge to let Gear tell him the *real* answer. Gear would insist on saying more. Telling him what the lantern and the red light *actually* were.

Closer. Moving fast now, and in a direction of travel across Anderson's field of vision, which would also take it across the stripe of the Milky Way that stretched diagonally from the upper right to lower left of Anderson's sightlines.

He could have irised out his perception, gone to virtual remote sensing via Gear's input. But he didn't. He waited and watched.

The two lights and what was between them, a line of something that looked and moved very like antlers bouncing up and down, crossed the Milky Way in front of Anderson's unaided eyes.

Had to be a few hundred meters out. Had to be very, very close to see this much detail.

What could not be—*was*. Reindeer silhouettes. The red light was attached to what would be the nose of the most forward of those reindeer silhouettes. And to the rear, a sleigh followed along after the silhouettes. The lantern hung from its side, and you could clearly make out it was a globe inside some kind of containing contraption. Dark bands cut across the light.

Exactly like an old fashioned lantern in a picture.

And in the sleigh, lit by the lantern's light: a lumpy form, the form of a man. A man exposed to the vacuum. A man holding strips of darkness that might be reins.

A man calling out.

This was when Anderson knew it had to be fake, had to be some kind of stunt or something. Because he heard the distance voice of the man, a low-pitched, happy voice calling loudly, but contained, not a scream because he was out in empty space and ought to be quickly dying. Not that you could hear a scream in space. Not that *any* of this made sense.

"On Dasher, On Dancer, On Comet, and Cupid—"

Enough! Unmute!

The tiny click in his hearing that let him know Gear was now speech enabled.

All right, tell me. What is that, Gear?

What is *what*, Anderson? I do not understand to what you are referring.

Out there! Anderson found himself speaking aloud, something that he almost never did with Gear, something that was for newbies and babies. "What is that thing out there that looks like Santa and his reindeer?" he asked loudly, his voice trembling.

Out where?

"Outside my window!"

Gear was silent for a moment, then answered matter-of-factly. **Interesting. Remote sensing indicates a quantum foam anomaly. It is traversing local composed reality in discrete instantiations of seventeen point eight micro-millimeters separation from a position Solar system north-northwest to south-southeast. No observable point of origin.**

What?

A foam anomaly is a region—although "region" is not a precise characterization—of space-time that is unformatted. The information content has been temporarily removed from the underlying space-time structure. These anomalies can occur around an area of extreme quantum resolution such as the Sphere, where artificial states of quantum entanglement are generated and resolved on a scale an order of magnitude greater than what would be space-time normal.

Gear, I see Santa and his reindeer outside my window.

As stated, quantum foam anomalies *are* statistically more likely near the Sphere. This is the first instance on record of one occurring, however.

That's not a quantum foam whatever you call it, Gear. I see Santa!

But he didn't anymore. He craned to the right, but whatever it was, the sleigh, the reindeer, the hallucination, had drawn out of sight.

Another long moment of silence. Anderson squeezed the snow globe in his hand tightly, tensely, knowing it would never break. Still no answer. When Gear didn't talk for a perceptible second or two, you could be sure there was some massive computing going on.

Finally, Gear replied.

I have no further information, Anderson.

What do you mean? And then, just to be sure he was understood, he also spoke the question aloud. "What do you mean you have no further information? You *always* have further information, Gear."

I have no further information, Anderson.

"Did I just see Santa? Analyze me!"

Accomplished, Gear answered. **You are telling the truth.**

"No I'm *not*!" He was shouting now, but he didn't care. "Gear, take a reading on my brain-state. Make sure I'm not going crazy!"

Accomplished, Gear said. **Although you are at present in an excited condition, all parameters fall within acceptable norms. You are not insane, or going insane, Anderson.**

"Then why did I just see Santa Claus out my window?" he said. "Check my memories. Come on, Gear!"

The Altblock Conventions limit my access of individual thoughts and memories to volitional communications.

"I'm *giving* you permission," Anderson said. "Look at my brain and *tell me* what I just saw."

You are specifically offering permission to access recent observational memory storage within your nervous system?

"Yes!"

I refuse.

What? "Why?"

Your recent observations have characterized a null portion of space-time. You have balanced the sum total of information in the universe. If I access your observational data, the anomalous region will either return to a null state or become irrevocably resolved.

"Like that cat you were telling me about. In the black box?"

Schrödinger's Cat is a thought experiment. This is a situation with real consequences.

I don't mind knowing the truth, Gear. I'm twelve now. I'm old enough to take it—especially if it keeps me from thinking I'm going spring-sprung crazy.

That is not what I refer to. Observation of your state of observational uncertainty will cause that state to resolve. This poses a danger to the Sphere. A vacuum cannot exist without information to structure it. The Sphere's hull may communicate such information and lose form itself.

"You mean there might be a hull breach?" A breach. It was supposed to be impossible, but this was the great nightmare of everyone who lived in the Shell. To be sucked *out there*. The layer between life and death felt so very thin in this part of the Sphere.

"Precisely," said Gear.

"But I know I couldn't have actually seen Santa."

Really, Anderson? Do you know that?

"Mom and Dad told me Santa is fake. *You* told me he doesn't exist. You gave me that whole lecture on the origins of the myth."

Were you actually listening, Anderson?

"No, but that's not the point."

But that *is* exactly the point, said Gear. **You were not convinced.**

"I know there's no such thing as Santa!"

Some part of you doesn't know that at all, Anderson.

"How can that possibly be true?" Anderson stomped his feet. He jumped up and down on the soft-pad floor of his room. "There's no such thing as Santa! There's no such thing as Santa!" he yelled. "See?"

***Something* brings the toys.**

What, are you trying to pull over on me—that it's alien elves or something? Mom and Dad bring the toys!

Something makes your mother and father want to put out toys in the dead of night.

"Myth does," he replied. "You said it yourself. The power of myth because of the way humans evolved. We *needed* myth in the old days to explain stuff. Now it's all like, you know, *leftover* material. Like food you have to eat because you're not supposed to let anything go to waste. Santa is garbage. Leftover garbage that only kids believe in."

Like gravity.

That's different. You can feel gravity. It affects things.

Any gravity you feel in the Sphere is a quantum trick, Anderson. As the controlling A.I., I compute it and I make it for you.

"That's not the same as Mom and Dad pretending to be Santa and putting stuff under the Christmas tree for me. They never met Santa."

And I have never experienced gravity. All I know is what people have told me. That is all I know about anything, as a matter of fact.

Anderson held up the snow globe. He shook it. The little bubble trapped inside shook up the snow, or whatever the white flecks were. The sleigh remained motionless, frozen in time, always and never delivering its load of toys.

There is no Santa, Gear.

Believe, Anderson. It could save many lives.

He shook his head. "I can't."

You must.

There are over three hundred billion children in the Sphere.

I know. And I know most of them well.

"Why *me*?"

You were the only one looking in the right place at the right time.

Anderson gave the snow globe one more shake, then dropped it. It made a thump against the soft nubs of the floor covering.

"There's no Rudolph in there," he said. He raised his eyes to look out the window again. "Or out there. And whatever it was is long gone,"

Is it?

Anderson looked to his right. There, at about two o'clock in the sky, seemingly emerging from the center Cassiopeia itself, was the red light again. It had zigged away, and now it was zagging back toward him.

Very close now.

Headed straight for his window.

Enough light from the lantern on the sleigh to see by.

Reddish face, but that could just be the lantern glow. White beard. Red suit.

How is he going to get in? Is he going to cause a hull breach? Is the whole contraption going to splat up against the window in a bloody smear? "How is this even happening?"

Magic, perhaps.

"That explanation from *you*, Gear? Is that all you've got?"

As a famous fictional character once said: "when you have eliminated the impossible, whatever remains, however improbable, must be the truth."

I know! That's Sherlock Holmes. I read the stories. He's made up, Gear!

Yet Sherlock Holmes is who my chief programmer had in mind when he made *me*. Or actually my programmer modeled me on Sherlock's brother, Mycroft.

Would you cut it out with the history lesson. Santa is about to crash into my window!

It will be interesting to see how the quantum states resolve themselves.

Aren't you worried? For me, at least?

I think you will be all right, Anderson.

You're sure of that?

No.

"Do something!"

This is up to you.

Outside, the forever night sky burned with stars.

And then he heard it. The clanking of the bells, in tandem with the canter of nine reindeer. And the laugh. The deep, throaty laugh. All sounded as if it were coming from outside, from vacuum. From nothing at all.

Drawing nearer.

I believe, he told himself. "I believe!"

The *basso profundo* laugh. "Ho, ho, ho!"

"But I *don't* believe. I can't believe this," Anderson said, "But I *have* to believe it." He bent down, reached for the floor, but never took his eyes off the window. His hands closed on the snow globe. He picked it up, stood up straight. No Rudolph. But Christmas on the way.

What if the snow globe did break after all these hundreds of years? What if tonight was the end for it? Even its hardened shell couldn't survive a hull breach, could it?

"Ho, ho, ho," cried the voice. "Merry Christmas!"

Believe.

Did he? Maybe. Was it enough?

Merry Christmas, Gear.

Merry Christmas, Anderson.

"Tell Mom and Dad, will you? In case."

You will tell them yourself, tomorrow, Gear replied, then added: **in all likelihood.**

The sleigh was very close now. The reindeer were huffing and puffing nonexistent mist. The man on the sleigh was smiling.

Nearer.

Behind the man, the Big Dipper. Draco. Cassiopeia. And the great glowing smudge of the Milky Way chalked across the sky.

Anderson held his snow globe and waited for another moment only.

Christmas arrived.

INTRODUCTION
🌺
CHRISTMAS CARD

I DON'T THINK I CAN WRITE about this delightful gem without giving too much away, so I'll mention that this was one of the prolific Ms. Willis' early stories, and it may or may not have appeared in a semi-professional magazine (if it did, she was not sent a copy) years ago, so this may be its first time in print. She was reluctant to let the original version be published without a rewrite. Not having seen the original, I can't say whether or not she was being too hard on an early piece, but we should all be grateful that this story has finally seen the light of day. Thank you, Santa—er, Connie.

🌲 🌲 🌲

CONNIE WILLIS has won eleven Nebula Awards, seven Hugo Awards, four *Locus* Awards, the John W. Campbell Memorial Award, and the Damon Knight Memorial Grand Master Award from the Science Fiction Writers of America for lifetime achievement. Willis writes in her introduction to her short story collection, *Miracle*, that she loves Christmas, and, appropriately, all the stories in *Miracle* are Christmas stories, so if you enjoyed "Christmas Card," there are more yuletide goods in that book, not to mention a terrific Christmas novella in her recently published *The Best of Connie Willis*, a compilations of all her Hugo and Nebula Award winning stories.

CHRISTMAS CARD

❧❀❧

by Connie Willis

I HAVE JUST RECEIVED ANOTHER TRACT. It has a box of sixty-four Crayolas on the cover and is entitled (aren't they all?) "Broken Crayons." This one is from the ETCLU and begins, "Whether you know it or not, you are committing a crime by denying the Crayoni the right to vote," which is better than the Interplanetary Religious Council's, which began, "Exploiters of the alien downtrodden! Repent or else!"

As head exploiter, I am not in a position to do what I would really like to do with these tracts. In the first place, I am in full view of half my downtrodden, who are here clogging up my office to talk to me about my Christmas plans. And in the second place, the organization heads and tract authors down whose throats I would frankly like to stuff them, are not here on rhinoRogetselectricaltransformer-sunshineyellowfig. They are safely back on earth and have never actually met a Crayoni. (The lucky dogs!)

In their absence, I am sorely tempted to rip the tract (the nineteenth I have received this morning), into shreds, but that might be misinterpreted (since the Crayoni misinterpret virtually everything else they hear or see—or read), and, frankly, I can't afford any more misinterpretations right now.

And I can't afford to ignore the tract, since my secretary is watching me with an eagle eye. So I flip quickly through the pages, reading the section titles and hoping my face's turning purple will be misinterpreted as empathy. (Or a fondness for celery.)

The tract's subheads are printed in rainbow-colored letters and say things like, "Second-Class Citizens!" and "Why the Crayoni Deserve Full Interplanetary Alliance Voting Status" and "How would you feel if you were a Crayoni?"

Frankly, I have no idea. How *do* the Crayoni feel? Perplexed? Muddled? Contrary? (I could think of better words if I had my Thesaurus.) Willfully slow-witted? Utterly deranged?

I don't know, but definitely not second-class or disenfranchised or downtrodden. If anything, *I* am the downtrodden one here. The Crayoni are happy as larks, clams, and the day is long. And the last thing they should be given is the right to vote, though the state of our Interplanetary Congress being what it is, an argument could be made that there is no way they could make things worse.

But these are the Crayoni we're talking about, and yes, they could. Plus, to achieve this representation, rhinoRogetselectricaltransformersunshineyellowfig would have to send delegates to Earth, and frankly, you do *not* want that.

I know what you're going to say, that all sentient beings deserve the right to be full citizens, and what terrible previous exploiters both on and off Earth you're going to compare me to for saying that (Romans, plantation owners, and Arcturian Neo-Legreeists spring to mind), but, trust me, this is entirely different. And frankly, if you had to put up with the Crayoni on a daily basis as I do, you would all be lying down with sick headaches (like my two predecessors) before the week was out.

On my way to work I am besieged by orange and mustard and jade green reporters, all of them demanding to know my intentions regarding the upcoming holiday. The entire royal family, sporting mustaches and varying shades of aqua (as on Earth, the royalty here are blue bloods) are waiting for me in my office when I arrive, as are dozens of raw umber and lilac and crimson vendors and merchants and mongers and whatever you call those people who sell things from a hole in the sidewalk. (As I said before, if I had my Thesaurus, I could give you the exact word for that.) My secretary, who is a blinding neon yellow-green, is sitting at my desk, poised to jump up and ask me if I have made up my mind yet.

"No," I say before she has the chance. I hand her the tract and tell her to file it with the others.

"Under what?" she asks.

"Trains," I say, which is a joke (and a pun—get it? train tracts?), but she does not laugh, nor does the rest of the crowd. The Crayoni do not have a sense of humor.

They have everything else that I have happened to leave on my desk, however, and everything else I've ever happened to mention or even refer obliquely to. Mind you, I'm not accusing them of theft. They're perfectly willing to give everything back (which is part of the current problem) and they don't even always steal the things they like. They simply copy them, as in the case of my mustache.

There is no malice in their actions, and they are more than willing to do whatever we want them to (though they don't always understand what that is). They love us. They adore our Earth culture, our ships, my neckwear. And what they love, they attach themselves to with ferocity and without regard to who actually owns it. The rest, an inexplicable assortment of things including logic, ice cube trays, potato famines, flip-flops, parentheses, coconut macaroons, Dante, and puns, they simply ignore. There is no rhyme or reason to it.

They like feathers, but not plumes. They have no interest in windchimes or ukuleles, but adore bagpipes, and they ignore lipstick, sideburns, neckties, and eye shadow (which you would think they'd like because it comes in an array of interestingly-named colors—emerald, amethyst, lapis lazuli, lampblack), only to develop a passion for cravats and mustaches (but only the small, dashing, Civil War-era type I wear, not bushy soupstrainers, sinister Fu Manchus, Hitlerian toothbrushes, or handlebars, though they like other handlebars. But not bicycles).

Frankly, it is enough to . . . (if I seem to overuse the word "frankly," it is because the word is one of the few things about me they do not care for and have left alone. And since they have appropriated my cravat (which I thought made me look like Rhett Butler), my mustache, and my Thesaurus, I cling to it (the word, not the Thesaurus, which as I say has vanished) and to the few other things they don't want. Rather neurotically, I'm afraid. My writing has become unreadably cluttered with parenthetical remarks, and I have acquired an unhealthy delight in puns. Frankly, I am deteriorating.

Take my mustache. They took one look at it and immediately all began sporting one just like it. Or rather, all the females did. And the babies.

Or take my Thesaurus. (We did, thank you.) It illustrates my point even better. As you of course know, the inhabitants of rhinoRogetselectrical . . . etc. are brightly colored. Each family line is a different hue, with varying shades depending on age, height, and agility at doing the native foot-stomping ritual, and the effect of them in crowds is very nice. But before we came, their words for colors were limited. Red, blue, green, yellow, purple was about it. And since they all named themselves color names, it was all a bit repetitious and confusing. It's completely understandable that when they found out there were other possibilities, they latched onto them.

How they found out about these other color names, I don't know. (*I* didn't do it.) Perhaps one of the first expedition got to flirting with a pretty young blue thing and complimented her on her azure tresses. Or, more likely, one of the ship's crew swore at one of them for absconding with a lab specimen or the macrodrive. (Astronauts have long been known for their colorful language.) Or perhaps they picked up on the fact that we were calling them the Crayoni (only because rhino . . . etc. was too long and unwieldy) and figured it out for themselves. I mean, frankly, they're not stupid, just . . . alien.

Only that doesn't even begin to cover it. The Voracians are perfectly rational, if a bit irritable. The Frostal Lichens and the Rigello both have recognizable thought patterns. But the Crayoni are downright odd.

At any rate, the next thing you know, my Roget's Thesaurus is missing, and every Crayoni (or rhino . . . etc.) has renamed him or herself Ultramarine, Amber, Lettuce Green, and Vermilion. Very understandable. Even logical. So far.

But at some point their minds begin to drift away from the original idea like a bunch of hot-air balloons (which the Crayoni also love) coming loose from their moorings and drifting off into the wild blue (or royal or slate or baby blue) and they . . . blow it. (Oh, if I only had my Thesaurus, I could explain this *much* better!)

The point is, the names they chose have *nothing* to do with their actual color. The khaki-colored courier who delivers all my tracts named himself Tangerine. The royal family (blue, remember?) christened themselves Fuschia, Puce, Mauve, Ashes of Roses, and Banana. And my secretary, for whom "chartreuse" is an understatement, is currently strutting around my office sporting *my* mustache, my cravat, and a name for bright-red previously reserved for Southern belles and sentimental songs about ribbons.

"Why that particular shade?" I asked her. "There are other bright reds. Carmine, for instance. Or Flame. Or Inferno. Or why not a name that matches your actual color, say Neon Green or Absinthe or something?"

She frowned through her mustache. "Green?" she said blankly.

You see what I mean? And it's not just names or colors. They do the same thing with everything they come in contact with. In fact, my job here consists entirely of attempting to prevent them from coming in contact with anything else Earth-related.

But they had already heard about Christmas (the ship's crew had put up a Christmas tree) and the Crayoni had focused mostly on Yule logs and the multicolored tree lights, which they appropriated for their native foot-stomping ritual, resulting in assorted injuries and several new color names (Blood Red, Ashes of Anemia, and Gang Green (Sorry)

They had paid no attention at all to the concept of Christmas gifts, and I assumed it was one of those things they'd decided to ignore. Plus, I was just being funny. And I thought we were alone in the room. I was talking to one of the ship's crew about what to get the captain, and I said, "It's not what you give that's important," pause and punch line, "Its what you get."

Unfortunately, although it was a joke (and a not very good one), it was not a pun. And my red-nomered enterprising Girl Friday was apparently listening at the door because she promptly, in true Crayoni fashion, dropped the last part, turned the first around, did a little of the twisted something that passes for thinking around here, and came up with a thrilling new custom: Not-gifts for Christmas. Then she told everyone she knew, and five minutes later all of the Crayoni were walking around eating Yule logs and announcing, "I don't give a saberin fur to you."

This is not as simple or inexpensive as it may sound. You are simply not familiar with the intricate customs they are capable of weaving, given ten minutes' time. For example, a lover not-gives the above saberin. But another lover *gives* the saberin and not gives a Pez dispenser (higher on the scale and, according to my secretary, hopelessly romantic), so he wins and our saberin friend gets called an uncomplimentary color.

However, the winner can still be beaten out if somebody chooses a not-gift above his, like rice spools, and gives the whole gamut of gifts under it on the list. Follow? There are entire elaborate hierarchies.

Six days ago (and a mere twenty minutes after I told the joke) a list was subtly placed on my desk, entitled (not so subtly) "A List of Possible Not-Gifts for the Head of Crayoni Affairs." Bridges, underpasses, dams, wraparound sunglasses, anaerobic bacteria, courthouses, stars, galaxies, pinking shears, all neatly numbered and with humble hints in the margin as to how non-receipt would likely be taken by the populace. The bottom two were labeled "instant death" and the top five "probable godhood."

So I have spent the last week grappling with the thorny problem of what not to give them, making pathetic puns about being "marooned" here, and attempting to keep a grip on my ever-loosening sanity. Would you believe that on the way to work just now (post-reporters and pre-tract), I heard an old lavender gentleman reminiscing on the wonderful not-gifts of his youth?

And my hirsute secretary? "I don't always give my mother a yellow hip pin," she said to me last night, "and I guess I'll don't give bias eggs to the staff. Last year I don't gave Taupe four cravats and a catalpa leaf, but . . . by the way, have you decided?"

And yes, amid all the din and chaos, I have. Frankly, I kept hoping I would think of some miraculous way out of the mess—some not-gift that would enchant the entire planet and not cost the government a cent. Or make the Crayoni magically disappear in a burst of nonsense. But in the end, I had to abandon all hope and enter into a perfectly ordinary political decision, nondescript even, and in the exact middle of my list. Nevertheless, it gives me an incredible amount of pleasure to announce it.

I call my blazingly 1960s-lime-green secretary in. She flounces in like her literary namesake (except for the mustache), wearing a festive apron made out of tracts and my cravat (though this time it was wrapped around her heel—she has apparently been doing the foot-stomping ritual again).

"Well?" she says. "Have you decided?"

"Yes," I say. I snatch the cravat from her bleeding heel and tie it around my neck.

"I have," I say, curling my mustached lip as I speak. "Frankly, Scarlet, I don't give a dam."

INTRODUCTION
❧❀❧
AWAY IN A MANGER

THERE'S NO SIGN that the very unusual characters in this enigmatic but comical tale have ever heard of Christmas, though it's obviously getting near that time of year. And just how this situation came about and what has happened to certain absent entities is for the reader to wonder about. But then, Christmas is a time of wonders, and they certainly got a gift they weren't expecting . . .

🌲 🌲 🌲

JOHN W. CAMPBELL Award Winner Wen Spencer resides in paradise in Hilo, Hawaii with two volcanoes overlooking her home. Spencer says that she often wakes up and exclaims "Oh my god, I live on an island in the middle of the Pacific!" This, says Spencer, is a far cry from her twenty years of living in land-locked Pittsburgh. According to Spencer, she lives with "my Dalai Lama-like husband, my autistic teenage son, and two cats (one of which is recovering from mental illness). All of which makes for very odd home life at times." Spencer's love of Japanese anime and manga flavors her writing. The Elfhome series opener, *Tinker*, won the 2003 Sapphire Award for Best Science Fiction Romance and was a finalist for the *Romantic Times* Reviewers' Choice Award for Fantasy Novel. *Wolf Who Rules*, the sequel to *Tinker*, was chosen as a Top Pick by *Romantic Times* and given their top rating of four and a half stars. Other Baen books include SF adventure thriller *Endless Blue* and the third Tinker novel, *Elfhome*. Her latest novel is *Eight Million Gods*.

AWAY IN A MANGER

by Wen Spencer

IT WAS SO COLD IN THE TOWER when Jack woke, his breath turned to smoke as he breathed out. From the windows of the overlook, dawn's pale light revealed no telling glitter of frost on the asphalt below. Nor was there any on the patches of green among the tall buildings that they'd deemed pasture and hay field. The wind carried the scent of autumn leaves but nothing of grass sheared by the cold.

"So we have at least one more day?" Renard yawned, showing off his mouth full of sharp teeth, and then stretched lazily.

"How could you tell?"

"Your tail."

Jack glanced at his backside and saw that the white stub of his tail was indeed wagging. "Traitor."

The cat laughed as he strutted toward the nearest window and thumbed the latch. "Honestly you're as easy to read as a book with big bold font and little bitty words. That little tail is shouting 'yay, yay, let's make hay.'"

"What are you doing?"

"I'm going to catch my breakfast."

"Don't let the cold in." Jack trotted to the opening. "And make sure you don't catch anything that can talk."

"If it can talk, I'll thank it kindly for its brave sacrifice."

Jack huffed out a cloud that wisped away on the bitter cold wind. He hated the idea of eating anything you could argue morality with, but the simple truth was that they were losing the luxury every moment as the world turned colder. Last winter they barely survived. "Go on, let me shut the window. The cold is going to get to the bird."

Renard glanced across the room at the jury-rigged nest. "Too late."

"What?" Jack's tail stopped wagging.

"I told you it was too little, too late in the year."

Jack bound to the nest and peered into it. The tiny featherless bird inside lay on its side, smelling of death. Despite the heat lamp and curtain to keep out wind, the chick had been dead for hours. "Damn."

"Not your fault; they always die."

Which was nicer than what Renard usually said. Jack realized that the cat was still staring intently at the body.

"Fine! Take it."

The cat picked the dead chick up in its mouth and slunk away.

Alfie was asleep in the small room off the garage. Jack could never understand how the pony slept standing up. The little hairdressing robot was fussing with Alfie's long silky black tail that contrasted sharply with his gleaming golden hide. The robot had brushed out all the dirt and matted knots and was currently tying bits of bright colored ribbons into it.

Jack had learned to keep a safe distance from the sleeping pony. "Yo, Alfie! Alfie! Time to make hay!"

A flick of the ear was the only warning that the pony was waking up. His rear hoof lashed out, caught the hairdresser square on and kicked it across the room.

Jack winced, torn between the knowledge it could have been him that gotten kicked and the fact he would have to fix the robot if Alfie had broken it. "Hey, watch it now. That's the last one. I won't be the one pulling briars out of your tail if you broke this one too."

Jack righted the hairdresser. "You all right?"

"All right." The robot stated but it still sounded a little whoozy.

"Alfie, look what you did." Jack pointed to a hoof-shaped dent in the hairdresser's chassis.

Alfie snorted. "Serves it right; it's an annoying little fucker." He flicked his tail in irritation. "Stupid little bows."

Jack shook his head. "Come on, let's get cracking. Got to get this hay stored before the frost hits."

They had been working most of the year toward surviving the next winter. The last one had been the first for all of them to experience, so it had taken them off guard. Jack and Renard pulled through thanks to the fact they could eat everything from bugs to mice, but Alfie was skin and bones by the time the grass started to grow again. It had taken all summer for him to regain all his weight. He didn't have the fat to survive another brutal winter.

Renard researched ponies and learned about hay. They'd found a field with the correct mix of grasses. They'd watched over it all summer, watching it grow tall and lush. But when they went to cut it, their plans fell apart. The starter battery on the forklift was dead. Some idiot had designed the forklift to disconnect from the broadcast power grid while not in use. The only way to reconnect it was through a start procedure that needed a minimum charge in the starter battery. Jack couldn't understand why anyone would think it was a good idea, but there it was, blocking all their plans. Worse, it was a design flaw common on every semi–manual vehicle they could track down. The only thing operational was the fully automated systems but they all had a mind of their own. It'd taken half the autumn to build a battery charger once they discovered how screwed they were. With Alfie plodding in a tight circle as he powered the generator, Jack finished the modifications to the controls.

Unfortunately, it left the pony too much time to think.

"I still don't understand why we can't just use the lawnmower down by the river. We took the blade off it. Can't we move it to the hay field and put the blade back on it?"

Jack sighed from deep inside the forklift's motor housing. He'd tried to explain this before to Alfie. The pony was heaped high with common sense but was completely thickheaded when it came to machines. "The lawnmower knows where it's supposed to be and what it's supposed to do and what it's not supposed to do. It's supposed to cut the grass in the afternoon when it's reached a certain height, avoid all obstacles whether stationary or mobile while doing so . . ."

"So it could cut the grass in the hay field."

"No, it would just map its way back to the park and cut grass there."

"But why?"

"I don't know!" Jack cried and then swore as the bolt he'd been trying to coax into place slipped through his fingers and tumbled into the engine's guts. He peered through the machinery, searching for the bolt. "It just will and I can't change that. It's not the simple lever and gears and belts and hydraulics that I know how to fiddle with. It's the thinking part."

Jack spotted the bolt deep inside the housing, but his stubby fingers couldn't quite reach it. He squirmed, growling, trying to wedge himself closer.

"Jack?" Renard called from the forklift's bench seat. He'd returned an hour ago licking his lips and presented Jack with a frog as a peace offering. (The gift would have been more impressive if he hadn't obviously found the frog in one of Jack's frog traps and then complained that it had peed in his mouth.) "You okay?"

"Dropped the fucking bolt!" Jack barked out a series of words he knew were curses and some words he only suspected were curses.

"That last word does not mean what you think it means," Renard said with annoying calmness. "And it's impossible for bolts to fuck, at least in the sexual manner."

"Just shut up!" Jack snarled. He needed the bolt. It was aluminum, so using a magnet on a string wouldn't help. Could he reach it from underneath? He eyed all four of the access holes at the bottom of the housing, trying to judge if he stuck his hand up thru one of them, he'd be able to reach the bolt.

Something dark moved through the shadows under the forklift and his nose told him that it was a mouse. Sometimes the mice would fetch things for him if he asked nicely, but if he called to the mouse, he'd attract Renard's attention. Besides, he didn't actually "talk" to mice so much as "pantomime."

"And you can't fix the mower on the hayfield?" Alfie clip-clopped around the idea of what they were trying to do.

Jack brushed his right thumb and forefinger together in a whisper of a snap to attract the mouse.

Renard didn't seem to notice the sound, snickering at the conversation. The cat understood the machines only marginally better than the pony but he recognized the circular nature of their conversation.

As Jack waited to see if the mouse realized he was asking for help, Jack stared at his outstretched hand. There were times it seemed horribly wrong. It wasn't much different from Renard's but still the fingers seemed too short or the thumb seemed too long or both or neither.

No mouse appeared.

Jack answered Alfie's question to cover a second quiet snap. "We had to fry the brain on that mower which is why we need to tow it with the forklift to make hay." They'd discussed simply having Alfie tow the mower but the hay field was on a fairly steep hillside (which was probably why there were no buildings on it.) There was a chance that the mower would simply knock the pony down and run him over. Alfie would also work off any little fat that he had, rendering the whole process a negative gain.

"Before we can do that, we need to change over this forklift's controls because . . ." Which required the dropped bolt. Which was out of reach from the access hole in the bottom of the housing. Maybe if he used a bent wire . . .

A mouse popped up through the far right access hole.

So far for Jack communication hadn't hit the level of exchanging real names. He'd given nicknames to a dozen that he could recognize by sight and smell. This mouse was black with a torn ear and a surprisingly large set of gonads. Jack had named it Notch.

The mouse waved in greeting but didn't call out, probably because he understood that Renard was in ear shot.

Jack pointed at the bolt. Notch scanned the housing, spotted the bolt, and scurried to it. Picking it up with his mouth, Notch climbed up through the motor to drop it into Jack's outstretched palm. Unfortunately, there was no way to thank the mouse. Jack would have to owe Notch a treat.

"Because?" Renard prompted.

Jack frowned, screwing the retrieved bolt into place. What had he been talking about? "Because—because whoever built this world clearly did not have me in mind."

"God," Renard said.

"What?"

"God made the world." Renard expanded, marking his place in his reader with a flick of his paw. "In the beginning, God created the heavens and the earth. Yadayadayada, I don't remember it all. Just the cool parts. Darkness was over the surface of the deep, and the Spirit of God was hovering over the waters. And God said, 'Let there be light,' and there was light. God saw that the light was good . . ." Renard trailed off as Jack cocked his head in confusion. "Do you not read anything?"

"I read the instruction manual for this thing." Jack disappeared back into the motor housing of the forklift again. "I know how this is supposed to work." He came bounding out, tail wagging with excitement despite his irritation. He jumped up onto the seat beside Renard and posed with his paws on the steering wheel and then looked meaningfully at the foot pedals down in the darkness. "And this world wasn't built with me in mind."

"Nor me," Alfie muttered clopping through his paces in the endless circle of the power generator.

"More you than me," Jack called to the pony, and muttered lowly, "If you had hands and a more flexible spine."

Hay was cut and with a great deal of fiddling and swearing, eventually stacked to dry in the vast garage as planned. Of course, the heating system refused to acknowledge that temperatures were now low enough to kick on, and thus aid in the drying process.

Jack was deep in the heat ducts trying to trace the thermostat leads when he next saw Notch.

The black mouse appeared in front of him and waved. "*Ohayougozaimasu!*"

"Hi Notch! Thanks for the help with the bolt. I owe you."

"*Tasukete! Akachan no seigyo ga dame desu! Kite onegaishimasu!*"
The mouse gestured back the way Jack had come.

"I don't understand," Jack said.

Notch fell silent a moment and then started again, this time with
acting. Mouse pantomime was very entertaining although not very
informative. "*Akachan!*" Notch squeaked and put his paws over his
head and then stomped around in circle, roaring. Or at least, that's
what it looked like he was attempting to do but what was coming out
was ear-piercing squeaks.

"Okay, okay, okay." Anything to stop the squeaks. Obviously
something larger than a mouse was terrorizing the rodent tribe. "I do
owe you. I'll come and help."

Just about anything was bigger than a mouse, but it might be even
bigger than Jack. Backup would be a wise idea.

Alfie was grazing in the meadow by the river, stoically trying to
ignore the sabotaged mower that continued to march across the field.
Wheel tracks marked the mowers frustrated attempts at its assigned
task.

"This is not a pasture for livestock!" the mower complained. It
had not taken well to losing its cutting blades. "This is a public
recreational facility. We have laws against the likes of you." It avoided
a pile of Alfie's manure. "And we have scooper rules! And you! You're
supposed to be on a leash."

This was directed at Jack.

"I'm on a leash," Jack pointed out. They'd learned that the mower
could summon animal control if they broke certain laws and he never
wanted to go through that again.

The mower paused to eye him with a telescoping camera. It took
in the collar, the piece of thread, and the mouse in the carry basket,
holding onto the end of the "leash."

"*Ohayougozaimasu, robotto no kamisama!*" Notch squeaked.

There was a long, long silence, and finally, the mower whirled and
rolled away, muttering, "It still isn't a pasture for livestock."

🌲 🌲 🌲

"I don't understand how this is our problem," Alfie complained as they worked their way through the city.

"Where would you be if I hadn't come looking to see what was making that god-awful noise?"

"Stupid machines," Alfie muttered. "Damn milk dispenser dried up and then the stable door broke. I couldn't get back in."

This part of the story Jack had never heard before. It sounded similar to his first memories. He'd been raised in a place warm and snug with machines catering to his every need, and then suddenly he found himself in the barren empty city. "How'd you end up in that pit?"

"Got lost. Fell."

Jack had heard Alfie from half a mile away, as the pony gave loud wordless cries of terror. It had taken two hours to calm him down and three whole days to get the much larger animal out of the hole. It required a great deal of cable, pulleys, a sling, and a well-timed roping of a street sweeper's bumper. Renard had helped but only under protest as he was sure the pony would eat them once they freed him. They'd had to stop and actually look up Alfie's species before Renard was pacified.

Renard would call Jack stupid for helping the mice since the cat viewed the mice as food. It seemed only right though to help the mice out since they had fetched nuts and bolts for Jack that had fallen out of reach.

"I want to see what got the mice upset. There aren't many others around. There are us, the mice, and the birds."

"And the birds are god awful stupid."

True. They did kill themselves with great regularly by running into windows. If birds could talk, they chose never to speak to Jack, even after several peacemaking attempts. At least the birds put the mice farther down the possible dinner list.

Notch squeaked something, tugging lightly on Jack's leash. The black mouse pointed excitedly at the building that they were about to pass. There were words etched into the heavy glass of the doors.

"What does that say?" Alfie couldn't read. He contended it was because he didn't have hands. Jack wasn't sure if this were true or not;

he'd been trying to teach Alfie but the pony seemed unable to grasp the difference between letters. Jack had always been able to read, just as he had always been able to talk.

"Mayflower," Jack read the first word. It was plastered all over the place as if it meant "the." He didn't know the second word. He tried to sound out the syllables for Alfie. "K-re-ch-e. Maybe. Kre-cheh. Kreesh."

"What does it mean?" Alfie asked.

"I'm not sure."

"Mayflower *Hoikuen*," Notch squeaked climbing down out of the carry basket. He scurried up the ramped edge of the staircase to one of the small round portals that the mice used to enter buildings. There was an invisible barrier that kept Jack's paw from passing through the hole but the mice popped through it without slowing down.

Notch appeared on the other side of the glass doors and waved at them.

Automatic doors never worked for Jack. He apparently was too small to activate them, but they recognized Alfie bulk and movement. They slid open as the pony plodded up to them and into the building.

"And so it begins," Alfie grumbled.

Notch led them through several doors, moving deep into the building. The air inside was twenty degrees warmer than outside; the heating was working in the building. The last door opened to a vast dim room, filled with odd pieces of equipment, and a rank smell of excrement. Something fairly large was alive in the room.

"*Ohayou!*" Notch squeaked.

There was a squeal in reply, too loud to be a mouse, but just as ear-piercing.

"*Nigeru! Nigeru!*" a swarm of mice squeaked as they came charging toward Jack.

With a patter of feet, the pursuing creature rounded the corner, running on its back legs, front legs raised over its head. It stood at least two feet taller than Jack. It was mostly white with a long black mane. It stopped as it came in view and stood a moment, blinking in surprise at the dog and pony.

Then it gave this odd gurgling laugh, which ended with another loud, ear-piercing shriek, and charged.

Alfie snorted loudly and took off running the other way.

"Hey!" Jack dodged an attack and raced after the fleeing pony. "Why are you running from it?"

"Because it's chasing me!"

"You're bigger than it!"

"It apparently knows something I don't!"

They outdistanced it easily as the creature wasn't very stable on its back legs. It flailed its forelegs, laughing and shrieking and occasionally falling flat on its face.

"What is it?" Alfie snorted and pranced.

"I don't know!" For some strange reason, every time it fell, Jack had the overwhelming urge to run back to it and make sure it wasn't hurt. The weird instinct was warring with the knowledge that it was twice his size and obviously fearless.

The soft uneven patter of feet marked the approaching animal.

"Here it comes." Jack scanned room. The area was full of odd plastic equipment of unknown function in bright primary colors. "We need some kind of a plan to catch. . . . Oh crap!" This was because Alfie had bolted again, leaving him alone as the creature rounded the corner. It spotted Jack and squealed. Jack scrambled desperately after the pony. "Alfie, this is getting us no where!"

"It's getting us away from it!"

"We're running in loops!"

Alfie dodged right. "Now we aren't!"

The right had been a mistake. It led them into a virtual maze of the brightly dyed plastic equipment. There were ramps and slides and inexplicable pits filled with multi-colored balls.

Alfie suddenly jerked to a halt, his feet splayed wide, his eyes wide with fear. "Jack," the pony whimpered. "I think it's on my back."

It was definitely sprawled across Alfie's back having leapt from one of the pieces of equipment. It had two paws clenching tight to Alfie's mane.

"Get it off!" Alfie wailed.

"Hold on a minute."

Not exactly what Jack had in mind of "catching" the creature, but far as he could tell, it wasn't actually hurting the pony. The back feet seemed to be lacking in claws and the front feet seemed more like Jack's than Renard's.

"Jack, I'm scared."

"Nothing to be scared of," Jack lied.

"But—but—but what if it *falls*?"

Jack cocked his head in confusion. "You—you don't want it to fall?"

"Falling would be bad. Head injuries. Spinal damage. Broken limbs. Falling needs to be avoided at all cost. There should be a saddle."

"What's a saddle?"

"I don't know! It—it—it goes on my back and I shouldn't blow up my stomach when the girth is tightened."

"The girth?"

"Get it off before it falls!" Alfie wailed. "I don't like this!"

Jack circled the pony, trying to figure out how to get the creature who was twice his size off the pony's back without hurting any of them. "Can you lie down?"

Thus they ended up leaving the crèche with the creature carrying Jack as a very much-relieved Alfie walked ahead of them. Over the creature's shoulder, Jack could see mice appearing on the top step of the building, seemingly hundreds of them. There were more than he ever imagined there being.

Notch was easily identifiable by the missing part of his ear. He waved at Jack. "*Domo arigatougozaimashita, inu-sama! Kouun! Sayonara!*"

"Let me get this straight." Renard was perched on the highest point of the garage after the creature had attempted to pick him up by his tail. "The mice gave you this—this—thing and you brought it home."

"It doesn't seem dangerous." Jack had managed to stay free after they arrived by distracting the creature with his chew toy. For some reason, though, the creature kept flinging it across the room. Jack needed to retrieve it over and over again, but it made the creature laugh every time he dropped the toy at its feet. "It doesn't bite . . ."

"Yes, it does," Renard snapped.

"Very hard," Jack amended.

"I suppose we could keep it as emergency food rations," Renard stated.

"Don't ever say that again." Jack warned with a growl that he was serious.

"What? It doesn't talk. That's your criteria for food, right?"

"Don't!" Jack barked.

"Hm, both of you are acting weird for something that you just found." Renard leapt to a slightly lower perch that gave him access to the door. "I'm going to look it up. Find out what it is."

"It's a human." Renard returned to the perch a short period time later. "Judging by the shape of the eyes, the color and straightness of the mane, its breed is most likely East Asian descent. Male of the species."

"How do you get male?" Jack cocked his head at it.

"It's wearing fabric clothing. The white isn't really part of its skin."

Jack reached out and lifted the front hem. "Oh! Yeah, male."

"Human are omnivores. They eat everything, including ponies, dogs and cats."

"Still don't think he's dangerous."

"It will grow," Renard warned. "It will get bigger just like Alfie. Remember how little he was compared to now?"

"So you're saying it's just a baby now?"

Renard breathed out in disgust. "This is going to be like one of those damn baby birds? They always die, you know."

"If it dies, it dies," Jack said.

Renard slunk away.

He'd learned the trick to keep baby birds alive the longest was to keep them warm. Last winter while desperately foraging for food to keep Alfie alive, he'd found a big plastic bin labeled Non-structured Carbohydrates. They carefully rationed it out to Alfie all winter as they'd learn that he'd eat himself sick if given a chance. Jack rinsed the bin out and pushed it to the most protected corner of Alfie's garage. With the stacks of cut hay, the garage was now much warmer than the overlook.

He set up the heat lamp that he used with the baby birds, trying to nail it solid to the wall since so far the baby had upended almost everything in the garage. The hardest part was getting the baby into the bin and asleep.

"Maybe we should take it back," Alfie whispered when the garage was finally quiet and still.

Jack caught himself growling. "There is no place to take it back to! Don't you see? The proof is all around us. The birds are how it should be. When we were small and helpless, we should have had someone taking care of us. Someone alive. Someone who loved us enough that they wouldn't stop caring for us until they knew we could take care of ourselves. But we had machines just like the lawnmowers and the hairdressers. They knew what they were supposed to do and what they weren't supposed to do. They fed us and kept us warm and cleaned up after us. And like the lawnmower that stops trying to cut the grass at dusk, the machines stopped taking care of us because—because—I don't know—we'd gotten big enough to fly."

"Since when can we fly?" Alfie asked.

"It's a metaphor," Renard muttered from the doorway. Seeing that the baby was safely asleep, he stalked across the garage, tail twitching with annoyance. "The baby birds leave the nest once they're ready to fly."

"Exactly," Jack said. "I don't think your milk dispenser dried up and the door broke, I think whatever machines were feeding you decided they weren't supposed to take care of you anymore."

Like the baby, Jack had been locked in a kennel with toys and running water but no food. Starving and nearly driven mad by the silence, he'd managed to climb up and use a piece of wire to short the lock to get out of his cage. This baby, though, wasn't as capable as he had been when he was abandoned by the system.

"It seems to me a stupid way of doing things," Alfie said. "Even birds know better. They might be stupid as shit, but they take care of their chicks, day and night, until they're ready to be on their own. This randomly spit out babies and hoping someone takes care of them; sheer stupidity."

"Whoever came up with the design didn't think everything through," Jack said. "Like the forklift starter battery. Obviously they thought the battery wouldn't go dead because it wouldn't if someone was using it day in and day out."

"The designer is an idiot then." Renard snorted with disgust. "Because only an idiot thinks that things will always work out the way he images. He planed for the good but not the bad, or the horrible nor the utter disasters."

"Something has gone very wrong. And if we don't take care of…" Jack paused as he realized that they couldn't keep calling the baby simply "it." "If we don't take care of whatever we name the baby, he will die."

"So what do we call it?" Alfie asked.

They considered the sleeping baby curled inside the blue food bin. Renard suddenly snickered.

"What?" Jack and Alfie both asked.

"You put it in a manger?" the cat laughed.

"What's a manger?" Jack asked.

"Something that holds food for ponies." Renard glanced up at the heat lamp. "Nice and warm here." He climbed into the bin to tuck himself against the baby's back.

"What are you doing?" Jack hissed, not wanting to wake the baby. "You don't like it."

"I can't help myself." Renard looked away, embarrassed, as he started to purr. "It's like this is home. This is where I'm meant to be and it kind of pisses me off even as I can't help wanting it. There's this little voice that I don't think is actually mine, whispering how wonderful it would be to both read a book together and then sit discussing the story."

"We'll have to name him," Jack said.

Renard snorted. "His name is Jesus."

"Jesus?"

"And this shall be a sign unto you." Renard quoted something.

"You shall find the babe wrapped in swaddling clothes, lying in a manger."

🌿 Place Your Own Footnotes 🌿

1   Jack is a Jack Russell Terrier. Renard named him.
    Jack doesn't realize his name is a joke.

2. Renard misread his breed the only time he looked it up.
    Instead of Persian, he read it as Parisian. He believes he's
    French, hence his name. He chose the name of a popular
    French fairytale character known for being clever.
    Unfortunately he did not realize the character was named
    for its species, which was "Fox."

3. Alfie's full name is Alfalfa Hay Eater. Renard can be cruel.
    He's always careful, however, only to use it when he's out of
    kicking and biting range.

4. Alfie is a genetic mishmash that is part Shetland pony
    crossed with the Akhal-Teke, a breed of horses from
    Turkmenistan. They are famous for the natural metallic
    shimmer of their coats.

5. Renard complained about the frog peeing in his mouth not
    only because he found it disgustingly uncivilized but also he'd
    had the overwhelming urge to meow "Look I'm a mighty
    hunter" until Jack took ownership of the frog's body.

6. Let it be noted that all rodents have large gonads in
    proportion to their overall body-size.

7. *Ohayougozaimasu* is a greeting in Japanese.

8. *Tasukete! Akachan no seigyo ga dame desu! Kite onegaishimasu!*
Help! The toddler is out of control. Come!

9. Birds are swallows, not pigeons, but this doesn't seem to
eliminate window collisions.

10. *Hoikuen* means crèche.

11. A force field over the barrier only drops to allow
the mice to enter.

12. *Nigeru* means "Run away!"

13. *Domo arigatougozaimashita, inu-sama! Kouun! Sayonara!*
Notch is saying "Thank you very much, much obliged,
Sir Dog. Good luck. Goodbye!"

INTRODUCTION

HAPPY BIRTHDAY, DEAR JESUS

FREDERIK POHL is known for his sharp cutting satire, and this one, from the mid-1950s, cuts deep. If you think that Christmas has gotten too commercialized, be thankful that things haven't gone as far as they have in this possible future . . . yet.

🌲 🌲 🌲

While Frederik Pohl didn't found the world's first science fiction magazine (probably due to age discrimination, since he was only about six and a half when Hugo Gernsback launched *Amazing Stories*) he has otherwise been everything and done everything in science fiction: writer, editor, agent, a talk show guest, all of which makes most other sf stars look like dilletantes. Beginning with a poem published in a 1937 *Amazing Stories*, his phenomenal writing career has produced enough novels, story collections, nonfiction books, and collaborative novels to fill a medium-sized library (his latest novel is *All the Lives He Led*), and has been honored with four Hugo Awards, three Nebula Awards, two John W. Campbell Memorial Awards, a U.S. National Book Award, the SFWA Grand Master award for lifetime achievement, and other awards. His celebrated novel *Gateway* won the Hugo, Nebula, *Locus*, and John W. Campbell Memorial Award for its year. While editor of *Galaxy* and *If* in the 1960s, he received three Hugo Awards for best magazine for *If*. As befits a legend, he has also been inducted into the Science Fiction Hall of Fame. And, from the beginning and continuing up to the present, he has been an enthusiastic fan of science fiction. Thank you, sir, for all of it. And you can thank him at his blog at www.thewaythefutureblogs.com.

HAPPY BIRTHDAY, DEAR JESUS

by frederik Pohl

IT WAS THE CRAZIEST CHRISTMAS I ever spent. Partly it was Heinemann's fault—he came up with a new wrinkle in gift-wrapping that looked good but like every other idea that comes out of the front office meant plenty of headaches for the rest of us. But what really messed up Christmas for me was the girl.

Personnel sent her down—after I'd gone up there myself three times and banged my fist on the table. It was the height of the season and when she told me that she had had her application in three weeks before they called her, I excused myself and got Personnel on the store phone from my private office. "Martin here," I said. "What the devil's the matter with you people? This girl is the Emporium type if I ever saw one, and you've been letting her sit around nearly a month while—"

Crawford, the Personnel head, interrupted me. "Have you talked to her very much?" he wanted to know.

"Well, no. But—"

"Call me back when you do," he advised, and clicked off.

I went back to the stockroom where she was standing patiently, and looked her over a little thoughtfully. But she looked all right to me. She was blond-haired and blue-eyed and not very big; she had a sweet, slow smile. She wasn't exactly beautiful, but she looked like a girl you'd want to know. She wasn't bold, and she wasn't too shy; and that's a perfect description of what we call "The Emporium Type."

So what in the world was the matter with Personnel?

Her name was Lilymary Hargreave. I put her to work on the giftwrap spraying machine while I got busy with my paper work. I have a hundred forty-one persons in the department and at the height of the Christmas season I could use twice as many. But we do get the work done. For instance, Saul & Capell, the next biggest store in town, has a hundred and sixty in their gift and counseling department, and their sales run easily twenty-five per cent less than ours. And in the four years that I've headed the department we've yet to fail to get an order delivered when it was promised.

All through that morning I kept getting glimpses of the new girl. She was a quick learner—smart, too smart to be stuck with the sprayer for very long. I needed someone like her around, and right there on the spot I made up my mind that if she was as good as she looked I'd put her in a counseling booth within a week, and the devil with what Personnel thought.

The store was packed with last-minute shoppers. I suppose I'm sentimental, but I love to watch the thousands of people bustling in and out, with all the displays going at once, and the lights on the trees, and the loudspeakers playing *White Christmas* and *The Eighth Candle* and *Jingle Bells* and all the other traditional old favorites. Christmas is more than a mere selling season of the year to me; it means something.

The girl called me over near closing time. She looked distressed and with some reason. There was a dolly filled with gift-wrapped packages, and a man from Shipping looking annoyed. She said, "I'm sorry, Mr. Martin, but I seem to have done something wrong."

The Shipping man snorted. "Look for yourself, Mr. Martin," he said, handing me one of the packages.

I looked. It was wrong, all right. Heinemann's new wrinkle that year was a special attached gift card—a simple Yule scene and the printed message:

The Very Merriest of Season's Greetings

From _____

To _____

$8.50

The price varied with the item, of course. Heinemann's idea was for the customer to fill it out and mail it, ahead of time, to the person it was intended for. That way, the person who got it would know just about how much he ought to spend on a present for the first person. It was smart, I admit, and maybe the smartest thing about it was rounding the price off to the nearest fifty cents instead of giving it exactly. Heinemann said it was bad-mannered to be too precise—and the way the customers were going for the idea, it had to be right.

But the trouble was that the gift-wrapping machines were geared to only a plain card; it was necessary for the operator to put the price in by hand.

I said, "That's all right, Joe; I'll take care of it." As Joe went satisfied back to Shipping, I told the girl: "It's my fault. I should have explained to you, but I guess I've just been a little too rushed."

She looked downcast. "I'm sorry," she said.

"Nothing to be sorry about." I showed her the routing slip attached to each one, which the Shipping Department kept for its records once the package was on its way. "All we have to do is go through these; the price is on every one. We'll just fill out the cards and get them out. I guess—" I looked at my watch—"I guess you'll be a little late tonight, but I'll see that you get overtime and dinner money for it. It wasn't your mistake, after all."

She said hesitantly, "Mr. Martin, couldn't it—well, can I let it go for tonight? It isn't that I mind working, but I keep house for my father and if I don't get there on time he just won't remember to eat dinner. Please?"

I suppose I frowned a little, because her expression was a little worried. But, after all, it was her first day. I said, "Miss Hargreave, don't give it a thought. I'll take care of it."

The way I took care of it, it turned out, was to do it myself; it was late when I got through, and I ate quickly and went home to bed. But I didn't mind, for oh! the sweetness of the smile she gave me as she left.

I looked forward to the next morning, because I was looking forward to seeing Lilymary Hargreave again. But my luck was out—for she was.

My number-two man, Johnny Furness, reported that she hadn't phoned either. I called Personnel to get her phone number, but they didn't have it; I got the address, but the phone company had no phone listed under her name. So I stewed around until the coffee break, and then I put my hat on and headed out of the store. It wasn't merely that I was interested in seeing her, I told myself; she was just too good a worker to get off on the wrong foot this way, and it was only simple justice for me to go to her home and set her straight.

Her house was in a nondescript neighborhood—not too good, not too bad. A gang of kids were playing under a fire hydrant at the corner—but, on the other hand, the houses were neat and nearly new. Middle-class, you'd have to say.

I found the address, and knocked on the door of a second-floor apartment.

It was opened by a tall, leathery man of fifty or so—Lilymary's father, I judged. "Good morning," I said. "Is Miss Hargreave at home?"

He smiled; his teeth were bright in a very sun-bronzed face. "Which one?"

"Blond girl, medium height, blue eyes. Is there more than one?"

"There are four. But you mean Lilymary; won't you come in?"

I followed him, and a six-year-old edition of Lilymary took my hat and gravely hung it on a rack made of bamboo pegs. The leathery man said, "I'm Morton Hargreave, Lily's father. She's in the kitchen."

"George Martin," I said. He nodded and left me, for the kitchen, I presumed. I sat down on an old-fashioned studio couch in the living room, and the six-year-old sat on the edge of a straight-backed chair across from me, making sure I didn't pocket any of the souvenirs on the mantel. The room was full of curiosities—what looked like a cloth of beaten bark hanging on one wall, with a throwing-spear slung over the cloth. Everything looked vaguely South-Seas, though I am no expert.

The six-year-old said seriously, "This is the man, Lilymary," and I got up.

"Good morning," said Lilymary Hargreave, with a smudge of flour and an expression of concern on her face.

I said, floundering, "I, uh, noticed you hadn't come in and, well, since you were new to the Emporium, I thought—"

"I *am* sorry, Mr. Martin," she said. "Didn't Personnel tell you about Sundays?"

"What about Sundays?"

"I must have my Sundays off," she explained. "Mr. Crawford said it was very unusual, but I really can't accept the job any other way."

"Sundays off?" I repeated. "But—but, Miss Hargreave, don't you see what that does to my schedule? Sunday's our busiest day! The Emporium isn't a rich man's shop; our customers work during the week. If we aren't staffed to serve them when they can come in, we just aren't doing the job they expect of us!"

She said sincerely, "I'm terribly sorry, Mr. Martin."

The six-year-old was already reaching for my hat. From the doorway her father said heartily, "Come back again, Mr. Martin. We'll be glad to see you."

He escorted me to the door, as Lilymary smiled and nodded and headed back to the kitchen. I said, "Mr. Hargreave, won't you ask Lilymary to come in for the afternoon, at least? I hate to sound like a boss, but I'm really short-handed on weekends, right now at the peak of the season."

"Season?"

"The Christmas season," I explained. "Nearly ninety per cent of our annual business is done in the Christmas season, and a good half of it on weekends. So won't you ask her?"

He shook his head. "Six days the Lord labored, Mr. Martin," he boomed, "and the seventh was the day of rest. I'm sorry."

And there I was, outside the apartment and the door closing politely but implacably behind me.

Crazy people. I rode the subway back to the store in an irritable mood; I bought a paper, but I didn't read it, because every time I looked at it all I saw was the date that showed me how far the Christmas season already had advanced, how little time we had left to make our quotas and beat last year's record: the eighth of September.

I would have something to say to Miss Lilymary Hargreave when she had the kindness to show up at her job. I promised myself. But, as it turned out, I didn't. Because that night, checking through the day's manifolds when everyone else had gone home, I fell in love with Lilymary Hargreave.

Possibly that sounds silly to you. She wasn't even there, and I'd only known her for a few hours, and when a man begins to push thirty without ever being married, you begin to think he's a hard case and not likely to fall slambang, impetuously in love like a teenager after his first divorce. But it's true, all the same.

I almost called her up. I trembled on the brink of it, with my hand on the phone. But it was close to midnight, and if she wasn't home getting ready for bed I didn't want to know it, so I went home to my own bed. I reached under the pillow and turned off my dreamster before I went to sleep; I had a full library for it, a deluxe model with five hundred dreams that had been a present from the firm the Christmas before. I had Haroun al Rashid's harem and three of Charles Second's favorites on tape, and I had rocketing around the moon and diving to Atlantis and winning a sweepstakes and getting elected king of the world; but what I wanted to dream about was not on anybody's tape, and its name was Lilymary Hargreave.

🌲 🌲 🌲

Monday lasted forever. But at the end of forever, when the tip of the nightingale's wing had brushed away the mountain of steel and the Shipping personnel were putting on their hats and coats and powdering their noses or combing their hair, I stepped right up to Lilymary Hargreave and asked her to go to dinner with me.

She looked astonished, but only for a moment. Then she smiled ... I have mentioned the sweetness of her smile. "It's wonderful of you to ask me, Mr. Martin," she said earnestly, "and I do appreciate it. But I can't."

"Please," I said.

"I *am* sorry."

I might have said please again, and I might have fallen to my knees at her feet, it was that important to me. But the staff was still in the shop, and how would it look for the head of the department to fall at the feet of his newest employee? I said woodenly, "That's too bad." And I nodded and turned away, leaving her frowning after me. I cleared my desk sloppily, chucking the invoices in a drawer, and I was halfway out the door when I heard her calling after me:

"Mr. Martin, Mr. Martin!"

She was hurrying toward me, breathless. "I'm sorry," she said, "I didn't mean to scream at you. But I just phoned my father, and—"

"I thought you didn't have a phone," I said accusingly.

She blinked at me. "At the rectory," she explained. "Anyway, I just phoned him, and—well, we'd both be delighted if you would come and have dinner with us at home."

Wonderful words! The whole complexion of the shipping room changed in a moment. I beamed foolishly at her, with a soft surge at my heart; I felt happy enough to endow a home, strong enough to kill a cave bear or give up smoking or any crazy, mixed-up thing. I wanted to shout and sing; but all I said was: "That sounds great." We headed for the subway, and although I must have talked to her on the ride I cannot remember a word we said, only that she looked like the angel at the top of our tallest Christmas tree.

Dinner was good, and there was plenty of it, cooked by Lilymary herself, and I think I must have seemed a perfect idiot. I sat there, with the six-year-old on one side of me and Lilymary on the other, across from the ten-year-old and the twelve-year-old. The father of them all was at the head of the table, but he was the only other male. I understood there were a couple of brothers, but they didn't live with the others. I suppose there had been a mother at some time, unless Morton Hargreave stamped the girls out with a kind of cookie-cutter; but whatever she had been she appeared to be deceased. I felt overwhelmed. I wasn't used to being surrounded by young females, particularly as young as the median in that gathering.

Lilymary made an attempt to talk to me, but it wasn't altogether successful. The younger girls were given to fits of giggling, which she had to put a stop to, and to making what were evidently personal remarks in some kind of a peculiar foreign tongue—it sounded like a weird aboriginal dialect, and I later found out that it was. But it was disconcerting, especially from the lips of a six-year-old with the giggles. So I didn't make any very intelligent responses to Lilymary's overtures.

But all things end, even eating dinner with giggling girls. And then Mr. Hargreave and I sat in the little parlor, waiting for the girls to— finish doing the dishes? I said, shocked, "Mr. Hargreave, do you mean they *wash* them?"

"Certainly they wash them," he boomed mildly. "How else would they get them clean, Mr. Martin?"

"Why, *dishwashers*, Mr. Hargreave." I looked at him in a different way. Business is business. I said, "After all, this is the Christmas season. At the Emporium we put a very high emphasis on dishwashers as a Christmas gift, you know. We—"

He interrupted good-humoredly. "I already have my gifts, Mr. Martin. Four of them, and very fine dishwashers they are."

"But Mr. Hargreave—"

"Not Mister Hargreave." The six-year-old was standing beside me, looking disapproving. "*Doctor* Hargreave."

"Corinne!" said her father. "Forgive her, Mr. Martin. But you see we're not very used to the—uh, civilized way of doing things. We've been a long time with the Dyaks."

The girls were all back from the kitchen, and Lilymary was out of her apron and looking—unbelievable. "Entertainment," she said brightly. "Mr. Martin, would you like to hear Corinne play?"

There was a piano in the corner. I said hastily, "I'm crazy about piano music. But—"

Lilymary laughed. "She's good," she told me seriously. "Even if I do have to say it to her face. But we'll let you off that if you like. Gretchen and I sing a little bit, if you'd prefer it?"

Wasn't there any TV in this place? I felt as out of place as an Easterbunny-helper in the Santa Claus line, but Lilymary was still looking unbelievable. So I sat through Lilymary and the twelve-year-old named Gretchen singing ancient songs while the six-year-old named Corinne accompanied them on the piano. It was pretty thick. Then the ten-year-old, whose name I never did catch, did recitations; and then they all looked expectantly at me.

I cleared my throat, slightly embarrassed. Lilymary said quickly, "Oh, you don't have to do anything, Mr. Martin. It's just our custom, but we don't expect strangers to conform to it!"

I didn't want that word "stranger" to stick. I said, "Oh, but I'd like to. I mean, I'm not much good at public enfertaining, but—" I hesitated, because that was the truest thing I had ever said. I had no more voice than a goat, and of course the only instrument I had ever learned to play was a TV set. But then I remembered something from my childhood.

"I'll tell you what," I said enthusiastically. "How would you like something appropriate to the season? 'A Visit from Santa Claus,' for instance?"

Gretchen said snappishly, "What season? We don't start celebrating—"

Her father cut her off. "Please do, Mr. Martin," he said politely. "We'd enjoy that very much."

I cleared my throat and started:

'Tis the season of Christmas, and all through the house
St. Nick and his helpers begin their carouse.
The closets are stuffed and the drawers overflowing
With gift-wrapped remembrances, coming and going.

What a joyous abandon of Christmastime glow!
What a making of lists! What a spending of dough!
So much for—

"Hey!" said Gretchen, looking revolted. "Daddy, that isn't how—"

"Hush!" said Dr. Hargreave grimly. His own expression wasn't very delighted either, but he said, "Please go on."

I began to wish I'd kept my face shut. They were all looking at me very peculiarly, except for Lilymary, who was conscientiously studying the floor. But it was too late to back out; I went on:

So much for the bedroom, so much for the bath,
So much for the kitchen—too little by half!
Come Westinghouse, Philco! Come Hotpoint, G.E.!
Come Sunbeam! Come Mixmaster! Come to the Tree!
So much for the wardrobe—how shine Daddy's eyes
As he reaps his Yule harvest of slippers and ties.
So much for the family, so much for the friends,
So much for the neighbors—the list never ends.
A contingency fund for the givers belated
Whose gifts must be hastily reciprocated.
And out of—

Gretchen stood up. "It's our bedtime," she said. "Good night, everybody."

Lilymary flared, "It is not! Now be still!" And she looked at me for the first time. "Please go on," she said, with a furrowed brow.

I said hoarsely:

And out of the shops, how they spring with a clatter,
The gifts and appliances words cannot flatter!
The robot dishwasher, the new Frigidaire,
The doll with the didy and curlable hair!
The electrified hairbrush, the black lingerie,
The full-color stereoscopic TV!
Come, Credit Department! Come, Personal Loan!

Come, Mortgage, come Christmas Club, come—

Lilymary turned her face away. I stopped and licked my lips.

"That's all I remember," I lied. "I—I'm sorry if—"

Dr. Hargreave shook himself like a man waking from a nightmare. "It's getting rather late," he said to Lilymary. "Perhaps—perhaps our guest would enjoy some coffee before he goes."

I declined the coffee and Lilymary walked me to the subway. We didn't talk much.

At the subway entrance she firmly took my hand and shook it. "It's been a pleasant evening," she said.

A wandering group of carolers came by; I gave my contribution to the guitarist. Suddenly angry, I said, "Doesn't that *mean* anything to you?"

"What?"

I gestured after the carolers. "That. Christmas. The whole sentimental, lovable, warmhearted business of Christmas. Lilymary, we've only known each other a short time, but—"

She interrupted: "Please, Mr. Martin. I—I know what you're going to say." She looked terribly appealing there in the Christmassy light of the red and green lights from the Tree that marked the subway entrance. Her pale, straight legs, hardly concealed by the shorts, picked up chromatic highlights; her eyes sparkled. She said, "You see, as Daddy says, we've been away from—civilization. Daddy is a missionary, and we've been with the Dyaks since I was a little girl. Gretch and Marlene and Corinne were born there. We—we do things differently on Borneo." She looked up at the Tree over us, and sighed. "It's very hard to get used to," she said. "Sometimes I wish we had stayed with the Dyaks."

Then she looked at me. She smiled. "But sometimes," she said, "I am very glad we're here." And she was gone.

Ambiguous? Call it merely ladylike. At any rate, that's what I called it; I took it to be the beginning of the kind of feeling I so desperately wanted her to have; and for the second night in a row I let Haroun's harem beauties remain silent on their tapes.

🎄 🎄 🎄

Calamity struck. My number-two man, Furness, turned up one morning with a dismal expression and a letter in a government-franked envelope. "Greeting!" it began. "You are summoned to serve with a jury of citizens for the term—"

"Jury duty!" I groaned. "At a time like this! Wait a minute, Johnny, I'll call up Mr. Heinemann. He might be able to fix it if—"

Furness was shaking his head. "Sorry, Mr. Martin. I already asked him and he tried; but no go. It's a big case—blindfold sampling of twelve brands of filter cigarettes—and Mr. Heinemann says it wouldn't look right to try to evade it."

So there was breaking another man in, to add to my troubles.

It meant overtime, and that meant that I didn't have as much time as I would like for Lilymary. Lunch together, a couple of times; odd moments between runs of the gift-wrapping machines; that was about it.

But she was never out of my thoughts. There was something about her that appealed to me. A square, yes. Unworldly, yes. Her family? A Victorian horror; but they were *her* family. I determined to get them on my side, and by and by I began to see how.

"Miss Hargreave," I said formally, coming out of my office. We stepped to one side, in a corner under the delivery chutes. The rumble of goods overhead gave us privacy. I said, "Lilymary, you're taking this Sunday off, as usual? May I come to visit you?"

She hesitated only a second. "Why, of course," she said firmly. "We'd be delighted. For dinner?"

I shook my head: "I have a little surprise for you," I whispered. She looked alarmed. "Not for you, exactly. For the kids. Trust me, Lilymary. About four o'clock in the afternoon?"

I winked at her and went back to my office to make arrangements. It wasn't the easiest thing in the world—it was our busy season, as I say—but what's the use of being the boss if you can't pull rank once in a while? So I made it as strong as I could, and Special Services hemmed and hawed and finally agreed that they would work in a special Visit from Santa Claus at the Hargreave home that Sunday afternoon.

Once the kids were on my side, I plotted craftily, it would be easy enough to work the old man around, and what kid could resist a Visit from Santa Claus?

I rang the bell and walked into the queer South-Seas living room as though I belonged there. "Merry Christmas!" I said genially to the six-year-old who let me in. "I hope you kiddies are ready for a treat!"

She looked at me incredulously, and disappeared. I heard her say something shrill and protesting in the next room, and Lilymary's voice being firm and low-toned. Then Lilymary appeared. "Hello, Mr. Martin," she said.

"George."

"Hello, George." She sat down and patted the sofa beside her. "Would you like some lemonade?" she asked.

"Thank you," I said. It was pretty hot for the end of September, and the place didn't appear to be air-conditioned. She called, and the twelve-year-old, Gretchen, turned up with a pitcher and some cookies. I said warningly:

"Mustn't get too full, little girl! There's a surprise coming." Lilymary cleared her throat, as her sister set the tray down with a clatter and stamped out of the room. "I—I wish you'd tell me about this surprise, George," she said. "You know, we're a little, well, set in our ways, and I wonder—"

"Nothing to worry about, Lilymary," I reassured her. "What is it, a couple of minutes before four? They'll be here any minute."

"They?"

I looked around; the kids were out of sight. "Santa Claus and his helpers," I whispered.

She began piercingly: "Santa Cl—"

"Ssh!" I nodded toward the door. "I want it to be a surprise for the kids. Please don't spoil it for them, Lilymary."

Well, she opened her mouth; but she didn't get a chance to say anything. The bell rang; Santa Claus and his helpers were right on time.

"Lilymary!" shrieked the twelve-year-old, opening the door. "Look!"

You couldn't blame the kid for being excited. "Ho-ho-ho," boomed Santa, rolling inside. "Oh, hello, Mr. Martin. This the place?"

"Certainly, Santa," I said, beaming. "Bring it in, boys."

The twelve-year-old cried, "Corinne! Marlene! This you got to see!" There was an odd tone to her voice, but I didn't pay much attention. It wasn't my party any more. I retired, smiling, to a corner of the room while the Santa Claus helpers began coming in with their sacks of gear on their shoulders. It was "Ho-ho-ho, little girl!" and "Merry Christmas, everybody!" until you couldn't hear yourself think.

Lilymary was biting her lip, staring at me. The Santa tapped her on the shoulder. "Where's the kitchen, lady?" he asked. "That door? Okay, Wynken—go on in and get set up. Nod, you go down and hurry up the sound truck, then you can handle the door. The rest of you helpers—" he surveyed the room briefly— "start lining up your Christmas Goodies there, and there. Now hop to it, boys! We got four more Visits to make this afternoon yet."

You never saw a crew of Christmas Gnomes move as fast as them. Snap, and the Tree was up, complete with its tinsel stars and gray colored Order Forms and Credit Application Blanks. Snip, and two of the helpers were stringing the red and green lights that led from the Hargreave living room to the sound truck outside. Snip-snap, and you could hear the sound truck pealing the joyous strains of *All I Want for Christmas Is Two of Everything* in the street, and twos and threes of the neighborhood children were beginning to appear at the door, blinking and ready for the fun. The kitchen helpers were ladling out mugs of cocoa and colored-sugar Christmas cookies and collecting the dimes and quarters from the kids; the demonstrator helpers were showing the kids the toys and trinkets from their sacks; and Santa himself was seated on his glittering throne. "Ho-ho-ho, my boy," he was saying. "And where does your daddy work this merry Christmas season?"

I was proud of them. There wasn't a helper there who couldn't have walked into Saul & Cappell or any other store in town, and walked out a Santa with a crew of his own. But that's the way we do things at the Emporium, skilled hands and high paychecks, and you only have to look at our sales records to see that it pays off.

Well, I wanted to stay and watch the fun, but Sunday's a bad day to take the afternoon off; I slipped out and headed back to the store. I put in a hard four hours, but I made it a point to be down at the Special Services division when the crews came straggling in for their checkout. The crew I was interested in was the last to report, naturally—isn't that always the way? Santa was obviously tired; I let him shuck his uniform and turn his sales slips in to the cashier before I tackled him. "How did it go?" I asked anxiously. "Did Miss Hargreave—I mean the grown-up Miss Hargreave—did she say anything?"

He looked at me accusingly. "You," he whined. "Mr. Martin, you shouldn't have run out on us like that. How we supposed to keep up a schedule when you throw us that kind of a curve, Mr. Martin?"

It was no way for a Santa to be talking to a department head, but I overlooked it. The man was obviously upset. "What are you talking about?" I demanded.

"Those Hargreaves! Honestly, Mr. Martin, you'd think they didn't want us there, the way they acted! The kids were bad enough. But when the old man came home—wow! I tell you, Mr. Martin, I been eleven Christmases in the Department, and I never saw a family with less Christmas spirit than those Hargreaves!"

The cashier was yelling for the cash receipts so he could lock up his ledgers for the night, so I let the Santa go. But I had plenty to think about as I went back to my own department, wondering about what he had said.

I didn't have to wonder long. Just before closing, one of the office girls waved me in from where I was checking out a new Counselor, and I answered the phone call. It was Lilymary's father. Mad? He was blazing. I could hardly make sense out of most of what he said. It was words like "perverting the Christian festival" and "selling out the Saviour" and a lot of stuff I just couldn't follow at all. But the part he finished up with, that I could understand. "I want you to know, Mr. Martin," he said in clear, crisp, emphatic tones, "that you are no longer a welcome caller at our home. It pains me to have to say this, sir. As for Lilymary, you may consider this her resignation, to be effective at once!"

"But," I said, "but—"

But I was talking to a dead line; he had hung up. And that was the end of that.

Personnel called up after a couple of days and wanted to know what to do with Lilymary's severance pay. I told them to mail her the check; then I had a second thought and asked them to send it up to me. I mailed it to her myself, with a little note apologizing for what I'd done wrong—whatever it was. But she didn't even answer.

October began, and the pace stepped up. Every night I crawled home, bone-weary, turned on my dreamster and slept like a log. I gave the machine a real workout; I even had the buyer in the Sleep Shoppe get me rare, out-of-print tapes on special order—Last Days of Petronius Arbiter, and Casanova's Diary, and The Polly Adler Story, and so on—until the buyer began to leer when she saw me coming. But it didn't do any good. While I slept I was surrounded with the loveliest of them all; but when I woke the face of Lilymary Hargreave was in my mind's eye.

October. The store was buzzing. National cost of living was up .00013, but our rate of sale was up .00021 over the previous year. The store bosses were beaming, and bonuses were in the air for everybody. November. The tide was at its full, and little wavelets began to ebb backward. Housewares was picked clean, and the manufacturers only laughed as we implored them for deliveries; but Home Appliances was as dead as the January lull. Our overall rate of sale slowed down microscopically, but it didn't slow down the press of work. It made things tougher, in fact, because we were pushing twice as hard on the items we could supply, coaxing the customers off the ones that were running short.

Bad management? No. Looking at my shipment figures, we'd actually emptied the store four times in seven weeks—better than fifty per cent turnover a week. Our July purchase estimates had been off only slightly—two persons fewer out of each hundred bought air-conditioners than we had expected, one and a half persons more out of each hundred bought kitchenware. Saul & Cappell had been out of kitchenware except for spot deliveries, sold the day they arrived, ever since late September!

Heinemann called me into his office. "George," he said, "I just checked your backlog. The unfilled order list runs a little over eleven thousand. I want to tell you that I'm surprised at the way you and your department have—"

"Now, Mr. Heinemann!" I burst out. "That isn't fair! We've been putting in overtime every night, every blasted one of us! Eleven thousand's pretty good, if you ask me!"

He looked surprised. "My point exactly, George," he said. "I was about to compliment you."

I felt so high. I swallowed. "Uh, thanks," I said. "I mean, I'm sorry I—"

"Forget it, George." Heinemann was looking at me thoughtfully. "You've got something on your mind, don't you?"

"Well—"

"Is it that girl?"

"Girl?" I stared at him. "Who said anything about a girl?"

"Come off it," he said genially. "You think it isn't all over the store?" He glanced at his watch. "George," he said, "I never interfere in employees' private lives. You know that. But if it's that girl that's bothering you, why don't you marry her for a while? It might be just the thing you need. Come on now, George, confess. When were you married last? Three years? Five years ago?"

I looked away. "I never was," I admitted.

That jolted him. "Never?" He studied me thoughtfully for a second. "You aren't—?"

"No, no, no!" I said hastily. "Nothing like that. It's just that, well, it's always seemed like a pretty big step to take."

He relaxed again. "Ah, you kids," he said genially. "Always afraid of getting hurt, eh? Well, I'll mind my own business, if that's the way you want it. But if I were you, George, I'd go get her."

That was that. I went back to work; but I kept right on thinking about what Heinemann had said.

After all . . . why not?

🌲 🌲 🌲

I knew where to find her on Sunday. I waited impatiently, just after services, in an alcove ouside the church door.

I called, "Lilymary!"

She faltered and half-turned. I had counted on that. You could tell she wasn't brought up in this country; from the age of six on, our girls learn Lesson One: When you're walking alone at night, *don't stop*.

She didn't stop long. She peered into the doorway and saw me, and her expression changed as though I had hit her with a club. "George," she said, and hesitated, and walked on. Her hair was a shimmering rainbow in the Christmas lights.

We were only a few doors from her house. I glanced, half apprehensive, at the door, but no Father Hargreave was there to scowl. I followed her and said, "Please, Lilymary. Can't we just talk for a moment?"

She faced me. "Why?"

"To—" I swallowed. "To let me apologize."

She said gently, "No apology is necessary, George. We're different breeds of cats. No need to apologize for that."

"*Please.*"

"Well," she said. And then, "Why not?"

We found a bench in the little park across from the subway entrance. It was late; enormous half-tracks from the Sanitation Department were emptying trash cans, sprinkler trucks came by and we had to raise our feet off the ground. She said once, "I really ought to get back. I was only going to the store." But she stayed.

Well, I apologized, and she listened like a lady. And like a lady she said, again, "There's nothing to apologize for." And that was that, and I still hadn't said what I had come for. I didn't know how.

I brooded over the problem. With the rumble of the trash trucks and the roar of their burners, conversation was difficult enough anyhow. But even under those handicaps, I caught a phrase from Lilymary. "—back to the jungle," she was saying. "It's home for us, George. Father can't wait to get back, and neither can the girls."

I interrupted her. "Get back?"

She glanced at me. "That's what I said." She nodded at the Sanitation workers, baling up the enormous drifts of Christmas cards, thrusting them into the site burners. "As soon as the mails open up," she said, "and Father gets his visa. It was mailed a week ago, they say. They tell me that in the Christmas rush it might take two or three weeks more to get to us, though."

Something was clogging up my throat. All I could say was, "Why?"

Lilymary sighed. "It's where we live, George," she explained. "This isn't right for us. We're mission brats and we belong out in the field, spreading the Good News. . . . Though Father says you people need it more than the Dyaks." She looked quickly into my eyes. "I mean—"

I waved it aside. I took a deep breath. "Lilymary," I said, all in a rush, "will you marry me?"

Silence, while Lilymary looked at me.

"Oh, George," she said, after a moment. And that was all; but I was able to translate it; the answer was no.

Still, proposing marriage is something like buying a lottery ticket; you may not win the grand award, but there are consolation prizes. Mine was a date.

Lilymary stood up to her father, and I was allowed in the house. I wouldn't say I was welcomed, but Dr. Hargreave was polite— distant, but polite. He offered me coffee, he spoke of the dream superstitions of the Dyaks and old days in the Long House, and when Lilymary was ready to go he shook my hand at the door.

We had dinner. . . . I asked her—but as a piece of conversation, not a begging plea from the heart—I asked her why they had to go back. The Dyaks, she said; they were Father's people; they needed him. After Mother's death, Father had wanted to come back to America . . . but it was wrong for them. He was going back. The girls, naturally, were going with him.

We danced. . . . I kissed her, in the shadows, when it was growing late. She hesitated, but she kissed me back.

I resolved to destroy my dreamster; its ersatz ecstasies were pale.

"There," she said, as she drew back, and her voice was gentle, with a note of laughter. "I just wanted to show you. It isn't all hymnsinging back on Borneo, you know."

I reached out for her again, but she drew back, and the laughter was gone. She glanced at her watch.

"Time for me to go, George," she said. "We start packing tomorrow."

"But—"

"It's time to go, George," she said. And she kissed me at her door; but she didn't invite me in.

I stripped the tapes off my dreamster and threw them away. But hours later, after the fiftieth attempt to get to sleep, and the twentieth solitary cigarette, I got up and turned on the light and looked for them again.

They were pale; but they were all I had.

Party Week! The store was nearly bare. A messenger from the Credit Department came staggering in with a load of files just as the closing gong sounded.

He dropped them on my desk. "Thank God!" he said fervently. "Guess you won't be bothering with these tonight, eh, Mr. Martin?"

But I searched through them all the same. He looked at me wonderingly, but the clerks were breaking out the bottles and the runners from the lunchroom were bringing up sandwiches, and he drifted away.

I found the credit check I had requested. "*Co-Maker Required!*" was stamped at the top, and triply underlined in red, but that wasn't what I was looking for. I hunted through the text until I found what I wanted to know: "Subject is expected to leave this country within forty-eight hours. Subject's employer is organized and incorporated under laws of State of New York as a religious mission group. No earnings record on file. *Caution*: Subject would appear a bad credit risk, due to—"

I read no farther. Forty-eight hours!

There was a scrawl at the bottom of the page, in the Credit Manager's own handwriting: "George, what the devil are you up to? This is the fourth check we made on these people!"

It was true enough; but it would be the last. In forty-eight hours they would be gone.

I was dull at the Christmas Party. But it had been a splendid

Christmas for the store, and in an hour everyone was too drunk to notice.

I decided to skip Party Week. I stayed at home the next morning, staring out the window. It had begun to snow, and the cleaners were dragging away old Christmas trees. It's always a letdown when Christmas is over; but my mood had nothing to do with the season, only with Lilymary and the numbers of miles from here to Borneo.

I circled the date in red on my calendar: December 25th. By the 26th they would be gone.

But I couldn't, repeat couldn't, let her go so easily. It wasn't that I wanted to try again, and be rebuffed again; it was not a matter of choice. I had to see her. Nothing else, suddenly, had any meaning. So I made the long subway trek out there, knowing it was a fool's errand. But what kind of an errand could have been more appropriate for me?

They weren't home, but I wasn't going to let that stop me. I banged on the door of the next apartment, and got a surly, suspicious, what-do-you-want-with-*them*? inspection from the woman who lived there. But she thought they might possibly be down at the Community Center on the next block.

And they were.

The Community Center was a big yellow-brick recreation hall; it had swimming pools and pingpong tables and all kinds of odds and ends to keep the kids off the streets. It was that kind of a neighborhood. It also had a meeting hall in the basement, and there were the Hargreaves, all of them, along with a couple of dozen other people. None of them were young, except the Hargreave girls. The hall had a dusty, storeroom quality to it, as though it wasn't used much—and in fact, I saw, it still had a small Christmas tree standing in it. Whatever else they had, they did not have a very efficient cleanup squad.

I came to the door to the hall and stood there, looking around. Someone was playing a piano, and they were having a singing party. The music sounded familiar, but I couldn't recognize the words—

> *Adeste fideles*
> *Laeti triumphantes*
> *Venite, venite in Bethlehem.*

The girls were sitting together, in the front row; their father wasn't with them, but I saw why. He was standing at a little lectern in the front of the hall.

> *Natum videte, regem angelorum.*
> *Venite adoremus, venite adoremus—*

I recognized the tune then; it was a slow, draggy-beat steal from that old-time favorite, *Christmas-Tree Mambo*. It didn't sound too bad, though, as they finished with a big major chord from the piano and all fifteen or twenty voices going. Then Hargreave started to talk.

I didn't listen. I was too busy watching the back of Lilymary's head. I've always had pretty low psi, though, and she didn't turn around.

Something was bothering me. There was a sort of glow from up front. I took my eyes off Lilymary's blond head, and there was Dr. Hargreave, radiant; I blinked and looked again, and it was not so radiant. A trick of the light, coming through the basement windows onto his own blond hair, I suppose, but it gave me a curious feeling for a moment. I must have moved, because he caught sight of me. He stumbled over a word, but then he went on. But that was enough. After a moment Lilymary's head turned, and her eyes met mine.

She knew I was there. I backed away from the door and sat down on the steps coming down from the entrance.

Sooner or later she would be out.

It wasn't long at all. She came toward me with a question in her eye. She was all by herself; inside the hall, her father was still talking.

I stood up straight and said it all. "Lilymary," I said, "I can't help it, I want to marry you. I've done everything wrong, but I didn't mean to. I—I don't even want it conditional, Lilymary, I want it for life. Here or Borneo, I don't care which. I only care about one thing, and that's you." It was funny—I was trying to tell her I loved her, and I was standing stiff and awkward, talking in about the same tone of voice I'd use to tell a stock boy he was fired.

But she understood. I probably didn't have to say a word, she would have understood anyhow. She started to speak, and changed her mind, and started again, and finally got out, "What would you do in Borneo?" And then, so soft that I hardly knew I was hearing it, she added, "Dear."

Dear! It was like the first time Heinemann came in and called me "Department Head!" I felt nine feet tall.

I didn't answer her. I reached out and I kissed her, and it wasn't any wonder that I didn't know we weren't alone until I heard her father cough, not more than a yard away.

I jumped, but Lilymary turned and looked at him, perfectly calm. "You ought to be conducting the service, Father!" she scolded him.

He nodded his big fair head. "Doctor Mausner can pronounce the Benediction without me," he said. "I should be there but—well, He has plenty of things to forgive all of us already; one more isn't going to bother Him. Now, what's this?"

"George has asked me to marry him."

"And?"

She looked at me. "I—" she began, and stopped. I said, "I love her."

He looked at me too, and then he sighed. "George," he said after a moment, "I don't know what's right and what's wrong, for the first time in my life. Maybe I've been seffish when I asked Lilymary to go back with me and the girls. I didn't mean it that way, but I don't deny I wanted it. I don't know. But—" He smiled, and it was a big, warm smile. "But there's something I do know. I know Lilymary; and I can trust her to make up her own mind." He patted her lightly.

"I'll see you after the service," he said to me, and left us. Back in the hall, through the door he opened, I could hear all the voices going at once.

"Let's go inside and pray, George," said Lilymary, and her whole heart and soul was on her face as she looked at me, with love and anxiousness.

I only hesitated a moment. Pray? But it meant Lilymary, and that meant—well, everything.

So I went in. And we were all kneeling, and Lilymary coached me through the words; and I prayed. And, do you know?—I've never regretted it.

INTRODUCTION
❧☙
SHEPHERDS AND WOLVES

AT CHRISTMAS TIME, how are you supposed to feel if you've been declared not to be human? And what do you do when someone you never expected to see again shows up, reminding you of the sordid past you thought you had left behind—and endangering the safety and sanctuary you thought you had finally found?

🌲 🌲 🌲

SARAH A. HOYT won the Prometheus Award for her novel *Darkship Thieves*, published by Baen, and has authored *Darkship Renegades* and *A Few Good Men*, two more novels set in the same universe, as was "Angel in Flight," a story in the first installment of *A Cosmic Christmas*. *Darkship Renegades* also was a Prometheus Award nominee. She has written numerous short stories and novels in a number of genres, science fiction, fantasy, mystery, historical novels and historical mysteries, much under a number of pseudonyms, and has been published—among other places—in *Analog*, *Asimov's* and *Amazing*. For Baen, she has also written three books in her popular shape-shifter fantasy series, *Draw One in the Dark*, *Gentleman Takes a Chance*, and *Noah's Boy*. Her *According to Hoyt* is one of the most interesting blogs on the internet. Originally from Portugal, she lives in Colorado with her husband, two sons and the surfeit of cats necessary to a die-hard Heinlein fan.

SHEPHERDS AND WOLVES

by Sarah A. Hoyt

IT STARTED WITH THE CALL ON CHRISTMAS EVE. I was at the distress console, a job that the Sisters of St. Lucia of the Spaceways always give to their oldest novice. "Old enough to be responsible, young enough to stay awake all night," Mother Magdalene said, and I wouldn't argue.

I'd been living with the Lucias for five years, a welcome respite from my life before, and the doubts I had about professing had nothing to do with not liking the life, the house or the rule. They had to do with myself. And I'd been wrestling with them in the dark of the night when the call came.

"Ship in distress," it said. "Ship in distress." There followed coordinates, so many degrees from Gilgamesh basin, to the north of Memphis City so many miles.

I wrote down the numbers and the names, but didn't think about them—couldn't think about them—because the voice sounded familiar. I flicked the com signal on. "What ship, and what is your call sign? State the nature of your trouble."

I was working by rote. These were the questions I'd been told to ask.

The answer came, faint, distant, scratchy, "We have crashed

87

through a failure of the—" static. "Our call number is—" static. "We have ten people." The last made me sit back hard on the chair. Ten people. So it couldn't be the normal miner craft. It had to be another sort of transport.

The static did not bother me so much. After all, on Ganymede, half the equipment worked badly, and the other half worked not at all. Mars might now be a semi-civilized planet in the dawning glory of the twenty-sixth century, but Ganymede, once a forsaken wasteland, for many years a forgotten colony, remained a backwater: terraformed, but not comfortable, populated but poor, striving but forsaken. Ganymede was the basis of operation of asteroid miners— mostly desperate men who had long given up on seeking redemption—and of the women who amused them, most of them also desperate and seeking only to live another hour, another day, another week.

It is said—well, Mother Magdalene says it—that the order of St. Lucia was formed with the intent to go forth to the most desolate human colonies, to follow the ragged edges of the human diaspora out of Earth, burner in one hand and cross in the other.

We comforted the afflicted, fed the hungry, gathered in the lost— usually ten minutes before they died—and, because Mother Magdalene insisted, ran an unofficial rescue for anyone who crash landed near enough we could find them and bring them in to safety. The atmosphere in Ganymede was still thin, even after centuries of terraforming, and the nights became cold very fast. A broken ship could mean death.

Most of the people we helped were miners, in their two-men craft, often crashed through sheer mechanical failure. The ones I hated were the rescues in space. But we had to get to them before the scavengers did. Like all places at the edge of survival, Ganymede bred scavengers and pirates aplenty.

I bit my lip, wondering if this crashed craft could be a pirate vessel. Ten people . . . yes, I could see the advantages of ten people when it came to boarding other ships, stealing the result of their mining labors. Or even, of course, scavenging stranded ships.

At the same time, ten people seemed excessive. Most miner craft had two men, poorly armed. What overcame them was superior weaponry and better—pirate—craft. And four people would be plenty for that.

I looked up at the wall, measuring the hours of Ganymede night. Three hours until early service, and until then all my sisters and Mother Magdalene would be tucked away in their beds. Of course, I had permission to rouse any or all of them, if I so chose, if I deemed the emergency was important enough.

Did I? Ten people in a downed craft. I could take the bigger flyer, the one we used to transport all of us on the rare occasions we needed to make an appearance somewhere. When the Pope flew through Ganymede, we'd all of us gone to the Spaceport for a blessing, because it couldn't be thought that His Holiness would travel into the countryside to our poor abode. I could transport ten people, if a little cramped. The twenty of us had been cramped enough.

Why would I need help? If I woke up the house, or even one of the two novices more junior than I, just because I was afraid to go and collect the people in distress on my own, Mother Magdalene wouldn't get half sarcastic.

I sighed. It wasn't so much that I feared her sarcasm, but I liked her too much to want to incur her displeasure. She would ask me if I didn't have a burner. And yes, I had a burner, and I'd taken the training, though we were always cautioned not to shoot to kill, not before the sinner could get absolution.

Nodding to myself, I clicked the com and asked again, just in case, "What is your call sign?" There was no answer but the steady beep, beep, beep of a distress beacon, and I sighed. Likely their com had given up the ghost, but even on Ganymede, ships made sure their distress signal was working.

I got up, headed for the back door to our compound, passing the doors to the cells of my sisters—little rooms, provided only with a bed and pegs on the wall for our two extra habits—on my right, and the dormitories for our charity cases on the left. There were two large dormitories, one for males and one for females. I was mildly surprised that this one time I did not hear sounds to indicate that the inhabitants of one were visiting in the other. I was sure if I looked closely I would find a few couples snuggled in a single bed, but my job was rescue not policing, and besides, Mother Magdalene knew as well as I did what happened almost every night. She'd once muttered something on the subject of comfort and excusable sin, and that was that. She was more concerned with those who smuggled in interesting hallucinogenic substances, or those who tried to rob others.

Down the hallway there were the baths and showers, and past that a sort of hallway that also served as a cloak room. I stopped and got a cloak with a hood. It wasn't a matter of modesty. Yes, my novice's habit, adapted to the sort of work we did in space, consisted of white pants and pale blue shirt, and it might be consider to reveal too much of my body. His holiness had talked to Mother Magdalene on the subject of allowed variations to the habit, or some such, during their ten minute conference. But the more important consideration was that it would be very cold outside, somewhere below freezing. The suit was indoor wear, and even my white wimple and veil wouldn't keep out the chill. The heavy blue cloaks we wore outside kept us warm even in the worst weather.

I strapped on two burners—after checking the charge on them—and made my way to the flyer.

Attuning it to distress beacon took a bit of fiddling. I think we'd bought this thing used and fifth hand or so. But I managed it at last, set it on auto-pilot, standing by to rescue myself if the auto-pilot cut out. Flying over the mostly dark expanse of terrain, my mind returned to the fact that the voice on the com had sounded familiar. Awfully familiar. Something at the back of mind stirred, tried to wake up.

That voice, my mind told me, in no uncertain terms, *sounded like Joe.*

I ignored it. Joe was dead. Had to be after all these years, and given when and where we'd parted company.

I told myself, as I looked out at the expanse where lights were as sparsely scattered as the stars on the cloak of St. Lucia, that this was just my fear of professing, my fear of polluting the order with my presence. I was calling Joe to mind, because Joe and what Joe had been and what I'd been, and what we'd done together were probably reason to disqualify me from professing ten times over. Or more.

The flyer started heading downward before I could see anything resembling a ship. The site the beacon beamed from was inside a crater, dark in the shadow of night. It took landing next to it to see that it was a large ship—very large, doubtless equipped for interplanetary travel. And if it only had ten people in it, the travel it was fitted for had to be more than the jumps to Mars and back. For those little ships were used. This one clearly had supplies or cargo for much longer.

My alarms were ringing, and I had my hand on my burner handle as I called over the speaker outside, "Come out with your hands in full view. I want to see how many of you there are. And state your call code."

There was a moment of silence, and then they started coming out of the ship. Two men, followed by eight . . . juveniles, male and female. Four male, four female, all looking very young and awkward, at that age when humans have stopped growing but haven't yet gotten used to adult movements and poise. I counted them in the dim light, and looked them over. I couldn't see weapons on any of them, and all of them were dressed in pants-and-tunic suits that looked more flimsy than my habit. The young ones appeared to be in sandals!

Appalled, I opened the door at the rear of the flyer, and spoke again over the speaker, "Come in, one by one."

They did, first the adult males, slowly enough that I got the idea they were being very careful to display their lack of bad intentions, and then the boys and girls, half running, clearly anxious to be in out of the cold.

I closed the door with a whoosh behind them, ordered them to sit and strapped down, set home on the beacon, and tried to figure out where we would house all these people. I could put the two adult men in the male dormitory. They were well-built enough and looked capable of defending themselves. But the young ones . . . It would be a crime akin to throwing kittens into a lion cage to put them in with the drug-and-madness addled refuse of Ganymede.

I heard a seat belt unbuckle and turned to yell at my passenger to sit down, but before the words left my lips, I realized the man standing in the aisle, a few steps from me was Joe. My old friend Joe, whom I'd left on Mars. When I'd last seen him, five years ago, he'd been seized by interplanetary customs for the theft of valuable property: his body. I'd barely managed to escape the like fate, by leaving the landing area on the arm of a gentleman who'd sworn I was his wife. No one would think to test the wife of a rich man from Earth. Or at least, they'd not think of it twice.

For five years I'd assumed Joe had been killed. It was the normal penalty for artifacts who hid what they were and their origins and, further, who were capable of escaping their tightly controlled existence and freeing themselves. But there he was, in the middle of the aisle, his green eyes wide open, his red hair mussed as if he'd been in a fight. A three-day red growth glinted on his face, and I had a feeling he had blanched under his reddish tan.

I said, "Joe," at that same time he said "Blossom," and for a moment we stared at each other as the five years disappeared. We'd grown up together at the same crèche, Joe and I, destined to be Joy-bringers. But it wasn't till we'd been sold to a brothel, in our teens, that we'd developed our friendship, or perhaps love. I'd thought it was love at the time, but it's easy to convince someone like me of love. After all, born from a test tube and raised in a crèche, love was the human thing I had never hoped to experience.

The brothel didn't care what we did in our own time, and Joe and I had become friends; then we'd made mad plans for a future we'd known could never be. And then we'd put the plans into action, and escaped the brothel. A misbegotten adventure that had landed us in Mars Customs where our grand plans had come to an end.

I'd made my way to Ganymede, partly because it was the only place I could think of where no one would follow me and test me. And after a week of hospitality by the Lucias, I'd decided to become a novice. I wasn't even a Catholic at the time. I wasn't anything. All major religions agreed my kind lacked souls.

Over the last five years I'd come to wonder if that was true. More importantly, I'd come to believe there was something as souls—at least on my off hours, and when I squinted and wished really hard.

But now there was Joe and all the years rolled back. "Joe!" I said again. And then, at the same time, we both said, "I didn't know—"

"An old friend is she?" the other adult man said. "I didn't know you did nuns, Joe." I turned, outraged, not because of the implication, but because the other man had got off his seat while I was talking to Joe, and had approached me on the other side, on my blind side, while I was looking at Joe, with no eyes for anyone else.

"Please, get back to your seat," I said, reaching in my belt for the burner. The man was tall and blond, with a face crisscrossed with scars, and I had a feeling he was bad news, though I might be judging a miner by his kit.

"Listen, Avery," Joe said. He sounded panicked. "It's not like that. Listen, Blossom—"

I'd turned to look at him as he spoke, and I never heard the end of the sentence. Something hit me a sharp blow above the ear, and I went down into darkness.

I woke up, or rather I became aware of being awake while being pushed forward. I was on my feet. My hands were tied behind my back. I wasn't so naïve that I couldn't tell the pressure in the middle of my back was a burner muzzle. Likely my own burner. And there was a man behind me, pushing me just enough to keep me walking, while saying, "Steady, steady. Don't even think of screaming. If you don't scream, we won't hurt anyone. We don't want to have to hurt anyone."

My vision cleared. We were in the cloak room of the convent.

I didn't think of screaming. For one the voice was Avery's. I might or might not be able to claim some special favor and protection from Joe, but Avery was likely to give me no quarter. For another, Mother Magdalene would just about have my hide if I got myself shot by engaging in what she called heroics.

My only worry was Mother and my sisters, and the other people in the house. It was dawning on me slowly that I'd miscalculated. I should have taken another sister with me. I'd just brought two very bad men back with me. My heart clutched a little at the thought that Joe was a bad man, but I could hear him talking in an undertone to someone—the young people?—and I couldn't lie to myself.

The question was, what did they want in coming back to the convent? Supposing their vehicle, despite its fortuitous positioning in the crater, really had been wrecked, what did they expect to get in the convent? Couldn't they as easily have stolen my flyer and gone to Memphis City or elsewhere where they might hide or transact their business?

The certainty that their business was illegal and that they were in fact bad men made the presence of the eight young people something I didn't want to think about. Unfortunately my mind wasn't listening to my reluctance. I didn't want to believe that after all this time, Joe—Joe, who knew what it was like—was selling young artifacts into slavery of that kind, but a glimpse of the juveniles, out the corner of my eye, told me that they had the beauty that few natural born humans possessed: their features were almost too regular and all too pleasing, their bodies were lithe and uniformly well-formed. Not a pudgy one in the bunch, nor a short one, nor one with spots. But more than that, they had the passive demeanor of crèche-raised children, beaten into submission one too many times.

My heart sank somewhere to near my boots, and I thought it would have been better if he were dead.

Avery was still holding the burner to the middle of my back, but now Joe was whispering at him, and he was whispering back.

Then Joe approached, where I could see him. He pulled my hood back, with a quick gesture. "Listen, Blossom," he said. "Listen. We don't want to hurt you or your . . . sisters," there was a slight smirk at that, as though he found my presence here even odder than I did myself. "Or anyone, but you have to help us. You don't want me to die, do you?"

Strangely I didn't. Despite what I'd just thought, I didn't want him to die. Five years ago, he'd given me a desperate sign, behind his back, telling me to flee, and I'd gone back, and ingratiated myself to an Earth gentleman just getting his luggage. I'd mourned him for five years. I didn't wish to mourn him anymore.

I must have shaken my head because he said, "Good girl," in that tone he used to talk in when he was trying to convince me to be calm. "Look, we need to send a coded message. Will you help me? Will you take me to the com room?"

I nodded. He whispered something to Avery, and I led Joe down the dark corridor, past the cell doors of my sleeping sisters, and the dormitories of our charity cases, to the small room at the back, where the com was. Less than an hour ago, I'd been here—

Joe sat at the com. He looked it over thoroughly, then threw the shield. We had a shield over our communications. Nothing much, understand, just enough that when we needed to send a message to the bishop in Memphis City, or get one back, no one could break it and— No, I never understood it really. What was anyone to make of our communications, except the list of obits, the list of births, an account of those helped, or a request for a confessor?

But Ganymede's authorities made a big deal of not interfering with Catholic communications, possibly because the church was one of the few unified authorities in the system, or maybe because the Lucias, through unrelenting charity, commanded a lot of loyal protection against people with very few scruples.

Joe threw the shield now, and started punching what looked like random keys.

"I'm surprised at you," I said. It was really my mouth running away with me, though I hoped against hope that I could find something which would allow me to make sure Mother and my sisters and all our refugees stayed safe. "Trafficking in joy-bringers."

He gave me a frowning look over his shoulder, and half shook his head, but his fingers went on, busily pushing keys. I didn't expect him to answer, but he did. "Not joybringers," he said. "Donors."

It took me a moment to appreciate what he'd said, and then I gasped, "Joe!"

"Oh, don't go moral on me, Blossom. What did you expect me to do, exactly, having broken out of penal servitude on Mars? What did you expect me to undertake? Did you expect me to find a cozy place, like what you got here? No, thank you. I won't go where people say I have no soul. And if I have no soul why should I care if they think I'm evil?"

I sat down on the spare chair in the room. My hands were still bound behind my back, or I might have been tempted to throttle him. "There are always better options than murder," I said, and realized my prim tones echoed the way Mother Magdalene spoken.

His grin was reflected in the polished panel of the com. "Oh, come off it, honey. They're not more human than I am, or than you are. Vat grown every one of them. Grown to provide rich elderly people with fresh organs. Nothing more, nothing less. They wouldn't exist but for the need. According to the law, they don't exist, since the traffic in humans for such purpose is illegal in all the worlds."

"Organs can be vat grown," I said. "They can be printed. You don't need to grow whole persons."

"Except that you do, at least if you want the organs to last. And growing them anacephalous is no answer, either. They don't grow properly and don't develop the right way. Come on, Blossom, who are you to stand in the way of people's attempts to survive."

I shook my head. One thing I was sure of. "You can't and shouldn't kill others to survive. That is wrong." By now I was awake enough to start moving my hands, stealthily, with the cover of the chair back, sliding one slowly against the other. They'd tied me with the belt from my habit. Not well enough, since the belt was slightly elastic. No matter how good their knots, as I slid my hands back and forth it loosened them little by little.

He frowned at me in the reflection on the panel, then said, "They really got to you, didn't they. They and their talk of all humans being important and all that. I've heard all that too, you know. Only if you ask them if they'd take you they always say their order is not allowed to take artifacts." He made a face as if he'd like to spit. "It's all nonsense. They don't think we're human any more than anyone else does. And no one thinks those kids are human either. Not even themselves. They know what they're destined for. Do you see them trying to escape? At least they're not bound for what we were sold into. Think about it. I am being merciful."

My hands were now free, and I was merciful too. I dove forward, towards the burner that Joe had discarded next to the keyboard of the com console so he could use both hands to message. Grabbing it I turned with it pointed at Joe.

For a moment he looked at me, and he thought he'd try something. There was a little chuckle as he tried to be indulgent, but I said, "Don't even think about it. I will not kill you. We're told not to kill. But I know a hundred places I can burn you and at least one you'd hate to lose in Ganymede away from regen." I backed up, till my back was against the wall, my burner steady, pointed at his crotch.

He blinked. The idea that I was serious must have penetrated because he said a word in a dialect I couldn't understand. The tone of it made me think I didn't want to understand it. Then he said, "Why? All we want is to meet with the buyers here. They take the kids, Avery and I go back to the ship and you go back to whatever you're doing here. I'm not going to tell anyone what you really are. I'm not going to disturb your life in any way. I never meant to, you know? We'd never have laid this trap if it weren't for the fact that we were tracked here, to Ganymede. The interplanetaries are after us. If they catch us, they kill us, and those kids. All artifacts. All illegal. Yes, even Avery. No owner. The kids should never have been created, and Avery and I have gone rogue and pretended to be human. If they catch you, you'll be gone too. Is that what you want?" he said. "You want to bring the police here?"

I shook my head. I wasn't sure what I wanted, exactly, but I knew what I wanted specifically. "No," I said. "I want you to leave and take Avery with you. Leave those children. Don't touch a hair on their heads. You don't have the right to kill them just to make money."

He gave a hollow, disbelieving laugh. "I'm not going to kill them."

"You're handing them over to be killed. I can't let you do that."

"Where have you been? All over this solar system, artifacts are killed, handed over to be killed, created only to be tortured to death, and no one cares. These kids will go easy, under anesthesia. They'll give the gift of life to real people who are in pain now. Just because it's illegal, doesn't mean it's bad."

"It's bad," I said. "They're people. Just as we were people in the crèche, Joe. And you will not hand them over to be killed. You say no one cares, but I care. And now that they're under my roof, I can't let them die like that. Get up, Joe."

He got up.

"Turn around, Joe," I said.

He did. I half expected him to do something—to try to grab me, to fight me. But he probably still remembered our tussles where, while he might be stronger, I was faster. I tied him. I wasn't stupid enough to use elastic material. I tied his hands together. I put my burner in the small of his back. "Did you send the message for your buyers?" I asked. He nodded. His lips were pale, and there was a very odd look in his eyes. Once, on Mars, I'd seen a dog who'd been run into a corner, and was surrounded on all sides by hostile people. He'd had the same look in his eyes.

"Walk out, just ahead of me," I said. "Don't run or I shoot you."

He walked. Just ahead of me. He walked slowly down the hallway the way we'd come. I opened the door, careful to hide behind him. I spoke from behind him. "Avery," I said. "Take your burner and slide it towards me, on the floor. The floor is smooth and it will slide easily. If you don't, I shoot Joe."

A flash of light, a scream, a smell of burning, and Joe tottered to the side, and I saw Avery grinning at me, his burner still glowing from flaming Joe. Joe sagged against the arm I'd put out to support him. He'd fall if I let him. Avery smiled, a wolfish grin, "That dumb artifact? He don't mean nothing to me."

I must have fired. I've confessed it, in fact, but I have no memory of lifting the burner, of aiming it, of shooting. I just realized my arm was lifted, and Avery was falling. There were eight kids, in the room, staring at me. Joe was on the floor, probably dead—I had no time to check—and Avery was most certainly dead.

From behind me, in the cool dark hallway came a clearing of the throat, a gentle voice. "Blossom," the voice said. "What is this?"

It was Mother Magdalene. I was almost weak with relief, but had to tell myself the danger wasn't past. Turning around, quickly, I told her the essentials. Not of my past with Joe. Not about what I was. There would be time enough for that, and now I knew I'd tell her before defiling the convent with my professing. But I told her what Joe and Avery had been doing, what I'd tried to do to get them to leave, and the traffickers in human organs even now headed for our door.

Mother Magdalene is sixty, with white hair and pale blue eyes and looks like everyone's favorite grandmother. I'd never seen her look shocked. She didn't look shocked now. She said, "I see." And then, "It would seem to be imperative to hide the young people." She looked them over. They stood still in a group, their hands in front of them. "Are they brain damaged or on some drug? They don't seem to react."

"No. They're perfectly normal," I said. "You see, in the crèches they beat us until we—" I stopped, realizing what I'd said.

Mother Magdalene didn't look even slightly surprised. "I see," she said again, and then she clapped her hands as she did when she was trying to get the attention of the novice group. "Children, come with me."

"Where?" I said. "Where are you taking them?"

She shook her head. "Better if you don't know." And to what must be my alarmed look, "No, I won't harm them. Surely you know better, sister. You, go wake sister Anne, and sister Dolores. Take these men to the morgue. And tell Sister Dolores—"

"That you want her to help defend the convent?" I said.

Mother Magdalene smirked. "Heavens, no. How would we do that? No. Tell sister Dolores to let any men inquiring after the children or these men in, and show them the morgue and the rest of the convent. The two men shot each other, and they had no children with them. That is our story. And you, go to bed. Sleep or pretend to sleep, so long as you remember if anyone should ask you've never been out of the convent today."

I probably would never be allowed to profess, but I had given my word to obey, and I went to bed and stayed there. I was vaguely aware of the door opening, of voices outside, then the door closed again softly. I must have fallen asleep because, presently, Sister Dolores was shaking me, reminding me I would be late for early service.

The mass was said by a priest who does a circuit of Parishes and worship houses between Memphis City and Kittu Crater. I took my place in the choir of my sisters, and he made it fast, but not so fast that I didn't discover, in the mass of amorphous Ganymede refuse the fresh faces of eight young people. Mother couldn't have hid them there; too easy to find. But now . . . now we could feed them and care for them, and find them a different place to sleep, away from the derelicts, and . . . I didn't know, but I knew Mother would take care of it.

Only one thing marred my joy at their rescue and at having got out of the night's troubles with so little tragedy. No, two things. The first and most important one was that Joe had died and, worse, Joe had died thinking himself unworthy and not human. The second was that I'd have to leave the convent. Now Mother knew what I was. I had no soul. I'd never be allowed to profess. The idea of losing this community, this sisterhood, cut through my soul like knife through flesh, but it had to be done. I couldn't wish myself on the Lucias as one of them. Perhaps they'd let me stay on and look after the poor and afflicted.

After mass, I went to see Mother and told her that. It all came out in a rush, the story of what had happened to me and Joe, and what we'd done, and what I'd done to survive, and what I was, the story of Joe's last words to me, of my sorrow he'd died thinking himself not human. And then I said I knew I could never profess, but I'd stay and serve, and help the poor. It didn't matter I had no soul, did it? I could do real good for real humans.

I'd caught Mother in her cell, writing something in a notebook. She had the archaic habit of using real paper and real pencils, her one luxury, sent to her from her wealthy family on earth. She started tapping the pencil on the paper as I spoke. "Blossom, you know the story as well as I do of the man who was beaten by robbers and left to die, and whose wounds were bound and who was treated like family by a man from another tribe, a man he too would not consider human. The reason for the prohibition. . . . Most artifacts are so damaged that the soul within them is afraid to show itself. No. Put another way, they are like your friend Joe or even more like Avery. They hate themselves so much there's no love left in them. But you risked yourself for those children. You are willing to serve the poor and unfortunate, even though you have no illusions about them. I'd say, Blossom, that your soul is in right order, and if you wish to profess the order will be happy to have you."

I couldn't believe it, there was a roaring in my ears, and I almost missed the next words, "And your friend Joe will be all right, sister Anne says. We had him in the morgue, until the traffickers left. Safest place to hide him, and he was cold enough in the refrigerated drawer.

But we brought him out immediately, we applied regen. He was in shock, but he'll live. Whether his soul will live too, I don't know. If you want some moments with him."

I wanted some moments with him. I found him in the white infirmary, very pale, his hair the only shock of color amid the white bed, the white covers, the white walls.

"Blossom," he said, and smiled a little. The smile was bitter. "You thought Avery would care for me? That he wouldn't shoot me?"

I nodded.

"Why?"

"He was your partner in this venture," I said. "Wasn't he? How long?"

"A year, two."

"Poor man," I said.

"Me?"

"No, him. To work that long with you and not care, not know you're human, he must have felt very sure that no artifact could be human. He must have hated himself very much."

He blinked at me. "If your Mother Superior found out—"

"She knows," I said. "I told her."

"And she'll let you stay?" I said.

"She'll let me profess," I said.

He raised his eyebrows. "And you want to? You could come with me, Blossom. We could—"

"Run from place to place, looking for a humanity that always eludes us? I've found my home, Joe, and my place." I took a deep breath. "Mother says you can stay here until you're well. Until you've recovered. And then we'll find . . . what you want to do. She says she has connections. She can give you ID papers. You can be free."

"Free?" he said.

"Free from self-hatred and the fear they'll discover you're not human. Free from the fear of not being human." I pulled back his disarrayed hair. He felt cold to the touch. "You see, the thing is, we are humans. Humans also are never sure they are . . . real. Usually they find their humanity in others. When you see others are human and worth caring for, then you too must be."

He blinked at me. "I want to believe you, Blossom. I thought I loved you once."

"You loved me once. There was no way I could have disarmed you, unless you wanted me to," I said, confidently.

He blinked again. He sighed. "I can't promise anything. You don't know what I've done, the things I've said and contrived and—"

"You don't have to promise," I said. "You just have to try. It's all humans do. All the rest is left for a greater power."

On the way out of the infirmary and just in case, I stopped before the statue of St. Lucia in its niche in the hallway. She smiled serenely, the veil covering her head and caught in her hands, wide open. There was a crown of stars on her head, made of something that sparkled in the darkness. And the inside of her mantle was deep blue spangled with white stars.

I looked up at her face, sculpted from holos taken while she was alive. Such regular features, so perfect. In someone living, I'd know that face belonged to an artifact. But it couldn't be. In her day, centuries ago, artifacts would never be allowed even the benefit of the doubt.

And yet, I had a feeling she understood as I whispered a prayer that Joe's heart and soul might be healed, as well as his body. I'd come home and found my family. My love for him was now more memory and a warm sense of solidarity. But I wanted him to find what I had found. I wanted him to discover his mission in life and to be happy.

I had the impression the saint smiled at my back as I turned and went to serve breakfast to our charity cases. There would be cakes and cinnamon toast because it was Christmas. I couldn't wait to see how the crèche children reacted to the treats.

INTRODUCTION
❧◈❧
IN THE SPIRIT
OF CHRISTMAS

THE MINISTRY OF PECULIAR OCCURRENCES investigates the mysterious, the bizarre, and the unknown that leaves Scotland Yard baffled. They protect Her Majesty Queen Victoria's subjects from the occult, the paranormal, and those agents bent on bringing down the empire. And it is on Christmas Eve when the Ministry is called upon to help liberate a local solicitor out of a precarious arrangement from an old friend. Welcome to a steampunk spin on a beloved Christmas classic. *Ectoplasm sold separately*

🌲 🌲 🌲

TEE MORRIS began his writing career with the 2002 historical epic fantasy, *MOREVI: The Chronicles of Rafe & Askana* from Dragon Moon Press. In 2005 Tee took *MOREVI* into the then-unknown podosphere, making his novel his first book podcast in its entirety. That experience led to the founding of Podiobooks.com, collaborating with Evo Terra and Chuck Tomasi on *Podcasting for Dummies*, and podcasting *The Case of the Singing Sword: A Billibub Baddings Mystery*, winning him the 2008 Parsec Award for Best Audio Drama. Today, Tee podcasts *The Shared Desk* with his wife, Pip Ballantine, and the Parsec-winning *Tales from the Archives*.

Tee and Pip continue to write together in the award-winning Ministry of Peculiar Occurrences series, their third installment *Dawn's Early Light* hitting the shelves in 2014. Between books, they have released *Ministry Protocol: Thrilling Cases of the Ministry of Peculiar Occurrences*, a collection of short stories set in their steampunk world .Find out more about Tee at TeeMorris.com.

IN THE SPIRIT OF CHRISTMAS

by TEE MORRIS

CHRISTMAS, 1895

WELLINGTON THORNHILL BOOKS, Esquire, had not planned for anything out of the ordinary this Christmas Eve. His agenda called for a candlelight service at his church, a special Christmas treat of goose for Archimedes when he got home, and then to bed, rising the next morning to a day of progress on his current work. He had solved the challenge of thrust. Now it was a matter of control over pitch and yaw. That mystery he planned to solve as a gift for himself. His Christmas plans did not include, in any way, shape, or form, investigation into an occurrence of any kind, peculiar or otherwise.

That was before Eliza returned from the main level of Miggins Antiquities with a cylinder that she had, without a doubt, retrieved from the Scotland Yard pneumatic. That was before a quick conversation about the two of them being the only ones left in the building as it was Christmas Eve and everyone, including the

Director, has absconded for the holiday. That was before Wellington uttered seven words he knew he would regret.

"Very well, Miss Braun. If you insist."

He now bit his lip hard as he watched from his hiding place the third apparition appear. Not a single confirmed haunting, but a *third*. In the same location. In the same night. Not free floating orbs. Not wisps of mist. Not partial apparitions.

Full.

Body.

Apparitions.

This spirit appeared more imposing than the others. It was tall, wearing tattered, ancient robes that insinuated druidic origins, and while the shadows concealed its face, Wellington could easily make out pale bones protruding from the robes' cuffs.

His eyes immediately darted to the other side of the room. He could just make out the shoe tips of his partner. The curtain she concealed herself behind remained still, placid. They had already done this twice before in the evening. This third procedure should be effortless.

The old man had dropped to one knee—as they had planned— almost as if he were about to propose marriage. As the other spirits had appeared completely and totally cognizant to verbal and physical communication, it was a strategy to lower the next fantastic creature's defenses. Wellington felt more than confident this was the right strategy to play as each ghost garnered their own specific, tactical advantages. The previous one, for instance, appeared to sport its own girth as a weapon, but it was the children crouching within his robes that proved quite the adversaries.

Unlike the other visitations, however, this spirit fed on the very life in the room. Wellington felt despair well up inside him. The temperature in this already cold, dreary place felt as if it had dropped even further. He fought back a piteous sigh for he knew his breath would give his own hiding place away.

"I am in the presence of the Ghost of Christmas Yet To Come?" the old man spoke, his earlier confidence seeming dashed and destroyed.

No reply came from the ghost, save for a gesture. The ghost pointed downward, inclining its bony hand towards the frail, trembling soul before it.

"You are about to show me shadows of the things that have not happened, but will happen in the time before us," the old man, his words forming as puffs of fog around his mouth, pressed. "Is that so, Spirit?"

The ghost inclined its head. The only answer this bare apartments' sole occupant received.

Amazing, Wellington thought to himself. *It, too, is fully responsive to corporal beings. Never have I seen such* consistent *interaction, let alone such irrefutable spiritual activity, at one haunting.*

"Ghost of the Future!" the old man exclaimed, "I fear you more than any spectre I have seen. But as I know your purpose is to do me good, and as I hope to live to be another man from what I was, I am prepared to bear you company, and do it with a thankful heart. Will you not speak to me?"

Wellington furrowed his brow. *Laying it on a bit thick, aren't you?*

The specter gave no reply, but extended its hand straight before them.

"Very well." Then the old man rose to his feet, stepped back, and shouted, *"Get him!"*

With a grand flutter, the curtain opposite Wellington billowed out and parted to reveal Eliza D. Braun, throwing back the switch and safety lock on the Tesla-McTighe-Fitzroy Paraphysical Containment Rifle, or as the three inventors had nicknamed it, the "Phantom Confounder." A whine emitted from the small turbine mounted atop the chamber, but only a heartbeat or two later the weapon roared to life. The dark lenses of Eliza's goggles flickered from the tendrils of energy erupting from the Confounder's bell-shaped barrel. The electricity illuminated the room, the ethereal creature, and the old man, their shadows—*Dear Lord,* Wellington thought, *this spectre is so complete it has mass!*—dancing along the drab walls of the bedroom. Like pearl white claws, bolts wrapped themselves around the ghost, ensnaring it where it stood, but suddenly the rifle kicked in Eliza's arms and a pop rang out from the weapon's transistor. Several tendrils went wide, destroying two small figurines on the fire's mantelpiece and bouncing off the mirror over the same mantelpiece and striking a small gas lamp on the wall. The wall fixture exploded, making the phantom and old man recoil.

"Bugger!" Eliza spat. "Wellington, we have a problem!"

Dash it all.

"Throw the capacitor to Position Three!" Wellington emerged from his hiding place, sliding a small metal plate underneath the spirit. It was stumbling, so the creature was stunned. At present, this could work in their favour. The plate stopped just behind the ghost. "That should open a circuit and—"

The Confounder roared to life and threw another webbing of energy at and around the spirit. It reared back, making the tendrils whip and bow in mid-air.

"Eliza," Wellington said, his eyes watching the electro-pattern, "the stream is going to go wide."

"No, it's not," she returned.

"You're going to go wide."

"I've got this under control," she growled through gnashed teeth.

"Eliza!" Wellington grabbed the old man and dove. He was thankful that this man enjoyed the indulgence of a luxurious bed.

The creature jerked its body again and the bolt snapped outward, cutting through the air where the old man had once stood. Lightning scorched across the wall and sliced through a small statue of Eros located in the room's far corner.

"Right then," Eliza said, throwing the rifle's bolt forward, "I went wide. Apologies."

"Stay here, Mr. Scrooge," Wellington said before rolling away from the old man.

He opened the drawer of Scrooge's bed stand, and withdrew the small control box he had hidden there earlier. The green button made a hard *click* under Wellington's thumb, and the ghost lurched as the plate began to rattle. Wellington's throat constricted as he adjusted a pair of dials on the wireless in his grasp. The black spectre was still moving too much.

"Eliza," Wellington called, "a moment of your attention if you please."

"Just a moment if you please," she replied over her weapon's attempt to spin up to full power. "The generator is still warming up."

The plate rattled louder.

"We don't *have* a few minutes!"

"Just another—"

The phantom had been silent all this while. From underneath it, Wellington's trap hummed and shuddered, but not loud enough to drown out the low, guttural scream ripping from the dark void of the ghost's cowl.

Eliza threw back the bolt, and shifted the capacitor lever to the far right. "Close enough."

The Confounder exploded in a brilliant flash, pure energy cocooning the Ghost of Christmas Yet to Come in a wild, turbulent display. It released another howl as it wrestled against the Confounder.

"Bugger me, he's strong," muttered Eliza.

"Hold him there," Wellington said as he adjusted the settings on his controls what he hoped would be one final time, "and I've got him!"

His thumb lifted the guard and flipped the red switch to the "*Open*" position. The metal plate spilt, revealing a dark mass that churned and bubbled underneath the ghost. On sight of this, the ghost's struggle grew frantic, desperate. Its bony hands cut through the air, threatening to grab hold of anything that would come within reach of it. Try as it would, Wellington knew without a doubt the portal's pull would not falter. Eliza shut down the Confounder as shadows from this abyss reached up, grabbing hold of the phantom as the Confounder once had. The creature gave one final reach and a wail of panic before surrendering. The shadows constricted around it and yanked, dragging it into the murkiness of oblivion.

Wellington returned the switch to the "*Closed*" position, and the portal shut with a soft hum. He took a deep breath—that sound cutting through the moment's heavy silence—and afforded a smile.

Three spirits, three captures. Not bad for one evening.

"Apart from a momentary cock-up, that went rather well, I thought," Eliza said.

"Yes," Wellington replied, motioning to the massive device now resting across her shoulders, "about that?"

"It had to have been that second ghost. You saw the size of him, yes?" She motioned with her head to the Confounder. "I think its calibration might have been thrown off after packing him and his beasties up. I'll make sure to give it a once-over when we get back to the office."

Her smile, he always thought, was quite disarming. It was made even more so when she lifted her tinted goggles and rested them across her forehead. The soot and grime from the Confounder had darkened and stained her face, save for a small band of pale white skin across her eyes.

He was about to comment when he heard a soft scratching coming from the bed where he had left Ebenezer Scrooge. Wellington turned to find Scrooge muttering something to himself, and then quickly making notations on a small piece of parchment.

"Mr. Scrooge," Wellington began, "are you well?"

"As well as can be expected," Scrooge returned, his eyes noting the parchment as he turned to the two of them, "I would have been asleep hours ago had we not tonight to contend with."

"Well now, Mr. Scrooge, no need to worry," Eliza said, smiling warmly. "You can sleep more soundly now, thanks to the Ministry."

"Of that, I have no doubt." Scrooge's eyes looked over them both, his mouth stretching into a thin frown. "Though I still have no inkling exactly what Ministry you serve."

"Our policies unfortunately mean we must remain in shadow," she said.

"So it would seem. Very well. Makes no difference either way as you have seen to your obligations." He glanced at the parchment and then presented it to Wellington. "And now, your bill."

Wellington and Eliza both gave a start. The Archivist was still staring at the paper, the ink still quite fresh, when Eliza blurted, "Our what?"

"For damages to my estate." Scrooge motioned to the scorched mirror over the fireplace, the destroyed gas lamp, and the destroyed statue. "And let's not forget the parlour where you ensnared the Ghost of Christmas Present."

Eliza scoffed. "As much as I hate to repeat myself, but did you see the size of him?"

"You claimed this sort of thing to be a specialty. I was unaware that damage to personal property came with your unique services."

Her eyes quickly reviewed the paper in Wellington's hand, and then jumped back to Scrooge. "You billed us *for your time?*"

"In my occupation, I must be alert and well-rested. My mind is far more reliable than any difference engine in Her Majesty's service, provided I get enough sleep. As I am presently not asleep and working with you all, my time is therefore billable. And as I anticipate that I will not simply drift off to sleep in the wake of tonight's excitement, this is time billable to your organization as direct consequences to your actions."

"You've got some cheek, mate!" Eliza spat.

"I pay my taxes. And as I mentioned to some rather insistent annoyances earlier this day, my taxes help to support the establishments of our government. They cost enough. My taxes, however, should not be expected to be exempt from damages upon my personal property due to your incompetence."

Now Wellington took offense. "I crave a pardon, sir, but we *captured* your ghosts. How do you define that—"

"All but one," Scrooge said, his tone so sorrowful that it was insulting. "Marley's Ghost is still at large, I am afraid. And did your partner not admit to her own ineptitude with your contraption there while attempting to capture the final spirit?"

Her warning came colder than the apartments themselves. "Tread. Carefully."

Both men looked to Eliza whose fingers were splaying slowly around the butt of the Confounder.

"Mr. Scrooge," Wellington began, clearing his throat lightly, "please consider that your case would have been dismissed as the rantings of a mad old man if our Scotland Yard contact had not happened to relay it to our Ministry. Miss Braun and I happened to be in the office on its arrival, and we dropped everything in order to give your case our undivided attention."

"I applaud your dedication to your civic duty," Scrooge returned. His expression turned dark. "Now unless you wish me to adjust my invoice for the time you are continuing to take without any consideration to me, I suggest you collect your infernal devices and depart. Good evening."

He turned back to his four-poster bed and crawled between the sheets. He went to blow out his candle, but paused to see Wellington and Eliza still standing there.

"The front door has not moved since your arrival." He motioned with his head to the bedroom door. "Good evening."

Eliza's grumbling was the only sound Wellington could hear as they saw themselves out of the dark, dank apartments, their gear jostling lightly with each of their steps. It had just started to snow, meaning that even with their efforts to bundle against the elements, a long, cold walk home stretched before them. Wellington checked his watch and saw it was just past midnight. How these spirits could also alter time would have been something he would have loved to investigate. Could Scrooge's apartments been constructed at some sort of temporal convergence point?

His thoughts were scattered by Eliza, the Confounder's bulk looking rather odd against her heavy fur coat as she spat, "Jolly nice. We have to walk home, I suppose, after carrying out our civic duty."

"It seems that way," Wellington muttered.

She looked back up to the window that remained lit for a few moments, and then winked into darkness. "Old bugger really needs a taking to task, doesn't he?"

"He does seem a bit cantankerous," Wellington agreed.

They took a few steps further, and Eliza stopped. He turned to look at her in the gaslight. The grime across her face seemed darker now, making the area once protected by her goggles seeming to glow in the night.

"I'm sorry, Wellington."

Tonight was truly a night of surprises. "You're sorry, Miss Braun?"

"Welly, I am certain you probably had other plans for Christmas.

Perhaps a fine dinner with relatives or some such; but I was quite happy to have this case appear in the pneumatic system when it did."

"Well, of course you were happy. It was a chance to return to the field—"

"I did not look forward to another Christmas alone."

His brow furrowed. "You? The vivacious Eliza D. Braun, alone at Christmas?"

"Christmas is a time for family, and my own is…" Her voice trailed off, and now with the pronounced clean skin around her eyes, the tears welling in there were evident.

Wellington felt a warmth swell in his chest. Eliza had been insistent on him joining her on this case, but not to return to the life of a field agent. She had wanted to spend Christmas with family. Instead, she chose to spend the holiday with the next best thing.

"I'm flattered, Miss Braun." And he truly was. Tonight has been a delightful Christmas gift.

He then looked around himself and realised, "Oh, dash it all, I forgot the portalplate at Scrooge's."

"Better go get it then," Eliza said, sniffling a bit. "I'll wait here for you."

Wellington took a quick step back to the detestable man's apartments but stopped. He looked over to the wireless controller slung over his shoulder, looked back at Eliza, and then back towards Scrooge's.

"You know, Miss Braun," Wellington said, a smile forming across his face, "wireless telegraphy is an amazing technology of our age. Before it, we would have to be tethered to devices in order to make them work."

Eliza inclined her head to one side. "Yes," she said plainly, "and your point?"

"With wireless advances, we can now operate devices of all sorts," and he flipped the safety up of the portalplate's activation switch, "from great distances."

His thumb pushed the switch to *"Open"* and turned to look up to Scrooge's bedroom window as it exploded with light.

On hearing the old miser scream, he returned his attention to

Eliza. "Mr. Scrooge did say his time was valuable," Wellington said, "so now he can take them all at once, and have it over, yes?"

Eliza laughed at the frantic display erupting from Scrooge's window, then she looked back to Wellington, her smile brighter than the chaotic luminance coming from above them. "Alice will be off for the day, but I know a butcher who usually has a nice bit of New Zealand lamb. If you are available for Christmas dinner, Wellington, would you care to enjoy the holiday with a touch of Aotearoa?"

Wellington smiled. "I would be delighted."

He extended his arm to her, and with his peculiar wireless control slung over his shoulder and her Confounder resting on her shoulder, the two walked into the night, leaving fresh tracks in the gathering snow around them.

Another scream from Scrooge's apartments cut through the night.

"Merry Christmas, Eliza."

"Merry Christmas, Welly."

INTRODUCTION
❧✿❧
WORMHOLE MAGIC

HERE'S A SPRIGHTLY NARRATIVE of a distant future which has forgotten about Christmas and that fellow named Kris. But Kris hasn't forgotten, and if he has to go to the Moon to revive the tradition, well . . . who's to say that those reindeer can't go *anywhere*?

🌲 🌲 🌲

MARIANNE PLUMRIDGE is an Australian-born artist and writer who lives in Rhode Island, USA, with her husband, illustrator Bob Eggleton. In the last few years, Marianne has returned to her fine art roots by refining her oil painting techniques. As well as painting natural subjects, Marianne has combined birds and robots into an ongoing series of "technology lost in nature" paintings that include quirky tin toy robot adventures, to great acclaim. Her other continuing themes of cosmic whales and pointy rocket-ship paintings still enjoy success and popular favor. The results can be found online at: "Daub du Jour"—http://daubdujour.blogspot.com/

Marianne has published fiction, articles and essays in magazines and anthoogies, and also writes book reviews and notes on her second blog, "Muse du Jour"—http://musedujour.blogspot.com/ Currently, she is writing the text for a book called *Bob Eggleton's Ice Age America* for Impossible Dreams Press, in collaboration with her husband. It will feature essays and epic artwork and visions of prehistoric peoples, megafauna, and flora . . . and especially mammoths and mastodons. Meanwhile, Marianne and Bob's first collaboration as writer and artist, a children's picture book called *If Dinosaurs Lived in My Town*, will be released in November 2013 from Sky Pony Press.

WORMHOLE MAGIC

by Marrianne Plumridge

"GEEZ, WILL. You've been there, what, three months now?" Jen began.

Three months on the Moon, she meant. On my own, nominally in charge of Earthwatch Prime Station, and feeling rather like a superfluous janitor on a fully self-maintained automated space frigate rather than a paid intern with a momentous responsibility. And I'd never fully taken into account how lonely it would be out here. No one to talk to except by vid-screen, like I was doing now.

". . . and you still haven't decided on a topic for your Astrogation Thesis. Professor Jordan mentioned that a couple of days ago. In fact, he's been mentioning it a lot lately." Her face dissolved into a disapproving pout.

Professor Jordan harrumphs about that dangling thesis topic every time he sends a data burst—thankfully, only once a week. Whenever he prefaces a sentence with, "Now then, William, it's time to make a decision . . ." I know I'm going to hear the usual lecture on my future, career, commitment, and profitability, even though I know it by heart. I didn't want to hear a similar lecture from Jen. Even with her talking on the vid-com from the beacon point space station half a light beyond the orbit of Pluto, there were other things I wanted to hear her saying.

"I've got nine more months to think about it, Jen," I said.

"You're supposed to be *working* on it by now . . ." She emphasized with a roll of her eyes. "You've lost three months already. Then it'll be three more months, and three more after that, and *then* you'll only have three more months to cobble it together. The way to do something is to actually get busy and *do* it." I'd heard her say that before—it's one of her mottos, I think—and she was trying to be very serious with me, but she doesn't really do stern and serious well. She always seems on the verge of laughing. It's probably the dimples that do it. The first time she smiled at me, I'd lost all track of the conversation for about five minutes and missed out on a crucial piece of a spatial physics lesson she was imparting. I'd learned, since then, to record all of our conversations.

"You're there by yourself, without any distractions—" she continued.

Well, actually, I'm talking with a major distraction right now, I thought, but didn't say. A very pleasant distraction, of course. On my wall screen, Jen was perched in her command chair with legs and arms woven into one of those elegant knots only dancers or yoga masters seemed to achieve with any ease. Her long red-brown hair was tumbled haphazardly on top of her head and skewered there with what looked to be one of those very expensive light scribes for writing on virtual 3D panels. A data lens covered her right eye, but the other was its usual grey/green. I wiped a hand over my mouth to hide the goofy smile that always seemed to creep up whenever we talked. Today, she looked adorable. I found myself fascinated by her socks: rubber-soled to avoid static, but the resemblance to practicality ended there. They were a fluffy hot pink, animated by the near constant movement of her toes inside them. *Keep on distracting me, please*. But I didn't know how she would react if I said that aloud. Not yet, anyway.

So, I mentioned other distractions. "Actually, there are plenty of distractions. You should see the stuff stored here—masses upon masses of it. They must have wanted to keep some of history locally intact for future use so they hauled it up from Earth and stashed it here. Really fascinating antiques and artifacts covering . . . oh, *centuries*."

"Well . . . yeah," she said with a wistful sigh. We had talked before about some of the items I'd come across. Like most of us, she has a craving for all things "Earth," and she was a rapt audience when I waxed lyrical about my "finds."

And, even with the massive distance between us, I'd much rather talk to her than the Professor. She's much prettier and funnier than he. Jen's also a lot smarter than I am and knows exactly what she wants out of life. Professor Jordan adores her for that fact alone. (Of course, I can think of other reasons to adore her.) Several times a day I silently thank the Professor for assigning her to be my tutor six months ago. And believe me, I've been availing myself of every opportunity to get ahead—one way or another. Aside from being my tutor, Jen is also a fellow classmate at Gaia U.—studying for *her* astrogation thesis. The only difference is she knows exactly what to write for hers.

"I've got to go now, Will. Did my explanation of how the uncertainty principle affects navigation through wormholes help?"

Actually, I'd been paying more attention to her eyes, in spite of the data lens, and thinking of the laughter hiding in their depths. As usual, I'd recorded her explanations and would play it back later when I could keep my mind on the math.

"Sure it did, Jen. I'll try the exercise again," I said. Then thought maybe I could call her again tomorrow, so I added, "I'll call if I get stuck."

"Call whenever you need help, Will. If I'm out, the recorder will get it." She smiled and clicked off. Still bemused by the brief flash of her dimples, I hoped that I'd never get the recorder again. Ever.

I meant what I said to Jen, honest. But first I wanted to take another look at those things I found in Section C yesterday. I supposed the novelty of looking at ancient artifacts which actually originated on Earth would wear off soon enough, but I was enjoying exploring the outpost's treasures. Not to mention walking on the Moon's surface and looking up at the Earth. How many people had a chance to actually *see* ancestral Earth, and not just a vid of it?

Section C was filled floor to very high ceiling with endless multitudes of old plascrete crates. And I was having a perfectly fine afternoon, randomly poking into some of them until I got to a large area of crates full of something called "books." At least that was what the label on the crate at hand read. I popped the cryo-seal and took off the top. The contents were blocky and short, and stacked neatly inside. They smelled kind of musty though. Old, like the inside of well used space suits—only cleaner somehow. A moment of consideration and heavy thinking produced a solution to my puzzlement: these were paper products. I shivered in distaste, and nearly dropped the one I was holding. It fanned open. Bound sheets of fine white stuff, neatly covered with tiny text, flapped back at me. I fingered one in awe: these were once part of a living tree. Paper manufacture was one of a myriad of things that ultimately caused the creation of this outpost, Earthwatch Prime, in the first place. I felt like I was touching the distant chaotic past.

I must tell Jen about this, I thought.

As I carefully replaced the artifact in its receptacle, a splurge of color caught my eye. I gingerly plucked another blocky volume from the crate and inspected it. There was a small inset picture, but it didn't look real. Painted perhaps? They did things like that back then, or so I'm told. The little "painting" was primarily dark blue with white speckled all over it. Damage? Ash? I gently wiped a forefinger over it, but it didn't come off, and the surface was not pitted. It must really be part of the picture, I surmised. There was a structure with a sharply inclined roof, all lit up from inside, and something long in the sky behind it. I looked at it for a long time, but couldn't make believable sense of it, so I turned my attention to the label. The script was so ornate, that it was even more difficult to fathom. After some minutes, I managed to decipher "T'was The Night Before Christmas".

"Who, or what, is Christmas?" I mused aloud.

I had my hand on the edge of the book ready to open the cover to find out, when a klaxon alarm sounded overhead. A very loud klaxon alarm. It nearly deafened me. The voice of the main computer was even louder still.

"INTRUDER ALERT! INTRUDER ALERT! MAIN AIRLOCK! INTRUDER ALERT!"

It took a bare second to put the book back into its crate and seal it in. Taking a deep breath, I yelled into the air. 'Turn the alarm off, you stupid computer! I'm the only one here, for Earth's sake! You've got my attention!" By then, I was running for the station control room, via the weapons locker, and to the main airlock. All the while, my mind was feverishly turning over worst-case scenarios. Had the supply ship turned up a month early? Was someone shipwrecked on the Moon's surface outside the station? Raiders?

"Computer, scan occupants of airlock. Keep it sealed! Give me details." I puffed out loud. Damn, I've gotta get more exercise.

"ONE HUMANOID BIPED AND NINE SMALLER QUADRAPEDS. THE VEHICLE OUTSIDE THE AIRLOCK IS OF UNKNOWN ORIGIN AND CONTAINS AN UNIDENTIFIABLE POWER SOURCE. THERE ARE INTER-DIMENSIONAL IRREGULARITIES."

Oh, great! Pity the Computer couldn't understand sarcasm, or I'd let fly with a few choice witticisms. Its description told me bloody little. Could it be Scumvrates—aliens from the Orion Sector? I've never been able pronounce even the phonetic version of their race name, and gave up long after a general lack of ethics was found in some of their most flamboyant representatives by the Central Gov. on Gaia. Some journalistic wag had dubbed them Scumvrates in an editorial some years ago and it had stuck. Still, I was glad to have grabbed a plasma rifle instead of the skimpier stunner. Those reptilian rats were a bugger to knock out. The biped puzzled me, though: irony curled my lip, and I wondered if they'd brought an interpreter along with them. Sure, they like to be polite when they trash a place on a grab and run operation. Earthwatch was an official "ark" site and protected by all the worlds in the commonwealth. Those Scumvrate bastards were just looking for trouble, and they were really, really going to find it.

I finally came to a slithering halt before the airlock door. Something big was blocking the window of the inner hatch, and an ominous pounding from the other side of it reached my ears.

"Okay, Computer. Close and seal the Ready Room behind me." I dragged a heavy maintenance trolley out of its locker and shoved it in front of one of the more vulnerable work consoles, not sure if I was trying to protect it or me as I squatted behind it. I took a deep breath and hefted the rifle to the ready over my makeshift barricade. "Open the inner airlock door."

Assorted hisses and clangs announced that my orders were being obeyed. Last of all, the airlock door "fzzzzzzzztd" open.

A big red something snarled in the opening. "Well, it's about time!" Nine small furry heads with sticks on top framed the doorway around it, bad-tempered curiosity written on every face. One seemed to be in ill health, as its nose was demonstrably red.

Well, they weren't Scumvrates. Not even a close second. What filled the airlock was absolutely ludicrous. The giant in the red coat and trousers, and the silly hat—all trimmed in fluffy white stuff—was human. Tall, weighed about three hundred pounds, and grumpy as hell. Worse, he spotted me. I suppose he couldn't help it really: I'd stupidly risen from the barricade and stood transfixed with my mouth hanging open. Was this some kind of joke?

"You!" The red and white individual bellowed, advancing on me. He brushed my rifle aside, and reached over both trolley and console and grabbed me by the suit-front. I felt myself lifted up off the floor until I stood on tippy toes. Obviously, the in-house contrived Earthlike gravity meant as much to him as a spacesuit did. This close, yes he was definitely human: an iron grip, burly hands, biceps of steel, chubby red cheeks, long white beard, blazing angry eyes, smelling of candy.

And he'd arrived without a spacesuit. So had his little friends. Damn. It briefly crossed my mind that I might be hallucinating . . . but this kind of realism was going a bit too far.

The red-clad one was yelling again. Remotely, I thought I'd better pay attention.

". . . Where are they? Where did they go?"

"Wh . . . who? I'm the only one supposed to be here." Despite the shaking he was giving me, I thought I'd managed that rather well.

"Not here, you blockhead! On Earth! The planet's empty! Not one single soul is down there!" He shook me one more time, just to get the point across, then he let me go.

Rocking back and forward on my feet, trying to gain some balance,

I just stared at him. He must be mad, or something. "Sir." No sense in being disrespectful is there? "There hasn't been a human living on Earth for the last two hundred years. Preservation policy forbids it."

The intruder looked stricken. "Are you the only one left, then? You poor soul." He then covered his eyes with his meaty hands and groaned. He appeared genuinely distressed. Warily, I reached out and tentatively patted the broad red expanse of his shoulder. Relieved that he didn't seem like he was about to rip my hand off and slap me with the wet end, I patted a bit more firmly.

"A question woke me. I've slept far too long," he murmured from behind his hands. "Too long."

Feeling bold, I left my hand resting on his shoulder. "Sir, who are you?" I asked quietly. I certainly didn't want to rile him up again.

The old man, if that is what he was, stared into my eyes for a very long moment, then at his own attire, and at his creature companions. Finally he turned back to me with infinite sadness in his eyes, and whispered. "You don't know?"

I slowly shook my head.

The intruder wiped a hand across his eyes, and his shoulders sagged in defeat. "There have been many names for me over the eons, but you can call me Kris. I'm sorry to have been such a boor, but the silence down there was nigh deafening when I awoke. All I heard was someone asking "who, or what is Christmas?"

I very nearly choked. No! It couldn't be! It was impossible. Wasn't it? So was a human not requiring a spacesuit on the surface of the Moon. I didn't even want to think about the creatures he'd brought with him. I was flabbergasted. "Sir? I asked that self-same question only minutes ago."

The old man brightened visibly. "At least my internal direction finder is still working."

Eons? The word and the meaning finally penetrated. Carefully taking the mental measurement of it, I repeated the word again aloud on a breath of air. "Eons . . ." Clearly, there was way more mystery here than met the eye, and I felt a sudden hunger to hear his story. I smiled weakly. "Perhaps you had better come inside, then. I guess I could use the company."

It probably seemed a foolish move, inviting the old guy into the station like that, but curiosity had me by the scruff of the neck and wasn't about to let go. Inexplicably, a part of me felt like a naughty child feeling the first thrill of the unknown, and another felt like I was rolling in cotton candy.

"Computer. Unseal the Ready Room. Stand down from intruder alert."

Kris beamed. "Well, thank you kindly, young man." He reached back into the airlock and fetched out a rather large, lumpy red sack, and then shooed all the little creatures out into the spaciousness of the Ready Room proper. "Out you come, kiddies. It looks like we've been invited to supper. "

They didn't look so fierce, now, in the full light. It seemed that what I'd taken to be sticks were actually branching, pointy, bony structures attached to their furry heads. If you got too close though, it was possible to lose an eye. I fervently hoped that the computer could convince the food synthesizer to produce something for them to eat. *That* might take some doing.

After I'd introduced myself, our little group proceeded up to the living areas on level two. As we strolled along, I noticed Kris admiring the walls of the corridors and the many technological fixtures with something akin to puzzled bewilderment. "You have an interesting . . . er, house . . . here, William," he ventured finally. He appeared almost relieved when we reached the living quarters and oversized lounge area.

We took seats at the dining table while the little creatures, or reindeer as he called them, went off to investigate the furnishings. I winced, and hoped they wouldn't chew on anything important or needful, like life-support or gravity grid cables.

"Can I get you something to eat or drink? The food's not great, but it's edible." I turned back to my guest and offered with a smile, spreading my hands.

Kris chuckled. "Well, I never leave home without a supply of vittles. What say I furnish the feast, to make up for my earlier misbehavior?"

This I *had* to see. "Sure."

The old man took off his hat and tucked it into the pocket of his coat, which he then removed and hung over the back of his chair. Suspenders held up his red trousers, under which he wore a white, long-sleeved jersey. He looked like someone's grandfather from any backwoods planet out in the galactic rim—though somewhat cleaner. Kris happily rubbed his hands together and rummaged in his sack. What emerged was a huge woven hamper, and the smells emanating from it instantly made my mouth water. Out of the sack, he also took a large red cloth and laid it over the table. From the hamper, he began to pull an almost endless progression of hot goods and platters, identifying them for me as he laid them on the table. After a moment or two, the memory of the computer's assessment of "inter-dimensional irregularities" began to take on a deeper meaning. Nearly as deep as the food hamper. I seriously entertained the thought that Kris had a tiny wormhole in there, feeding him. One that small could probably make several fortunes for the creator. I angled my head, trying to see inside it.

"Oww!"

I rubbed the back of my hand where Kris had smacked it with a metal spoon. I hadn't realized I'd reached for the hamper at all, until that stinging thwack. How did one roast a pot anyway, I grumped, getting back to his culinary litany? Something stirred in the back of my mind, and I vaguely wondered what it would take to make Kris part with his hamper. If the Moon had a title deed of ownership, and I had access to it just then, I'd probably offer it to the old guy in exchange for that innocent looking basket. Not only would it be an answer to my career and success, but it would possibly feed me for the rest of my life, as well. Somehow though, I don't think Kris would accept the offer—he didn't seem to need or want anything at all, except maybe companionship.

I sighed and shook my head, as Kris finally brought out a steaming red jug and two red mugs. He appeared to really identify with that color. Each to his own, I guess. It certainly made a colorful and welcome contrast to the pastel and dun mediocrity of the base's committee-directed failure at cheerful decor. They seemed to forget that we caretakers had to live here as well as work here. But Kris' red fetish really seemed to brighten the place up, make it warmer somehow.

". . . and at last, Eggnog," he announced with a flourish. Filling both mugs, he presented one to me then appeared to think for a moment. "What's the date?" he inquired.

"Hmm, GM 837—20th, I think," I replied, sniffing cautiously at my mug. Then I caught him staring blankly at me. "Oh! Computer, what's today's date—old Earth calendar?"

'ACCORDING TO OLD EARTH STANDARD CALENDAR, TODAY IS 24TH DECEMBER, OF THE YEAR 3604.'

Kris seemed to beam, twinkle and sparkle all at once, he was so pleased. "Perfect!" He announced. "Merry Christmas, William!" And with that, the old man drained his mug.

I took a sip of mine, and then a deeper mouthful. Grief, that was good! I let him refill the mug again, before asking, "Is this it? Is this what Christmas is?" I indicated the laden table with an unoccupied hand.

"Ohh, ho, ho, no," my companion chuckled. "It all began for humanity a very long time ago. Would you like to hear about it?"

I thought he'd never ask! I nodded eagerly, but had to wait while he fed the reindeer, before Kris settled back in his chair. The bag produced three large flat pans filled with a kind of ground up . . . something. A grain of some kind? I'd sneak a sample for analysis later, if the little greedy gutses left any. They were chowing down very enthusiastically.

"Well, now. I've been around a mighty long time. Long before your species rose to walk the Earth, I slept beneath it and within it with many others of my kind. Our plane of existence greatly differs from yours. But sometimes the planes interconnect, for good or ill." Kris scratched his head ruefully, and I got the distinct impression that he was trying to figure out how to verbalize the impossible to an infant…me. "One event or another would awaken us, or humans would get too loud in their dealings, and we'd have to take steps. We've been called many things over time. Demons, gods, angels, ghosts, sprites, spirits, et cetera . . . hmmm, I've always liked that one: spirits. Well, there came a time when a child was born. A human child. A very special child, on a very special night, a very long time ago in a small town called Bethlehem. . . ."

I listened, totally entranced, while the old man wove an oral history of the human race. I was unashamed of the tears that laid silent tracks on my cheeks when he told of the death of that special child, and what it had portended for humanity. The journey had begun then, and was still in progress—only we didn't know it. He made it sound real, and worthy, and mighty in spirit. I'd automatically hit the record button on the rec's area computer link to capture his story, as I usually did Jen's. Kris ummed and erred a bit over several things during his telling, and I wondered if his story was as perfect as it sounded, particularly where humanity was concerned. We weren't a perfect race . . . far from it. But I had a good many burning questions to fill later hours, days, and months once left alone with the base computer and the masses of stored archives in the caverns below us. What he was describing resembled a primitive kind of worship. I wondered absently if it had ever gotten out of hand like the God wars between a set of planets out on the galactic rim a few hundred years back. I remembered bits of that from a history refresher course I took once. It wouldn't surprise me if it had.

Kris went on to explain how his role in Christmas came to be: "I woke one evening to find a man dying in the snow. His name was Kris Kringle, and he had a mighty errand to perform, but an accident made sure that this would never happen. He was crying out in despair with his body and soul—and that is why I heard him. He died there, while I held his hand, and I comforted him with the promise that I would finish his errand for him. So I became him for that night, and I delivered the items in his sack. It was a pitifully easy thing to do, but I distributed every wrapped package to every intended recipient, and then some. And I must say, that I enjoyed it so much that I got a bit creative with giving the humans in the village things to treasure: even if it was just a memory, or a smile, or enough to eat."

He paused. A smile softened his features as he remembered that far distant night.

"Anyway, I listened in the next day—a day in celebration of the birth of that child I mentioned before, incidentally—and how they mourned when the body of the real Kris Kringle was discovered in the forest. I read in the minds of some of the people of how they vowed to see Kris's sacrifice and compassion kept alive the next year, by doing the same thing in his honor. I was touched. They did it too, you know. I checked, and helped where I could, and whispered suggestions into specific ears. It became a habit after that, I suppose. One I really didn't want to break. And I became stronger as the rumor of the event spread across the continent and the seas, and people helped keep it alive by giving to those they loved, and helping those in need." Kris stopped briefly. "How's the turkey, son?"

I looked down at my plate, at the inroads I'd made into the feast. Once I'd gotten past the anatomical resemblance the "turkey" had to a semi-intelligent alien species on a planet in the Interior, I'd tucked in with gusto. Where did one get such food that tasted so good and looked so exotic? I finally looked back up and grinned. "Tastes like chicken."

"I'm not surprised!" Kris rolled his eyes and harrumphed a bit.

I blinked a bit in shock. Did he really know what "chicken" tasted like, let alone what it was? That old adage was a running joke where I came from, and usually alluded to "I don't know for sure, but it tastes great," I squinted at him, suspiciously. There were gaps in the world records after the chaotic 21st through 23rd centuries, old Earth time. Knowledge was lost, along with many people, and many species of native flora and fauna. I felt an urgent need to know whether "chicken" was animal, vegetable, or mineral.

"Er, Kris . . ." I began casually. "What exactly IS chicken?"

He frowned at me as if to say, *"Really?"* After he'd stretched the moment to its ultimate, he finally said with a degree of withering pity, "It's a bird, son. Like a turkey, only smaller. Has feathers, but can't fly far. The females lay eggs."

My eyes widened. The chicken and egg theory. . . . but that was just a myth. Wasn't it?

And it was a bird? Well that explained it then. The most powerful avian virus the world had ever known took out most of the bird species mid 22nd century. But I needn't tell him that just yet. I gazed at my companion with new respect and a touch of awe, as he got on with his story.

"It was fine for many years", he said, then his voice grew more somber. "But progress shot forward in both technological, and spiritual senses. Over time, the meaning and spirit of what Christmas was really about, got lost." Kris looked very tired and old just then. "When this happened, I slept longer and longer, and then didn't wake up at all. Rapid change just took over, and people forgot in all the rush." He looked up at me and smiled. "And then you asked your question, and I woke up and came looking for you."

"Wow." It was all I could manage just then. The magnitude of his story made me feel very small. I looked Kris over for a very long moment, absorbing his costume and accoutrements. Finally, I just had to ask: "Kris, have you always looked like you do now?"

The big guy chuckled his peculiar ho-ho-ho-ing laugh. "No, William. I change with people's perceptions and with their fashionable trends. Thankfully, they've let me keep my beard, and sent me Rudolph to lead the reindeer team in recent years." He averred fondly—the little creature with the ruddy nose wandered over and nuzzled his hand before bounding off again. I dragged my mind back from wondering if the little reindeer's nose was something akin to an implanted laser pointer or laser weapon. Kris caught me gazing first at his red jacket, the table cloth and jug, and then finally back to the retreating reindeer nose. He drew himself up to his full awesome height, and sniffed disdainfully. "What's wrong with red anyway? *I* like it very much." He sounded a bit defensive about it. "It's festive and all, and expresses the season and the sentiment splendidly. And the other Christmas colors like green, blue and silver always seemed a bit blah to me." Kris finished in a faint grumble.

Okay, you had to be an extrovert to do what he did, so perhaps garish, loud, warming, wonderful red made people smile over the long years. And it also stood out against the whiteness of snow and frost as a safety issue. I laughed. "It's a grand color, Kris. And it suits you very well. Hmm, I guess I should tell you what happened while you slept."

The old man sat forward with an eager expression on his red cheeks. "That would be most gratifying, William. Yes, please."

"Well, probably several centuries after you went into your long sleep, the Earth was starting to really deteriorate physically. Overpopulation, pollution, and waste took its toll, and it started to die. Not as many children were born each year, species of animals and plants disappeared, natural catastrophes took their toll along with health ones, and so on. The ecology couldn't keep up under the onslaught of humanity's foibles, no matter how much we tried to fix it. It was too little, much too late."

A sudden bleakness crossed my companion's features at these disclosures. I felt his discomfort enough to ask what was wrong.

"No wonder I had no energy and couldn't wake up," he noted broodingly. "If Earth was dying, then so were we."

We'd never known that we were killing off Kris' people as well as our own, along with everything else. It was hard to swallow around the sudden lump in my throat. And I thought I knew helplessness. Now I knew better. Kris waved me to continue after a moment.

"In spite of everything wrong on Earth, we somehow floundered our way into space. WorldCom co-opted everything into extending our reach by promoting colonial settlements on other worlds. The discovery of temporary wormholes in the space-time continuum and the development of the Ellison Drive enabled us to travel farther and faster than we ever had before. Control was a bit wild at first, but the scientists eventually got it under control, under budget and viable. Short high energy bursts and a tame wormhole got the first interstellar spaceship out of the solar system and to our nearest neighbor, Alpha Centauri. There were no planets we could use, so we kept going. Eventually, we found a solar system like ours further inward along our arm of the galaxy. It had three planets out of nineteen that were suitable. Planet number six became the new home of the human race. We called it Gaia—the rest is history."

I stared at nothing for a bit, still awed by that massive undertaking. Then I shook myself and continued. "As for here, Worldgov evacuated the Earth, and put an inviolate satellite cordon around it, forbidding landing there. On the planet surface, teams spent twenty years replanting anything they could lay their hands on, and cloning animals to be released. Then the home-world was left on its own to regenerate. That was nearly two hundred years ago. It'll be another four hundred or so before the Commonwealth government lets anyone move back again for study and evaluation. This station, Earthwatch Prime, was built here on the Moon to house some of the artifacts from planetside, and to monitor the status of re-growth progress." I tied up my nutshell version of Earth history, and smiled at my guest. I was startled to find Kris gazing at me in stunned amazement.

"You mean you're not the only human left? That there're more of you?" he demanded, echoing his earlier belligerence.

"No, no, no! Humans just moved out for the duration! The central seat of government is on Gaia—where I was born. There are at least 12 billion, or so, of us spread across twenty-nine worlds. I'm just on contracted assignment as Caretaker here for a year, so I can finish studying for my Astral Navigation degree." I spread my hands in apology, for letting him think that humans had died out. Oh, grief!

"Well," he mused thoughtfully, after a few calming breaths, "It explains why I can't hear them, and maybe why Christmas has been forgotten."

I had an inspiration about then. "But it's such a beautiful story, and you have to tell it again: to anyone who will listen. Look, how do you feel about public speaking? My professor at Gaia Central University could help you reach people. Earth history and culture is very, very popular among the worlds—everyone dreams of one day going 'home', even though they never can. Humans aren't as long lived as you obviously are. Maybe you could bring the story to them. Then you'd hear 'them'—the people—again."

Kris appeared to be thinking it over, methodically stroking his beard while he did so. His blue eyes blazed with sharp speculation. "How far is it, to this Gaia?"

"If you had no problem getting here on the strength of a question, then I'd say that you'd have no problem getting there, or anywhere else. How do you navigate?" I pressed eagerly.

"By thoughts and feelings—the stronger the better. I believe that I find thoughts on Christmas to be the best pin-pointers. I sort of browse around when I get wherever it is I arrive at." Kris supplied, catching some of my excitement. "I'll do it," he finished firmly, grinning, and swatted me on the back with one of his meaty paws.

The impact nearly threw me off my feet. Rubbing the offended spot, I half grimaced, half grinned back at him. He'd be all right.

"Good, I'm going to send you to a friend who is a caretaker on another station, and then she will send you on to Gaia, and the Professor." Plans ran wild in my head. Even the reindeer must have caught on to it, because they milled around us excitedly, butting gently with their head-sticks.

Kris and I shook hands on it, beaming at each other.

"I will have to return to Earth periodically, to renew my energy with it, and to sleep," he said gravely. "Would you mind if I dropped in to visit you now and then?"

I grinned. "Not at all. It would break up my study quite nicely. Besides, it gets to be too quiet here, some days. Please come, you'll be very welcome."

Kris half-turned and snapped a crisp command at the table. The hamper rose on four spindly legs, and stepped neatly over the debris of our feast. Its large handle split into two and became arms ending with hands and long dexterous fingers. They deftly shoved platters and things back into its open maw. I still couldn't see the wormhole inside, and I wondered if it was because my eyes were bulging so hard they hurt. I tried very hard not to have hysterics just then.

While Kris oversaw this operation, I excused myself and quickly ducked down to the hydroponics dome. As soon as the door whooshed closed behind me, I pelted the computer with rapid fire questions. I even got some answers I could use. When I came back, I'd finally gotten my sanity under control, and I presented him with something. It was a transparent plastic tube filled with soil from Earth, some leaves and twigs and pebbles: a little bit of everything. I had tied a flower to it with a bit of long grass. I felt a bit awkward, and shuffled a bit in explanation. "It's from Earth. So you can take a little bit of it with you, when you go away. Merry Christmas, Kris."

He looked gobsmacked, and very touched. When he suddenly hugged me, I think he surprised both of us. I felt slightly ashamed of my earlier covetous thoughts about his food hamper.

"Merry Christmas, William. And thank you."

Then I handed him a small carisac filled with hybrid apples and few quickly pulled carrots with the green bits still attached. "They're for your reindeer. The computer said that they might like them," I added softly. Rudolf approached again and I tweaked one of his headsticks. Antlers, the computer had called them. They were finely fuzzy beneath my fingertips. I suddenly wondered what the names of the other reindeer were. But that would have to wait for another day.

Kris grinned as he accepted the bulging sack and Rudolf nudged it with his overly bright nose. "I thank you on behalf of the kiddies."

"Okay. You get ready to go, and I'll call Jen." I wasn't even going to try to explain all this to her. Let her find her own adventure. For the life of me, I couldn't stop smiling.

Kris was soon back outside the airlock, settled into his vehicle, strange as is was, and all the little reindeer were nestled into their harness, with Rudolf in front. Funny, I could see his little nose glowing very brightly even from the control-room window.

I called Jen.

"Hi Will, how're things?" came her cheerful voice over the vid-com. "Did the equation work out?" She was still folded into her command chair, but her hair had come down around her shoulders and the light scribe pen was now tucked behind her right ear.

"Haven't gotten to it yet. Something came up." I grinned back. "Listen, I'm sending you a visitor. He's really nice and quite harmless, but he's got one hell of a story. I really think you'd get a kick out of hearing it."

Jen's face looked out at me with a quizzical expression that clearly said: "am I going to regret this?" Her puzzlement cleared, and her mouth made an "o" shape when I added: "It's about Earth."

Then we got to the silly bit. I took a deep breath, and went on. "Okay, I need you to close your eyes and think hard about something you've always wanted, but never got. Now, say this: what is Christmas? Repeat it." Taking my eyes off Jen reluctantly parroting my words, I saw Kris give me a "thumbs up."

His "ship" swooped spaceward and disappeared in a flash of white light. What wouldn't I give to write a thesis about that? I longed wistfully after the magic hamper for a moment, and then smiled, ever practical. I probably wouldn't have been able to figure out how it worked on my own anyway. And I was still kind of dealing with its sudden sprouting of appendages.

When I looked back at the vid-screen, Jen's image was gazing out at me in exasperation. I heard a sudden bang and clatter from her end of the line, and saw her duck.

"Crap! Something just landed on the control-room roof!" she frantically threw back at me. Then her gaze was drawn off to the side by something. Her control room window or security camera screen, I hazarded. Jen's mouth dropped open. "Gack!! He's not wearing a space-suit!"

"Jen! Jen!" I had to call her several times to get her attention. She finally responded, wide-eyed. "It's okay, really," I told her. "Send him on to Prof. Jordan when he wants to leave. Merry Christmas, love. Call me later." With that, I smiled and ended the transmission. The "love" had just slipped out. Whether she noticed or not suddenly didn't seem to matter anymore.

Then I got quietly drunk—happy, but drunk.

When I staggered out into the dining area the next morning, I found a small pile of packages, a little tree with colored balls on it, and a hot jug of eggnog on the table. Sipping the eggnog from a familiar red mug, I opened the packages. There were a number of data chip texts with titles like "Wormholes for Dummies," "Transdimensional Travel," and an "Inter-dimensional Irregularities and Wormhole Travel: Theory and Practice" by one Kris Kringle; a real book like the one down in Section C, labeled "A Christmas Carol," and some music discs tagged "Christmas Carols," Grinning to myself, I began thinking about my next data-burst to Professor Jordan, and my decision to write my thesis on "Inter-dimensional Irregularities and Travels As Used by a Christmas Spirit." Prof. Jordan probably wouldn't believe me at first, but changing that would only be a matter of time. I raised my mug and toasted the Earth loitering in its usual position over the Moon horizon in the dining room window.

"Merry Christmas, old girl. It seems that there's hope for us yet."

🌲 🌲 🌲

INTRODUCTION

A CHRISTMAS IN AMBER

IN TIMES OF WAR, disease, disasters, Christmas can seem out of place, yet it can also bring comfort and a reminder of how life goes on. Here's a story of a disaster of a magnitude almost beyond comprehension—and of a human connection that made all the difference . . .

🌲 🌲 🌲

SCOTT WILLIAM CARTER has had over fifty short stories published in *Asimov's, Analog, Ellery Queen, Realms of Fantasy, Weird Tales,* and other popular magazines. His first novel, *the Last Great Getaway of the Water Balloon Boys,* was praised by *Publishers Weekly* as a "touching and impressive debut," and won the prestigious Oregon Book Award. Since then, he has published ten novels, the latest being *The Ghost Detective.* Another recent novel, *Wooden Bones,* chronicles the untold story of Pinocchio and was singled out for praise by the Junior Library Guild. Born in Minnesota and raised in Oregon, he graduated from the University of Oregon with an English degree, and makes that state his home, along with his wife, two young children, two indifferent cats, a faithful dog, and thousands of imaginary friends. Visit him online at www.scottwilliamcarter.com.

A CHRISTMAS IN AMBER

by Scott William Carter

THE SNOWFLAKES barely touched the glass before they melted, the moisture swept aside by his humming windshield wipers, but Alan was still mesmerized. Not a word had been said about snow on any of the Evacuation Updates. Rain had been the forecast. Lots and lots of rain. It had been many years since he had seen real snow—twenty or thirty at least, back when Janis was still alive. And that had been at a ski resort, not Los Angeles. The last time he could remember it snowing in Los Angeles was when he was still in his twenties, some fifty years back, and he could *never* remember it snowing on Christmas Day.

The snowflakes wafted through the golden halos surrounding the streetlights before they vanished on the glistening pavement. He was amazed at how deserted the streets were. *That* never would have happened if not for the evacuation. There'd be gobs of kids outside trying to make snowballs. Every house in the subdivision looked the same, with gabled windows and brick facades, posh and expensive in every respect, so identical Alan was surprised when the autopilot turned the van into a driveway. He had been to the house lots of times, but still he couldn't tell it apart from the others. Only when he saw Michelle's face pressed against the bay window, hands cupped on either side, did he know he was in the right place.

She wore the purple A's baseball cap he had bought her when they attended the game the previous year. The blinking holiday lights around the window made her face green one moment, red the next. When she saw him, she waved excitedly and disappeared through the part in the curtains. So they hadn't told her. If they had told her, he doubted she would be smiling.

A sharp sadness stabbed at his heart. For a moment, he wondered if this was a good idea.

"Open all doors," he said.

The van's computer beeped in acknowledgement. The two front doors, the sliding side door, and the back doors all popped open. In his haste to get to his son's house on time, he had forgotten his jacket, and the chill wind sliced right through his thin cotton sweater. If Janis was still alive, he knew what she would say. Stepping out onto the pavement, he could hear her voice.

You trying to get pneumonia, Alan? Is that what you want?

"It's not like it matters now, dear," he said, catching himself when he realized he was speaking out loud. He had been hearing her a lot lately, and he had been trying hard not to answer. If the kids heard him, they'd worry.

The driveway was lit by two lamps, one on either side of the garage. The air smelled like the old pines that lined the street. The front door to the house slid open and Rick emerged, bulging brown leather suitcases under each arm. His hands were covered with thick mittens. He was dressed in the type of heavy blue parka somebody on an expedition up Mount Everest might wear, as well as bright red ski pants, a brown wool cap with ear flaps, and yellow rain boots, all of which looked brand new. Under all that garb his face was tanned a deep bronze, which Alan knew was a requirement of the part Rick had been playing—a professional surfer on that soap opera. This amused Alan to no end; as far as he knew, Rick had never been surfing. He hated both swimming and the ocean.

An image of Rick surfing in his current outfit flashed through Alan's mind, and he chuckled.

"What's so funny?" Rick asked, breath fogging. His curly black hair ruffled in the breeze. Janis had always called him muffin head because of his dome-like hair.

"Nothing," Alan said.

"It's cold."

"Yes, it is."

He made a motion to take the bags, but Rick shook his head and walked past. Katherine came out next, also dressed in a heavy coat and pants, also carrying bulging suitcases. The difference was that her clothes matched: they were solid white, hugging her model-thin body, and stylishly designed. Her blond hair was pulled back into a braided pony tail, sticking out the side of her Russian-style fur hat. Michelle came out right behind her, dressed in the same coat as her mother, but otherwise in rumpled jeans faded in the knees, dirty tennis shoes, and of course, the baseball cap. He knew her hair was as blond as her mother's, but it was cut so short you couldn't see it underneath the hat. A black backpack was slung over her shoulders, and he saw the eyepiece of her microscope jutting out the top.

How her parents had ever ended up with a child so dissimilar to them Alan couldn't say, but he was glad for it. She was more like him than his son had ever been. She was even saying she wanted to grow up to be a paleontologist. The thought of that made his chest tighten, and he forced it away.

"I'll help you," he said to Katherine, taking one of her bags.

"Oh, thank you," Katherine said, breathing a sigh. Up close, he saw that she was perspiring, her cheeks pink. Alan wondered if she had lifted anything that heavy in years. It must have been hard being without servants, he thought sarcastically, and then felt guilty for thinking it. He and Katherine had never gotten along great—hell, he and Rick had never gotten along great—but he needed to be positive now.

"*Dear*," Rick said from behind the van, "think of his back."

"I'm fine," Alan said, but he did feel a twinge. Damn thing had been bothering him for years.

Rick made a noise that sounded like *hummmph*. It was a sound Janis used to make, a sort of disgusted resignation. Janis had been in the business, too, a television director. They had always been close, Janis and Rick. They had a bond that Alan could never understand.

Kind of like he and Michelle.

"Hey, sport," he said to her.

She beamed up at him, smiling with sealed lips. He knew she was embarrassed about the gap in her teeth. She had lost them a few months earlier, a couple days shy of her sixth birthday. He also remembered that her parents, obsessed with the preparations they needed to make after they received winning lottery numbers, had forgotten to put money under her pillow. Grandpa had given her a ten, telling her the tooth fairy had come to his house by mistake. She was a smart kid, too smart to believe this, but she had nodded just the same.

The snowflakes dotted the brim of her cap before turning into dark watermarks.

"You all packed, huh?" he said.

"Yeah," she said. "Hey Grandpa, guess what? We get to go on a spaceship!"

"I know," Alan said.

As if Alan might drop the bag at any moment, Rick quickly snatched the bag from him, scooting it into the van. Then he helped Katherine with her other bag. Alan helped his granddaughter take off her backpack, all while she chatted nonstop.

"Mommy says only a few people get to take a ride on the spaceship and we're lucky," she said. "She says we're going to be gone a while so I better take all the stuff I want to play with, so I made sure to bring my microscope."

"I see that," Alan said. "You bring any of your fossils?"

"No," she answered glumly. "Mommy says they're too heavy."

"Well, she's probably right."

"But I do have this!"

She reached into her pocket and pulled out an object that fit into the palm of her hand. When the lamps shined on the yellowish plastic, he knew what it was. He had bought it for her when they visited the California Academy of Sciences in June. The plastic looked more yellow than honey-colored; it was meant to look like amber, a facsimile of a new species of termite that had been found in Columbia, encased in amber, perfectly preserved after sixty million years. He had offered to buy her a t-shirt, but she had insisted on the little keepsake.

"Ah," he said, and for a moment he couldn't speak.

With the luggage secured, they boarded the van, everyone absorbed in grim silence. Except for Michelle. She talked about how she had never been in a spaceship and how it would be so much fun to tell everyone at school about it—when she started going to school again, whenever that was. Alan punched in the coordinates of the airport, and Rick, in the passenger seat, struggled to leaf through their evacuation paperwork with his mittens. As they pulled away from the house, Alan tried to think of something to say, something to lighten the mood.

"What's wrong, Mommy?" Michelle asked.

"Hmm?" Katherine said softly. "Oh, nothing."

"But you're crying. Did you hurt your hand on the seat belt?"

"Yes, dear. That's it."

"Okay. I'm sorry. I hurt my finger once on one of Grandpa's seat belts too. It hurts."

"I've got an idea," Alan said. "Why don't we sing some Christmas carols? I think that would be a lot fun." He tried to sound jovial, but he knew his voice wasn't ringing true. "Jingle Bells, anyone?"

"Maybe we should focus on watching the road," Rick said. "There might be some crazies out there, and the autopilot doesn't always know what to do."

"I'd like to sing," Michelle protested.

Katherine sniffled. "Yes, let's."

"All right, fine," Rick said. "Just don't let the van drive too fast, okay? We have plenty of time. We don't need to hurry. Hurrying will just get us in an accident."

Alan felt his irritation rise, then let it go. He was amazed he could feel irritated even today of all days. He cleared his throat and began to sing with his scratchy voice, and Katherine and Michelle quickly joined him. Rick focused his attention on his papers for a few blocks, as if there was something there that he could have possibly missed, but soon even he was singing. And that's how they passed the time as they made their way along the slick roads, the vents blasting warm air, the tires sloshing through water, soon out onto the ghostly highway, hardly a car on it. So many people, already gone, and those that weren't had headed somewhere in the middle of the country, though he knew it could hardly help them. The asteroid coming their way was bigger than the United States.

When they finished that song, they launched immediately into Frosty the Snowman, then Silent Night, then Rudolph the Red-Nosed Reindeer. He couldn't remember them singing like this *ever*, and here they were singing fools. When they were nearly to LAX, he wondered if they should be talking more seriously, but he didn't know what the point of it all would be. What needed to be said had been said well enough in the previous months. Now there was only the parting.

The only person he *hadn't* talked to about what was happening was Michelle, and he wasn't sure he could bring himself to do that.

It wasn't long before they had reached the airport, navigated through three different checkpoints manned by soldiers, past tanks and jeeps with guns trained on them, down a special road to a gated area full of hundreds of cars parked in neat rows separated by red cones. Papers were checked, retinas scanned. At the last gate, they had to get out, and their car was thoroughly searched, their bags run through an X-ray machine before being tagged and dropped into the back of a pickup truck. In the gated area bright fluorescent lights mounted high in the air gave the place the feel of a sporting event. Hundreds of people were making their way slowly to the far end, where out in the middle of the tarmac sat the white transport plane, it too surrounded by enough artillery and soldiers to subdue a small country. The transport ships, fat, white, and ungainly in appearance, had been nicknamed "spaceducks." Now, surrounded by all that army green, it seemed all the more like a duck—a duck sitting on a grassy bank.

For the past two months, all over the world, the spaceducks had been ferrying the lucky few up to *Little Earth*. And *that* ship, as big as a hundred football fields, with a self-contained ecosystem that could theoretically (but only theoretically) maintain itself indefinitely, would carry a little over ten thousand passengers and crew to *RNL-875*—a planet around a star much like the sun, some 157 light years away. The best scientists in the world had determined that planet, out of the hundred or so identified, to have the best chance of having an environment hospitable to humans.

Alan knew that scientists had pegged the actual odds at something like one in ten thousand, and that was mostly guesswork and wishful thinking, but nobody talked about that much. In any case, it would be hundreds of generations before the ship arrived.

They parked the van and fell in line with the others, heading toward the last X-ray and retina arch before the tarmac; a dozen yards beyond that were the stairs up to the ship. The snowflakes were gone now, the air thick with a wet mist that clung to his skin. Michelle took his hand. Her fingers were small but warm within his own.

"Why is everybody crying?" she asked.

Rick and Katherine trailed behind, and he heard Katherine start crying again, Rick shushing her. All around them, much the same thing was happening. The line was moving quickly. They would be to final gate in no time, Alan knew. He just had to keep moving. One foot in front of the other.

Alan swallowed. "It's hard saying goodbye."

"But they seem so sad," Michelle said.

"Yes."

"Are they sad because they don't get to go on the spaceship?"

He didn't answer. They were only ten or eleven people from the front, and a woman near the gate suddenly threw herself against the fence and was shouting someone's name, soldiers quickly pulling her back. Was it Frank? Or Hank? Watching this, Alan knew he could no longer lie to Michelle. The truth may have brought out some ugly things in people, but at least it was truth. When she was older, he knew she would most likely look back on this day with sadness, but he didn't want her to look back feeling betrayed.

"No," he said, looking down at her, attempting a smile. "They're sad because . . . because they're leaving. Leaving and not coming back."

He saw the skin underneath her eyes quiver. "What?"

"I'm sorry, honey. We didn't tell you until now because we didn't want you to be upset."

"But why?"

"Well, there's this asteroid that's heading toward Earth—"

"Jimmy across the street told me about that," she said quickly. "Daddy said they shot it down with a laser. They said it won't hurt anyone." Her grip on his hand tightened.

Alan nodded. "Your daddy told you that because he didn't want you to worry about me. You see, dear, I'm not going with you."

Michelle stopped, looking at him with an expression of shock and hurt he wished immediately he had never seen. There was only one group ahead of them, a family of five, and the arch beeped as each child passed underneath.

"I'm sorry," he said. "You see, only a few people can go on the ship that's going to take you to a new home. Old people like me don't get to go, but you and your parents are lucky ones."

He was waiting for her to cry, but the tears didn't come. Instead she looked furious, releasing his hand and clenching her fists.

"But I don't want to go without you!"

"I'm sorry, dear."

"They can't make me."

Katherine touched her daughter's shoulder. "Honey," she began, but Michelle pulled away.

"No! I'm staying if Grandpa stays!" She grabbed Alan's hands and looked up at him with a pleading expression. "Please don't make me go, Grandpa! Please, I want to stay with you."

They were to the last arch; the plastic was bright yellow, like a children's playground toy. The soldiers waited silently, but he could see the impatience in their eyes. He wondered why any of them were even bothering doing this, then he knew that they must have also been lucky ones. They just had one last job to do before they got to board a transport ship of their own.

He bent down in front of Michelle and took her gently by the shoulders. "You know I love you," he said.

She swallowed. The tears still hadn't come, but he knew they weren't far away now. "I love you too, Grandpa."

"But you've got to go with your Mommy and Daddy. They need you very, very much. And I want you to grow up and be happy, and you can't be happy here with me."

"Yes, I can—"

He put a finger on her lips, quieting her. "Please, don't argue. Just go."

She nodded, though she now looked dazed. He kissed her forehead, looking away so he wouldn't see her crying. If he saw her crying, he knew his strength would desert him. He'd end up just like that woman throwing herself against the fence. He hugged Katherine, then Rick, said a few words of goodbye that had already been said, and then the three of them were ushered through the archway. Alan got to watch them for only a moment before a soldier escorted him out of the line and to a roped-off area where dozens of people stood along the fence. There were no lights in this area, and their faces were shadowy and dark. Alan wondered if it had been deliberate. He didn't want to see these people's faces.

He took his place along side them, and by then Rick, Katherine, and Michelle were entering the ship. He saw Michelle looking around frantically. He waved, but she didn't see him.

"Michelle!" he shouted.

She turned, perhaps not seeing exactly where he was, but definitely looking in his direction. Then she was in the ship. He knew he shouldn't have done it, but he wasn't the only one. Lots of people shouted. He heard a sound, a heavy thumping, and for a moment he thought it might be the asteroid crashing through the atmosphere, since he had no idea what that would sound like, and then he realized it was the pounding of his own heart. A few minutes later the rest of the passengers were in the ship. A woman in an orange jumpsuit was at the hatch, closing it. This is it, Alan thought. They're really leaving.

And then, before the hatch was closed, he saw the woman in orange stumble to the side. A figure emerged, short, dressed in a white jacket, running down the steps. When he recognized Michelle, he cried out, reaching as if he could grab her, his hand finding only the cold and damp metal fence. All around him others were crying out as well. It was as if she had fallen into an ocean full of sharks and they all stood helplessly on the boat.

The two soldiers at the bottom, who had turned aside, now turned back, but Michelle was already at the bottom. She ran for Alan. "Grandpa! Grandpa!" she cried.

She was surprisingly fast for such a little girl, so fast she may have surprised the soldiers, because she was halfway to Alan before they broke into a run. They gained on her quickly, but she was nearly to Alan already, slowing when she got close to the fence.

"Grandpa?" she said.

He hesitated for a second, but then his resolve broke. "Here," he said. "Here, Michelle, here!"

She dashed to the fence with the soldiers, two thin men with assault weapons slung over their shoulders, close behind. Other soldiers were also approaching. Alan bent down to meet her, reaching to embrace her, forgetting that there was a fence in the way. His fingers closed around the gaps, and then her smaller fingers were over his own.

"Grandpa!"

The light was bad, but he saw the grim horror on her face, the desperation. All of these soldiers here to prevent the unexpected, he thought, and all it took was a six year-old girl to disrupt them. The first two soldiers grabbed her and began to pull, but she released Alan's fingers and grabbed onto the fence, screaming. Try as they might, they couldn't pull her away. They had her whole body in the air and still they couldn't pry her off the fence.

"Damn kid," one of them muttered.

"Don't hurt her!" Alan said.

"Grandpa! Grandpa!" Michelle cried.

The other soldiers had reached them now, a half dozen of them all looking the same in the dark. A tall, bald man with a silver mustache stepped between the two who were holding Michelle. "Put her down," he said.

The two obeyed, putting Michelle back on her feet. Her white-fingered grip on the fence didn't slack, and she pressed up against the metal.

"I won't go!" she said.

"Please, Michelle," Alan said.

"No!"

"If you don't go," the man with the silver mustache said, "you'll be left behind."

"I want to stay with Grandpa!"

"Don't you want to be with your parents?"

"I want to stay with Gandpa!"

"Oh, for heaven's sake," the man with the silver mustache said. "We don't have time—"

"Wait," Alan said. "Let me come over there. I'll walk her up."

The man with the silver mustache looked at him skeptically. All those guns, Alan thought.

"Please," he begged.

The man with the silver mustache looked at him a moment more, then nodded back toward the gate. As Alan ran, some of the soldiers on the other side jogged along side him. There was a moment of fuss at the arch, a few words spoken on radios, and then he was ushered through the beeping mechanism, the soldiers on the other side guiding him back to Michelle. He was still a few steps away from her when she turned and threw herself into his arms.

"I don't want to go!"

He stroked her hair, feeling the warmth of her face through his damp sweater. He knew there was nothing now he could say to comfort her. The truth was what it was. With his own private army accompanying him, he turned and headed for the plane. Two people in orange jumpsuits, a man and a woman, watched him from the top of the steps. Michelle's body shook with each breath. The yelling and shouting from the spectators had stopped; he knew they were all watching. When he started up the stairs, feet clanging on the metal, the soldiers stopped and gathered at the bottom.

With each step, his legs seemed heavier. He wasn't sure he was going to make it, but then there he was, at the top, placing Michelle on her feet between the two people in orange.

"There now," he said, his throat constricting.

She looked up at him with wet eyes, cheeks glistening. He steadied her with a hand on her shoulder.

"Grandpa," she said.

"It's for the best, honey. Please do it for me."

"But—"

"I know."

"I want—"

"Yes, but you still have to go."

Her chin dropped, and she looked down for a moment before turning toward the ship. Then she turned back suddenly, her hand reaching into her jacket pocket and emerging with the amber-like keepsake. She thrust it at him.

"I want you to have this," she said.

"But it's yours."

"But I want *you* to have it."

He nodded and took it from her, kissing the back of her hand when he did so. She turned, not a trace of emotion on her face, and the two people in orange closed in behind her. He placed the keepsake in his pocket, then without waiting, turned and started back down the steps. He had to go quickly. He would not even wait for the ship to take off. He had to get out of there.

When the hatch clanged shut, he jumped. The soldiers watched him as if he was the walking dead, and he knew that to them perhaps he was. When he reached the bottom, a few patted him on the shoulder. The man with the silver mustache personally saw him back to the viewing area, shaking his hand and saying something inaudible before turning and leaving. Some people in the crowd asked him questions, but he didn't listen. He moved close to the fence, pressing his face up against the cool metal, and watched the plane.

The regular engines started turning, rumbling; the plane lurched forward. Even where he stood, he felt the frigid air pushing against him. He knew when it was up higher, the rocket engines would take over for the last leg of the journey. Science, his old friend, would see his family into space.

"Some Christmas," he heard Janis say behind him.

The plane taxied along the runway, gathering speed. As he watched the ungainly white bird sail up into the darkness, he thought about Christmases past and Christmases future. He thought about a huge hunk of rock hurtling toward the Earth. He thought about little girls with microscopes and insects encased in amber. He thought about the meaning of the word hope.

"The best ever," he said.

INTRODUCTION
❧⊛❧
SPACE ALIENS SAVED
MY MARRIAGE

AS I WROTE IN *A Cosmic Christmas*, S.N. Dyer has a brilliantly twisted sense of humor. Last time, she gave us two tales of vampires, a witch, and a werewolf for Christmas. This time, she wonders what things would be like if *The Weekly World News* (no longer with us, alas) and similar supermarket tabloids were reporting nothing but the real, incontrovertible truth. And at Christmas time, too . . .

🌲 🌲 🌲

Beginning in the 1970s and continuing into the 1990s, S. N. Dyer wrote an amazing number of hysterically funny sf and fantasy stories under more than one name. The author now pursues a medical career, and fiction's loss is medicine's gain, but I'm sure I'm not the only one who hopes Dyer will someday return to writing her strikingly individual bizarre tales.

SPACE ALIENS SAVED MY MARRIAGE

❦

by S.N. Dyer

WHEN I GOT HOME FROM WORK, Tim was still in the kitchen, drinking coffee and reading the sports page. Construction's slow in December. The kitten began rubbing up against my leg and purring the minute I came in.

"What do you think, honey?" I asked, petting the kitten. "Shouldn't we give Mittens two names? I mean, she does have two heads, and all."

Tim said, "Whatever you want," but Stacy stopped splashing her spoon in her Count Chockula and pointed at each head. "Muffin. Tiffany."

"Good names," I told her, pouring Muffin and Tiffany a saucer of milk. As usual, the two heads began squabbling over their treat.

"Any newspapers, Bobby June?" asked Tim.

When the new tabloids come out, I get to take home the old ones, along with the day-old bread and mushy bananas. I'd already read them all, of course. The Quik-Stop-Shop gets real slow after around 2 A.M. "Look here: HOUSE WIFE SEES ELVIS IN LAUNDROMAT. It happened in our town!"

"Forget it," said Tim. "People are always seeing Elvis. Didn't that spaceship, Voyager or whatever it was, see his face on Mars?" This was the longest conversation we'd had since we were visiting my Aunt Martha in Austin and saw the ghost of Uncle Edgar in the closet. So I figured maybe this is the time to bring it up.

"Tim honey, it's Christmas Eve tomorrow. Don't you have any relatives you'd like to invite for dinner, to meet me and Stacy and all?"

"No," he said, and went off to read the papers somewhere else.

I have trouble sleeping when I work third-shift, so I took Stacy shopping for shoes. It's incredible how quick she seems to outgrow them—she's only four, and already in a grown-up size 6. She has her dad's feet, I guess, but luckily she has my nose.

Anyway, the mall was pretty crowded, what with it being the day before the day before Christmas. We did a little last-minute shopping for presents, and we were buying this cute little dog and cat salt and pepper set for Jesse, my friend-at-work, when a woman shrieked.

"Oh, my god!" she yelled, pointing up at a black velvet painting of Elvis. Tears seemed to be pouring from his eyes.

"Why's he crying, Mommy?" asked Stacy.

The clerk got up on a ladder and pulled down the painting, to check for leaks or something in the wall, but nothing else was wet.

The woman who'd seen it first reached over and touched the tears, then raised her finger to her mouth. "It's salty," she said. "Those are real tears!"

I looked at the painting, and it seemed that the wet eyes were staring deep into my own. And suddenly this thought was there, in my mind. *You'd better go to County Mercy General. There's been an emergency.*

When we got to the hospital, it seemed they'd been looking for me. Grannie had had this bad stomach ache, and they'd been worried she'd bled into a big old fibroid tumor she'd had for a long time, only they hadn't wanted to operate before, what with her being so old and all, but now they'd had to operate after all, and her doctor wanted to talk with me, right outside the operating room.

He was still wearing green clothes and a paper hat and booties, just like on TV. He didn't mince words, just started right out. "Your grandmother's had a baby."

"But that's impossible," I said. "Gran's seventy-eight!"

He got that narrow-eyed little look that doctors get when they think you don't believe them, and said, "Of course it's possible—it happened. It seems your grandmother had been pregnant with twins over fifty years ago, but only one of them actually got born."

Then he talked about ovulation, and hibernation, and a lot of other complicated stuff I didn't get, cause I mean, I dropped out in eleventh grade to work and all. But the long and the short of it seemed to be that this baby had been in her womb for fifty-five years, and in fact was my late daddy's twin. They'd compared footprints, and it was true.

"But that's not the end of it," the doctor continued. "I've seen a lot of weird stuff—I've delivered babies wearing ancient Egyptian amulets, or tattooed with holy symbols, and once I saw a woman give birth to a Cabbage Patch Doll. But never in all my years of practicing has one of my newborns ever spoken in the delivery room before!"

"What'd he say?"

"When I slapped his little behind, he didn't even cry, he just looked me in the eye and said 'The Twin returns. Love him tender and don't be cruel.' He wouldn't say anything more, and now he's acting just like a regular baby." The doctor took off his paper hat and scratched his head. "*The Twin.* Must be himself he means, right?"

"No. No, it isn't." I didn't know yet what he meant, back then, but I knew that something big was going on, or about to happen.

What with staying with Gran all afternoon, and then making dinner for Stacy and Tim, I only had a few hours' sleep before going to work. I was a couple minutes late, but Ralph always covers for me—he's a real good guy. He was this World War II veteran who they found after drifting alone in a life raft in the Bermuda Triangle for forty years, but he didn't let that ruin his attitude.

"Congratulate me, I'm gonna get hitched," Ralph told me while he was putting on his muffler and overcoat.

"Who to?" I didn't even know he was dating. As far as I knew, his only real friend was this guy Eddy he'd known in basic training, who'd looked him up after seeing his picture in the paper.

"I' m marrying Eddy," Ralph said, sort of blushing. "No really, it's not like that. See, he was struck by lightning last year, and it turned him into a woman!"

"Wow!" I remembered reading about it, but never realized who it had been. "Well, good luck and everything." We'd have to put on a shower for them.

Jesse had been in back, and now he came in to restock the chips. "Heard about Ralph and Eddy?" he asked. He's got this real velvety deep voice, but I never could figure out his accent.

"I hope they'll be happy," I said, started thinking about me and Tim, and choked a little. Jesse came over to hug me—we're only friends, really—and I told him how me and Tim just didn't seem to communicate anymore. Then I wiped away my tears, and looked at Jesse. "Hey! You've been losing weight."

"It's that *eat all you want and lose a pound a day diet.* Works!" A customer came in to pay for some gas, so Jesse went back to restock the Oreos and Pecan Sandies.

The customer—he was paying with a credit card—said, "Your stock clerk looks a lot like Elvis, don't you think?"

"No, not really . . ." I mean, I just thought of him as my friend Jesse, and never really thought much about his face, you know?

"Yeah," continued the customer, pointing to some cigarettes, so I had to ring him up all over again. "Yeah, they've been seeing Elvis all over—the post office in Decatur, a McDonald's in Fresno, the Baseball Hall of Fame . . . Now I've seen him here in a convenience store. Think I'll make the papers?"

We laughed a little about that. Another customer, buying milk and bread, put her stuff down on the counter. "Don't laugh," she said. "Yesterday, totally unexpected, my cat dragged in an old monophonic record album, looking brand new. It was *Blue Hawaii.*"

We were pretty impressed by how strange that was, including Jesse, who'd come over to listen. "I tell you," the lady continued, "something's brewing. It feels kind of like a storm, about to break." She noticed Jesse. "Hey, anyone ever said you look like Elvis?"

"No ma'am. Maybe Roy Orbison," he answered.

She looked him over again. "Yeah, guess you're right. Well, Merry Christmas everyone."

Things stayed quiet for a while and, around midnight, Brian, the night supervisor came by to check on us. I didn't like Brian much, he was always acting like he thought you were stealing money from the store, but I was real pleasant, and didn't suspect much when he sent Jesse in back to inventory all the cookies and sodas, to see what we'd need extra to last over the holidays.

"Come here!" Brian called, from over the back aisle, where the candy and toys are.

"Uh oh," I thought. Some kids must've snuck in while I wasn't paying attention, and taken some toys and left the plastic containers behind. They do that if you don't watch careful.

But everything looked okay on the novelty rack. "What's wrong?" I asked.

"Nothing's wrong," said Brian. "I just wanted to wish you a Merry Christmas," and he started to kiss me.

"Hey!" I said, trying to make like it was a joke. I mean, I needed the job, you know? "Hey, there's no mistletoe here." I pushed him away—and then he opened his mouth and showed me these fangs like the plastic Dracula teeth we sell at Halloween, only his looked real.

"Brian, what the . . ."

And suddenly he was biting me on the throat, and I couldn't call for help . . .

I seemed to be sliding down this long dark tunnel, and there was a light at the end, and my parents, and my grandparents (except for Gran of course), and everyone I knew who ever died including my ninth grade boyfriend who fell in the drainage ditch, and all the dogs and cats I ever owned, were there to welcome me. Only when I got to the end of the tunnel, there was this view like in an old movie house with just one big screen, and it was showing Earth, and this big old rocky asteroid heading right for it. At first I thought it was something out of a Star Trek movie, but then I realized it was for real. And then the space scene was gone, and Elvis was there—Elvis himself—smiling at me. Just smiling. And he raised up one hand and said to me, "Go back and warn them."

Next thing I knew, I was on the floor back in the Quik-Stop-Shop, and Jesse was putting cold rags on my forehead.

"I thought you'd died," he said.

"I did!" I tried to sit up, making it the second time, and noticed the floor was all wet with milk, and this slimy yellow and red gunk I didn't recognize, but smelled awful. "What happened—is that stuff Brian?"

Jesse nodded. "I threw milk on him—it dissolves vampires. Too wholesome or something, I dunno, but it works every time. Mind, you have to use whole milk. Skim or two percent just won't work."

"Jesse, you got to listen to this dream I just had." I told him about the tunnel, and the asteroid, and Elvis. Jesse just rocked back and forth on his heels. Finally he said, "It ain't no dream, Bobby June. It's for real, and we must act quick if we're to save the planet."

I was still kind of dazed, what with dying and coming back and all, so I didn't hardly protest when he closed up the store, and we started driving. I didn't even really care where we were going. I just sat wrapped in a blanket—his pickup didn't have heat—and looked out the window at the big old full moon.

"You see, this is the culmination of my stay upon the Earth," Jesse said.

"Huh?"

"I'm the Twin who returned," he said. "The one your little baby uncle was talking about."

"Huh?" The night was weird enough without old Jesse getting bizarre on me. I looked at him like for the first time. He did look like Elvis. "Who are you?"

"Like I said, I'm the Twin. Elvis's twin brother, Jesse, who supposedly died at birth, but who was really taken off planet and raised in a UFO."

"You mean the UFO people who steal missing children and eat them?"

"Nope—those guys're from Andromeda."

"Then, the UFO people who take your pets or lawn ornaments for company, and return them a year later?"

"Nope—Betelgeuse."

"Then how about the ones who hover outside your window and won't let you eat junk food?"

"Those busybodies? I should hope not. No, my UFO was from the Southern Cross, and they're real benevolent folk there."

I suddenly began to snuffle. "Poor Jesse. Taken away from your family and raised with weird aliens."

He took his hand off the wheel long enough to pat me on the shoulder. "It wasn't that bad. The scenery was nice, and we got *Lucy* reruns on the radio telescope. Besides, I'm half-space alien myself, so I had kinfolk."

His face got real sad. "Poor brother Elvis, he never even knew the truth about his heritage. That's why he ate too much, and drank, and did drugs. Earth food didn't have all the essential vitamins and minerals he needed."

"Oh!" Suddenly it made sense, Jesse's always sucking on a Tic Tac. "Your breath mints are from space too!"

"Right. They're to compensate for dietary deficiencies, and to protect me from the pollution."

Lots more was making sense. Like those Elvis sightings, all over the country. They'd been Jesse, just wandering about waiting for whatever it was he'd been sent to our planet to stop to happen so he could stop it. As he drove, he told me a little about how he traveled around, always one step ahead of reporters, and the KGB, and bad aliens who didn't want him to save the Earth.

Then we got to where we were going, which was the observatory up near the university. I hadn't been there since a field trip in second grade. Jesse got us inside—he could be real impressive—but the egghead types there were snooty, and wouldn't believe us.

"Asteroid coming in to destroy us? Give me a break," said the professor in charge, but then Jesse took him aside and whispered in his ear for a while, and when they came back, the man was pale. "Turn the scope around," he ordered, and began searching the sky.

"What'd you say?" I asked Jesse.

He shrugged. "I just told him things only he knew about himself—like, he really doesn't like sushi, and he always wanted to be a fireman, and he's got this secret crush on Vanna White."

It took a while, but then the professor came back, even paler, said, "You were right!" and began making lots of important phone calls.

Pretty soon—well, really it was hours later, but I slept through the flight to Washington and was still half-asleep when we met the President and the Joint Chiefs of Staff—pretty soon we were at the United Nations. They'd let me call Tim from the White House, and the President's wife, who was pretty nice, told them to send a plane to pick up Tim and Stacy so they could be with me.

So we were all up there at the UN. First the professor talked, and a bunch of other professors from all sorts of countries agreed with him. Then everyone got in a panic, because this asteroid was going to hit the Earth in a month or so, and smash us to bits, and we didn't have any missiles big enough to stop it.

I was kind of mad about that, thinking about Stacy not even getting old enough for kindergarten, and I said to the President, "Here I voted for you, and you spend all this money on bombs and stuff, and you can't even stop one lousy asteroid." He looked sort of upset, which got me feeling bad, so I apologized.

"It's okay," he told me. "We're all a bit on edge."

Then Jesse got up, and talked about how he had a plan and would need lots of cooperation. Our professor did some calculations and said it'd work. But lots of them still didn't believe Jesse.

"I guess I'll just have to convince you, then," he said, and asked someone to fetch him a guitar, and right there in the UN assembly hall, he started to sing. And maybe his voice wasn't much better than his brother's, who you have to admit was the greatest singer ever lived, but Jesse'd been trained by aliens, and he knew how to use that extra nine-tenths of the brain that none of the rest of us uses, so it was the best singing anyone ever thought they'd ever hear. Pretty soon everyone didn't know if they wanted to cry or applaud, and when they'd all calmed down and the medics had taken away the delegates who'd passed out or had heart attacks, everyone voted to go with Jesse's plan.

So there it was, Christmas Eve day, and Jesse had a radio hookup to everywhere on Earth. They asked if he wanted translators, but he said no—and sure enough, when he started talking, slow and kind of loud, everyone understood him, no matter what language they usually talked.

"I want everyone in the Western Hemisphere and Europe and Africa to just stand real still," he said into the radio. I was kind of awed, thinking how everyone all over the world was hearing my friend Jesse's words. And trusting and believing him too, because he sounded like his brother, and everyone on Earth knows about Elvis. "And I want everyone in the East, in China and Japan and . . ." Well, I'll just skip the list of countries, 'cause I don't exactly know where most of them were, or how to spell them either.

". . . I want every one of you to go get a kitchen chair exactly eighteen inches tall—that's forty-six centimeters—"

It was real impressive how smart Jesse was.

"You can put some books or plywood on the seat if it isn't exactly eighteen inches. Now I want you to get up on those chairs, every one of you. Come on now." He waited a bit, so folks who were old or young or maybe had arthritis could get onto their chairs. "Now when I say 'Go'—hold on, not yet—when I say 'Go', I want everyone to jump. Okay, all ready?"

He looked over at me, and I smiled and crossed my fingers.

He leaned close to his microphone. "Okay. Ready, set—jump!"

And all over China and Japan and all those other countries, people jumped off their kitchen chairs.

The ground shook a little, and Stacy began to cry. I comforted her, and Tim put his arm around my shoulder.

The professor was talking on the phone to some other scientists, who were somewhere or other doing stuff, and he put his hand over the receiver and shouted. "It worked! It worked! When the Asians all jumped, they pushed the Earth slightly out of its orbit, so now that asteroid is going to miss us. We're saved!"

Everyone began to cheer and hug each other. Then we got quiet, because we'd all noticed a day-glow orange UFO hovering outside the windows.

Jesse came over and took my hands. "You've been a right good friend, Bobby June, and I'm gonna miss you."

Stacy said, "You goin' somewhere, Uncle Jesse?"

He put a hand on her head—and her hair's been blond and naturally curly ever since—and said, "My job, and my brother's, is over, Stacy. I'm going home. But first . . ."

He took Tim aside a bit. "Now Tim," he said, "I know you love your wife, but you have to talk with her."

"But if I do, if she learns the truth about me," Tim answered, "she wouldn't love me no more."

"Now, you know that isn't true. Don't be afraid," Jesse told him.

Tim said to me, "Bobby June, I wouldn't blame you if you leave me when I tell you this. The reason we never visit my relatives, and the reason I have so much trouble finding shoes that fit—sweetheart, I'm Bigfoot.

"Well, I'm not really Bigfoot," he continued. "I'm just his little brother. But you get the idea."

I said, "Honey, I wouldn't care if you were the Loch Ness Monster, you're still my man," and I hugged Tim, and Stacy jumped up and down cause she could tell things were going to be okay from now on.

Jesse went to the window, stepping onto a gangplank from the UFO. "Wouldn't you and your family like to spend the holiday with your relatives, Tim?"

"Sure would," said Tim. "But we couldn't get no flight to Oregon on Christmas Eve, and anyway, we don't have no presents either."

"Forget airplanes," grinned Jesse. "We can drop you off on our way. And I'm sure we can find something around the saucer for you to give your folks." He waved us to the gangplank.

"Oh boy!" cried Stacy. "This is going to be the best Christmas ever! And I also predict major conflict in the Mideast, a startling new career development for Linda Evans, and all the dogs in Denver will lose their hair but learn to speak . . ."

♣ ♣ ♣

INTRODUCTION
✎✎✎
ZWARTE PIET'S TALE

TO MANGLE VOLTAIRE (though I'm sure if he weren't dead, he'd defend to the death my right to mangle it), if Santa Claus didn't exist, it would be necessary to invent him. And after Mars was colonized, that was just what happened, though the results were sometimes unexpected . . .

♣ ♣ ♣

ALLEN M. STEELE, JR.'S first published story was "Live from the Mars Hotel" in 1988. Since then he has written many more short stories, some of which have been collected in five volumes, nineteen novels, and essays, with his work appearing in England, France, Germany, Spain, Italy, Brazil, Russia, the Czech Republic, Poland, and Japan. His novella, "The Death Of Captain Future," received the 1996 Hugo Award for Best Novella, won a 1996 Science Fiction Weekly Reader Appreciation Award, and received the 1998 Seiun Award for Best Foreign Short Story from Japan's National Science Fiction Convention. It was also nominated for a 1997 Nebula Award by the Science Fiction and Fantasy Writers of America. Altogether, he has won three Hugo Awards, along with the *Locus* award, the *Analog* AnLab Award (the story you're about to read won one, in addition to being a Hugo nominee), the *Asimov's* Reader's Award, and other honors, most recently the Robert A. Heinlein Award for fiction promoting the exploration of space. Born in Nashville, Tennessee, he earned a B.A. from New England College and an M.A. from the University of Missouri. He lives in Massachusetts with his wife Linda and their dogs. His web site is www.allensteele.com

ZWARTE PIET'S TALE

❧❀❧

by Allen Steele

PEOPLE OFTEN SPEAK OF CHRISTMAS as being a season of miracles. Indeed, it sometimes seems that's all you hear about during the holiday season; download the daily newsfeed, and you're sure to find at least one doe-eyed story about a lost child reunited with his parents, a stray pet finding his way home, a maglev train that barely avoids colliding with another, a house burning down without anyone being killed. These things can happen at any time, and often do, but when they occur at Christmas, a special significance is attached to them, as if an arbitrary date on the Gregorian calendar somehow has a magical portent.

That sort of thing may go smoothly on Earth, but anyone on Mars who believes in miracles is the sort of person you don't want to be with during a habitat blowout or a dust storm alert. Belief in miracles implies belief in divine intervention, or luck at the very least; that kind of attitude has killed more people out here than anything else. Luck won't help you when a cell of your dome undergoes explosive decompression, but having paid attention during basic training will. I've known devoutly religious people who've died because they panicked when a wall of sand came barreling across the plains, while atheists who kept their heads and sprinted to the nearest shelter have

165

survived. Four people returning to Wellstown from a water survey were killed on Earth's Christmas Day back in m.y. 46, when the driver of their rover rolled the vehicle down a twenty-meter embankment; there was no yuletide miracle for them.

I'm sorry if this may seem cynical, but that's the way it is. Almost a million aresians now live on Mars, and we didn't face down this cold red world by believing in Santa Claus. Luck is something you make for yourself; miracles occur when you get extra-lucky. I've been here for over twenty years now, and I've never seen it work differently, whether it be on Christmas, Yom Kippur, or First Landing Day.

Yet still . . . there's always an exception.

Sure, we celebrate Christmas on Mars. We just don't do it the same way as on Earth.

The first thing you have to remember is that we count the days a bit differently. Having 39.6 more minutes each day, and 669 days—or sols, as we call 'em—in a sidereal period, meant that aresians threw out both Greenwich Mean Time and the Gregorian calendar in a.d. 2032, long before the Pax Astra took control of the near-space colonies, way before Mars declared its independence. The Zubrin calendar has twelve months, ranging from 48 to 66 sols in length, each named after a Zodiac constellation; it retroactively began on January 1, 1961, which became Gemini 1, m.y. 1 by local reckoning. The conversion factors from Gregorian to Zubrin calendars are fairly complex, so don't ask for an explanation here, except to say that one of the first things newcomers from Earth have to realize is that April Fool pranks are even less funny at Arsia Station than they were back in Indiana.

Indeed, aresians pretty much did away with Halloween, Thanksgiving, Guy Fawkes Day, Bastille Day, and virtually every other Earth holiday. Our New Year's is out of whack with the rest of the solar system, and instead of Columbus Day we have First Landing; when Mars succeeded from the Pax Astra in 2066, or m.y. 57, we began commemorating the event with our own Independence Day. A few religious holidays continue to be observed at the same time as they are on Earth. West Bank, the small Jewish settlement on the western slope of the Tharsis bulge, celebrates Hanukkah in accordance with the traditional Hebrew calendar; I was once there for the third night of Hanukkah, and watched as the family with whom I was staying lit its menorah when the colony's DNAI calculated the sun had set in Jerusalem.

Christmas has been imported as well, yet because the aresian year was nearly twice as long as Earth's, it comes around half as often. The first colonists tried having their Christmas promptly on December 25th, but it felt odd to be celebrating Christmas twice a year, sometimes in the middle of the Martian summer. When the colonies formally adopted the Zubrin calendar in m.y. 38, it was decided that the aresian Christmas would fall only once two Earth years; this meant that we had to devise our own way of observing the holiday. So instead of designating one single sol in Taurus as being Christmas Day, aresians picked the second week of the month as Christmas Week, beginning on Ta.6 and continuing through Ta.13; it was roughly adapted from the Dutch tradition of observing December 6 as the Feast of St. Nicholas. During that week, everyone would take a break from all but the most essential labor, and this would give families and clans a chance to get together and exchange gifts. Devout Christians who wished to continue unofficially observing December 25 as Jesus' birthday were welcome to do so—New Chattanooga and Wellstown took two sols off each aresian year for a terran-style Christmas—but it wasn't marked on the Zubrin calendar.

Most of the original Seven Colonies, with the exception of West Bank, accepted Christmas Week as a respite from the hard work of settling the Martian frontier. As more immigrants from Earth and the Moon began establishing new colonies along the eastern equator, they adopted Christmas Week as well. Yet, as time went on, the aresian Christmas began to lose much of its original meaning.

Indeed, as some noted, the week never had that much meaning to begin with. Since it wasn't held to celebrate of the birth of Christ, it had little religious significance. Families and clans tended to live in the same colonies, often sharing the same quarters, so there wasn't much point in setting aside an entire week for them to get together. These colonists lived on the verge of poverty; Pax trade tariffs and the enormous cost of importing items from Earth made Christmas presents beyond the reach of most people, and giving someone a new helmet liner is hardly the stuff of romance. So what usually happened during Christmas Week was that people congregated in taprooms to get ripped on homebrew and weed; when the taprooms closed, louts roamed the corridors looking for trouble. By mid-century, Christmas Week had degenerated into debauchery, random violence, and the occasional fatal accident. It wasn't a lot of fun.

Worse yet was the fact that the first generation of aresians to be born on Mars was growing up with only second-hand knowledge of what Christmas was supposed to be like. They'd read old microfiche stories about Rudolph and Santa Claus, the Grinch and Scrooge, or watch disks of ancient films like *It's A Wonderful Life* and *Frosty the Snowman*, and then go to their parents asking why Santa didn't drop down their chimney to leave wrapped and ribboned gifts beneath a tree strung with lights and tiny ornaments. Perhaps you can successfully explain to a four-year-old why there aren't any reindeer and Douglas firs on Mars, or even point out that your two-room apartment doesn't have a hearth, let alone a chimney . . . but try telling a small child that there's no such person as Santa.

Mars was in desperate need of a St. Nicholas, a Father Christmas, a Santa Claus. In m.y. 52, he arrived in the form of Dr. Johann Spanjaard.

Despite the fact that I'm one of the few people on Mars who knew him well, there's very little I can tell you about Doc Spanjaard. That's not much a surprise, though; folks came here for many different reasons, and not always the best ones. Frontiers tend to attract people who didn't quite fit in the places they came from, and on Mars it's impolite to ask someone about their past if they don't voluntarily offer that information themselves. Some aresians will blabber all day about their home towns or their old job, but others I've known for twenty years and still don't know where they were born, or even their real names.

Johann Spanjaard fell somewhere between these extremes. He was born in Holland, but I don't know when: around a.d. 2030 is my best guess, since he appeared to be in his early forties when he arrived at

Arsia Station. He was trained as a paramedic, and briefly worked on Clarke County; and later at Descartes Station. He was a Moon War vet; he told me that he witnessed the Battle of Mare Tranquillitatis, but if he had any combat medals he never showed them to me. He returned to Earth, stayed there a little while, left again to take a short job as a beltship doctor, then finally immigrated to Mars. There were at least two women in his past—Anja, his first wife, and Sarah, his second—but he seldom spoke of them, although he sent them occasional letters.

No children. In hindsight, that may be the most significant fact of all: even after marrying and leaving two wives, Doc didn't have any kids. Save that thought.

Doc Spanjaard immigrated to Mars in m.y. 52, five aresian years before the colonies broke away from Pax. By then Arsia Station had become the largest colony; nearly a hundred thousand people lived in reasonable comfort within the buckydomes and underground malls that had grown up around the base camp of the original American expedition, just south of the Noctis Labyrinthis where, on a nice clear day, you could just make out the massive volcanic cone of Arsia Mons looming over the western horizon. The colony had finally expanded its overcrowded infirmary into a full-fledged hospital, and Doc was one of the people hired to staff its new emergency ward.

I came to know Doc because of my job as an airship pilot. One of Arsia General's missions was providing medical airlifts to our six neighbor colonies in the western hemisphere; although they had infirmaries of their own, none possessed Arsia General's staff or equipment. The hospital had contracted my employer, AeroMars, to fly doctors out to these remote settlements and, on occasion, bring back patients for treatment. Within two sols of Doc's arrival at Arsia General, I flew him over the Valles Marineris to Wellstown so he could treat a burn victim from an explosion at the fuel depot. We ended up hauling the poor guy back to Arsia Station that same day; the sortie lasted twenty-seven hours, coming and going, and when it was over we were too wired to go to bed, so we wandered over to the Mars Hotel and had a few beers.

That trip established a regular pattern for us: fly out, do what had to be done, fly back, hand the case over to the ER staff, then head to the nearest taproom to decompress. However, I seldom saw Doc Spanjaard get loaded; three beers was his limit, and he never touched hard liquor. Which was fine with me; I'm a featherweight drinker myself, and two beers was the most I'd allow myself because I never knew when I'd get beeped to drag *Miss Thuvia* back into the sky again. But the three of us logged a lot of klicks together; once I had the princess tied down in her hangar and Doc had washed someone else's blood off his hands, we'd park our rumps in a quiet bar and tap mugs for a job well done.

We were a mutt-'n-jeff team if there ever was one. Doc was tall and preposterously skinny, with solemn blue eyes and fair skin that helmet burn had freckled around his trim white beard; imagine an underfed St. Nicholas and you've got it down. I was the short, dumpy black sidekick from Tycho City who had a thing for Burroughs classics and loved old Eddie Murphy movies even though I had never spent more than two weeks on Earth (what can I say? he made me laugh). But Doc had a wry sense of humor that most people didn't see, and I was the only airlift pilot who wouldn't panic when he had to perform a emergency tracheotomy at twelve hundred meters with a utility knife and a pen.

We saw a lot of action over the course of the next nine months; by my count, we saved at least thirty lives and lost only four. Not bad for two guys whose biggest complaint was losing a lot of sleep. *The Martian Chronicle* caught wind of our act and wanted to do a story on us. We talked it over during a ride back from Sagan, then radioed back to Arsia General and arranged for the reporter to meet us at the Mars Hotel after we got home. The reporter was there, along with his photographer and one of Doc's former patients, a sweet young thing from West Bank whose heart was still beating again due to Doc's ministrations and my flying skills, but gee gosh, we forgot where we were supposed to meet them and went to Lucky Pierre's instead. Two more missed interviews, followed by profuse apologies and sworn promises that we'd at the right place next time, went by before the *Chronicle* finally got the message. On Mars, the phrase "mind your own business" is taken seriously, even by the press.

But it wasn't always funny stuff. Our job took us places you'd never want to see, the settlements established along the equatorial zone surrounding the Valles Marineris. Over forty Earth years had elapsed since First Landing, and humankind had made substantial footholds on this big red planet, yet beyond the safe, warm confines of Arsia Station life could be pretty grim. New Chattanooga was infested with sandbugs, the seemingly indestructible mites which lived in the permafrost and homed in on any aquifer large enough for them to lay eggs; the colony's water tanks were literally swimming with them, and despite the best filtration efforts they were in every cup of coffee you drank and every sponge-bath you took. DaVinci was populated by neocommunists who, despising bourgeois culture and counterrevolutionary influences, wanted little to do with the rest of the colonies, and therefore turned down most aid offered by Arsia Station; their subsurface warrens were cold and dimly-lit, their denizens hard-eyed and ready to quote Mao Tse Tung as soon as you entered the airlock. Viking, the northernmost settlement, was located on the Chryse Planitia near the Viking I landing site: two hundred people huddled together in buckydomes while eking out the most precarious of existences, and every time we visited them, the population had grown a little smaller. And people spoke only in hushed tones about Ascension, the settlement near Sagan just south of the Valles Marineris that had been founded by religious zealots; living in self-enforced isolation, running short of food and water, finally cut off from the neighboring colonies by the planetwide dust storm of m.y. 47, its inhabitants began murdering one another, then cannibalizing the corpses.

Doc and I saw a side of the Martian frontier that most people on Earth didn't even know existed: hypothermia, malnutrition, disease, injuries caused by carelessness or malfunctioning equipment, psychosis, and not a few deaths. We did what we could, then we flew home and tried to drown our sorrows in homemade brew. There's many wonderful things about Mars, but it's not Earth or even the Moon; this is a place with damned little mercy, and those it doesn't kill outright, it conspires to drive insane.

Perhaps we went a little stir-crazy ourselves, for one night in the Mars Hotel we got to talking about what we missed about Christmas.

♣ ♣ ♣

It was the third week of Aries, m.y. 53. Christmas was only a couple of weeks away, and already the taprooms were brewing more beer for the festivities to come. We had just returned from delivering medical supplies to the poor schmucks at Viking, and were watching the bartender as he strung some discarded fiberoptics over the bar.

"I miss mistletoe," I murmured. I was working on my second beer by then, so I wasn't conscious of my alliteration. "Mistletoe and Christmas trees."

"You don't know mistletoe and Christmas trees," Doc said.

"Sure do. Had them in my family's apartment. My mother and father, they used to kiss beneath the . . ."

"You grew up on the Moon. You had vinyl mistletoe and plastic Christmas trees. Bet you've never smelled the real thing."

"No, but it was close enough."

"Not in the slightest. You'd know the difference." Doc sipped his beer. "But I get the point. Out in the belt, we'd get together in the wardroom on Christmas Eve and sing carols. You know caroling . . . ?"

"Sure. 'Silent Night,' 'The First Day of Christmas,' 'Jingle Bell Rock' . . ."

"'Santa Claus Is Coming To Town,' that's my favorite. And then we'd exchange gifts. Sarah gave me a ring with a little piece of gold from an asteroid ore our ship had refined." He smiled at the memory. "Marriage didn't last, but I held onto the ring."

"My favorite was a little rocket from my Dad. I was eight . . . nine, I guess. He made it for me in his lab. About two meters long, with a hollow nose cone. We put a little note with our squid number in the cone, then went EVA and hiked up to the crater rim, set the trajectory, fueled it up and fired it at Earth." Once again, I remembered that little rocket's silent launch, and how it lanced straight up into the black sky over Tycho. "Dad told me that it would eventually get there and land somewhere, and maybe someone would find it and send back a letter."

"Anyone ever fax you?"

"Naw. It probably never got to Earth . . . or if it did, it probably burned up on entry." I shrugged. "But I like to think that it made the trip, and just landed some place where no one ever found it."

"But it meant something, didn't it? Like Sarah's ring. No Christmas gift is ever insignificant. There's always a little of your soul in whatever you give someone." Doc scowled at the lights being strung above the bar. "Here, it's just an excuse for people to get drunk and stupid, and the next day everyone has to apologize to each other. Sorry for banging on your door. Sorry for keeping you awake last night. Sorry for making a pass at your wife . . ."

"What do you expect? Rudolph the green-nosed reindeer?"

"*Red*. Rudolph the *red*-nosed reindeer. Don't they teach you selenians anything?"

"Oh, yeah. Red-nosed reindeer." I polished off my second and last, shoved the mug across the bar. "Yeah, I know, but all that Santa stuff doesn't make a lot of sense out here, y'know?"

"It doesn't? Why shouldn't it?"

I could tell that he was spoiling for a fight. "Aw, c'mon, Doc . . . does this look like Earth to you? Cheststuff smoking on an open fire, jackass stepping on your toes . . ."

"You can't even get the lyrics right! 'Chestnuts roasting on an open fire, Jack Frost nipping at your toes . . .'"

"What's a chestnut?"

"Never mind." He turned away from me. "Jeff, I'll have another one. Put it on his tab."

I didn't object. Doc was in a self-righteous mood; when he was this way, silence was the only way you could deal with him. I helped myself to some fried algae from the bowl the bartender had placed between us while I waited for him to calm down.

"I guess what I miss the most," he finally said, "is the look . . . no, not just the look, the *glow* . . . children have on Christmas morning. Until I came here, I'd never seen a kid who didn't think it was the best day of the year. Even out in the Belt, it was something they could look forward to. But here . . ."

"I know what you mean." My gaze wandered to the line of ceramic liquor bottles lined up on the shelf. "The best some of them can hope for is that their folks won't be too hung over to make breakfast for them. I mean, some people try to do better, but . . . I dunno, something's missing."

"I'll tell you what's missing." Doc tapped his finger against the bar top. "It isn't just trees or presents. Magic, that's missing. There's no Sinterklass"

"Yeah. No Santa Claus."

"Did I say Santa Claus? I didn't say Santa Claus. I said Sinterklass."

"There's a difference?"

For a moment, I thought he was going to brain me with his beer mug. "Hell, yes, there's a difference! Sinterklass arrives in Holland on a ship from Spain. He's a tall, slender gent with a long white beard who wears a red robe and bishop's minter. He rides into town on a white horse with his assistant Zwarte Piet, where he gives presents to all the good children on his list. Then he . . . what's so damn funny?"

"That's Santa Claus, you quack! Only the details are different! Reindeer, elves, a sleigh from the North Pole . . . it's still the same mook, right down to the extortion racket."

"True, but Sinterklass came first . . . or St. Nicholas, if we want to call him by his proper name." He swigged his beer. "He was brought to America by the Dutch, but just like everything else brought over from Europe, he was changed until virtually no one remembered his origins."

"Tell me about it. Same thing happened to my African ancestors . . . although not by choice."

"Then you'd appreciate the similarity between Santa's elves and Zwarte Piet. It means Black Peter . . . he's a Moor."

I shrugged. "Sounds like a demotion. My great-grandfather used to play Santa every Christmas at a shopping mall. There weren't many black Santas back then, I'm told."

"Your grandfather played Santa Claus?" He raised an eyebrow. "Now there's a coincidence. My father played Sinterklass in our village, as did my grandfather."

"No kidding?"

"Goes with the genes." He stroked his trim white beard. "Men in my family have the right whiskers for the job. All we have to do is let our beard grow out and . . ."

He stopped just there. To this day, I'll never forget his slack-jawed expression as he stared at me in wonderment. He had just spoken of the glow that children have on Christmas morning; in that instant, I saw something like that appear in his own face. Wonder and joy, wonder and joy; tidings of wonder and joy . . . I don't believe in telepathy any more than I do in Santa Claus, yet I suddenly knew exactly what he was thinking.

"Oh, no, you don't," I said, turning to hop off the stool and book out of there. "Don't even think for a minute . . ."

"Oh, shut up and sit down." Doc grabbed my wrist before I could make it to the door. "Let's see if we can work this out."

Against my better judgment, I stayed. Doc finished his beer, and then we switched to coffee, and by the end of the evening I had a new name.

Sinterklass and Zwarte Piet live in the caldera of Olympus Mons, within an invisible buckydome which contains their secret toyshop. When they're not making toys or teaching sandbugs to perform tricks for their flea circus, they watch all the boys and girls of Mars through magic telescopes that can peer through walls, putting together a long list of who's been naughty and who's been nice.

Then, on the first sol of Christmas Week, they load their gifts aboard their airship, climb aboard, and fly away from Olympus Mons. Over the next seven sols they visit the colonies one by one, stopping at each to distribute presents to the good children of Mars. They may stay overnight at a settlement, because sometimes Black Peter gets too tired to fly St. Nicholas to the next colony, but if they do stay, the children should try to leave the pair alone, or next Christmas they may find the boots of their skinsuits filled with sand instead of candy.

That's the story that we artfully disseminated through the Marsnet. It was posted on all the usual sites kids would mouse, plus a few that their parents would find. It isn't hard to create a myth, if know what you're doing, but Doc and I didn't do it all by ourselves, and not without running into a little trouble.

Arsia Station's board of selectmen were skeptical when we formerly pitched the idea to them at the next weekly meeting. They thought Doc and I had dreamed this up as a sneaky way of earning overtime until Doc explained that we would also be transporting food, medical supplies, and replacement parts to the settlements. Not only that, but since we would hitting each settlement in turn, we could take stuff from one place to another, in much the same way supply caravans presently operated, yet in a shorter time-span and for more charitable reasons. The selectmen were all too aware of the ill-will some of the smaller settlements felt toward Arsia; our plan would make for good colonial relationships. So they found a few extra megalox in the budget to fund an extended medical sortie, not the least of which was subcontracting *Miss Thuvia* from AeroMars for a seven-sol sortie.

When we contacted the other five colonies and informed them of our proposal, we received mixed reactions. Wellstown, Sagan, Viking, and New Chattanooga were mystified by the notion of a Martian Santa, but otherwise interested, albeit not wildly enthusiastic; if anything, it meant they would receiving a previously unscheduled visit from Arsia General, and a few freebies to boot. West Bank was initially cool to the idea—they didn't observe Christmas Week, after all—until we agreed to knock off the Sinterklass routine and perform as if it was just another airlift. But DaVinci was the aresian home of Ebenezer Scrooge; after a few days of stone silence, we received a terse fax from its Proletariat, stating that the free people of DaVinci had decided to reject St. Nicholas as an archaic symbol of capitalistic society and Black Peter as a shameful holdover of racist imperialism. Well, tough boots: no candy for the commies.

Most people went for it, though, and once word leaked out about what Doc and I intended to do, we received assistance from various individuals, sometimes without us soliciting them for help. Aresians have a strong tradition of looking out for the other guy, after all, and the citizens of Arsia Station came out for us. A textile shop volunteered to make toys for us: tiny Mars landers, statuettes of men in skinsuits, some inflatable replicas of *Miss Thuvia*. A food-processing firm turned out several kilos of hard candy; it looked weird and tasted the same, or at least so I thought, but Doc field-tested samples on kids passing through the ER ward and none of them spit it out. A lady I was dating from Data One hacked out a game pak which she stored on a handful of spare disks; one of them was a little hide-and-seek involving Sinterklass and Zwarte Piet chasing each other through a three-dimensional maze. She made sure that the odds of Black Peter winning the match were always in my character's favor, something which Doc resented when he tried playing it.

Yet the best efforts were those on behalf of our skinsuits. It wouldn't do for us to cycle through airlocks looking like any other dust-caked aresian coming in from the cold. Sinterklass and Zwarte Piet were magical, after all; we had to look the part. So we hired Uncle Sal, Arsia's premier skinsuit tailor, to come up with a some hempcloth overgarments which closely mimicked the traditional costumes worn in the Netherlands. Doc's outfit was bright red and white, with a long scarlet cape whose ribbed hood, when pulled over his helmet, looked much like a bishop's minter. My costume was dark blue, with a plumed white collar around the neck and puffed-out sleeves and leggings. To add to the effect, Sal weaved colored microfilaments through the garments; when we switched them on, we looked like walking Christmas trees.

The only problem we had was with Doc's beard. He stopped trimming it once our plan was approved, and within a couple of weeks it flowed down his face like a pale waterfall. It looked terrific and his girlfriends loved running their fingers through it, but he had the damnedest time tucking it into his helmet. He finally figured out what that hearty "ho-ho-ho" business was all about; it allowed him to spit out the whiskers in his mouth.

Altogether, it was an impressive effort, doubly so by the fact that we pulled it all together in less than three weeks. On Ta.6, m.y. 53, Doc and I climbed aboard *Miss Thuvia* and set sail from Arsia Station. The blimp had been temporarily festooned with multicolored lights. I turned them on as soon as we were clear of the hangar, and watched from the gondola windows as a small crowd of aresians waved us farewell.

It was a good beginning, but our first stop, at twilight on the first day of the tour, was a bust. West Bank didn't want anything to do with Christmas, so I kept the lights turned off when we approached the settlement on the western slope of the Tharsis volcano range, and we weren't wearing our outfits when we exited the blimp's airlock. The settlers were cordial enough; we handed out sweets and toys to the handful of kids we met inside, and once their folks unloaded the supplies they had requested—which wasn't much, because West Bank took pride in its self-sufficiency—we had a meal and a glass of wine in the commissary before we were shown the way to the hostel. Nothing lost, but nothing really gained either, save for fuel and a night's rest; by dawn the next morning we were airborne again. The only thing which made the trip worthwhile was seeing the sunrise over Pavonis Mons as we flew eastward toward the upper edge of the Noctis Labyrinthis.

That was the longest leg of the journey. Over a thousand klicks lay between West Bank and Wellstown, and although Doc stood watch in the cockpit while I bunked out for a couple of hours, I did little more than doze. Questions ran through my mind even while my eyes were shut, murmuring like the incessant drone of *Miss Thuvia*'s props. What were we doing, two grown men dressing up like the Dutch Santa and his Moorish apprentice? I could be home now, trying to find an unattached lady with whom I could share some holiday cheer. What were we trying to achieve here? The children at West Bank had shown only slight interest in us; a little girl had stoically gazed at the toy lander Doc placed in her hand, and a small boy had made a sour face when he ate the candy I had given him. Yeah, so maybe Christmas wasn't part of their culture, but the Jewish friends with whom I had been raised on the Moon knew what it was, if only for the spirit of the season. Perhaps Christmas didn't belong on Mars. So why did any of this matter?

When I finally got up and went forward, I could see that Doc had been contemplating the same thought. "It'll go better in Wellstown," he said softly, but I don't think he believed it either.

We ate cold rations as the sun went down behind us, drank some more powdered coffee, and said very little to one another until the lights of Wellstown appeared before us, a tiny cluster of white and amber lights against the cold darkness of the Martian night. Almost reluctantly, we pulled on our skinsuits. I almost forgot to switch *Miss Thuvia*'s Christmas lights until we were above the landing field.

A handful of men grabbed our mooring lines, dragged us in, tied us down. It was only the second time we had worn our costumes on EVA; Doc stepped on his cape and nearly fell down the gangway, and the puffed-out legging of my suit forced me into a bow-legged gait. We looked stupid as we made our way to the airlock of the nearest buckydome. The final touch came when Doc couldn't fit inside, and he had to lower the peaked hood of his cape.

The outer hatch shut behind us; we got a chance to study each other as the airlock cycled. Two fools in gaudy, luminescent skinsuits. A bad dream come to life. We had been flying for the past twelve hours, but I would have gladly flown straight home if I thought it would save me any further humiliation. Why did I ever let Doc talk me into . . . ?

Then the green light flashed above the inner hatch. Doc and I were unclasping our helmets when the lockwheel began turning its own. The inner hatch was thrown open from outside. Bright light rushed into the airlock, and along with it, the excited squeals of the dozens of children waiting outside.

At that instant, it all made perfect sense.

Even after all these years, I still consider that first Christmas tour to be our best. We ran short of candy and toys before we were through, and we were bone-tired by the time we left Sagan for the last leg of the circuit back to Arsia Station, yet we brought home with us the most exciting discovery since microfossils were found in the Noctis Labyrinthis.

St. Nicholas was alive and well and living on Mars. How could nearly three hundred kids possibly be wrong?

Sometimes it was tough. The children at Viking broke our hearts: grimy, hungry, wearing cast-off clothes, but enchanted the moment we stepped through the airlock. None rejected our awful candy, and they fought jealously over the crude toys from Doc's bag until we made sure that everyone had something to take home. They took turns sitting in Sinterklass's lap, and he listened to stories of hardship and loss that would have horrified the worst curmudgeon. Several kids were sallow and feverish with lingering illnesses that required Doc to play physician as well as holiday saint; we were prepared for that, so after a sneaky sort of examination ("How long is your tongue? I bet you've got the longest one here. Open your mouth and let Sinterklass see. Oh, yes, you do, don't you . . . ?") he'd send the sick ones over to Black Peter for a card trick and a couple of pills; later, we'd give the rest of the prescription to their parents.

Sometimes it was funny. A little girl in New Chattanooga was adamant in her outspoken belief that Sinterklass was a fake; the brat kept yanking at Doc's beard, tearing out white hair by its roots in her dogged attempt to dislodge his mask. She got candy and a toy—no child came away empty-handed during that first tour—but before we left the following morning I tracked down her skinsuit in the community ready-room and filled her boots with handfuls of sand. She was much nicer to us the next year. Sagan's resident nymphomaniac decided that the holiday season wasn't complete until, in her words, she had "made Santa's bells jingle." She started by sitting in his lap and whispering something in Doc's ear that succeeded in turning his nose bright red. At any other time, Doc might have obliged, once they were safely away from the little ones, but he decided that this might set a bad precedent. To her credit, she took his refusal with good grace . . . and then she asked me why I was called Black Peter.

And, yeah, sometimes it was scary. A slow leak in one of her hydrogen cells caused *Miss Thuvia* to lose altitude as we were flying from Viking to New Chattanooga. The pressure drop occurred while we were flying over Cupri Chasm, one of the deepest parts of the Valles Marineris; for a few minutes, it looked as if we would crash in the red-rock canyon dozens of kilometers below us. I awoke Doc from his nap and he scrambled into the gondola's rear to open the ballast valves. When that wasn't enough, he shoved some cargo containers out the airlock—including, much to our regret, one containing several bottles of homemade wine we were freighting from Wellstown to the other colonies. We jettisoned enough weight from the princess to keep her aloft just long enough to clear the chasm, but she left skid marks when she landed at New Chattanooga. And then we had to put on our costumes and pretend that we hadn't just cheated death by only a few kilos.

But it was fun, and it was exhilarating, and it was heart-warming, and it was *good*. Even before we arrived back at Arsia Station, where we were greeted not by the small handful who had witnessed our departure a week earlier but by hundreds of skinsuited colonists who surrounded the crater and threw up their arms as *Miss Thuvia* came into sight, Doc and I swore to each other that we'd make the same trip again next year.

It wasn't because our newfound fame—we still ducked the *Martian Chronicle* when it came to us for an interview—or the lure of adventure, or even another shot at our cuddly friend in Sagan. It was simply because we'd brought something pure, decent and civilized to Mars. Perhaps that was a Christmas miracle in itself. If so, then we wanted another one, and another one after that.

We'd eventually received our miracle. But it wasn't one I would have ever expected.

In 2066, the Pax Astra underwent a political upheaval when the Monarchists overthrew the ruling New Ark Party on the Clarke County space colony near Earth. The *coup d'état* was led by former New Ark members frustrated with the economic stagnation brought on by the Pax's government by consensus. They formed an opposition party with the intent of recasting the Pax Astra as a democratic monarchy, and eventually deposed the New Ark in a near-bloodless revolution. Yet shortly after Queen Macedonia had been crowned, the aresian representatives to the new Parliament realized that Martian interests were a very low priority in the new order. The diplomats caught the next cycleship home; no sooner had they arrived at Arsia Station that they formally announced that Mars was seceeding from the Pax Astra and that its colonies were declaring political independence.

This was the beginning of the great Martian immigration. Within a year, our world began receiving the first shiploads of refugees from the Pax. Most were New Ark loyalists who had quickly discovered that Monarchist democracy was restricted to those who supported the royal agenda, which mainly involved keeping itself in power and persecuting anyone who objected. Since the Moon was part of the Pax and life on Earth was intolerable to those who had been born in low-gee environments, Mars became their only sanctuary.

But we hadn't built a Statue of Liberty anywhere on our planet, and even Arsia Station was ill-equipped to handle the dozens, then hundreds, of refugees—drybacks, you want to use the impolite term—who came to us during the long winter of m.y. 57. Human survival on Mars has always been a frail and precarious matter; even with mandatory water rationing and voluntary birth control, the six colonies were unable to support everyone from the Pax who wanted to move here. Ascension was reopened and West Bank relaxed its standards to admit non-Jewish immigrants. When their resources were exhausted, the colonies sent messages to the Pax pleading for it to stop sending more bodies our way. Yet the Monarchists turned a deaf ear to us; since Mars was no longer within the Queen's domain, it was a convenient dumping ground for its dissidents, low-lifes, and criminals. When its escapees began to include people they wanted to keep to themselves, they revoked exit visas and began searching outbound vessels. But they couldn't stop everyone from leaving, and it was a rare week when the contrail of another lander wasn't spotted streaking across our pink skies.

Some of the newcomers came equipped to establish new settlements; this was how we got Nova America in the Solis Planum south of Arsia Station, Graceland in the Margaritifer northeast of New Chattanooga, and Thankgod up on southern edge of the Acidalia Plantia. Others arrived with little more than a second-rate skinsuit and a handful of useless Pax lox that the Mars colonies had stopped accepting as hard currency. They often came down in cramped landers stripped of all but the most essential hardware. Many arrived safely; one way or another, they managed to survive, even prosper. But a few crashed in remote areas. Decades later, explorers were still finding their remains: sad and lonesome skeletons, desiccated by dust storms, half-buried within cold red drifts.

As the month of Taurus rolled around once more, Doc and I found little free time to prepare for Christmas Week. I had received paramedic training by then, so I could assist Doc when we flew out on a sortie; good thing, too, because Arsia General's resources were stretched to the limit. Besides the fact that many immigrants had sustained injuries during landing, just as many had become ill during their long flight from near-space. Radiation sickness, calcium deficiency, dysentery, bronchitis, malnutrition, Tibbet's disease, a half-dozen different strains of influenza . . . .you name it, they had it. We had already logged sixteen hundred hours aboard *Miss Thuvia* by Christmas, and were seldom seen in the bars at Arsia Station.

Yet just because the colonies were in crisis didn't mean that Sinterklass and Zwarte Piet got a break. Indeed, their presence was needed more than ever before; the children whom we had visited during our first tour were now teenagers and young adults, but their ranks had been filled by yet more kids, many of whom were toddlers born on Clarke County and the Moon. Uprooted from their homes by the Monarchist revolution, bewildered and frightened by their harsh new environment, some sick, most living in awful poverty, they needed Christmas just as much as they needed air, food, and medicine.

Our annual Christmas tour had become a major part of aresian life by now. The West Bank elders finally decided that a little gentile culture wasn't such a bad thing after all, so they allowed us to wear our costumes when we came to call, and since DaVinci's socialist government had crumbled a couple of years earlier, St. Nicholas and Black Peter were now welcome as the next stop after Viking. Along with the revived Ascension colony and three new settlements, the tour now had nine stops, not including our home port at Arsia Station.

This meant that Doc and I spent the entire holiday week on the road, sometimes making two stops a day. Fortunately, the older colonies had learned to not depend upon Arsia Station to make the holiday season for them; as well as offering room and board if we stayed overnight and to refuel *Miss Thuvia* when she touched down, they began making gifts of their own for their neighbor settlements. Since *Miss Thuvia* has a limited payload capacity, and therefore couldn't haul thousands of kilos of Christmas presents from one settlement to another, a rather clever system of gift-giving had been devised: each colony gave presents to the next settlement on our route. Arsia Station gave to West Bank, West Bank to Wellstown, Wellstown to Viking, Viking to DaVinci, and so forth. Every other year, Doc and I reversed the schedule so that DaVinci gave stuff to Viking, etc. And the gifts themselves ranged from the simple to the elaborate; West Bank made wonderful handcrafted dreidels that spun forever, Wellstown could be depended on to supply excellent wine, DaVinci distributed illustrated chapbooks of poetry and short stories, Viking's artists contributed tiny yet endlessly fascinating sand paintings, and Sagan's gliders could fly for almost a quarter-klick. And, of course, Arsia Station continued to send candy and small toys to every child who wanted one.

The new settlements were still too impoverished to spend the time or energy to make gifts of their own, though, so I sent email to representatives at each of the older colonies, telling them that Black Peter would be reserving a little extra cargo space aboard Sinterklass's magic dirigible for gifts to Nova America, Graceland, and Thankgod. No one objected to the deviation from standard operating procedure, and we were promised extra goodies from everyone when *Miss Thuvia* lifted off from Arsia on Sag. 6.

For the past four years, the Christmas tour had been blessed with good flying weather. Our luck couldn't last forever, though; by the time we arrived at DaVinci, Marsnet had posted nowcasts of a severe dust storm developing in the Amazonis Plantia, due west of the Tharsis Montes range. West Bank, which we had left only eighteen hours earlier, was already reporting high winds. They warned us that *Miss Thuvia* wouldn't be able to handle the storm, and suggested that we deflate our craft and hunker down at DaVinci until the worst was over.

That might be good advice at any other time, but during Christmas Week it posed a real problem. Dust storms have been known to last for days or weeks, even months on certain historic occasions. If Doc and I chose to ride out the storm in DaVinci, we might be celebrating New Year's there. About two dozen immigrants in Thankgod were barely holding out in shelters little more sophisticated than those built by the First Landers; they were in dire need of the food, water, and medicine aboard *Miss Thuvia*. And we quietly regarded DaVinci as our least favorite of stopovers; we hadn't forgotten the snubbing we'd received during our first tour, and more than a few hard-line neocommies still hadn't warmed up to us.

We managed to get the station manager to loan us a long-range rover. It was about six hundred and fifty klicks from DaVinci to Thankgod, but since the rover burned methane/oxygen and carbon dioxide, it was capable of manufacturing its own fuel from the atmosphere and from recaptured water vapor from the condensers, and ditto for cabin air. Using the rover would be slower than taking the blimp, but flying Miss Thuvia in this sort of weather was out of the question. The rover had a top speed of seventy klicks per hour, so the round-trip to Thankgod would take about nineteen or twenty hours. If we budgeted two hours for our appearance at Thankgod and add two more as a fudge-factor, and with luck—there's that word again—we'd only lose a sol. Thus we figured the storm should blow itself out by the time we made it back to DaVinci; then we'd be able to reinflate the blimp and head for New Chattanooga.

The kids at the remaining colonies on our tour might have to wait a bit for their Christmas, but there were limits to even Sinterklass's magic. However, we had little doubt that we'd make it to Thankgod.

That's what we told ourselves. In hindsight, I think we were counting on miracles we hadn't earned.

So Doc and I loaded our stuff into the rover and set out from DaVinci near the middle of the same sol. The wind was already rising from the west as we followed the line of compacted rover tracks away from the colony into the high country northeast of the Valles Marineris. We hadn't covered a hundred klicks before Doc had to switch on the windshield blowers.

Well, no problem. You've seen one dust storm, you've seen a dozen. I brewed some more coffee, then sacked out in the shotgun seat. When I woke up, my first thought was that I had overslept and that night had already fallen, until Doc told me that it was only late afternoon. The road had completely disappeared behind rippling curtains of red sand; despite the rover's lights, visibility had diminished to only a few meters ahead of the front bumper.

We were driving into the throat of the worst winter storm in . . . well, forget the stats. It was nasty, and that's all there was to it.

Yet we weren't worried. Not really. We had a clear satellite fix on our location, so there was no real danger of getting lost out here. Although our ground speed had dropped to fifty klicks, the rover's six tandem wheels continued to move through the dense sand that scurried around us. We had air, we had hot coffee, we had Nashville music on the CD player; the howling wind buffeted the rover as if it was a boat on high seas, but it was Christmas, and we were Sinterklass and Zwarte Piet. We couldn't be stopped, storm or no storm.

I had just switched off with Doc, and he was rummaging through the food locker in search of cold rations which wouldn't taste too much like cardboard, when we received a microbeam transmission from Arsia Station. I thought it was just a courtesy call: the folks back home making sure we weren't in trouble. The reception was bad, and I was fumbling for a headset when Doc came forward and told me to keep my hands on the yoke, he'd take care of it.

I didn't catch most of it; my attention was focused on avoiding boulders and craters. Doc played the keys until he got a semi-clear channel, listened for a few minutes, scribbled some stuff on a pad, murmured a few words, then clicked off and turned to me.

"Problem."

"Big or small?"

"Dunno. Phobos Station spotted a lander making atmospheric entry about a half-hour ago. Probably from a Pax freighter that made orbit earlier today. Arsia Traffic locked onto its transponder and followed it down until they lost it in the storm."

"Where did it come down?" Then I shook my head. "Oh, no. I can guess this one . . ."

"Edge of the Acidalia, about a hundred and fifty klicks southeast of Thankgod."

"Aw, for the love of . . ."

It figured this might happen, if only because it had happened before; the commander of a Pax refugee ship tried to drop his lander on one of the new colonies without first informing Arsia of his intentions. Pax Royal Intelligence, in an attempt to stop the hemorrhage of its best and brightest from Clarke County and the Moon, had recently begun spreading ugly rumors that we'd launch missiles at any immigrant ships arriving in aresian space. This played into the hands of freighter captains taking aboard drybacks as unlisted passengers; they'd load them aboard a lander, drop 'em near a new settlement, then swing around the planet, make a periapsis burn, and scoot for home before anyone was the wiser. The commander and his crew make out like bandits from the megalox they've taken from their desperate passengers; meanwhile, we're saddled with another dozen or so immigrants who didn't know they were being taken for a ride, both literally and figuratively.

Only in this case, the freighter captain had deposited his human cargo in the middle of a dust storm. Perhaps he wasn't fully aware of the ferocious nature of the Martian climate, but I couldn't bring myself to give him to benefit of the doubt. More likely he knew that dead men don't tell tales, let alone disclose ship registry numbers.

I was still fuming about this while Doc played with the high-gain. "I've got something," he murmured after a few moments. "Weak, but it's there."

"Vox or transponder?"

"Transponder. You think we're going to get local vox through this shit?"

Good point. Unless the drybacks were bouncing signals off one of the satellites, they probably couldn't transmit anything through the storm. Landers that came down intact, though, were programmed to broadcast a shortwave distress signal as soon as they touched down, even if it was only a repeating Morse-code dit-dot-dit that could be received for hundreds of kilometers. "Mayday cast?" I asked, and Doc nodded without looking up. "Can you get a lock on it?"

Doc dickered with the keypad a little while longer before he spoke again. "Yeah, got it. I'm feeding the coordinates to your board."

A topo map appeared on the flat just above the yoke. The signal source was approximately a hundred and fifty kilometers east-southeast of Thankgod, about forty klicks west of our beeline from the colony. Doc looked at me, I looked at him, and that was it. We didn't even discuss the matter; there was no question of whether or not we'd head for the crash site. We were Sinterklass and Zwarte Piet, but before that we were meds, and this is what we did, plain and simple.

"Pain in the ass," I murmured as I began punching the new coordinates into the nav system.

"Yeah. Kind of screws up Christmas, don't it?" Doc lurched out of his seat and headed aft again. "So what do you want? Cheese and tomato, ham and cheese, or turkey?"

It was close to midnight when we located the downed lander.

One moment, it wasn't there; the next, it was in our high-beams, a gargantuan manta ray that had mysteriously been thrown across space and time. Its starboard landing skid had buckled during touchdown, so the craft listed sharply to one side, its right wing half-buried in the sand, the wind driving dust into its engine intakes. The cockpit faced away from us, but there was a dim glimmer of light from within the main hatch porthole.

I halted the rover about ten meters away, and tried one last time to raise someone on the radio. As before, there was no answer, not surprising since the ship had sustained heavy damage during landing. I went aft and found that Doc had already suited up. Until that moment, it hadn't occurred to either of us to strip off all the Father Christmas stuff, but now we didn't have time. So we switched on the holiday lights so we could see each other better in the darkness. Doc raised his hood and picked up his medical bag, then we cycled through the airlock.

We made our way to the lander with our heads down, our arms raised to shield our faceplates against windblown silt and gravel. Glancing back, I could make out the rover only by its lamps. I doubted that anyone within the lander had heard our approach through the storm. If, indeed, there were any survivors.

Typical of Pax spacecraft, the airlock was only large enough to accommodate one person at a time. I went first; Doc waited outside while I closed the outer hatch. The light we'd seen outside came from an emergency lamp in the ceiling, but there was sufficient power in the back-up electrical system to allow me to run the cycle-through routine. I went by the book, though, and didn't unlatch my helmet even after the green light appeared above the inner hatch.

For a moment, there was only darkness when I pushed open the hatch. Then a half-dozen flashlight beams swung my way, and muffled voices cascaded from the gloom:

". . . opening! Look, the hatch . . . !"

". . . the hell, where did he come . . . ?"

". . . it's a man! Daddy, there's a man in . . . !"

". . . everyone, stand back! Get back from the . . . !"

"It's okay. Everything's all right!" I raised a hand against the sudden glare. "I'm from Arsia Station! I'm here to rescue you!"

They couldn't hear me, of course; they were all shouting at once, and my voice didn't carry well through the closed helmet. Yet there were at least a dozen people in here, shadows backlit by flashlight beams. Moving awkwardly against the sloped deck, I stepped the rest of the way out of the airlock, then turned to close the hatch behind me.

Something slammed against my shoulder, hard enough to make me lose my balance. I collapsed against the airlock hatch. It fell into place, then a hand grabbed my shoulder and twisted me around, shoving me back against the portal.

"Don't move!" a voice yelled at me. "Keep your hands where I can see 'em!"

"Hey, cut it out!" I yelled back. "I'm just trying to . . . !"

There's nothing like having a gun shoved in your face to kill conversation. Even in the dim light, I could make out the maw of a Royal Militia blaster, a miniature particle-beam cannon capable of ending all debate over my hat size.

The guy holding it didn't look too pleasant, either: a large gent with a selenian helmet tan, his dark eyes narrowed with rage. His breath fogged my faceplate—it must be pretty cold in here for it to do that—but above the heavy sweater he wore was a blue uniform jacket. Its epaulets told me it was from the Pax Astra Royal Navy. I had a hunch that it wasn't military surplus.

"Kyle, cut it out!" A woman's voice somewhere behind the ring of flashlights. "Can't you see he's . . . ?"

"Shut up, Marcie." Kyle let go of me and backed away a few centimeters, but kept his weapon trained on my face. "Okay, Mars boy, I.D. yourself."

I took a deep breath. "Look, calm down, okay? Don't shoot. I'm not here to . . ."

"Jeez, lieutenant, let him take off his helmet." This from another man elsewhere in the compartment. "How can you hear him?"

"Kyle . . ." Marcie said.

"Everyone shut up!" Kyle braced his feet against the deck. "Okay, open up . . . slowly."

"Okay, all right. Take it easy." I slowly moved my hands to my suit collar, began unlatching the ring. I heard a child crying from somewhere in the darkness.

I was getting a bad feeling about my friend Kyle. If he was a former PARN officer, then he was doubtless a deserter. Worse, he had most likely heard the Pax agitprop that aresians are cannibals who raid dryback landers. My Christmas gear didn't help matters much; it wasn't your usual standard-issue skinsuit, so to him I probably looked like the Martian equivalent of a wild native wearing a grass skirt and a shrunken head. The man was desperate and afraid, and hiding his fear behind a gun.

"Look," I said once I had removed my helmet, "you're not in any danger, I promise you. We're a med team from Arsia Station. Our rover's just outside. We picked up your transponder signal and . . ."

"There's more than one of you?" His eyes flickered to the hatch behind me. "How many are out there?"

Great. Now he thought he was surrounded. "Just one other guy. I promise you, we're not armed. Please, just put down the gun and we can see about getting you out of this jam, okay?"

"Kyle, would you listen to him?" The woman who had spoken before, Marcie, stepped a little closer. Now I saw that her neck was wrapped in thick swatches of torn fabric. A crude neck brace; she probably suffered whiplash during the crash. "He doesn't mean us any harm, and we're . . ."

"Dammit, Marcie, did you hear what he just said? Nobody drives from Arsia Station in a rover. If there was going to be rescue mission, why didn't it come from Thankgod?" Kyle's gun didn't budge an millimeter. "I'm not about to take this guy at his word. He's just going to have to . . ."

Whatever Kyle was about to propose that I do—I suspect it wasn't pleasant—it was forgotten when the hatch suddenly clunked.

Everyone heard the sound. They froze, staring past me. I felt the hatch nudge my back, and I automatically moved aside before I realized what I was doing.

"Doc," I yelled, "don't come in!"

"Shut up!" Kyle shifted his gun first to cover me, then aimed it at the hatch. "You there, listen up! I've got a gun on your pal, so you'd better stop right . . . !"

"Ho, ho, ho! Mer-r-r-ry Christmas! Mer-r-r-r-r-ry Christmas!"

Then the hatch was pushed fully open, and in walked Sinterklass.

Doc had removed his helmet and had lowered his hood. In the darkness of the cabin, the lights of his suit glowed like a childhood fantasy. Motes of dust swirled from his red cape and caught in his long white beard like flakes of fresh-fallen snow.

"Mer-r-r-r-ry Christmas!" he bellowed again, and gave another jolly laugh.

In that instant, he was no longer Doc Spanjaard. He had become every holiday legend. Sinterklass, St. Nicholas, Father Christmas . . .

"Santa!"

The little girl I had heard earlier bolted from the gloom. Before Kyle or Marcie or anyone else could grab her, she rushed across the dark cabin.

"It's Santa Claus!" she screamed. "Santa's on Mars! Mama, you were right! There's a Santa Claus on Mars!"

As Doc bent to catch her in his arms, I heard another child call out, then another, and suddenly two more kids darted past the legs of the bewildered adults surrounding us. They were all over Doc before anyone could stop them, least of all Kyle, who suddenly didn't seem to know what to do with the gun in his hands, and Doc was laughing so hard that I thought he was going to lose his balance and fall back into the airlock with three children on top of him, and everyone else was yelling in relieved surprise . . .

Then Marcie turned to Kyle, who stood in gape-jawed confusion, his blaster now half-raised toward the ceiling so that it wasn't pointed at any of the kids.

"So what are you going to do?" she murmured. "Be the guy who shot Santa Claus?"

He stared at Doc, then at me. "But it isn't Christmas yet."

"Welcome to Mars," I said quietly. "We do things a little different here."

He nodded, then put the gun away.

And that was our Christmas miracle.

We dispensed some food from the lander; the three children were handed toys from Doc's sack and the adults were given two bottles of wine. Doc spent a couple of hours treating injuries while I went back to the rover and radioed both Thankgod and Arsia to tell them that we had located the lander. Arsia informed me that the storm was ebbing in our region and that DaVinci had already volunteered to send out a couple of rovers to pick up the new arrivals. I relayed the news to Kyle, whom I learned was their leader; he couldn't look me straight in the eye when he tendered an apology for his behavior, but I accepted it anyway.

By the time Doc and I left the crash site, the first light of dawn was appearing on the eastern horizon; it might be mid-summer back on Earth, but here it was the third sol of Christmas. Peace on Mars, good will towards men.

We completed that long, hard tour, and returned to Arsia Station only a little later than usual. Once I had put *Miss Thuvia* to bed, Doc and I decompressed in the Mars Hotel. For the first time since we had started this little homecoming ritual, we allowed ourselves to get drunk. No wonder Doc rarely got blotto; he didn't hold his liquor very well. He sang dirty songs and made jokes no one understood; it's a good thing no children were present, because he would have ruined Christmas for them forever. The last I saw of him that night, he was being helped out of the bar by two of his girlfriends, neither of whom seemed likely to let him quietly pass out before they gave him the mistletoe treatment.

We made eight more Christmas tours before I retired from service. By then I was married and running AeroMars; my wife and business partners didn't want me leaving Arsia Station for several sols each year to haul candy and toys to distant settlements. Nor was it necessary for me to play Black Peter any longer; now there were nineteen self-sustaining colonies scattered across the planet, and nearly every one of them had their own homemade Sinterklass and Zwarte Piet costumes.

Doc, though, continued to play his role every year, if only to take a rover out to nearby settlements. He was the first and best Sinterklass on Mars, and everyone wanted to see him. He relished the job, and continued it longer after he set up a private practice at Arsia. Toys and candy for all the children, wine for the adults, and a different Zwarte Piet everywhere he went. It was what he did, period. And whenever he came home, we got together for drinks and small talk.

Twelve years after we made the Acidalia rescue mission, though, Doc didn't come back to the bar. He went out alone to Ascension during another dust storm and . . . well, vanished. No final transmissions, and no one ever found his vehicle. He simply disappeared, just like that.

I miss Doc, but I think this is an appropriate way to go. Mars is full of mystery; so is Christmas, or at least it should be. The holiday got ruined on Earth because everything wonderful about it was gradually eroded, the magic sucked away. Out here, though, we've got a great Christmas, and a patron saint all our own.

He lives in the caldera of Olympus Mons.

INTRODUCTION
❧❀❧
HOW THORVALD THE BLOODY-MINDED SAVED CHRISTMAS

NOW FOR A TALE OF A WARRIOR of mighty thews and minimal brain who was enlisted in the cause of righteousness, whether he wanted to join the cause or not. It does not pay to argue with a saint, even one who's dead. Particularly, one who's dead . . .

♣ ♣ ♣

ESTHER FRIESNER is winner twice over of the coveted Nebula Award (for the Year's Best short Story, 1995 and 1996) and is the author of almost forty novels, including the *USA Today* best-seller *Warchild*, and nearly two hundred short stories. For Baen she edited the five popular "Chicks in Chainmail" anthologies, with another politically incorrect installment forthcoming. Her works have been published in the UK, Japan, Germany, Russia, France and Italy. She lives in Connecticut with her husband, is the mother of two, and harbors cats.

HOW THORVALD THE BLOODY-MINDED SAVED CHRISTMAS

by Esther M. Friesner

FAR TOO REPEATEDLY UPON A TIME in Northumbria there was a Viking named Thorvald the Bloody-Minded. He was a rather large and bilious barbarian whose Danish mother had mated with a troll during a more than ordinarily rebellious adolescence. Her intention was to teach her parents that a maiden could do worse things than stay out all night consorting with bards and other societal filth, but her juvenile attempts at parental education came a cropper when the troll followed her home, devoured her mother, and bit her father in a delicate anatomical area before falling to the sword of his victim, Bjarni the Shortened.

Thus Thorvald, that unfortunate product of a broken-and-slightly-gnawed home, grew up to be half man, half monster, and half witted. Fortunately for him, he also grew up to be a strapping lad with a mighty arm, a loyal heart, and the independent intelligence of a very small cheese. Such an ideal fighting machine would not go begging

197

long. Thus it was that young Thorvald had barely celebrated his fifteenth birthday before he was recruited into the Great Army of those plunder-hungry rulers, Ivar (the Boneless) and Halfdan (the Much Bonier Than Ivar) for their assault upon the western island kingdom of the Anglo-Saxons.

The Great Army of Danes assaulted East Anglia in the Year of Their Victims' Lord, 865. It was a lovely first combat experience for Thorvald, who earned a battlefield promotion and his *nom de massacre* after King Ivar saw what the lad singlehandedly did to the twelve Anglo-Saxons fool enough to gang up on him. Like the common rat that was his favorite breakfast treat, Thorvald the Bloody-Minded fought best when cornered and facing impossible odds. By the time the dust and eyeballs settled, the Danish forces realized that they were the lucky proprietors of the world's first Weapon of Mass Destruction (if you didn't count those Indian peoples already in possession of vindaloo curry).

Yes, Thorvald was gifted, a natural, an idiot *savant/sauvage* born to go on viking. Though he grew sullen and suspicious when asked to deal with complex matters, such as words of more than one syllable, he had little trouble living the principles behind them, such as *maraud, pillage, destroy, ravish* and *annihilate*. (Notheless he was quite grateful when his friend and shield-mate, Hvitis the Eloquent, taught him their more mnemonic, utilitarian synonyms, *raid, rob, wreck, rape* and *splat*.) Many of his fellow soldiers remarked that the young man was destined for great achievements, all of them involving a high body-count and plenty of sloppy collateral damage.

In other words, if there were one career path that no sane and sighted human being would have predicted for Thorvald, it was that of saint.

Funny old thing, Vile Circumstance. Not funny *ha-ha*, you understand; more like funny *aaaaaaaaiiiiiieeeeeee*! but there you have it.

It was in the second year of the reign of good king Ethelred of Wessex that the little Northumbrian seaport of Streaneshalch was overrun by a Viking horde and given what-ho. On the cliffs high above the sea, the venerable monastic community was introduced to the sword, the torch, and the plummet into said sea. Monks howled and fled, nuns hid, ecclesiastic treasures were plundered and all that could be put to the torch went up in a plume of smoke and flame. It was simply dreadful.

When the screaming stopped and the smoke cleared, there were Vikings all over the place. Like raspberry seeds between the teeth, it was next to impossible to dislodge them without a good deal of concentrated effort. Alas, after the raid, the only concentrated effort to which the good citizenry of Streaneshalch felt equal was tying tourniquets around spurting arteries and trying to locate one's other arm.

To the victor belong the spoils, and to the despoiler belongs the victory. Most of Thorvald's companions gazed about the prospect of Streaneshalch, found it agreeable, and decided to put down roots. And who was going to stop them? Your common or garden Viking does not raid for the sheer destructive joy of hands-on devastation. No, he is a pragmatic man who has taken up his sword and shield for the eminently practical purpose of survival. The northern lands whence his family tree springs are not Odin's gift for plentiful, arable acreage, and there is just so much herring a man can eat before he goes stark mad.

Ecclesiastical gold and silver plundered from the churches is all very well and good, but give a Viking a few hides of decent land and he'll be more likely to make mead than mayhem. A fine farm, a buxom wife, a clutter of children at the hearthside, a few slaves to keep the children from catching fire, and a break from all of that damned herring: Of such simple joys were even the most savage Viking warrior's dreams made.

Except, of course, Thorvald.

Thorvald was not the farming type. Plows confused him. Marriage seemed to him to be a needless complication to what was otherwise quite a simple carnal transaction. Children made him nervous. He didn't mind herring. There was little question in his mind as to whether he ever would so much as consider remaining at Streaneshalch.

There was little *anything* in Thorvald's mind, as a rule.

Thus it came as a surprise to no one more than himself when his good friend, Hvitis the Eloquent, informed him that the pair of them would be among those of Ivar and Halfdan's Great Army who'd be staying on.

"But I don't *want* to stay!" Thorvald bellowed, stamping his feet like a petulant child.

It was as this point that he noticed something of general interest, a patent fact which good old Hvitis, true to his name, underscored most eloquently, viz.:

"I'm afraid you've got no choice, Thorvald, old man. Also no left leg as such."

It was so. At some point in the great battle, a Saxon had gotten in a lucky slash of the battle ax, hacking Thorvald's leg just below the knee. It was the last bit of luck he enjoyed, for an enraged Thorvald promptly returned the compliment with a sword-stroke of such flair and power that the Saxon actually was able to exclaim, "Well, I guess *I* showed that bloody herring-eater how we do things here in Streaneshalch!" before his head fell off.

But the damage had been done.

Poor Thorvald! Hvitis never ceased from telling him how lucky he was that the Great Army's healer—a man of medicine, magic, and applied mold—had been able to staunch the bleeding and save his life. He felt neither gladness nor gratitude. Of what use was it to breathe the summer's air if one could not exhale that same breath in a ferocious battle-cry? What good did it do him to hobble peg-legged along the top of the Streaneshalch cliffs, gazing off across the wild waves, when he knew he'd go no more a-roving the whale-road, spreading fear and terror wherever he went?

A Viking who can no longer go *on* viking is not a happy Viking. Q.E.D.

Hvitis was a good man, if not half so dedicated a pillager as his friend Thorvald. He used the impetus of the Sack of Streaneshalch as collateral to obtain himself a dear old farmstead (nothing a month and nothing down unless you counted the previous owner), took (literally) a local girl to be his bride, and settled down to plow them both. Of course he invited his former shield-chum to share his home, if not his wife. "*Mi casa es su casa*," said Hvitis, albeit in Danish.

"Will there be mead?" said Thorvald.

"Well, *d'uh!*" Hvitis replied, again in Danish.

Years passed, as they will, willy-nilly. The Northmen who'd chosen to remain at Streaneashlach soon went from being those bellowing, bloodthirsty, baby-eating, dreadful, disease-riddled Danish demons who would devour your living heart as soon as look at you to Good-old-Hvitis-up-the-hill-nice-enough-bloke-funny-accent-but-give-you-the-bearskin-off-his-back-if-you-asked-him-for-it-our-eldest-rather-fancies-his-girl-Frida. The Danes saw no dishonor in peace. Underneath it all, they were as averse to spilling blood as the next man, particularly when there was the chance of it being their own.

This did not apply when the next man was Thorvald. He had not taken well to the years of concord. His hair and beard turned white as the wintry wave-tops, his shield was pressed into service as an emergency cradle when Hvitis' wife (in an access of enthusiasm) gave birth to twins, his hunger was more often sated by mutton than herring, but other than that, he was unchanged.

The wooden peg that had replaced his lost limb was now a formidable piece of lumber that he'd improved upon over many winters, adding some rather explicit carvings of men, women, and livestock *au naturel* in poses *trés* un*naturel*. Whenever Hvitis brought the whole family to town, the common greeting was: "H'lo, Hvitis, Missus Hvitis, kids, don't-you-dare-look-at-Mister-Thorvald's-leg-Osbert-I-don't-care-if-it-*is*-educational-I'll-give-you-such-a-clout, Mister Thorvald, and how are you all this fine day?"

That was bad enough, but Thorvald had also girdled the lower end of the artificial leg with an iron ring liberally starred with spikes. It made for rough going when the roads were deep in mud, but it also gave substantial teeth to any kicks Thorvald might wish to distribute. No stray dogs came to give him a friendly sniff more than once, no beggars repeatedly tried his patience or his purse, and cats, being wise, gave him a wide berth without putting to empirical proof his theoretical reactions to any sociable overtures. Away from the farm,

Thorvald was left alone with his ever-growing bitterness of spirit. He liked it that way.

One chill November day it so happened that Hvitis had to come to town with a considerable amount of silver, part of his share of the booty gleaned during his time with the Great Army. Now it was going to be put to use providing a dowry large enough to convince Edric Fairhair (still the richest man in Streaneshalch despite the Viking incursion and thus, by inference, the cleverest as well) to marry his son Edgar to Hvitis' middle daughter, Thora.

Wisely, Hvitis asked Thorvald to accompany him, as a deterrent to thieves on the road. Just as wisely, once they reached town, Hvitis strongly suggested that Thorvald pass the hours until dusk as far away from the site of the betrothal negotiations as possible.

"Why?" Thorvald demanded. "I like Thora. You named her for me. If that Saxon meat doesn't want her for a daughter-in-law, I'll soon set him straight."

"I'm sure you would, and I appreciate your moral support no end," Hvitis assured him, nervously eyeing the way that Thorvald's hand remained staunchly attached to the pommel of his old battle-blade. (Every day, rain or shine, Thorvald stumped out to the nearest woodland and kept up his swordsmanship. Hvitis hadn't had to clear an extra hide of land with his own hands in years, though the farm was beginning to suffer a firewood shortage.) "However, my dear friend, this is a matter best settled by the immediate parties concerned."

"I like parties," Thorvald said hopefully.

Hvitis gave his friend a short lesson on synonyms, then said, "Here, take this, go have your own party, and I'll find you afterwards."

Grudgingly, Thorvald accepted his friend's gift of several small silver bits. Hvitis frequently gave him money when they came to town, on the unspoken understanding that Thorvald would take himself to the nearest drinking establishment and methodically consume enough beer or stronger spirits to put himself into a harmless (to others) stupor. In that stupor he would remain until Hvitis came by to collect him and take him home. Thorvald's subsidized binges were the best insurance Hvitis and all Streaneshalch had to guarantee that the former warrior would keep his sword sheathed and his spiked pegleg to himself. Though Thorvald took the money and drank the beer, he detested the whole process. He knew he was useless as a Viking, but he hated to be reminded that he was equally useless in every other capacity except that of sometime bodyguard and full-time drunk.

Perhaps it was this entrenched sense of self-loathing that inspired him to rebellion on that fateful day. Taking himself to the Severed Arms, he slammed his payment down and demanded a take-away order of the most potent spirits so much coin might buy. The master of the house made no demur (he was in fact overjoyed to hear the big man say "take-*away*"), and soon, carrying a huge stone jug of Mother Gudrun's Fortified Mead and Wolf Repellent, Thorvald was hiking his way up the perilous steps that led from the town of Streaneshalch to the abbey ruins on the cliff above.

There, amid tumbled stone and charred wood, Thorvald settled himself down with his drink and his memories. The Great Army had done rather a thorough job of turning a once-thriving religious settlement into a wildlife refuge. Where formerly a community of monks had worked and prayed side-by-side with an equally devout group of nuns, in separate yet neighboring establishments, now weeds sprouted, badgers burrowed, and voles cavorted with immunity (except from the badgers).

"Good times," Thorvald said with a sigh as he regarded the well-remembered spot where he had personally reduced an altar and all its non-marketable furnishings to shards, splinters, and ash. He cast a fond eye over the site of indiscriminate slaughter and guzzled the last of the jug that was his only companion. "Good times." With that, he toppled over into a sodden slumber.

He awoke with his head submerged in a bucket of sea-water and to the sensation of someone doggedly kicking him in the ribs. He thrust himself clear of the brine and, with a mighty roar, drew his sword, ready and eager to give his assailant a first (and last) lesson in manners.

"Put that down," said the little woman before him. "Now."

Thorvald froze. The fingers he'd had wrapped around the hilt of his sword went numb, releasing their grip as if struck by lightning. It was night, and a full moon cast cold shadows through the abbey ruins. Part moonlight and part moonshadow, a woman half his height stared at him severely, the abandoned bucket of sea-water at her feet.

"Sit down," she said. "I need to talk to you."

Thorvald sat. He didn't want to, but he did it anyway. Resistance was more than futile: It hurt. Any independent action he attempted to take that could not be classified as obedience to that strange little woman's direct orders was as painful as sticking his head in a beehive. Thorvald knew this as fact, not simile, having stuck his head in a beehive several times as a young man after his friends convinced him that certain breeds of bee made honey while others cut out the middleman entirely and made mead.

"That's fine," said the woman. She seated herself on a fallen block of stone and folded her arms. "I am Hilda, abbess of Streaneshalch. It was a very nice abbey until you broke it. Well? What do you intend to do about that, young man?"

Thorvald was speechless. He rubbed his eyes, unwilling to trust their evidence, for the longer he gazed upon the irascible woman before him, the more insubstantial she became. He could see right through her body, a vision so clear that he could even make out the mottled markings on the stone where she perched. His old grandsire's tales of ghosts came back to him in a rush until finally he found tongue enough to say, "Oh. You're dead."

"So are you, soon enough, so don't put on airs just because you're still breathing them. All flesh is grass, though in your case I'd call it cabbage." She thrust her hands deep into the sleeves of her habit and glared at him.

Thorvald was not what most people would call a quick study, but on occasion his neglected higher processes came through, such as when it was time to divide plunder or show a perfidious swordsmith that he'd tried to pass off substandard work on the wrong Viking. He had heard conflicting reports as to the powers of ghosts. Some said that they were incapable of physically affecting the living, beyond rendering certain pieces of real estate unsalable to high-strung potential buyers. Some said that, on the contrary, ghosts could not only achieve physical contact with the living, but contact of the sort that caused bruises, bleeding, and more permanent damage. Perhaps it was their little way of meeting recruitment goals.

On the evidence of his brine-soaked head and bruised ribs, Thorvald determined that this spectre was of the latter type and determined to treat her accordingly.

"What do you want me to do so you won't hurt me any more?"

The abbess harrumphed. "You're a blunt thing. Perhaps that's all to the good. Hark, barbarian! Before I can say fully what I require of you, I'd best inform your ignorance, may God give me the strength to do so. Some two hundred years ago, this abbey was the site of the Synod of Streaneshalch at which it was determined that the Church of Angle-land would leave the Celtic rites and submit wholeheartedly to the rulings of Rome. It was my honor to both host and attend this Synod, and to hear the compelling arguments of— Stay *awake* when I'm talking to you, you toad!"

She followed up her admonition with a solid thwack to Thorvald's nodding head, a feat all the more miraculous not only for the strength and heft of her phantom hand but for the fact that she was seated well out of arm's-reach. He snapped to attention.

"Sorry, sorry," he muttered. Then, slyly: "Maybe the reason I'm having such trouble harking and all that is 'coz I'm no Christian. There's a still a few of 'em left, down in the town. Why don't I go fetch old man Aethelbert for you? Drunk or sober, I bet he'd hark better'n me."

Hilda's ghost said nothing. Her expression said all.

"Well, it was only a suggestion. No need to get your beads in a bunch," said Thorvald (who actually did know something of the practices of Christians from drinking with old man Aethelbert). "Talk about putting on airs, what kind of a *real* Christian hits a poor crippled man when he's helpless, eh?" He waved his pegleg at her.

Hilda curled her lip in distaste at Thorvald's dubiously adorned extremity. "I apologize," she said in a tone whose sincerity left much room for skeptical debate.

"That's not the way it goes," Thorvald countered, sly again. "I know; I heard. You're not supposed to hit a fellow in the face unless you let him hit you in the face, too!"

"Your grasp of the dram is firmer than your grasp of the doctrine," Hilda replied coolly. "What we are taught is that if anyone strikes a *Christian* on the cheek, he should offer up his other cheek as well. Hitting *others* is perfectly all right, if done to some worthy purpose."

"Oh." Thorvald was crestfallen. A horrid doubt seized him. Cradling his own recently-injured cheek, he asked, "Here, this doesn't mean you've made me a Christian, does it? Without my leave?" He eyed the water-bucket askance. If he knew about rosary beads he certainly knew about baptism as well.

"You should be so lucky," said Hilda. "Very few men receive the Faith at the hands of a saint, you know. Not in these times."

"You're a saint?" He'd heard about those, too. In fact, he rather enjoyed hearing about them, especially the ones with *Martyr* after their names. Thorvald never fell asleep during *those* stories. "How'd they kill you, all at once or by bits?" He hugged himself in gleeful anticipation.

Abbess Hilda rolled her ghostly eyes. "I misspoke: I dwell where all Knowledge dwells, and so I often jump the gun—There, I've done it again. What I meant to say is that I will be *made* a saint a scant four hundred years from now. However, I feel that is no excuse to slack off in the meantime. Of what profit is my sainthood if the very spot whence I took my first Heavenward step has tumbled back into the mire of ungodliness? I can not rest idle in eternal bliss, knowing that my beloved Streaneshalch is—*Asleep* again? That does it!"

This time Thorvald's wake-up call took the form of the empty Wolf Repellent jug. He gasped, groaned, spit out one of his seven remaining teeth, and swore he'd only closed his eyes the better to concentrate. For a miracle—perhaps one of Hilda's own—he went on to prove that he had been paying attention by saying: "So the reason you're in a snit is the Christian shortage hereabouts? Well, what did you expect? When Hvitis and me came through here with the Great Army, it rather took its toll, and those folks what were left afterwards—them as didn't lose their lands or just run for their lives on the spur of the moment—didn't really see the point of keeping up with religion and all that. Some said that if Christianity'd been doing its job, then how'd us Danes take everything in a walkover?"

"O weak of spirit!" Hilda said bitterly.

"Nah, just simple folk who saw which way the wind blew. That, and they didn't much care for what happened after, how the odd leftover monk'd come knocking at their doors. always at suppertime, begging for money to rebuild. Bother a man while he's eating and then can't even take the trouble to pronounce his name right, I ask you!"

"Never mind," said Hilda. "I'm sure you'll do a much better job of it."

"What? Me? Now just a—!"

"Oh, stop whinging," the abbess commanded, and Thorvald was cut off in mid-whinge. "It's not as though I'm asking you to *be* a Christian. I just want you to use your considerable strength of . . . *persuasion* to remind the good people of Streaneshalch of their true religious heritage."

"Hunh!" Thorvald snorted. "And what'll it take to convince you I've done my job? Would you be happy if I got, say this many folks up here to tell you they're Christians again?" He held up the fingers of both hands. "Or this many?" He flashed the hands twice, then a third time to show willing. "Or is it going to take my getting your whole bloody abbey rebuilt? Because if that's it, I can save us both the time by jumping off the cliffs right now: It's not going to happen."

"You will do no such thing!" Hilda informed him. "To take your own life is a grievous sin."

"To die in bed's the greatest sin I can think of," said Thorvald. "But that's all I've got to look forward to."

Now it was Hilda's turn to look sly. "Thorvald, dear," she wheedled. "What would you say if I promised to restore your lost leg?"

"I'd say you were full of shit," the former Viking replied in a matter-of-fact manner. He got another thwack for that, but thought it was worth it.

"Listen to me, you jackass: I'm a saint, or will be. I've already performed miracles. I saved the region's entire crop by banishing flocks of ravenous birds that would have despoiled the harvest."

"No miracle, bird-scaring; not with *that* face," Thorvald muttered. "Ow," he added, as he learned about the keenness of saints' ears.

"Another time—" Hilda spoke on through clenched teeth.

"Another time our land was bedeviled by a plague of serpents, but by the grace of God I was able to cast them all into the sea where they turned to stone. You can still see their bodies on the strand, if you don't believe me."

"I can see a lot of things," said Thorvald. "That doesn't mean *you* put 'em there. But I'll tell you what, give me back my leg and I'll give you anything you ask for: A pile of bodies, a pile of Christians, a pile of stones built up into a new abbey, anything. This wooden leg's the only thing that's holding me back from a man's *real* work. All I want is the chance to go back on viking and die as a man should die, one sword in my hand and another in my skull, because that's what it'll take to do the job!"

Abbess Hilda heard him out, understood that he was serious, and turned her gaze upward. "O Lord, You granted a vision of your Glory to the ignorant shepherd Caedmon while he slept, and he awoke to share that gift of holy poetry with Thy servants. Indeed, because it was Thy will that he at last seek the shelter of this very abbey under my rule, I somehow came to believe that it was possible to turn any sleeping man into a vessel for Thy service. Forgive a foolish woman for her misapprehension, and for ever having dared to hope that our earthly trials end at the grave. Seriously, *You* try talking some sense into this one; I give up."

To Thorvald she said: "If *you* are typical of the sort of person who'll be settling down in Angle-land, I am tempted to give you back your leg here and now, unconditionally, if only to get rid of you before it's too late. Go find some corner of a foreign field to wreak your uninvited havoc. If you really cared about fighting as much as you claim you do, a little thing like a chopped-off leg wouldn't hold you back. But no: Moaning and groaning about how keen you are to be off to the slaughter if only you could, wah, wah, wah! You sound just like a general. Well, whose lead did you follow to these shores, eh? Ivar the Boneless! Poor man couldn't stand on his own two feet, but did that stop him? Did that even slow him down? No! It was hoi-hoop-hopla, *up* onto a shield and off he went, carried into the thick of battle! Not that I am endorsing warfare *per se*, but one does have to admire the fellow's spunk.

"You know, all I was going to ask you for, in exchange for your leg, was one last Christmas service here, at the old abbey, or what's left of it. Oh, how I did love Christmas! It gave one such a sense of *hope* for seeing the end of winter's icy grip on the land and on the spirit. We'd sing, and our cooks would make a special dish or two to honor the birth of Our Lord, and the halls would be fragrant with the scent of evergreens. Sometimes one of the older sisters would bring in bunches of holly and ivy and mistletoe, with such a dear, mysterious smile on her lips that we quite believed she was guarding some precious secret. And what harm did it do to let the poor old thing have her way?"

Here Hilda sighed. "Christmas. Even after I was dead, I'd lean down from the very gates of Heaven to catch a thread of song or a whiff of smoke from the great log burning on the abbey hearth. If I could only have some hint of that sweet holy day celebrated here again, I'd give you *two* new legs. No, why stop there? I'd turn you into a centipede! But I'd best face facts: I'd have better luck preaching to that lump of stone under your rump than to that lump of stone atop your neck. Go." She waved a watery hand weakly. "Go back to your guzzling and your groaning and your give-up-and-die attitude. But go quickly. Here."

And with another wave of her hand, Thorvald's artificial leg vanished like a blown candle flame, instantly replaced by a limb of flesh and blood and good, strong sinew. His specially cut breeches didn't shield it from the cold, nor had the saint-to-be provided him with a new shoe, but Thorvald didn't care. He goggled at the miracle, let out a whoop, seized Hilda by the shoulders and whisked the ghost around the ruins in a dance of joy that lasted until he stubbed his restored toes against a slab of broken abbey.

When he was done cursing, he caught his breath and asked, "Why'd you do that for me? I never yet gave my word to do anything for you."

"Perhaps I wanted you to see that there can be more to Christianity than target practice," Hilda replied. "Or call it an early Christmas present." She shook her head sadly. "To think I sat here, bargaining like a fishmonger for my Faith. It's a good thing that I'm centuries away from full sainthood; I've still got a lot to learn. Now go,

Thorvald, and if anyone asks you where you got that brand new leg, just give them a thump in the head for being nosey. I'd really rather you kept my name out of it, if at all possible. God be with you and good night."

With that, the abbess' ghost was gone.

The *Anglo-Saxon Chronicle* (Morning Edition) notes the year of Abbess Hilda's passing, likewise the incursions of the Danes, but an event of equal magnitude was not deemed noteworthy by that venerable record. That a one-legged man might return to his friends—all right, to his *friend*—restored in body was a miracle overlooked. It happens. The world is full of wonders, some of which are bound to slip between the cracks.

However, that this selfsame man—once feared, once contented to give his fellow men the reciprocal wide berth they preferred to give him—should suddenly take to seeking out his Saxon countrymen, tirelessly urging them to return to the Faith of their fathers, was considered by all to be a local phenomenon. If that were not enough, at the same time he was doing all within his power to encourage his Danish shield-brethren to give this Christianity thing a bit of a chance, no, really, it's not half so bad once you get used to it. This was accounted a prodigy.

The crowning marvel was, in the words of Hvitis the Eloquent, this: "It's not just that Thorvald's grown himself a fresh leg. His mother mated with a troll, so who knows? She might've had some on the side with a starfish. Never question a lady. And it's not just that he's preaching Christianity everywhere that new leg takes him. No, what's really making everyone take notice is the fact that he's actually able to talk it up *sensibly*, which means that when old man Aethelbert swore he was giving our Thorvald *lessons* about the old religion, it wasn't just the drink talking. Which means Thorvald's actually been able to *retain* something in that half-troll skull of his besides six teeth, meat and mead. I don't know about you, but any god that can make Thorvald learn someting beyond sword-goes-in-here has got my vote! Besides, he said he'd thump me in the head if I didn't convert in time for Christmas."

And that was how, on a crisp December night, a procession of the newly made or lately restored Faithful trooped up the cliffside steps in the wake of their priest. He was a young man named Leofwine, and he had almost as much difficulty believing his luck at having secured a parish of his own so soon as he did the local bishop's letter, for it claimed the spiritual recapture of an entire town in the space of less than a month. Least credible of all—and growing steadily more mind-boggling with every glance that Father Leofwine cast at the man in question—was the purported source of this pious reawakening. Father Leofwine had baptized him with his own hands, and still he could not believe that such a person had joined the Church at less than sword's-point.

Come to think of it, such a person would probably have bitten off said sword's point if it tried prodding him in any direction he did not personally wish to go.

Ah well, Father Leofwine was never one to look a gift parish in the mouth, even when that mouth was buried in the snowy beard of Thorvald the Bloody-Minded.

Once the crowd reached the abbey ruins, Father Leofwine might still have been the priest, but it was Thorvald who was the boss. He directed the disposal and ignition of a huge log in one of the least rubbish-heaped hearths of the old abbey. He chivvied the women along as they set out a few special dishes on the scattered stones. He urged the children on in their strewing of holly and ivy, evergreen boughs and mistletoe. Last but not least, he got a good old sing-song going among those young people with the strongest voices. It was a drinking song, but it made mention of a monk who owned a very large set of rosary beads, so he thought it would do.

And then, before the priest could begin the holy service, Thorvald called for silence and you can bet he got it. In that sweet hush, while the people awaited the commemoration of a centuries'-old miracle, the former Viking lifted his face to the stars and called out:

"Thanks for the leg, old girl! I reckoned since it came from you, it was Christian already, so I had the rest of me brought along to keep it company. And the rest of *this* is my Christmas gift to you." He spread his arms wide, embracing the massed worshippers and all the improvised trappings of the holiday. "What d'you think of that?"

The people gasped to hear a female voice descend with the starlight from on high, a voice as sturdy and stubborn as Thorvald's own: "*I* think—" it said. "*I* think it's a very lovely present, Thorvald. I haven't gotten anything else like it. I also think that you're up to your old tricks, pillaging and plundering all the credit for what's happening here. And so, because these good folk have given me something so precious, I now will give unto them a gift of equal worth. May they forever cherish and appreciate it, for it is foreknowledge of a miracle to come, a marvel whose telling will rival that of how I turned the snakes to stones. Behold!"

And all eyes sought the heavens as the stars themselves spelled out the name STREANESHALCH, only to have those glittering letters crumble, melt, and re-form themselves into the simpler, shorter blazon: WHITBY.

"Well, that's a miracle *and* a mercy," Father Leofwine remarked. "At least it'll be easier to spell."

"What's 'spell'?" asked every other happily illiterate Streaneshalchian present.

And Thorvald the Bloody-Minded was busy for the rest of the night, thumping unquestioning gratitude into them all, a fine tradition that was soon adopted by many a father whose thankless children refused to show proper enthusiasm over the Yuletide gift of socks and smallclothes.

For to quote the wisdom of Whitby's unsung son and uncanonized saint, that sterling proponent of extremely muscular Christianity: "Merry Christmas. Or else."

It sounds better in Danish.

INTRODUCTION

JULIAN:
A CHRISTMAS STORY

WARTIME puts a strain between what one wishes to do and what one *has* to do—or, sometimes, what one must refuse to do. At Christmastime, the strain becomes even more unavoidable, even if the war is seemingly far away. And friendship, one of the greatest gifts, becomes more important than ever.

♣ ♣ ♣

BORN IN 1953, ROBERT CHARLES WILSON has been a full-time professional writer since 1986. He has published 14 novels, numerous short stories, and several non-fiction pieces and book reviews. His novel, *Spin*, won the Hugo Award for best novel, and the story you are about to read was also a Hugo nominee. He is a three-time winner of the Aurora Award for Canadian imaginative fiction for his novels *Darwinia* and *Blind Lake*, and his short story, "The Perseids," and also won the John W. Campbell Memorial Award for his novel, *The Chronoliths*, the Philip K. Dick Award for his novel, *Mysterium*, and the Theodore Sturgeon Memorial Award for his short story, "The Cartesian Theater." His novels and stories have been published in French, Spanish, German, Italian, Hungarian, and other foreign editions, and his work in translation has received the Geffen Award (Israel), the Kurd Lasswitz Prize (Germany), the Grand Prix de l'Imaginaire (France), the Seiun Award (Japan), and the Czech Academy of Science Fiction, Fantasy and Horror Award. He lives in Concord, Ontario, with his wife Sharry, a professional proofreader.

JULIAN:
A CHRISTMAS STORY

by Robert Charles Wilson

❧ 1 ❧

THIS IS A STORY ABOUT JULIAN COMSTOCK, better known
as Julian the Agnostic or (after his uncle) Julian Conqueror. But it
is not about his conquests, such as they were, or his betrayals, or
about the War in Labrador, or Julian's quarrels with the Church of
the Dominion. I witnessed many of those events—and will no
doubt write about them, ultimately—but this narrative concerns
Julian when he was young, and I was young, and neither of us was
famous.

2

IN LATE OCTOBER OF 2172—an election year—Julian and I, along with his mentor Sam Godwin, rode to the Tip east of the town of Williams Ford, where I came to possess a book, and Julian tutored me in one of his heresies.

It was a brisk, sunny day. There was a certain resolute promptness to the seasons in that part of Athabaska, in those days. Our summers were long, languid, and hot. Spring and fall were brief, mere custodial functions between the extremes of weather. Winters were short but biting. Snow set in around the end of December, and the River Pine generally thawed by late March.

Today might be the best we would get of autumn. It was a day we should have spent under Sam Godwin's tutelage, perhaps sparring, or target-shooting, or reading chapters from the Dominion History of the Union. But Sam was not a heartless overseer, and the kindness of the weather had suggested the possibility of an Outing, and so we had gone to the stables, where my father worked, and drawn horses, and ridden out of the Estate with lunches of black bread and salt ham in our back-satchels.

We rode east, away from the hills and the town. Julian and I rode ahead; Sam rode behind, a watchful presence, his Pittsburgh rifle ready in the saddle holster at his side. There was no immediate threat of trouble, but Sam Godwin believed in perpetual preparedness; if he had a gospel, it was BE PREPARED; also, SHOOT FIRST; and probably, DAMN THE CONSEQUENCES. Sam, who was old (nearly fifty), wore a dense brown beard stippled with wiry white hairs, and was dressed in what remained presentable of his tan-and-green Army of the Californias uniform, and a cloak to keep the wind off. He was like a father to Julian, Julian's own true father having

217

performed a gallows dance some years before. Lately he had been more vigilant than ever, for reasons he had not discussed, at least with me.

Julian was my age (seventeen), and we were approximately the same height, but there the resemblance ended. Julian had been born an aristo; my family was of the leasing class. His skin was clear and pale where mine was dark and lunar. (I was marked by the same Pox that took my sister Flaxie to her grave in '63.) His hair was long and almost femininely clean; mine was black and wiry, cut to stubble by my mother with her sewing scissors, and I washed it once a week or so—more often in summer, when the brook behind the cottage ran clean and cool. His clothes were linen and, in places, silk, brass-buttoned, cut to fit; my shirt and pants were course hempen cloth, sewn to a good approximation but obviously not the work of a New York tailor.

And yet we were friends, and had been friends for three years, since we met by chance in the forested hills west of the Duncan and Crowley Estate, where we had gone to hunt, Julian with his fine Porter & Earle cassette rifle and me with a simple muzzle-loader. We both loved books, especially the boys' books written in those days by an author named Charles Curtis Easton.[1] I had been carrying a copy of Easton's *Against the Brazilians*, illicitly borrowed from the Estate library; Julian had recognized the title, but refrained from ratting on me, since he loved the book as much as I did and longed to discuss it with a fellow enthusiast (of which there were precious few among his aristo relations)—in short, he did me an unbegged favor, and we became fast friends despite our differences.

In those early days I had not known how fond he was of blasphemy. But I had learned since, and it had not deterred me. Much.

We had not set out with the specific aim of visiting the Tip; but at the nearest crossroad Julian turned west, riding past cornfields and gourdfields already harvested and sun-whitened split-rail fences on which dense blackberry gnarls had grown up. The air was cool but the sun was fiercely bright. Julian and Sam wore broad-brimmed hats to protect their faces; I wore a plain linen pakool hat, sweat-stained,

---

[1] Whom I would meet when he was sixty years old, and I was a newcomer to the book trade—but that's another story.

rolled about my ears. Before long we passed the last rude shacks of the indentured laborers, whose near-naked children gawked at us from the roadside, and it became obvious we were going to the Tip, because where else on this road was there to go?—unless we continued east for many hours, all the way to the ruins of the old towns, from the days of the False Tribulation.

The Tip was located far from Williams Ford to prevent poaching and disorder. There was a strict pecking order to the Tip. This is how it worked: professional scavengers hired by the Estate brought their pickings from the ruined places to the Tip, which was a pine-fenced enclosure (a sort of stockade) in a patch of grassland and prairie flowers. There the newly-arrived goods were roughly sorted, and riders were dispatched to the Estate to make the high-born aware of the latest acquisitions, and various aristos (or their trusted servants) would ride out to claim the prime gleanings. The next day, the leasing class would be allowed to sort through what was left; after that, if anything remained, indentured laborers could rummage among it, if they calculated it worthwhile to make the journey.

Every prosperous town had a Tip; though in the east it was sometimes called a Till, a Dump, or an Eebay.

Today we were fortunate: several wagonloads of scrounge had lately arrived, and riders had not yet been sent to notify the Estate. The gate was manned by a Home Guard, who looked at us suspiciously until Sam announced the name of Julian Comstock; then the guard briskly stepped aside, and we went inside the enclosure.

Many of the wagons were still unloading, and a chubby Tipman, eager to show off his bounty, hurried toward us as we dismounted and moored our horses. "Happy coincidence!" he cried. "Gentlemen!" Addressing mostly Sam by this remark, with a cautious smile for Julian and a disdainful sidelong glance at me. "Anything *in particular* you're looking for?"

"Books," Julian said promptly, before Sam or I could answer.

"Books! Ordinarily, I set aside books for the Dominion Conservator . . ."

"The boy is a Comstock," Sam said. "I don't suppose you mean to balk him."

The Tipman reddened. "No, not at all . . . in fact we came across something in our digging . . . a sort of *library in miniature* . . . I'll show you, if you like."

This was intriguing, especially to Julian, who beamed as if he had been invited to a Christmas party. We followed the stout Tipman to a freshly-arrived canvasback wagon, from which a laborer was tossing bundled piles into a stack beside a tent.

These twine-wrapped bales were books . . . old, tattered, and wholly free of the Dominion Stamp of Approval. They must have been more than a century old; for although they were faded they had obviously once been colorful and expensively printed, not made of stiff brown paper like the Charles Curtis Easton books of modern times. They had not even rotted much. Their smell, under the cleansing Athabaska sunlight, was inoffensive.

"Sam!" Julian whispered. He had already drawn his knife and was slicing through the twine.

"Calm down," suggested Sam, who was not an enthusiast like Julian.

"Oh, but—*Sam!* We should have brought a cart!"

"We can't carry away armloads, Julian, nor would we ever have been allowed to. The Dominion scholars will have all this. Though perhaps you can get away with a volume or two."

The Tipman said, "These are from Lundsford." Lundsford was the name of a ruined town thirty or so miles to the southeast. The Tipman leaned toward Sam Godwin, who was his own age, and said: "We thought Lundsford had been mined out a decade ago. But even a dry well may freshen. One of my workers spotted a low place off the main excavations—a sort of *sink-hole*: the recent rain had cut it through. Once a basement or warehouse of some kind. Oh, sir, we found good china there, and glasswork, and many more books than this . . . most were mildewed, but some had been protected under a kind of stiff oilcloth, and were lodged beneath a partially-collapsed ceiling . . . there had been a fire, but they survived it . . "

"Good work, Tipman," Sam Godwin said.

"Thank you, sir! Perhaps you could remember me to the great men of the Estate?" And he gave his name (which I have forgotten).

Julian had fallen to his knees amidst the compacted clay and rubble of the Tip, lifting up each book in turn and examining it with wide eyes. I joined him in his exploration.

I had never much liked the Tip. It had always seemed to me a haunted place. And of course it *was* haunted: that was its purpose, to house the revenants of the past, ghosts of the False Tribulation startled out of their century-long slumber. Here was evidence of the best and worst of the people who had inhabited the Years of Vice and Profligacy. Their fine things were very fine, their glassware especially, and it was a straitened aristo indeed who did not possess antique table-settings rescued from some ruin or other. Sometimes one might find silver utensils in boxes, or useful tools, or coins. The coins were too plentiful to be worth much, individually, but they could be worked into buttons or other adornments. One of the high-born back at the Estate owned a saddle studded with copper pennies all from the year 2032. (I had occasionally been enlisted to polish it.)

But here also was the trash and inexplicable detritus: "plastic," gone brittle with sunlight or soft with the juices of the earth; bits of metal blooming with rust; electronic devices blackened by time and imbued with the sad inutility of a tensionless spring; engine parts, corroded; copper wire rotten with verdigris; aluminum cans and steel barrels eaten through by the poisonous fluids they had once contained—and so on, almost *ad infinitum*.

Here, too, were the in-between things, the curiosities, the ugly or pretty baubles, as intriguing and as useless as seashells. ("Put down that rusty trumpet, Adam, you'll cut your lip and poison your blood!"—my mother, when we had gone to the Tip many years before I met Julian. There had been no music in the trumpet anyway; its bell was bent and corroded through.)

More than that, though, there was the uneasy knowledge that these things, fine or corrupt, had survived their makers—had proved more imperishable than flesh or spirit (for the souls of the secular ancients were almost certainly not first in line for the Resurrection).

And yet, these books . . . they tempted; they proclaimed their seductions boldly. Some were decorated with impossibly beautiful women in various degrees of undress. I had already sacrificed my personal claim to virtue with certain young women at the Estate, whom I had recklessly kissed; at the age of seventeen I considered myself a jade, or something like one; but these images were so frank and impudent they made me blush and look away.

Julian simply ignored them, as he had always been invulnerable to the charms of women. He preferred the larger and more densely-written material—he had already set aside a textbook of BIOLOGY, spotted and discolored but largely intact. He found another volume almost as large, and handed it to me, saying, "Here, Adam, try this— you might find it enlightening."

I inspected it skeptically. The book was called A HISTORY OF MANKIND IN SPACE.

"The moon again," I said.

"Read it for yourself."

"Tissue of lies, I'm sure."

"With photographs."

"Photographs prove nothing. Those people could do anything with photographs."

"Well, read it anyway," Julian said.

In truth the idea excited me. We had had this argument many times, Julian and I, especially on autumn nights when the moon hung low and ponderous on the horizon. *People have walked there*, he would say. The first time he made this claim I laughed; the second time I said, "Yes, certainly: I once climbed there myself, on a greased rainbow—" But he had been serious.

Oh, I had heard these stories before. Who hadn't? Men on the moon. What surprised me was that someone as well-educated as Julian would believe them.

"Just take the book," he insisted.

"What: to keep?"

"Certainly to keep."

"Believe I will," I muttered, and I stuck the object in my back-satchel and felt both proud and guilty. What would my father say, if he knew I was reading literature without a Dominion stamp? What would my mother make of it? (Of course I would not tell them.)

At this point I backed off, and found a grassy patch a little away from the rubble, where I could sit and eat some of the lunch I had packed, and watch Julian, who continued to sort through the detritus with a kind of scholarly intensity. Sam Godwin came and joined me, brushing a spot on an old timber so he could recline without soiling his uniform, such as it was.

"He sure loves those old books," I said, making conversation.

Sam was often taciturn—the very picture of an old veteran—but he nodded and spoke familiarly: "He's learned to love them. I helped teach him. I wonder if that was wise. Maybe he loves them too much. It might be they'll kill him, one of these days."

"How, Sam? By the apostasy of them?"

"Julian's too smart for his own good. He debates with the Dominion clergy. Just last week I found him arguing with Ben Kreel[2] about God, history, and such abstractions. Which is precisely what he must *not* do, if he wants to survive the next few years."

"Why, what threatens him?"

"The jealousy of the powerful," Sam said, but he would say no more on the subject, only sat and stroked his graying beard, and glanced occasionally, and uneasily, to the east.

The day went on, and eventually Julian had to drag himself from his nest of books with only a pair of prizes: the INTRODUCTION TO BIOLOGY and another volume called GEOGRAPHY OF NORTH AMERICA. Time to go, Sam insisted; better to be back at the Estate by supper; in any case, riders had been sent ahead, and the official pickers and Dominion curators would soon be here to cull what we had left.

But I have said that Julian tutored me in one of his apostasies. Here is how it happened. We stopped, at the drowsy end of the afternoon, at the height of a ridge overlooking the town of Williams Ford, the grand Estate upstream of it, and the River Pine as it cutthrough the valley on its way from the mountains of the West. From this vantage we could see the steeple of the Dominion Hall, and the revolving wheels of the grist mill and the lumber mill, and so on,

---

[2] Our local representative of the Council of the Dominion; in effect, the Mayor of the town.

blue in the long light and hazy with woodsmoke, colored here and there with what remained of the autumn foliage. Far to the south a railway bridge crossed the gorge of the Pine like a suspended thread. *Go inside*, the weather seemed to proclaim; *it's fair but it won't be fair for long; bolt the window, stoke the fire, boil the apples; winter's due.* We rested our horses on the windy hilltop, and Julian found a blackberry bramble where the berries were still plump and dark, and we plucked some of these and ate them.

This was the world I had been born into. It was an autumn like every autumn I could remember. But I could not help thinking of the Tip and its ghosts. Maybe those people, the people who had lived through the Efflorescence of Oil and the False Tribulation, had felt about their homes and neighborhoods as I felt about Williams Ford. They were ghosts to me, but they must have seemed real enough to themselves—must have *been* real; had not realized they were ghosts; and did that I mean I was also a ghost, a revenant to haunt some future generation?

Julian saw my expression and asked me what was the matter. I told him my thoughts.

"Now you're thinking like a philosopher," he said, grinning.

"No wonder they're such a miserable brigade, then."

"Unfair, Adam—you've never seen a philosopher in your life." Julian believed in Philosophers and claimed to have met one or two.

"Well, I *imagine* they're miserable, if they go around thinking of themselves as ghosts and such."

"It's the condition of all things," Julian said. "This blackberry, for example." He plucked one and held it in the pale palm of his hand. "Has it always looked like this?"

"Obviously not," I said, impatiently.

"Once it was a tiny green bud of a thing, and before that it was part of the substance of the bramble, which before that was a seed inside a blackberry—"

"And round and round for all eternity."

"But no, Adam, that's the point. The bramble, and that tree over there, and the gourds in the field, and the crow circling over them—they're all descended from ancestors that didn't quite resemble them.

A blackberry or a crow is a *form*, and forms change over time, the way clouds change shape as they travel across the sky."

"Forms of what?"

"Of DNA," Julian said earnestly. (The BIOLOGY he had picked out of the Tip was not the first BIOLOGY he had read.)

"Julian," Sam warned, "I once promised this boy's parents you wouldn't corrupt him."

I said, "I've heard of DNA. It's the life force of the secular ancients. And it's a myth."

"Like men walking on the moon?"

"Exactly."

"And who's your authority on this? Ben Kreel? The *Dominion History of the Union*?"

"Nothing is changeless except DNA? That's a peculiar argument even from you, Julian."

"It would be, if I were making it. But DNA *isn't* changeless. It struggles to remember itself, but it never remembers itself perfectly. Remembering a fish, it imagines a lizard. Remembering a horse, it imagines a hippopotamus. Remembering an ape, it imagines a man."

"Julian!" Sam was insistent now. "That's *quite* enough."

"You sound like a Darwinist," I said.

"Yes," Julian admitted, smiling in spite of his unorthodoxy, the autumn sun turning his face the color of penny copper. "I suppose I do."

That night, I lay in bed until I was reasonably certain both my parents were asleep. Then I rose, lit a lamp, and took the new (or rather, very old) HISTORY OF MANKIND IN SPACE from where I had hidden it behind my oaken dresser.

I leafed through the brittle pages. I didn't read the book. I *would* read it, but tonight I was too weary to pay close attention, and in any case I wanted to savor the words (lies and fictions though they might be), not rush through them. Tonight I wanted only to sample the book; in other words, to look at the pictures.

There were dozens of photographs, and each one captured my attention with fresh marvels and implausibilities. One of them showed—or purported to show—men standing on the surface of the moon, just as Julian had described.

The men in the picture were evidently Americans. They wore flags stitched to the shoulders of their moon clothing, an archaic version of our own flag, with something less than the customary sixty stars. Their clothing was white and ridiculously bulky, like the winter clothes of the Inuit, and they wore helmets with golden visors that disguised their faces. I supposed it must be very cold on the moon, if explorers required such cumbersome protection. They must have arrived in winter. However, there was no ice or snow in the neighborhood. The moon seemed to be little more than a desert, dry as a stick and dusty as a Tipman's wardrobe.

I cannot say how long I stared at this picture, puzzling over it. It might have been an hour or more. Nor can I accurately describe how it made me feel . . . larger than myself, but lonely, as if I had grown as tall as the stars and lost sight of everything familiar. By the time I closed the book the moon had risen outside my window—the *real* moon, I mean; a harvest moon, fat and orange, half-hidden behind drifting, evolving clouds.

I found myself wondering whether it was truly possible that men had visited that celestial body. Whether, as the pictures implied, they had ridden there on rockets, rockets a thousand times larger than the familiar Independence Day fireworks. But if men had visited the moon, why hadn't they stayed there? Was it so inhospitable a place that no one wished to remain?

Or perhaps they *had* stayed, and were living there still. If the moon was such a cold place, I reasoned, people residing on its surface would be forced to build fires to keep warm. There seemed to be no wood on the moon, judging by the photographs, so they must have resorted to coal or peat. I went to the window and examined the moon minutely for any sign of campfires, pit mining, or other lunar industry. But I could see none. It was only the moon, mottled and changeless. I blushed at my own gullibility, replaced the book in its hiding place, chased these heresies from my mind with a prayer (or a hasty facsimile of one), and eventually fell asleep.

❧ 3 ❧

IT FALLS TO ME TO EXPLAIN something of Williams Ford, and my family's place in it—and Julian's—before I describe the threat Sam Godwin feared, which materialized in our village not long before Christmas.[3]

Situated at the head of the valley was the font of our prosperity, the Duncan and Crowley Estate. It was a country estate (obviously, since we were in Athabaska, far from the eastern seats of power), owned by two influential New York mercantile families, who maintained their villa not only as a source of income but as a kind of resort, safely distant (several days' journey by train) from the intrigues and pestilences of city life. It was inhabited—ruled, I might say—not only by the Duncan and Crowley patriarchs but by a whole legion of cousins, nephews, relations by marriage, high-born friends, and distinguished guests in search of clean air and rural views. Our corner of Athabaska was blessed with a benign climate and pleasant scenery, according to the season, and these things attract idle aristos the way strong butter attracts flies.

It remains unrecorded whether the town existed before the Estate or vice versa; but certainly the town depended on the Estate for its prosperity. In Williams Ford there were essentially three classes: the Owners, or aristos; below them the leasing class, who worked as smiths, carpenters, coopers, overseers, gardeners, beekeepers, etc., and whose leases were repaid in service; and finally the indentured laborers, who worked as field hands, inhabited rude shacks along the west bank of the Pine, and received no compensation beyond bad food and worse lodging.

---

[3] I beg the reader's patience if I detail matters that seem well-known. I indulge the possibility of a foreign audience, or a posterity to whom our present arrangements are not self-evident

My family occupied an ambivalent place in this hierarchy. My mother was a seamstress. She worked at the Estate as had her parents before her. My father, however, had arrived in Williams Ford as a transient, and his marriage to my mother had been controversial. He had "married a lease," as the saying has it, and had been taken on as a stable hand at the Estate in lieu of a dowry. The law allowed such unions, but popular opinion frowned on it. We had few friends of our own class, my mother's blood relations had since died (perhaps of embarrassment), and as a child I was often mocked and derided for my father's low origins.

On top of that was the issue of our religion. We were—because my father was—Church of Signs. In those days, every Christian church in America was required to have the formal approval of the Board of Registrars of the Dominion of Jesus Christ on Earth. (In popular parlance, "The Church of the Dominion," but this was a misnomer, since every church is a Dominion Church if it is recognized by the Board. Dominion Episcopal, Dominion Presbyterian, Dominion Baptist—even the Catholic Church of America since it renounced its fealty to the Roman Pope in 2112—all are included under the Dominionist umbrella, since the purpose of the Dominion is not to *be* a church but to *certify* churches. In America we are entitled by the Constitution to worship at any church we please, as long as it is a genuine Christian congregation and not some fraudulent or satanistic sect. The Board exists to make that distinction. Also to collect fees and tithes to further its important work.)

We were, as I said, Church of Signs, which was a marginal denomination, shunned by the leasing class, recognized but not fully endorsed by the Dominion, and popular mostly with illiterate indentured workers, among whom my father had been raised. Our faith took for its master text that passage in Mark which proclaims, "In my Name they will cast out devils, and speak in new tongues; they will handle serpents, and if they drink poison they will not be sickened by it." We were snake-handlers, in other words, and famous beyond our modest numbers for it. Our congregation consisted of adozen farmhands, mostly transients lately arrived from the southern states. My father was its deacon (though we did not use that name), and we kept snakes, for ritual purposes, in wire cages on our back acre, next to the outbuilding. This practice contributed very little to our social standing.

That had been the situation of our family when Julian Comstock arrived as a guest of the Duncan and Crowley families, along with his mentor Sam Godwin, and when Julian and I met by coincidence while hunting.

At that time I had been apprenticed to my father, who had risen to the rank of an overseer at the Estate's lavish and extensive stables. My father loved animals, especially horses. Unfortunately I was not made in the same mold, and my relations with the stable's equine inhabitants rarely extended beyond a brisk mutual tolerance. I did not love my job—which consisted largely of sweeping straw, shoveling ordure, and doing in general those chores the older stablehands felt to be beneath their dignity—so I was pleased when it became customary for a household amanuensis (or even Sam Godwin in person) to arrive and summon me away from my work at Julian's request. (Since the request emanated from a Comstock it couldn't be overruled, no matter how fiercely the grooms and saddlers gnashed their teeth to see me escape their autocracy.)

At first we met to read and discuss books, or hunt together; later, Sam Godwin invited me to audit Julian's lessons, for he had been charged with Julian's education as well as his general welfare. (I had been taught the rudiments of reading and writing at the Dominion school, and refined these skills under the tutelage of my mother, who believed in the power of literacy as an improving force. My father could neither read nor write.) And it was not more than a year after our first acquaintance that Sam presented himself one evening at my parents' cottage with an extraordinary proposal.

"Mr. and Mrs. Hazzard," Sam had said, putting his hand up to touch his cap (which he had removed when he entered the cottage, so that the gesture looked like a salute), "you know of course about the friendship between your son and Julian Comstock."

"Yes," my mother said. "And worry over it often enough—matters at the Estate being what they are."

My mother was a small woman, plump, but forceful, with ideas of her own. My father, who spoke seldom, on this occasion spoke not at all, only sat in his chair holding a laurel-root pipe, which he did not light.

"Matters at the Estate are exactly the crux of the issue," Sam Godwin said. "I'm not sure how much Adam has told you about our situation there. Julian's father, General Bryce Comstock, who was my friend as well as my commanding officer, shortly before his death charged me with Julian's care and well-being—"

"Before his death," my mother pointed out, "at the gallows, for treason."

Sam winced. "True, Mrs. Hazzard, I can't deny it, but I assert my belief that the trial was rigged and the verdict indefensible. Defensible or not, however, it doesn't alter my obligation as far as the son is concerned. I promised to care for the boy, Mrs. Hazzard, and I mean to keep my promise."

"A Christian sentiment." Her skepticism was not entirely disguised.

"As for your implication about the Estate, and the practices of the young heirs and heiresses there, I couldn't agree more. Which is why I approved and encouraged Julian's friendship with your son. Apart from Adam, Julian has no true friends. The Estate is such a den of venomous snakes—no offense," he added, remembering our religious affiliation, and making the common but mistaken assumption that congregants of the Church of Signs necessarily *like* snakes, or feel some kinship with them—"no offense, but I would sooner allow Julian to associate with, uh, scorpions," striking for a more palatable simile, "than abandon him to the sneers, machinations, ruses, and ruinous habits of his peers. That makes me not only his teacher but his constant companion. But I'm almost three times his age, Mrs. Hazzard, and he needs a reliable friend more nearly of his own growth."

"What do you propose, exactly, Mr. Godwin?"

"What I propose is that I take on Adam as a second student, full-time, and to the ultimate benefit of both boys."

Sam was usually a man of few words—even as a teacher—and he

seemed as exhausted by this oration as if he had lifted some great weight.

"As a student, but a student of *what,* Mr. Godwin?"

"Mechanics. History. Grammar and composition. Martial skills—"

"Adam already knows how to fire a rifle."

"Pistolwork, sabrework, fist-fighting—but that's only a fraction of it," Sam added hastily. "Julian's father asked me to cultivate the boy's mind as well as his reflexes."

My mother had more to say on the subject, chiefly about how my work at the stables helped offset the family's leases, and how difficult it would be to do without those extra vouchers at the Estate store. But Sam had anticipated the point. He had been entrusted by Julian's mother—that is to say, the sister-in-law of the President—with a discretionary fund for Julian's education, which could be tapped to compensate for my absence from the stables. And at a handsome rate. He quoted a number, and the objections from my parents grew considerably less strenuous, and were finally whittled away to nothing. (I observed all this from a room away, through a gap in the door.)

Which is not to say no misgivings remained. Before I set off for the Estate the next day, this time to visit one of the Great Houses rather than the stables, my mother warned me not to tangle myself too tightly with the affairs of the high-born. I promised her I would cling to my Christian virtues. (A hasty promise, less easily kept than I imagined.[4])

"It may not be your morals that are at risk," she said. "The high-born conduct themselves by different standards than we use, Adam. The games they play have mortal stakes. You do know that Julian's father was hung?"

Julian never spoke of it, but it was a matter of public record.

---

[4] Julian's somewhat feminine nature had won him a reputation among the other young aristos as a sodomite. That they could believe this of him without evidence is testimony to the tenor of their thoughts, as a class. But it had occasionally rebounded to my benefit. On more than one occasion, his female acquaintances—sophisticated girls of my own age, or older—made the assumption that I was Julian's intimate companion, in a physical sense. Whereupon they undertook to cure me of my deviant habits, in the most direct fashion. I was happy to cooperate with these "cures," and they were successful, every time.

I repeated Sam's assertion that Bryce Comstock had been innocent.

"He may well have been. That's the point. There has been a Comstock in the Presidency for the past thirty years, and the current Comstock is said to be jealous of his power. The only real threat to the reign of Julian's uncle was the ascendancy of his brother, who made himself dangerously popular in the war with the Brazilians. I suspect Mr. Godwin is correct, that Bryce Comstock was hanged not because he was a *bad* General but because he was a *successful* one."

No doubt such scandals were possible—I had heard stories about life in New York City, where the President resided, that would curl a Cynic's hair. But what could these things possibly have to do with me? Or even Julian? We were only boys.

Such was my naiveté.

4

THE DAYS HAD GROWN SHORT, and Thanksgiving had come and gone, and so had November, and snow was in the air—the tang of it, anyway—when fifty cavalrymen of the Athabaska Reserve rode into Williams Ford, escorting an equal number of Campaigners and Poll-Takers.

Many people despised the Athabaskan winter. I was not one of them. I didn't mind the cold and the darkness, not so long as there was a hard-coal heater, a spirit lamp to read by on long nights, and the chance of wheat cakes or headcheese for breakfast. And Christmas was coming up fast—one of the four Universal Christian Holidays recognized by the Dominion (the others being Easter, Independence Day, and Thanksgiving). My favorite of these had always been Christmas. It was not so much the gifts, which were generally meager—though last year I had received from my parents the lease of a muzzle-loading rifle of which I was exceptionally proud—nor was it entirely the spiritual substance of the holiday, which I am ashamed to say seldom entered my mind except when it was thrust upon me at religious services. What I loved was the combined effect of brisk air, frost-whitened mornings, pine and holly wreaths pinned to doorways, cranberry-red banners draped above the main street to flap cheerfully in the cold wind, carols and hymns chanted or sung—the whole breathless confrontation with Winter, half defiance and half submission. I liked the clockwork regularity of these rituals, as if a particular cog on the wheel of time had engaged with neat precision. It soothed; it spoke of eternity.

But this was an ill-omened season.

The Reserve troops rode into town on the fifteenth of December. Ostensibly, they were here to conduct the Presidential Election.

233

National elections were a formality in Williams Ford. By the time our citizens were polled, the outcome was usually a foregone conclusion, already decided in the populous Eastern states—that is, when there was more than one candidate, which was seldom. For the last six electoral years no individual or party had contested the election, and we had been ruled by one Comstock or another for three decades. *Election* had become indistinguishable from *acclamation*.

But that was all right, because an election was still a momentous event, almost a kind of circus, involving the arrival of Poll-Takers and Campaigners, who always had a fine show to put on.

And this year—the rumor emanated from high chambers of the Estate, and had been whispered everywhere—there was to be a movie shown in the Dominion Hall.

I had never seen any movies, though Julian had described them to me. He had seen them often in New York when he was younger, and whenever he grew nostalgic—life in Williams Ford was sometimes a little sedate for Julian's taste—it was the movies he was provoked to mention. And so, when the showing of a movie was announced as part of the electoral process, both of us were excited, and we agreed to meet behind the Dominion Hall at he appointed hour.

Neither of us had any legitimate reason to be there. I was too young to vote, and Julian would have been conspicuous and perhaps unwelcome as the only aristo at a gathering of the leasing class. (The high-born had been polled independently at the Estate, and had already voted proxies for their indentured labor.) So I let my parents leave for the Hall early in the evening, and I followed surreptitiously, and arrived just before the event was scheduled to begin. I waited behind the meeting hall, where a dozen horses were tethered, until Julian arrived on an animal borrowed from the Estate stables. He was dressed in his best approximation of a leaser's clothing: hempen shirt and trousers of a dark color, and a black felt hat with its brim pulled low to disguise his face.

He dismounted, looking troubled, and I asked him what was wrong. Julian shook his head. "Nothing, Adam—or nothing *yet*—but Sam says there's trouble brewing." And here he regarded me with an expression verging on pity. "War," he said.

"There's always war."

"A new offensive."

"Well, what of it? Labrador's a million miles away."

"Obviously your sense of geography hasn't been much improved by Sam's classes. And we might be *physically* a long distance from the front, but we're *operationally* far too close for comfort."

I didn't know what that meant, and so I dismissed it. "We can worry about that after the movie, Julian."

He forced a grin and said, "Yes, I suppose so. As well after as before."

So we entered the Dominion Hall just as the lamps were being dimmed, and slouched into the last row of crowded pews, and waited for the show to start.

There was a broad stage at the front of the Hall, from which all religious appurtenances had been removed, and a square white screen had been erected in place of the usual pulpit or dais. On each side of the screen was a kind of tent in which the two players sat, with their scripts and dramatic gear: speaking-horns, bells, blocks, a drum, a pennywhistle, *et alia*. This was, Julian said, a stripped-down edition of what one might find in a fashionable New York movie theater. In the city, the screen (and thus the images projected on it) would be larger; the players would be more professional, since script-reading and noise-making were considered fashionable arts, and the city players competed with one another for roles; and there might be a third player stationed behind the screen for dramatic narration or additional "sound effects." There might even be an orchestra, with thematic music written for each individual production.

Movies were devised in such a way that two main characters, male and female, could be voiced by the players, with the male actor photographed so that he appeared on the left during dialogue scenes, and the female actor on the right. The players would observe the movie by a system of mirrors, and could follow scripts illuminated by a kind of binnacle lamp (so as not to cast a distracting light), and they spoke their lines as the photographed actors spoke, so that their voices seemed to emanate from the screen. Likewise, their drumming and bell-ringing and such corresponded to events within the movie.[5]

"Of course, they did it better in the secular era," Julian whispered, and I prayed no one had overheard this indelicate comment. By all reports, movies had indeed been spectacular during the Efflorescence of Oil—with recorded sound, natural color rather than black-and-gray, etc. But they were also (by the same reports) hideously impious, blasphemous to the extreme, and routinely pornographic. Fortunately (or *unfortunately*, from Julian's point of view) no examples have survived; the media on which they were recorded was ephemeral; the film stock has long since rotted, and "digital" copies are degraded and wholly undecodable. These movies belonged to the twentieth and early twenty-first centuries—that period of great, unsustainable, and hedonistic prosperity, driven by the burning of Earth's reserves of perishable oil, which culminated in the False Tribulation, and the wars, and the plagues, and the painful dwindling of inflated populations to more reasonable numbers.

Our truest and best American antiquity, as the *Dominion History of the Union* insisted, was the nineteenth century, whose household virtues and modest industries we have been forced by circumstance to imperfectly restore, whose skills were practical, and whose literature was often useful and improving.

But I have to confess that some of Julian's apostasy had infected me. I was troubled by unhappy thoughts even as the torchieres were extinguished and Ben Kreel (our Dominion representative, standing in front of the movie screen) delivered a brief lecture on Nation, Piety, and Duty. *War*, Julian had said, implying not just the everlasting War in Labrador but a new phase of it, one that might reach its skeletal hand right into Williams Ford—and then what of me, and what of my family?

"We are here to cast our ballots," Ben Kreel said in summation,

---

5 The illusion was quite striking when the players were professional, but their lapses could be equally astonishing. Julian once recounted to me a New York movie production of Wm. Shakespeare's Hamlet, in which a player had come to the theater inebriated, causing the unhappy Denmark to seem to exclaim "Sea of troubles—(an unprintable oath)—I have troubles of my own," with more obscenities, and much inappropriate bell-ringing and vulgar whistling, until an understudy could be hurried out to replace him.

"a sacred duty at once to our country and our faith, a country so successfully and benevolently stewarded by its leader, President Deklan Comstock, whose Campaigners, I see by the motions of their hands, are anxious to get on with the events of the night; and so, without further adieu, etc., please direct your attention to the presentation of their moving picture, *First Under Heaven*, which they have prepared for our enjoyment—"

The necessary gear had been hauled into Williams Ford under a canvas-top wagon: a projection apparatus and a portable Swiss dynamo (probably captured from the Dutch forces in Labrador), powered by distilled spirits, installed in a sort of trench or redoubt freshly dug behind the church to muffle its sound, which nevertheless penetrated through the plank floors like the growl of a huge dog. This vibration only added to the sense of moment, as the last illuminating flame was extinguished and the electric bulb within the huge black mechanical projector flared up.

The movie began. As it was the first I had ever seen, my astonishment was complete. I was so entranced by the illusion of photographs "come to life" that the substance of the scenes almost escaped me . . . but I remember an ornate title, and scenes of the Second Battle of Quebec, recreated by actors but utterly real to me, accompanied by drum-banging and shrill pennywhistling to represent the reports of shot and shell. Those at the front of the auditorium flinched instinctively; several of the village's prominent women came near to fainting, and clasped the hands or arms of their male companions, who might be as bruised, come morning, as if they had participated in the battle itself.

Soon enough, however, the Dutchmen under their cross-and-laurel flag began to retreat from the American forces, and an actor representing the young Deklan Comstock came to the fore, reciting his Vows of Inauguration (a bit prematurely, but history was here truncated for the purposes of art)—that's the one in which he mentions both the Continental Imperative and the Debt to the Past. He was voiced, of course, by one of the players, a *basso profundo* whose tones emerged from his speaking-bell with ponderous gravity. (Which was also a slight revision of the truth, for the genuine Deklan Comstock possessed a high-pitched voice, and was prone to petulance.)

The movie then proceeded to more decorous episodes and scenic views representing the glories of the reign of Deklan Conqueror, as he was known to the Army of the Laurentians, which had marched him to his ascendancy in New York City. Here was the reconstruction of Washington, DC (a project never completed, always in progress, hindered by a swampy climate and insect-borne diseases); here was the Illumination of Manhattan, whereby electric streetlights were powered by a hydroelectric dynamo, four hours every day between 6 and 10 p.m.; here was the military shipyard at Boston Harbor, the coal mines and foundries and weapons factories of Pennsylvania, the newest and shiniest steam engines to pull the newest and shiniest trains, etc., etc.

I had to wonder at Julian's reaction to all this. This entire show, after all, was concocted to extoll the virtues of the man who had contrived the death by hanging of his father. I could not forget—and Julian must be constantly aware—that the current President was a fratricidal tyrant. But Julian's eyes were riveted on the screen. This reflected (I later learned) not his opinion of contemporary politics but his fascination with what he preferred to call "cinema." This making of illusions in two dimensions was never far from his mind—it was, perhaps, his "true calling," and would culminate in the creation of Julian's suppressed cinematic masterwork, *The Life and Adventures of the Great Naturalist Charles Darwin* . . . but that tale remains for another telling.

The present movie went on to mention the successful forays against the Brazilians at Panama during Deklan Conqueror's reign, which may have struck closer to home, for I saw Julian wince once or twice.

As for me . . . I tried to lose myself in the moment, but my attention was woefully truant.

Perhaps it was the strangeness of the campaign event, so close to Christmas. Perhaps it was the HISTORY OF MANKIND IN SPACE, which I had been reading in bed, a page or two at a time, almost every night since our journey to the Tip. Whatever the cause, I was beset by a sudden anxiety and sense of melancholy. Here I was in the midst of everything that seemed familiar and ought to be comforting—the crowd of the leasing class, the enclosing benevolence of the Dominion Hall, the banners and tokens of the Christmas season— and it all felt suddenly *ephemeral*, as if the world were a bucket from which the bottom had dropped out.

Perhaps this was what Julian had called "the philosopher's perspective." If so, I wondered how the philosophers endured it. I had learned a little from Sam Godwin—and more from Julian, who read books of which even Sam disapproved—about the discredited ideas of the Secular Era. I thought of Einstein, and his insistence that no particular point of view of was more privileged than any other: in other words his "general relativity," and its claim that the answer to the question "What is real?" begins with the question "Where are you standing?" Was that all I was, here in the cocoon of Williams Ford— a Point of View? Or was I an incarnation of a molecule of DNA, "imperfectly remembering," as Julian had said, an ape, a fish, and an amoeba? Maybe even the Nation that Ben Kreel had praised so extravagantly was only an example of this trend in nature—an imperfect memory of another century, which had itself been an imperfect memory of all the centuries before it, and so back to the dawn of Man (in Eden, or Africa, as Julian believed).

Perhaps this was just my growing disenchantment with the town where I had been raised—or a presentiment that it was about to be stolen away from me.

The movie ended with a stirring scene of an American flag, its thirteen stripes and sixty stars rippling in sunlight—betokening, the narrator insisted, another four years of the prosperity and benevolence engendered by the rule of Deklan Conqueror, for whom the audience's votes were solicited, not that there was any competing candidate known or rumored. The film flapped against its reel; the electric bulb was extinguished. Then the deacons of the Dominion began to reignite the wall lights. Several of the men in the audience had lit pipes during the cinematic display, and their smoke mingled with the smudge of the torchieres, a blue-gray thundercloud hovering under the high arches of the ceiling.

Julian seemed distracted, and slumped in his pew with his hat pulled low. "Adam," he whispered, "we have to find a way out of here."

"I believe I see one," I said; "It's called the door—but what's the hurry?"

"Look at the door more closely. Two men of the Reserve have been posted there."

I looked, and what he had said was true. "But isn't that just to protect the balloting?" For Ben Kreel had retaken the stage and was preparing to ask for a formal show of hands.

"Tom Shearney, the barber with a bladder complaint, just tried to leave to use the jakes. He was turned back."

Indeed, Tom Shearney was seated less than a yard away from us, squirming unhappily and casting resentful glances at the Reserve men.

"But after the balloting—"

"This isn't about balloting. This is about conscription."

"Conscription!"

"Hush!" Julian said hastily, shaking his hair out of his pale face. "You'll start a stampede. I didn't think it would begin so soon . . . but we've had certain telegrams from New York about setbacks in Labrador, and the call-up of new divisions. Once the balloting is finished the Campaigners will probably announce a recruitment drive, and take the names of everyone present and survey them for the names and ages of their children."

"We're too young to be drafted," I said, for we were both just seventeen.

"Not according to what I've heard. The rules have been changed. Oh, you can probably find a way to hide out when the culling begins—and get away with it, considering how far we are from anywhere else. But *my* presence here is well-known. I don't have a mob or family to melt away into. In fact it's probably not a coincidence that so many Reserves have been sent to such a little village as Williams Ford."

"What do you mean, not a coincidence?"

"My uncle has never been happy about my existence. He has no children of his own. No heirs. He sees me as a possible competitor for the Executive."

"But that's absurd. You don't *want* to be President—do you?"

"I would sooner shoot myself. But Uncle Deklan has a jealous bent, and he distrusts the motives of my mother in protecting me."

"How does a draft help him?"

"The entire draft is not aimed at me, but I'm sure he finds it a useful tool. If I'm drafted, no one can complain that he's excepting his own family from the general conscription. And when he has me in the infantry he can be sure I find myself on the front lines in Labrador—performing some noble but suicidal trench attack."

"But—Julian! Can't Sam protect you?"

"Sam is a retired soldier; he has no power except what arises from the patronage of my mother. Which isn't worth much in the coin of the present realm. Adam, is there another way out of this building?"

"Only the door, unless you mean to break a pane of that colored glass that fills the windows."

"Somewhere to hide, then?"

I thought about it. "Maybe," I said. "There's a room behind the stage where the religious equipment is stored. You can enter it from the wings. We could hide there, but it has no door of its own."

"It'll have to do. If we can get there without attracting attention."

But that was not too difficult, for the torchieres had not all been re-lit, much of the hall was still in shadow, and the audience was milling about a bit, and stretching, while the Campaigners prepared to record the vote that was to follow—they were meticulous accountants even though the final tally was a foregone conclusion and the ballrooms were already booked for Deklan Conqueror's latest inauguration. Julian and I shuffled from one shadow to another, giving no appearance of haste, until we were close to the foot of the stage; there we paused at an entrance to the storage room, until a goonish Reserve man who had been eyeing us was called away by a superior officer to help dismantle the projecting equipment. We ducked through the curtained door into near-absolute darkness. Julian stumbled over some obstruction (a piece of the church's tack piano, which had been disassembled for cleaning in 2165 by a traveling piano-mechanic, who had died of a stroke before finishing the job), the result being a woody "clang!" that seemed loud enough to alert the whole occupancy of the church, but evidently didn't.

What little light there was came through a high glazed window that was hinged so that it could be opened in summer for purposes of ventilation. It was a weak sort of illumination, for the night was cloudy, and only the torches along the main street were shining. But it registered as our eyes adjusted to the dimness. "Perhaps we can get out that way," Julian said.

"Not without a ladder. Although—"

"What? Speak up, Adam, if you have an idea."

"This is where they store the risers—the long wooden blocks the choir stands on when they're racked up for a performance. Perhaps those—"

But he was already examining the shadowy contents of the storage room, as intently as he had surveyed the Tip for ancient books. We found the likely suspects, and managed to stack them to a useful height without causing too much noise. (In the church hall, the Campaigners had already registered a unanimous vote for Deklan Comstock and had begun to break the news about the conscription drive. Some few voices were raised in futile objection; Ben Kreel was calling loudly for calm—no one heard us rearranging the unused furniture.)

The window was at least ten feet high, and almost too narrow to crawl through, and when we emerged on the other side we had to hang by our fingertips before dropping to the ground. I bent my right ankle awkwardly as I landed, though no lasting harm was done.

The night, already cold, had turned colder. We were near the hitching posts, and the horses whinnied at our surprising arrival and blew steam from their gaping nostrils. A fine, gritty snow had begun to fall. There was not much wind, however, and Christmas banners hung limply in the frigid air.

Julian made straight for his horse and loosed its reins from the post. "What are we going to do?" I asked.

"You, Adam, will do nothing but protect your own existence as best you know how; while I—"

But he balked at pronouncing his plans, and a shadow of anxiety passed over his face. Events were moving rapidly in the realm of the aristos, events I could barely comprehend.

"We can wait them out," I said, a little desperately. "The Reserves can't stay in Williams Ford forever."

"No. Unfortunately neither can I, for Deklan Conqueror knows where to find me, and has made up his mind to remove me from the game of politics like a captured chesspiece."

"But where will you go? And what—"

He put a finger to his mouth. There was a noise from the front of the Dominion Church Hall, as of the doors being thrown open, and voices of congregants arguing or wailing over the news of the conscription drive. "Ride with me," Julian said. "Quick, now!"

We did not follow the main street, but caught a path that turned behind the blacksmith's barn and through the wooded border of the River Pine, north in the general direction of the Estate. The night was dark, and the horses stepped slowly, but they knew the path almost by instinct, and some light from the town still filtered through the thinly falling snow, which touched my face like a hundred small cold fingers.

"It was never possible that I could stay at Williams Ford forever," Julian said. "You ought to have known that, Adam."

Truly, I should have. It was Julian's constant theme, after all: the impermanence of things. I had always put this down to the circumstances of his childhood, the death of his father, the separation from his mother, the kind but aloof tutelage of Sam Godwin.

But I could not help thinking once more of THE HISTORY OF MANKIND IN SPACE and the photographs in it—not of the First Men on the Moon, who were Americans, but of the Last Visitors to that celestial sphere, who had been Chinamen, and whose "space suits" had been firecracker-red. Like the Americans, they had planted their flag in expectation of more visitations to come; but the End of Oil and the False Tribulation had put paid to those plans.

And I thought of the even lonelier Plains of Mars, photographed by machines (or so the book alleged) but never touched by human feet. The universe, it seemed, was full to brimming with lonesome places. Somehow I had stumbled into one. The snow squall ended; the uninhabited moon came through the clouds; and the winter fields of Williams Ford glowed with an unearthly luminescence.

"If you must leave," I said, "let me come with you."

"No," Julian said promptly. He had pulled his hat down around his ears, to protect himself from the cold, and I couldn't see much of his face, but his eyes shone when he glanced in my direction. "Thank you, Adam. I wish it were possible. But it isn't. You must stay here, and dodge the draft, if possible, and polish your literary skills, and one day write books, like Mr. Charles Curtis Easton."

That was my ambition, which had grown over the last year, nourished by our mutual love of books and by Sam Godwin's exercises in English Composition, for which I had discovered an unexpected talent.[6] At the moment it seemed a petty dream. Evanescent. Like all dreams. Like life itself. "None of that matters," I said.

"That's where you're wrong," Julian said. "You must not make the mistake of thinking that because nothing lasts, nothing matters."

"Isn't that the philosopher's point of view?"

"Not if the philosopher knows what he's talking about." Julian reined up his horse and turned to face me, something of the imperiousness of his famous family entering into his mien. "Listen, Adam, there is something important you can do for me—at some personal risk. Are you willing?"

"Yes," I said immediately.

"Then listen closely. Before long the Reserves will be watching the roads out of Williams Ford, if they aren't already. I have to leave, and I have to leave tonight. I won't be missed until morning, and then, at least at first, only by Sam. What I want you to do is this: go home—your parents will be worried about the conscription, and you can try to calm them down—but don't allude to any of what

---

6 Not a talent that was born fully-formed, I should add. Only two years previously I had presented to Sam Godwin my first finished story, which I had called "A Western Boy: His Adventures in Enemy Europe." Sam had praised its style and ambition, but called attention to a number of flaws: elephants, for instance, were not native to Brussels, and were generally too massive to be wrestled to the ground by American lads; a journey from London to Rome could not be accomplished in a matter of hours, even on "a very fast horse" —and Sam might have continued in this vein, had I not fled the room in a condition of acute auctorial embarrassment.

happened tonight—and first thing in the morning, make your way as inconspicuously as possible into the Estate and find Sam. Tell him what happened at the Church Hall, and tell him to ride out of town as soon as he can do so without being caught. Tell him he can find me at Lundsford. That's the message."

"Lundsford? There's nothing at Lundsford."

"Precisely: nothing important enough that the Reserves would think to look for us there. You remember what the Tipman said in the fall, about the place he found those books? A low place near the main excavations. Sam can look for me there."

"I'll tell him," I promised, blinking against the cold wind, which irritated my eyes.

"Thank you, Adam," he said gravely. "For everything." Then he forced a smile, and for a moment was just Julian, the friend with whom I had hunted squirrels and spun tales: "Merry Christmas," he said. "Happy New Year!"

And wheeled his horse about, and rode away.

❧ 5 ❧

THERE IS A DOMINION CEMETERY in Williams Ford, and I passed it on the ride back home—carved stones sepulchral in the moonlight—but my sister Flaxie was not buried there.

As I have said, the Church of Signs was tolerated but not endorsed by the Dominion. We were not entitled to plots in the Dominion yard. Flaxie had a place in the acreage behind our cottage, marked by a modest wooden cross, but the cemetery put me in mind of Flaxie nonetheless, and after I returned the horse to the barn I stopped by Flaxie's grave (despite the shivery cold) and tipped my hat to her, the way I had always tipped my hat to her in life.

Flaxie had been a bright, impudent, mischievous small thing—as golden-haired as her nickname implied. (Her given name was Dolores, but she was always Flaxie to me.) The Pox had taken her quite suddenly and, as these things go, mercifully. I didn't remember her death; I had been down with the same Pox, though I had survived it. What I remembered was waking up from my fever into a house gone strangely quiet. No one had wanted to tell me about Flaxie, but I had seen my mother's tormented eyes, and I knew the truth without having to be told. Death had played lottery with us, and Flaxie had drawn the short straw.

(It is, I think, for the likes of Flaxie that we maintain a belief in Heaven. I have met very few adults, outside the enthusiasts of the established Church, who genuinely believe in Heaven, and Heaven was scant consolation for my grieving mother. But Flaxie, who was five, had believed in it fervently—imagined it was something like a meadow, with wildflowers blooming, and a perpetual summer picnic underway—and if that childish belief soothed her in her extremity, then it served a purpose more noble than truth.)

Tonight the cottage was almost as quiet as it had been during the mourning that followed Flaxie's death. I came through the door to find my mother dabbing her eyes with a handkerchief, and my father frowning over his pipe, which, uncharacteristically, he had filled and lit. "The draft," he said.

"Yes," I said. "I heard about it."

My mother was too distraught to speak. My father said, "We'll do what we can to protect you, Adam. But—"

"I'm not afraid to serve my country," I said.

"That's a praiseworthy attitude," my father said glumly, and my mother wept even harder. "But we don't yet know what might be necessary. Maybe the situation in Labrador isn't as bad as it seems."

Scant of words though my father was, I had often enough relied on him for advice, which he had freely given. He was fully aware, for instance, of my distaste for snakes—for which reason, abetted by my mother, I had been allowed to avoid the sacraments of our faith, and the venomous swellings and occasional amputations occasionally inflicted upon other parishioners—and, while this disappointed him, he had nevertheless taught me the practical aspects of snake-handling, including how to grasp a serpent in such a way as to avoid its bite, and how to kill one, should the necessity arise.[7] He was a practical man despite his unusual beliefs.

But he had no advice to offer me tonight. He looked like a hunted man who has come to the end of a cul-de-sac, and can neither go forward nor turn back.

I went to my bedroom, although I doubted I would be able to sleep. Instead—without any real plan in mind—I bundled a few of my possessions for easy carrying. My squirrel-gun, chiefly, and some notes and writing, and THE HISTORY OF MANKIND IN SPACE; and I thought I should add some salted pork, or something of that nature, but I resolved to wait until later, so my mother wouldn't see me packing.

---

7 "Grasp it where its neck ought to be, behind the head; ignore the tail, however it may thrash; and crack its skull, hard and often enough to subdue it." I had recounted these instructions to Julian, whose horror of serpents far exceeded my own: "Oh, I could never do such a thing!" he had exclaimed. This surfeit of timidity may surprise readers who have followed his later career.

♠ ♠ ♠

Before dawn, I put on several layers of clothing and a heavy pakool hat, rolled down so the wool covered my ears. I opened the window of my room and clambered over the sill and closed the glass behind me, after I had retrieved my rifle and gear. Then I crept across the open yard to the barn, and saddled up a horse (the gelding named Rapture, who was the fastest, though this would leave my father's rig an animal shy), and rode out under a sky that had just begun to show first light.

Last night's brief snowfall still covered the ground. I was not the first up this winter morning, and the cold air already smelled of Christmas. The bakery in Williams Ford was busy making nativity cakes and cinnamon buns. The sweet, yeasty smell filled the northwest end of town like an intoxicating fog, for there was no wind to carry it away. The day was dawning blue and still.

Signs of Christmas were everywhere—as they ought to be, for today was the Eve of that universal holiday—but so was evidence of the conscription drive. The Reservists were already awake, passing like shadows in their scruffy uniforms, and a crowd of them had gathered by the hardware store. They had hung out a faded flag and posted a sign, which I could not read, because I was determined to keep a distance between myself and the soldiers; but I knew a recruiting-post when I saw one. I did not doubt that the main ways in and out of town had been put under close observation.

I took a back way to the Estate, the same riverside road Julian and I had traveled the night before. Because of the lack of wind, our tracks were undisturbed. We were the only ones who had recently passed this way. Rapture was revisiting his own hoof-prints.

Close to the Estate, but still within a concealing grove of pines, I lashed the horse to a sapling and proceeded on foot.

The Duncan-Crowley Estate was not fenced, for there was no real demarcation of its boundaries; under the Leasing System, everything in Williams Ford was owned (in the legal sense) by the two great families. I approached from the western side, which was half-wooded and used by the aristos for casual riding and hunting. This morning the copse was not inhabited, and I saw no one until I had passed the snow-mounded hedges which marked the beginning of the formal gardens. Here, in summer, apple and cherry trees blossomed and produced fruit; flowerbeds gave forth symphonies of color and scent; bees nursed in languid ecstasies. But now it was barren, the paths quilted with snow, and there was no one visible but the senior groundskeeper, sweeping the wooden portico of the nearest of the Estate's several Great Houses.

The Houses were dressed for Christmas. Christmas was a grander event at the Estate than in the town proper, as might be expected. The winter population of the Duncan-Crowley Estate was not as large as its summer population, but there was still a number of both families, plus whatever cousins and hangers-on had elected to hibernate over the cold season. Sam Godwin, as Julian's tutor, was not permitted to sleep in either of the two most luxurious buildings, but bunked among the elite staff in a white-pillared house that would have passed for a mansion anywhere but here. This was where he had conducted classes for Julian and me, and I knew the building intimately. It, too, was dressed for Christmas; a holly wreath hung on the door; pine boughs were suspended over the lintels; a Banner of the Cross dangled from the eaves. The door was not locked, and I let myself in quietly.

It was still early in the morning, at least as the aristos and their elite helpers calculated time. The tiled entranceway was empty and still. I went straight for the rooms where Sam Godwin slept and conducted his classes, down an oaken corridor lit only by the dawn filtering through a window at the long end. The floor was carpeted and gave no sound, though my shoes left damp footprints behind me.

At Sam's particular door, I was confronted with a dilemma. I could not knock, for fear of alerting others. My mission as I saw it was to deliver Julian's message as discreetly as possible. But neither could I walk in on a sleeping man—could I?

I tried the handle of the door. It moved freely. I opened the door a fraction of an inch, meaning to whisper, "Sam?"—and give him some warning.

But I could hear Sam's voice, low and muttering, as if he were talking to himself. I listened more closely. The words seemed strange.

He was speaking in a guttural language, not English. Perhaps he wasn't alone. It was too late to back away, however, so I decided to brazen it out. I opened the door entirely and stepped inside, saying, "Sam! It's me, Adam. I have a message from Julian—"

I stopped short, alarmed by what I saw. Sam Godwin—the same gruff but familiar Sam who had taught me the rudiments of history and geography—was practicing *black magic*, or some other form of witchcraft: *on Christmas Eve!* He wore a striped cowl about his shoulders, and leather lacings on his arm, and a boxlike implement strapped to his forehead; and his hands were upraised over an arrangement of nine candles mounted in a brass holder that appeared to have been scavenged from some ancient Tip. The invocation he had been murmuring seemed to echo through the room: Bah-*rook*-a-*tah*-atten-*eye*-hello-*hey*-noo . . .

My jaw dropped.

"Adam!" Sam said, almost as startled as I was, and he quickly pulled the shawl from his back and began to unlace his various unholy riggings.

This was so irregular I could barely comprehend it.

Then I was afraid I *did* comprehend it. Often enough in Dominion school I had heard Ben Kreel speak about the vices and wickedness of the Secular Era, some of which still lingered, he said, in the cities of the East—irreverence, irreligiosity, skepticism, occultism, depravity. And I thought of the ideas I had so casually imbibed from Julian and (indirectly) from Sam, some of which I had even begun to believe: Einsteinism, Darwinism, space travel . . . had I been seduced by the outrunners of some New Yorkish paganism? Had I been duped by Philosophy?

"A message," Sam said, concealing his heathenish gear, "what message? Where is Julian?"

But I could not stay. I fled the room.

Sam barreled out of the house after me. I was fast, but he was long-legged and conditioned by his military career, strong for all his forty-odd years, and he caught me in the winter gardens—tackled me from behind. I kicked and tried to pull away, but he pinned my shoulders.

"Adam, for God's sake, settle down!" cried he. That was impudent, I thought, invoking God, *him*—but then he said, "Don't you understand what you saw? I am a Jew!"

A Jew!

Of course, I had heard of Jews. They lived in the Bible, and in New York City. Their equivocal relationship with Our Savior had won them opprobrium down the ages, and they were not approved of by the Dominion. But I had never seen a living Jew in the flesh— to my knowledge—and I was astonished by the idea that Sam had been one all along: *invisibly,* so to speak.

"You deceived everyone, then!" I said.

"I never claimed to be a Christian! I never spoke of it at all. But what does it matter? You said you had a message from Julian—give it to me, damn you! Where is he?"

I wondered what I should say, or who I might betray if I said it. The world had turned upside-down. All Ben Kreel's lectures on patriotism and fidelity came back to me in one great flood of guilt and shame. Had I been a party to treason as well as atheism?

But I felt I owed this last favor to Julian, who would surely have wanted me to deliver his intelligence whether Sam was a Jew or a Mohammedan: "There are soldiers on all the roads out of town," I said sullenly. "Julian went for Lundsford last night. He says he'll meet you there. Now *get off of me!*"

Sam did so, sitting back on his heels, deep anxiety inscribed upon his face. "Has it begun so soon? I thought they would wait for the New Year."

"I don't know *what* has begun. I don't think I know anything at all!" And, so saying, I leapt to my feet and ran out of the lifeless garden, back to Rapture, who was still tied to the tree where I had left him, nosing unproductively in the undisturbed snow.

I had ridden perhaps an eighth of a mile back toward Williams Ford when another rider came up on my right flank from behind. It was Ben Kreel himself, and he touched his cap and smiled and said, "Do you mind if I ride along with you a ways, Adam Hazzard?"

I could hardly say no.

Ben Kreel was not a pastor—we had plenty of those in Williams Ford, each catering to his own denomination - but he was the head of the local Council of the Dominion of Jesus Christ on Earth, almost as powerful in his way as the men who owned the Estate. And if he was not a pastor, he was at least a sort of shepherd to the townspeople. He had been born right here in Williams Ford, son of a saddler; had been educated, at the Estate's expense, at one of the Dominion Colleges in Colorado Springs; and for the last twenty years he had taught elementary school five days a week and General Christianity on Sundays. I had marked my first letters on a slate board under Ben Kreel's tutelage. Every Independence Day he addressed the townsfolk and reminded them of the symbolism and significance of the Thirteen Stripes and the Sixty Stars; every Christmas, he led the Ecumenical Services at the Dominion Hall.

He was stout and graying at the temples, clean-shaven. He wore a woolen jacket, tall deer hide boots, and a pakool hat not much grander than my own. But he carried himself with an immense dignity, as much in the saddle as on foot. The expression on his face was kindly. It was always kindly. "You're out early, Adam Hazzard," he said. "What are you doing abroad at this hour?"

"Nothing," I said, and blushed. Is there any other word that so spectacularly represents everything it wants to deny? Under the circumstances, "nothing" amounted to a confession of bad intent. "Couldn't sleep," I added hastily. "Thought I might shoot a squirrel or so." That would explain the rifle strapped to my saddle, and it was at least remotely plausible; the squirrels were still active, doing the last of their scrounging before settling in for the cold months.

"On Christmas Eve?" Ben Kreel asked. "And in the copse on the grounds of the Estate? I hope the Duncans and Crowleys don't hear about it. They're jealous of their trees. And I'm sure gunfire would disturb them at this hour. Wealthy men and Easterners prefer to sleep past dawn, as a rule."

"I didn't fire," I muttered. "I thought better of it."

"Well, good. Wisdom prevails. You're headed back to town, I gather?"

"Yes, sir."

"Let me keep you company, then."

"Please do." I could hardly say otherwise, no matter how I longed to be alone with my thoughts.

Our horses moved slowly—the snow made for awkward footing—and Ben Kreel was silent for a long while. Then he said, "You needn't conceal your fears, Adam. I know what's troubling you."

For a moment I had the terrible idea that Ben Kreel had been behind me in the hallway at the Estate, and that he had seen Sam Godwin wrapped in his Old Testament paraphernalia. Wouldn't that create a scandal! (And then I thought that it was exactly such a scandal Sam must have feared all his life: it was worse even than being Church of Signs, for in some states a Jew can be fined or even imprisoned for practicing his faith. I didn't know where Athabaska stood on the issue, but I feared the worst.) But Ben Kreel was talking about conscription, not about Sam.

"I've already discussed this with some of the boys in town," he said. "You're not alone, Adam, if you're wondering what it all means, this military movement, and what might happen as a result of it. And I admit, you're something of a special case. I've been keeping an eye on you. From a distance, as it were. Here, stop a moment."

We had come to a rise in the road, on a bluff above the River Pine, looking south toward Williams Ford from a little height.

"Gaze at that," Ben Kreel said contemplatively. He stretched his arm out in an arc, as if to include not just the cluster of buildings that was the town but the empty fields as well, and the murky flow of the river, and the wheels of the mills, and even the shacks of the indentured laborers down in the low country. The valley seemed at once a living thing, inhaling the crisp atmosphere of the season and breathing out its steams, and a portrait, static in the still blue winter air. As deeply rooted as an oak, as fragile as a ball of Nativity glass.

"Gaze at that," Ben Kreel repeated. "Look at Williams Ford, laid out pretty there. What is it, Adam? More than a place, I think. It's a way of life. It's the sum of all our labors. It's what our fathers have given us and it's what we give our sons. It's where we bury our mothers and where our daughters will be buried."

Here was more Philosophy, then, and after the turmoil of the morning I wasn't sure I wanted any. But Ben Kreel's voice ran on like the soothing syrup my mother used to administer whenever Flaxie or I came down with a cough.

"Every boy in Williams Ford—every boy old enough to submit himself for national service—is just now discovering how reluctant he is to leave the place he knows best. Even you, I suspect."

"I'm no more or less willing than anyone else."

"I'm not questioning your courage or your loyalty. It's just that I know you've had a little taste of what life might be like elsewhere— given how closely you associated yourself with Julian Comstock. Now, I'm sure Julian's a fine young man and an excellent Christian. He could hardly be otherwise, could he, as the nephew of the man who holds this nation in his palm. But his experience has been very different from yours. He's accustomed to cities—to movies like the one we saw at the Hall last night (and I glimpsed you there, didn't I? Sitting in the back pews?)—to books and ideas that might strike a youth of your background as exciting and, well, *different*. Am I wrong?"

"I could hardly say you are, sir."

"And much of what Julian may have described to you is no doubt true. I've traveled some myself, you know. I've seen Colorado Springs, Pittsburgh, even New York City. Our eastern cities are great, proud metropolises—some of the biggest and most productive in the world—and they're worth defending, which is one reason we're trying so hard to drive the Dutch out of Labrador."

"Surely you're right."

"I'm glad you agree. Because there is a trap certain young people fall into. I've seen it before. Sometimes a boy decides that one of those great cities might be a place he can *run away to*—a place where he can escape all the duties, obligations, and moral lessons he learned at his mother's knee. Simple things like faith and patriotism can begin to seem to a young man like burdens, which might be shrugged off when they become too weighty."

"I'm not like that, sir."

"Of course not. But there is yet another element in the calculation. You may have to leave Williams Ford because of the conscription. And the thought that runs through many boys' minds is, if I *must* leave, then perhaps I ought to leave on my own hook, and find my destiny on a city's streets rather than in a battalion of the Athabaska Brigade . . . and you're good to deny it, Adam, but you wouldn't be human if such ideas didn't cross your mind."

"No, sir," I muttered, and I must admit I felt a dawning guilt, for I had in fact been a little seduced by Julian's tales of city life, and Sam's dubious lessons, and the HISTORY OF MANKIND IN SPACE—perhaps I *had* forgotten something of my obligations to the village that lay so still and so inviting in the blue near distance.

"I know," Ben Kreel said, "that things haven't always been easy for your family. Your father's faith, in particular, has been a trial, and we haven't always been good neighbors—speaking on behalf of the village as a whole. Perhaps you've been left out of some activities other boys enjoy as a matter of course: church activities, picnics, common friendships . . . well, even Williams Ford isn't perfect. But I promise you, Adam: if you find yourself in the Brigades, especially if you find yourself tested in time of war, you'll discover that the same boys who shunned you in the dusty streets of your home town become your best friends and bravest defenders, and you theirs. For our common heritage ties us together in ways that may seem obscure, but become obvious under the harsh light of combat."

I had spent so much time smarting under the remarks of other boys (that my father "raised vipers the way other folks raise chickens," for example) that I could hardly credit Ben Kreel's assertion. But I knew little of modern warfare, except what I had read in the novels of Mr. Charles Curtis Easton, so it might be true. And the prospect (as was intended) made me feel even more shame-faced.

"There," Ben Kreel said: "Do you hear that, Adam?"

I did. I could hardly avoid it. The bell was ringing in the Dominion church, calling together one of the early ecumenical services. It was a silvery sound on the winter air, at once lonesome and consoling, and I wanted almost to run toward it—to shelter in it, as if I were a child again.

"They'll want me soon," Ben Kreel said. "Will you excuse me if I ride ahead?"

"No, sir. Please don't mind about me."

"As long as we understand each other, Adam. Don't look so downcast! The future may be brighter than you expect."

"Thank you for saying so, sir."

I stayed a while longer on the low bluff, watching as Ben Kreel's horse carried him toward town. Even in the sunlight it was cold, and I shivered some, perhaps more because of the conflict in my mind than because of the weather. The Dominion man had made me ashamed of myself, and had put into perspective my loose ways of the last few years, and pointed up how many of my native beliefs I had abandoned before the seductive Philosophy of an agnostic young aristo and an aging Jew.

Then I sighed and urged Rapture back along the path toward Williams Ford, meaning to explain to my parents where I had been and reassure them that I would not suffer too much in the coming conscription, to which I would willingly submit.

I was so disheartened by the morning's events that my eyes drifted toward the ground even as Rapture retraced his steps. As I have said, the snows of the night before lay largely undisturbed on this back trail between the town and the Estate. I could see where I had passed this morning, where Rapture's hoofprints were as clearly written as figures in a book. (Ben Kreel must have spent the night at the Estate, and when he left me on the bluff he would have taken the more direct route toward town; only Rapture had passed this way.) Then I reached the place where Julian and I had parted the night before. There were more hoofprints here, in fact a crowd of them —

And I saw something else written (in effect) on the snowy ground—something which alarmed me.

I reined up at once.

I looked south, toward Williams Ford. I looked east, the way Julian had gone the previous night.

Then I took a bracing inhalation of icy air, and followed the trail that seemed to me most urgent.

❧ 6 ❧

THE EAST-WEST ROAD through Williams Ford is not heavily traveled, especially in winter.

The southern road—also called the "Wire Road," because the telegraph line runs alongside it—connects Williams Ford to the railhead at Connaught, and thus sustains a great deal of traffic. But the east-west road goes essentially nowhere: it is a remnant of a road of the secular ancients, traversed mainly by Tipmen and freelance antiquarians, and then only in the warmer months. I suppose, if you followed the old road as far is it would take you, you might reach the Great Lakes, or somewhere farther east, in that direction; and, the opposite way, you could get yourself lost among washouts and landfalls in the Rocky Mountains. But the railroad—and a parallel turnpike farther south—had obviated the need for all that trouble.

Nevertheless, the east-west road was closely watched where it left the outskirts of Williams Ford. The Reserves had posted a man on a hill overlooking it, the same hill where Julian and Sam and I had paused for blackberries on our way from the Tip last October. But it is a fact that the Reserve troops were held in Reserve, and not sent to the front lines, mainly because of some disabling flaw of body or mind; some were wounded veterans, missing a hand or an arm; some were too simple or sullen to function in a disciplined body of soldiers. I cannot say anything for certain about the man posted as lookout on the hill, but if he was not a fool he was at least utterly unconcerned about concealment, for his silhouette (and that of his rifle) stood etched against the bright eastern sky for all to see. But maybe that was the intent: to let prospective fugitives know their way was barred.

Not *every* way was barred, however, not for someone who had grown up in Williams Ford and hunted everywhere on its perimeter.

Instead of following Julian directly I rode north a distance, and then through the crowded lanes of an encampment of indentured laborers (whose ragged children gaped at me from the glassless windows of their shanties, and whose soft-coal fires made a smoky gauze of the motionless air). This route connected with lanes cut through the wheat fields for the transportation of harvests and field-hands—lanes that had been deepened by years of use, so that I rode behind a berm of earth and snake rail fences, hidden from the distant sentinel. When I was safely east, I came down a cattle-trail that reconnected me with the east-west road.

On which I was able to read the same signs that had alerted me back at Williams Ford, thanks to the fine layer of snow still undisturbed by any wind.

Julian had come this way. He had done as he had intended, and ridden toward Lundsford before midnight. The snow had stopped soon thereafter, leaving his horse's hoof-prints clearly visible, though softened and half-covered.

But his were not the only tracks: there was a second set, more crisply defined and hence more recent, probably set down during the night; and this was what I had seen at the crossroads in Williams Ford: evidence of pursuit. Someone had followed Julian, without Julian's knowledge. This had dire implications, the only redeeming circumstance being the fact of a single pursuer rather than a company of men. If the powerful people of the Estate had known that it was Julian Comstock who had fled, they would surely have sent an entire brigade to bring him back. I supposed Julian had been mistaken for a simple miscreant, a labor refugee, or a youngster fleeing the conscription, and that he had been followed by some ambitious Reservist. Otherwise that whole imagined battalion might be right behind me . . . or perhaps soon *would* be, since Julian's absence must have been noted by now.

I rode east, adding my own track to these two.

Before long it was past noon, and I began to have second thoughts as the sun began to angle toward an early rendezvous with the southwestern horizon. What exactly did I hope to accomplish? To warn Julian? If so, I was a little late off the mark . . . though I hoped that at some point Julian had covered his tracks, or otherwise misled his pursuer, who did not have the advantage I had, of knowing where Julian meant to stay until Sam Godwin could arrive. Failing that, I half-imagined *rescuing* Julian from capture, even though I had but a squirrel rifle and a few rounds of ammunition (plus a knife and my own wits, both feeble enough weapons) against whatever a Reservist might carry. In any case these were more wishes and anxieties than calculations or plans; I had no fully-formed plan beyond riding to Julian's aid and telling him that I had delivered my message to Sam, who would be along as soon as he could discreetly leave the Estate.

And then what? It was a question I dared not ask myself—not out on this lonely road, well past the Tip now, farther than I had ever been from Williams Ford; not out here where the flatlands stretched on each side of the path like the frosty plains of Mars, and the wind, which had been absent all morning, began to pluck at the fringes of my coat, and my shadow elongated in front of me like a scarecrow gone riding. It was cold and getting colder, and soon the winter moon would be aloft, and me with only a few ounces of salt pork in my saddlebag and a few matches to make a fire if I was able to secure any kindling by nightfall. I began to wonder if I had gone quite insane. At several points I thought: I could go back; perhaps I hadn't yet been missed; perhaps it wasn't too late to sit down to a Christmas Eve dinner with my parents, raise a glass of cider to Flaxie and to Christmases past, and wake in time to hear the ringing-in of the Holiday and smell the goodness of baked bread and Nativity apples drenched in cinnamon and brown sugar. I mused on it repeatedly, sometimes with tears in my eyes; but I let Rapture continue carrying me toward the darkest part of the horizon.

Then, after what seemed endless hours of dusk, with only a brief pause when both Rapture and I drank from a creek which had a skin of ice on it, I began to come among the ruins of the secular ancients.

Not that there was anything spectacular about them. Fanciful drawings often portray the ruins of the last century as tall buildings, ragged and hollow as broken teeth, forming vine-encrusted canyons and shadowy cul-de-sacs.[8] No doubt such places exist—most of them in the uninhabitable Southwest, however, where "famine sits enthroned, and waves his scepter over a dominion expressly made for him," which would rule out vines and such tropical items[9]—but most ruins were like the ones I now passed, mere irregularities (or more precisely, *regularities*) in the landscape, which indicated the former presence of foundations. These terrains were treacherous, often concealing deep basements that could open like hungry mouths on an unwary traveler, and only Tipmen loved them. I was careful to keep to the path, though I began to wonder whether Julian would be as easy to find as I had imagined—Lundsford was a big locality, and the wind had already begun to scour away the hoofprints I had relied on for navigation.

I was haunted, too, by thoughts of the False Tribulation of the last century. It was not unusual to come across desiccated human remains in localities like this. Millions had died in the worst dislocations of the End of Oil: of disease, of internecine strife, but mostly of starvation. The Age of Oil had allowed a fierce intensity of fertilization and irrigation of the land, which had fed more people than a humbler agriculture could support. I had seen photographs of Americans from that blighted age, thin as sticks, their children with distended bellies, crowded into "relief camps" that would soon enough be transformed into communal graves when the imagined "relief" failed to materialize. No wonder, then, that our ancestors had mistaken those decades for the Tribulation of prophecy. What was astonishing was how many of our current institutions—the Church, the Army, the Federal Government—had survived more or less intact. There was a passage in the Dominion Bible that Ben Kreel had read whenever the subject of the False Tribulation arose in school, and which I had committed to memory: *The field is wasted, the land mourns; for the corn is shriveled, the wine has dried, the oil languishes. Be ashamed, farmers; howl, vinekeepers; howl for the wheat and the barley, for the harvest of the field has perished . . .*

---

[8] Or "culs-de-sac"? My French is rudimentary.

[9] Though Old Miami or Orlando might begin to fit the bill.

It had made me shiver then, and it made me shiver now, in these barrens which had been stripped of all their utility by a century of scavenging. Where in this rubble was Julian, and where was his pursuer?

It was by his fire I found him. But I was not the first to arrive.

The sun was altogether down, and a hint of the aurora borealis played about the northern sky, dimmed by moonlight, when I came to the most recently excavated section of Lundsford. The temporary dwellings of the Tipmen—rude huts of scavenged timber—had been abandoned here for the season, and corduroy ramps led down into the empty digs.

Here the remnants of last night's snow had been blown into windrows and small dunes, and all evidence of hoofprints had been erased. But I rode slowly, knowing I was close to my destination. I was buoyed by the observation that Julian's pursuer, whoever he was, had not returned this way from his mission: had not, that is, taken Julian captive, or at least had not gone back to Williams Ford with his prisoner in tow. Perhaps the pursuit had been suspended for the night.

It was not long—though it seemed an eternity, as Rapture short-stepped down the frozen road, avoiding snow-hidden pitfalls—before I heard the whickering of another horse, and saw a plume of smoke rising into the moon-bright sky.

Quickly I turned Rapture off the road and tied his reins to the low remnants of a concrete pillar, from which rust-savaged iron rods protruded like skeletal fingers. I took my squirrel rifle from the saddle holster and moved toward the source of the smoke on foot, until I was able to discern that the fumes emerged from a deep declivity in the landscape, perhaps the very dig from which the Tipmen had extracted THE HISTORY OF MANKIND IN SPACE. Surely this was where Julian had gone to wait for Sam's arrival. And indeed, here was Julian's horse, one of the finer riding horses from the Estate (worth more, I'm sure, in the eyes of its owner, than a hundred Julian Comstocks), moored to an outcrop . . . and, alarmingly, here was another horse as well, not far away. This second horse was a stranger to me; it was slat-ribbed and elderly-looking; but it wore a military bridle and the sort of cloth bib—blue, with a red star in the middle of it—that marked a mount belonging to the Reserves.

I studied the situation from behind the moon-shadow of a broken abutment.

The smoke suggested that Julian had gone beneath ground, down into the hollow of the Tipmen's dig, to shelter from the cold and bank his fire for the night. The presence of the second horse suggested that he had been discovered, and that his pursuer must already have confronted him.

More than that I could not divine. It remained only to approach the contested grounds as secretively as possible, and see what more I could learn.

I crept closer. The dig was revealed by moonlight as a deep but narrow excavation, covered in part with boards, with a sloping entrance at one end. The glow of the fire within was just visible, as was the chimney-hole that had been cut through the planking some yards farther down. There was, as far as I could discern, only one way in or out. I determined to proceed as far as I could without being seen, and to that end I lowered myself down the slope, inching forward on the seat of my pants over ground that was as cold, it seemed to me, as the wastelands of the Arctic north.

I was slow, I was cautious, and I was quiet. But I was not slow, cautious, or quiet *enough*; for I had just progressed far enough to glimpse an excavated chamber, in which the firelight cast a kaleidoscopic flux of shadows, when I felt a pressure behind my ear— the barrel of a gun—and a voice said, "Keep moving, mister, and join your friend below."

I kept silent until I could comprehend more of the situation I had fallen into.

My captor marched me down into the low part of the dig. The air, if damp, was noticeably warmer here, and we were screened from the increasing wind, though not from the accumulated odors of the fire and the stagnant must of what had once been a basement or cellar in some commercial establishment of the secular ancients.

The Tipmen had not left much behind: only a rubble of broken bits of things, indistinguishable under layers of dust and dirt. The far wall was of concrete, and the fire had been banked against it, under a chimney-hole that must have been cut by the scavengers during their labors. A circle of stones hedged the fire, and the damp planks and splinters in it crackled with a deceptive cheerfulness. Deeper parts part of the excavation, with ceilings lower than a man standing erect, opened in several directions.

Julian sat near the fire, his back to the wall and his knees drawn up under his chin. His clothes had been made filthy by the grime of the place. He was frowning, and when he saw me his frown deepened into a scowl.

"Go over there and get beside him," my captor said, "but give me that little bird rifle first."

I surrendered my weapon, modest as it was, and joined Julian. Thus I was able to get my first clear look at the man who had captured me. He appeared not much older than myself, but he was dressed in the blue and yellow uniform of the Reserves. His Reserve cap was pulled low over his eyes, which twitched left and right as though he were in constant fear of an ambush. In short he seemed both inexperienced and nervous—and maybe a little dim, for his jaw was slack, and he was evidently unaware of the dribble of mucous that escaped his nostrils as a result of the cold weather. (But as I have said before, this was not untypical of the members of the Reserve, who were kept out of active duty for a reason.)

His weapon, however, was very much in earnest, and not to be trifled with. It was a Pittsburgh rifle manufactured by the Porter & Earl works, which loaded at the breech from a sort of cassette and could fire five rounds in succession without any more attention from its owner than a twitch of the index finger. Julian had carried a similar weapon but had been disarmed of it; it rested against a stack of small staved barrels, well out of reach, and the Reservist put my squirrel rifle beside it.

I began to feel sorry for myself, and to think what a poor way of spending Christmas Eve I had chosen. I did not resent the action of the Reservist nearly as much as I resented my own stupidity and lapse of judgment.

"I don't know who you are," the Reservist said, "and I don't care—one draft-dodger is as good as the next, in my opinion—but I was given the job of collecting runaways, and my bag is getting full. I hope you'll both keep till morning, when I can ride you back into Williams Ford. Anyhow, none of us shall sleep tonight. I won't, in any case, so you might as well resign yourself to your captivity. If you're hungry, there's a little meat."

I was never less hungry in my life, and I began to say so, but Julian interrupted: "It's true, Adam," he said, "we're fairly caught. I wish you hadn't come after me."

"I'm beginning to feel the same way," I said.

He gave me a meaningful look, and said in a lower voice, "Is Sam—?"

"No whispering there," our captor said at once.

But I divined the intent of the question, and nodded to indicate that I had delivered Julian's message, though that was by no means a guarantee of our deliverance. Not only were the exits from Williams Ford under close watch, but Sam could not slip away as inconspicuously as I had, and if Julian's absence had been noted there would have been a redoubling of the guard, and perhaps an expedition sent out to hunt us. The man who had captured Julian was evidently an outrider, assigned to patrol the roads for runaways, and he had been diligent in his work.

He was somewhat less diligent now that he had us in his control, however, for he took a wooden pipe from his pocket, and proceeded to fill it, as he made himself as comfortable as possible on a wooden crate. His gestures were still nervous, and I supposed the pipe was meant to relax him; for it was not tobacco he put into it.

The Reservist might have been a Kentuckian, for I understand the less respectable people of that State often form the habit of smoking the silk of the female hemp plant, which is cultivated prodigiously there. Kentucky hemp is grown for cordage and cloth and paper, and as a drug is less intoxicating than the Indian Hemp of lore; but its mild smoke is said to be pleasant for those who indulge in it, though too much can result in sleepiness and great thirst.

Julian evidently thought these symptoms would be welcome

distractions in our captor, and he gestured to me to remain silent, so as not to interrupt the Reservist in his vice. The Reservist packed the pipe's bowl with dried vegetable matter from an oilcloth envelope he carried in his pocket, and soon the substance was alight, and a slightly more fragrant smoke joined the effluvia of the camp-fire as it swirled toward the rent in the ceiling.

Clearly the night would be a long one, and I tried to be patient in my captivity, and not think too much of Christmas matters, or the yellow light of my parents' cottage on dark winter mornings, or the soft bed where I might have been sleeping if I had not been rash in my deliberations.

♦7♦

I BEGAN BY SAYING this was a story about Julian Comstock, and I fear I lied, for it has turned out mainly to be a story about myself.

But there is a reason for this, beyond the obvious temptations of vanity and self-regard. I did not at the time know Julian nearly as well as I thought I did.

Our friendship was essentially a boys' friendship. I could not help reviewing, as we sat in silent captivity in the ruins of Lundsford, the things we had done together: reading books, hunting in the wooded foothills west of Williams Ford, arguing amiably over everything from Philosophy and Moon-Visiting to the best way to bait a hook or cinch a bridle. It had been too easy, during our time together, to forget that Julian was an aristo with close connections to men of power, or that his father had been famous both as a hero and as a traitor, or that his uncle Deklan Comstock, the President, might not have Julian's best interests at heart.

All that seemed far away, and distant from the nature of Julian's true spirit, which was gentle and inquisitive—a naturalist's disposition, not a politician's or a general's. When I pictured Julian as an adult, I imagined him contentedly pursuing some scholarly or artistic adventure: digging the bones of pre-Noachian monsters out of the Athabaska shale, perhaps, or making an improved kind of movie. He was not a warlike person, and the thoughts of the great men of the day seemed almost exclusively concerned with war.

So I had let myself forget that he was *also* everything he had been before he came to Williams Ford. He was the heir of a brave, determined, and ultimately betrayed father, who had conquered an army of Brazilians but had been crushed by the millstone of political intrigue. He was the son of a powerful woman, born to a powerful family of her own—not powerful enough to save Bryce Comstock from the gallows, but powerful enough to protect Julian, at least temporarily, from the mad calculations of his uncle. He was both a pawn and a player in the great games of the aristos. And while *I* had forgotten all this, Julian had *not*—these were the people who had made him, and if he chose not to speak of them, they nevertheless must have haunted his thoughts.

He was, it is true, often frightened of small things—I still remember his disquiet when I described the rituals of the Church of Signs to him, and he would sometimes shriek at the distress of animals when our hunting failed to result in a clean kill. But tonight, here in the ruins, I was the one who half-dozed in a morose funk, fighting tears; while it was Julian who sat intently still, gazing with resolve from beneath the strands of dusty hair that straggled over his brows, as coolly calculating as a bank clerk.

When we hunted, he often gave me the rifle to fire the last lethal shot, distrusting his own resolve.

Tonight—had the opportunity presented itself—I would have given the rifle to him.

I half-dozed, as I said, and from time to time woke to see the Reservist still sitting in guard. His eyelids were at half-mast, but I put that down to the effect of the hemp flowers he had smoked. Periodically he would start, as if at a sound inaudible to others, then settle back into place.

He had boiled a copious amount of coffee in a tin pan, and he warmed it whenever he renewed the fire, and drank sufficiently to keep him from falling asleep. Of necessity, this meant he must once in a while retreat to a distant part of the dig and attend to physical necessities in relative privacy. This did not give us any advantage, however, since he carried his Pittsburgh rifle with him, but it allowed a moment or two in which Julian could whisper without being overheard.

"This man is no mental giant," Julian said. "We may yet get out of here with our freedom."

"It's not his *brains* so much as his *artillery* that's stopping us," said I.

"Perhaps we can separate the one from the other. Look there, Adam. Beyond the fire—back in the rubble."

I looked.

There was motion in the shadows, which I began to recognize.

"The distraction may suit our purposes," Julian said, "unless it becomes fatal." And I saw the sweat that had begun to stand out on his forehead, the terror barely hidden in his eyes. "But I need your help."

I have said that I did not partake of the particular rites of my father's church, and that snakes were not my favorite creatures. This is true. As much as I have heard about surrendering one's volition to God—and I had seen my father with a Massassauga Rattler in each hand, trembling with devotion, speaking in a tongue not only foreign but utterly unknown (though it favored long vowels and stuttered consonants, much like the sounds he made when he burned his fingers on the coal stove)—I could never entirely assure myself that I would be protected by divine will from the serpent's bite. Some in the congregation obviously had not been: there was Sarah Prestley, for instance, whose right arm had swollen up black with venom and had to be amputated by Williams Ford's physician . . . but I will not dwell on that. The point is, that while I *disliked* snakes, I was not especially *afraid* of them, as Julian was. And I could not help admiring his restraint: for what was writhing in the shadows nearby was a nest of snakes that had been aroused by the heat of the fire.

I should add that it was not uncommon for these collapsed ruins to be infested with snakes, mice, spiders, and poisonous insects. Death by bite or sting was one of the hazards routinely faced by Tipmen, including concussion, blood poisoning, and accidental burial. The snakes, after the Tipmen ceased work for the winter, must have crept into this chasm anticipating an undisturbed hibernation, of which we and the Reservist had unfortunately deprived them.

The Reservist—who came back a little unsteadily from his necessaries—had not yet noticed these prior tenants. He seated himself on his crate, scowled at us, and studiously refilled his pipe.

"If he discharges all five shots from his rifle," Julian whispered, "then we have a chance of overcoming him, or of recovering our own weapons. But, Adam—"

"No talking there," the Reservist mumbled.

"—*you must remember your father's advice*," Julian finished.

"I said keep quiet!"

Julian cleared his throat and addressed the Reservist directly, since the time for action had obviously arrived: "Sir, I have to draw your attention to something."

"What would that be, my little draft dodger?"

"I'm afraid we're not alone in this terrible place."

"Not alone!" the Reservist said, casting his eyes about him nervously. Then he recovered and squinted at Julian. "I don't see any other persons."

"I don't mean persons, but vipers," said Julian.

"Vipers!"

"In other words—snakes."

At this the Reservist started again, his mind perhaps still slightly confused by the effects of the hemp smoke; then he sneered and said, "Go on, you can't pull that one on me."

"I'm sorry if you think I'm joking, for there are at least a dozen snakes advancing from the shadows, and one of them[10] is about to achieve intimacy with your right boot."

"Hah," the Reservist said, but he could not help glancing in the indicated direction, where one of the serpents—a fat and lengthy example—had indeed lifted its head and was sampling the air above his bootlace.

The effect was immediate, and left no more time for planning. The Reservist leapt from his seat on the wooden crate, uttering oaths, and danced backward, at the same time attempting to bring his rifle to his shoulder and confront the threat. He discovered to his dismay that it was not a question of *one* snake but of *dozens,* and he compressed the trigger of the weapon reflexively. The resulting shot went wild. The bullet impacted near the main nest of the creatures, causing them to

---

[10] Julian's sense of timing was exquisite, perhaps as a result of his theatrical inclinations.

scatter with astonishing speed, like a box of loaded springs—
unfortunately for the hapless Reservist, who was directly in their path.
He cursed vigorously and fired four more times. Some of the shots
careened harmlessly; at least one obliterated the midsection of the lead
serpent, which knotted around its own wound like a bloody rope.

"Now, Adam!" Julian shouted, and I stood up, thinking: My father's
advice?

My father was a taciturn man, and most of his advice had involved
the practical matter of running the Estate's stables. I hesitated a
moment in confusion, while Julian advanced toward the captive rifles,
dancing among the surviving snakes like a dervish. The Reservist,
recovering somewhat, raced in the same direction; and then I recalled
the only advice of my father's that I had ever shared with Julian:

*Grasp it where its neck ought to be, behind the head; ignore the
tail, however it may thrash; and crack its skull, hard and often enough
to subdue it.*

And so I did just that—until the threat was neutralized.

Julian, meanwhile, recovered the weapons, and came away from
the infested area of the dig.

He looked with some astonishment at the Reservist, who was
slumped at my feet, bleeding from his scalp, which I had "cracked,
hard and often."

"Adam," he said. "When I spoke of your father's advice—I meant
the *snakes.*"

"The snakes?" Several of them still twined about the dig. But I
reminded myself that Julian knew very little about the nature and
variety of reptiles. "They're only corn snakes," I explained.[11] "They're
big, but they're not venomous."

Julian, his eyes gone large, absorbed this information.

Then he looked at the crumpled form of the Reservist again.

"Have you killed him?"

"Well, I hope not," I said.

---

[11] Once confined to the southeast, corn snakes have spread north with the warming
climate. I have read that certain of the secular ancients used to keep them as pets—
yet another instance of our ancestors' willful perversity.

❧ 8 ❧

WE MADE A NEW CAMP, in a less populated part of the ruins, and kept a watch on the road, and at dawn we saw a single horse and rider approaching from the west. It was Sam Godwin.

Julian hailed him, waving his arms. Sam came closer, and looked with some relief at Julian, and then speculatively at me. I blushed, thinking of how I had interrupted him at his prayers (however unorthodox those prayers might have been, from a purely Christian perspective), and how poorly I had reacted to my discovery of his true religion. But I said nothing, and Sam said nothing, and relations between us seemed to have been regularized, since I had demonstrated my loyalty (or foolishness) by riding to Julian's aid.

It was Christmas morning. I supposed that did not mean anything in particular to Julian or Sam, but I was poignantly aware of the date. The sky was blue again, but a squall had passed during the dark hours of the morning, and the snow "lay round about, deep and crisp and even." Even the ruins of Lundsford were transformed into something soft-edged and oddly beautiful. I was amazed at how simple it was for nature to cloak corruption in the garb of purity and make it peaceful.

But it would not be peaceful for long, and Sam said so. "There are troops behind me as we speak. Word came by wire from New York not to let Julian escape. We can't linger here more than a moment."

"Where will we go?" Julian asked.

"It's impossible to ride much farther east. There's no forage for the animals and precious little water. Sooner or later we'll have to turn south and make a connection with the railroad or the turnpike. It's going to be short rations and hard riding for a while, I'm afraid, and if we do make good our escape we'll have to assume new identities. We'll be little better than draft dodgers or labor refugees, and I expect we'll have to pass some time among that hard crew, at least until we reach New York City. We can find friends in New York."

It was a plan, but it was a large and lonesome one, and my heart sank at the prospect.

"We have a prisoner," Julian told his mentor, and he took Sam back into the excavated ruins to explain how we had spent the night.

The Reservist was there, hands tied behind his back, a little groggy from the punishment I had inflicted on him but well enough to open his eyes and scowl. Julian and Sam spent a little time debating how to deal with this encumbrance. We could not, of course, take him with us; the question was how to return him to his superiors without endangering ourselves unnecessarily.

It was a debate to which I could contribute nothing, so I took a little slip of paper from my back-satchel, and a pencil, and wrote a letter.

It was addressed to my mother, since my father was without the art of literacy.

You will no doubt have noticed my absence, I wrote. *It saddens me to be away from home, especially at this time (I write on Christmas Day). But I hope you will be consoled with the knowledge that I am all right, and not in any immediate danger.*

(This was a lie, depending on how you define "immediate," but a kindly one, I reasoned.)

In any case I would not have been able to remain in Williams Ford, since I could not have escaped the draft for long even if I postponed my military service for some few more months. The conscription drive is in earnest; the War in Labrador must be going badly. It was inevitable that we should be separated, as much as I mourn for my home and all its comforts.

(And it was all I could do not to decorate the page with a vagrant tear.)

Please accept my best wishes and my gratitude for everything you and Father have done for me. I will write again as soon as it is practicable, which may not be immediately. Trust in the knowledge

*that I will pursue my destiny faithfully and with every Christian virtue
you have taught me. God bless you in the coming and every year.*

That was not enough to say, but there wasn't time for more.
Julian and Sam were calling for me. I signed my name, and added, as
a postscript:

*Please tell Father that I value his advice, and that it has already
served me usefully. Yrs. etc. once again, Adam.*

"You've written a letter," Sam observed as he came to rush me to
my horse. "But have you given any thought to how you might mail it?"

I confessed that I had not.

"The Reservist can carry it," said Julian, who had already
mounted his horse.

The Reservist was also mounted, but with his hands tied behind
him, as it was Sam's final conclusion that we should set him loose
with the horse headed west, where he would encounter more troops
before very long. He was awake but, as I have said, sullen; and he
barked, "I'm nobody's damned mailman!"

I addressed the message, and Julian took it and tucked it into the
Reservist's saddlebag. Despite his youth, and despite the slightly
dilapidated condition of his hair and clothing, Julian sat tall in the
saddle. I had never thought of him as high-born until that moment,
when an aspect of command seemed to enter his body and his voice.
He said to the Reservist, "We treated you kindly—"

The Reservist uttered an oath.

"Be quiet. You were injured in the conflict, but we took you
prisoner, and we've treated you in a more gentlemanly fashion than
we were when the conditions were reversed. I am a Comstock—at
least for the moment—and I won't be spoken to crudely by an
infantryman, at any price. You'll deliver this boy's message, and you'll
do it gratefully."

The Reservist was clearly awed by the assertion that Julian was a
Comstock—he had been laboring under the assumption that we were
mere village runaways—but he screwed up his courage and said,
"Why should I?"

"Because it's the Christian thing to do," Julian said, "and if this
argument with my uncle is ever settled, the power to remove your

head from your shoulders may well reside in my hands. Does that make sense to you, soldier?"

The Reservist allowed that it did.

And so we rode out that Christmas morning from the ruins in which the Tipmen had discovered the HISTORY OF MANKIND IN SPACE, which still resided in my back-satchel, vagrant memory of a half-forgotten past.

My mind was a confusion of ideas and anxieties, but I found myself recalling what Julian had said, long ago it now seemed, about DNA, and how it aspired to perfect replication but progressed by remembering itself imperfectly. It might be true, I thought, because our lives were like that—*time itself* was like that, every moment dying and pregnant with its own distorted reflection. Today was Christmas: which Julian claimed had once been a pagan holiday, dedicated to Sol Invictus or some other Roman god; but which had evolved into the familiar celebration of the present, and was no less dear because of it.

(I imagined I could hear the Christmas bells ringing from the Dominion Hall at Wiliams Ford, though that was impossible, for we were miles away, and not even the sound of a cannon shot could carry so far across the prairie. It was only memory speaking.)

And maybe this logic was true of people, too; maybe I was already becoming an inexact echo of what I had been just days before. Maybe the same was true of Julian. Already something hard and uncompromising had begun to emerge from his gentle features—the first manifestation of a new Julian, a freshly *evolved* Julian, called forth by his violent departure from Williams Ford, or slouching toward New York to be born.

But that was all Philosophy, and not much use, and I kept quiet about it as we spurred our horses in the direction of the railroad, toward the rude and squalling infant Future.